AMONG THE HOLLOW

by
Roman Ankenbrandt

Printed in the United States of America
Middleton, DE
First paperback edition, 2018

Paperback ISBN: 978-1-98040-382-1

Cover art by Jonathan Caridia
New Zealand

for Emmett

"This is the house where spirit was born. My bones and skin I leave like rags. I tear the veil and see the light I am. I feast on the silence of gods and the reticence of the world. Like smoke, like prayers I am lifted up."

-The Egyptian Book of the Dead, (trans. Normandi Ellis)

THE ARRUM EMPIRE

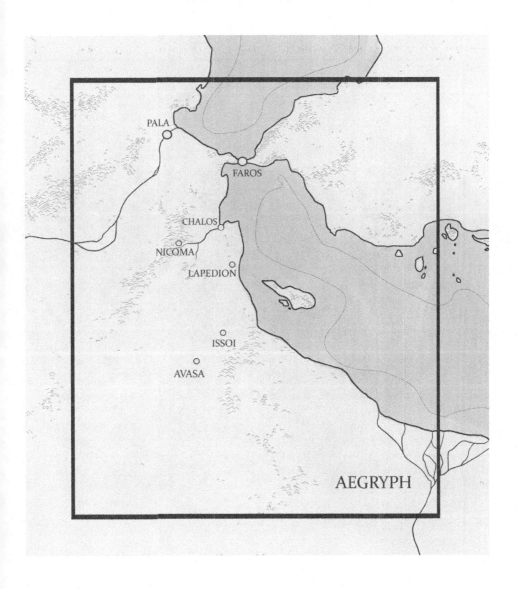

EXTENT OF THE ARRUM EMPIRE 200 YEARS PRIOR (LIGHT)
&
EXTENT OF THE ARRUM EMPIRE CURRENTLY (DARK)

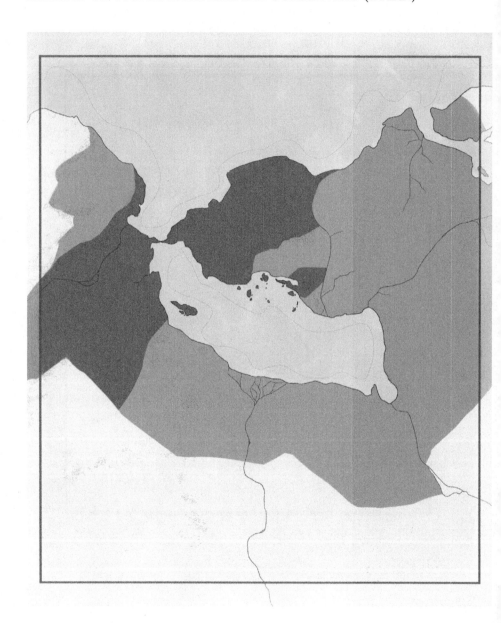

Chapter 1

Beneath a dim arch somebody stood in the doorway. Her face, obscured by a veil of bone-stitched cloth, revealed only her eyes which, when she turned her head, gleamed with a gold and owlish reflection. After a moment studying the rough-hewn liminal stone, she walked forward into the unlit room, crowded with a narrow corridor of slaughtered pigs. The carcasses dangled by their hind legs from the low-slung ceiling, bellies slit and emptied. Daintily so as not to bloody the fine silk and leather of her shoes, she stepped over the blood-drained corpse of a man in her path, then another, not once breaking stride, neither slowing nor hurrying until finally she paused.

The light from the doorway touched a streak of red painting the floor in a rough circle filled with hastily scrawled symbols and an assortment of abandoned tools: metal hooks, candles melted into puddles, a stained knife. In the shadow along the far wall a figure hunched, knees curled to chest. She cocked her head, then crouched down on her heels in the light just out of reach.

"What happened here?" she asked, her voice hard and raspy.

At the sound of her words the figure recoiled. Nothing of them could be seen beneath layers of ragged cloth and battered scraps of armour apart from their head, which hovered in place above broad shoulders like a shadow given form but no substance.

"I— I don't know." The shade had no mouth, only a pair of glowing slits for eyes. "Did I do this?"

"Doubtful," she answered. Glancing over her shoulder from beneath her long cowl, which flared around her narrow features like the hood of a desert snake, she scoffed. "Crude markings. A knife carved from the humerus instead of the femur. Pigs blood to supplement these dead guards. Clearly amateurs, whoever they were." As she shook her head in disgust, the veil shrouding her face faintly rattled. "I felt a tearing in the fabric of reality, and came searching, yet after all this way, the only thing I find is you: a disembodied soul with no memory. What a waste."

The shade flinched when she abruptly rose to her feet and dusted off her palms, long fingers clacking with many carnelian-studded rings at each knuckle. "Where are you going?" The spirit asked, a desperate tremble in their voice as the woman turned to leave.

"By the Abyss, you're needy." Glaring down at the spirit, she cast a dismissive wave at them. "Why would I help you? What could you possibly hope to offer me?" When their only response was an anguished silence, she sighed. "Perhaps once in life you were something, but now without a body you are nothing."

"My body —!" The shade stared up at her, scrambling to their knees to reach out, but stopping before they touched the light. "Please! Help me retrieve my body! I'll do anything!"

All of a sudden, she went very still. Wreathed in light from the doorway beyond, her eyes seemed to burn a molten gold, her pupils slitted like a serpent's. When at last she spoke, her voice was a hoarse rattling hiss. *"Anything?"*

She savoured the word on her tongue. Slowly she pulled down the veil to reveal her face, her sharp cheeks, her sharp chin, her shark-toothed smile. Quick as a bolt she snatched up the shade's outstretched hand, clasping the cold gauntlet that the spirit animated, and announced, "Contract accepted. I will help you get your body back, and for me you will do *anything.*"

"Thank you!" The spirit gasped, shivering as the full pressure of the pact settled over them, its unseen fetters digging deep.

She laughed, a sound devoid of warmth. "Oh, don't thank me, darling. This is not a favour."

She withdrew her hand, leaving the shade to stand on their own, then studied their hulking form as the shade rose, towering over her by a full head and shoulders. With a grimace of distaste, she plucked at their bloodied rags. "Did you scavenge these from the guardsmen?"

The spirit shuffled their booted feet sheepishly in reply.

Shooting them an incredulous look, she wiped her hand off on her bulky trousers as though that brief contact alone sullied her fingers. "First thing to be done is to find you some new clothes. I won't be seen with you in public like this."

Without another word, she walked to the open door. There she paused only to peer outside before stepping into the sun-drenched warmth. She engoldened in the harsh afternoon light, and everything about her seemed to glitter: her saffron-coloured silks trimmed with fine needlework, her gold-clapped wrists and fingers studded with wine-dark gems, her sweat-beaded skin. Tugging the veil back over her nose she turned to ask, "I don't suppose you have a name? Or is even that too much to ask?"

The shade lingered just out of the light's reach inside the doorway. Their glowing eyes narrowed in concentration, and when they shook their head blackness swirled through the air over their shoulders like ink.

"Hmm." She fiddled with one of the bracelets cinching her long sleeves from wrist to elbow. Finally, she announced, "Aurel. That's what I'll call you."

"Aurel?" The spirit repeated, reluctant to emerge from the safety of the butchery and into the bright unknown. "Why that name?"

"It means *golden*, and I like gold." She shrugged, brushing off the question with a wave of her hand and a dry comment. "Besides, it suits your sunny disposition."

Aurel scowled, but rather than bristle with a barbed retort, they asked, "And what should I call you?"

"Normally I prefer souls bound in eldritch contract to refer to me as *'Mistress.'* In this case however, you may call me Sevila." She planted her fists on her hips and snapped, "Now, are you just going to sulk in there, or are you going to come out sometime before the reign of the next Empress?" Sevila's voice lowered, and she muttered to herself, "Perhaps not the best comparison; they are dropping like flies these days."

Turning sideways so as not to scrape their shoulders against the door frame, Aurel at last stepped out into the light. They squinted, braced against the incoming glare, the sudden lash of heat, only to blink in confusion when neither manifested. High overhead the sun baked the dusty alleyway and the cracked wall-plaster, yet Aurel felt nothing. Curious, they reached out to trace the doorway with the leather-padded fingertips of one gauntlet, but the contact remained a blind numbness, bereft of even the bluntest sensation.

Sevila began walking towards the exit of the alleyway, and every step she took rattled faintly, like the sound of coin clattering against bone. "This way. I want to get out of this backwater before nightfall, and we still have a few things to do before then."

Aurel followed. The two of them emerged onto a main road, revealing a small town sparsely populated. An old man snored in the cool shadow of an awning, and a lanky dog scurried around a corner, its paws and muzzle black with what Aurel hoped was mud. A dry hot wind rustled a chime made of bronze and pitted plates each as small as fingernails.

"Where is everyone?" Aurel asked as they wandered down the street.

"It's market day," Sevila replied as though that were clear enough. "The busiest day of the week, where everyone is distracted. It's when I'd choose to murder you, too."

Aurel stared at her, aghast. "What makes you think I was murdered?"

Laughing throatily, Sevila paused at a street intersection to place her hand on Aurel's chest. "Darling, that scene back there wasn't one I would describe as overflowing with boundless love and affection." She rapped at Aurel's rags with the back of her hand. "Now, you should really take this off."

"I -!" Aurel stepped away, crossing their arms over their chest, shoulders sloping inwards, feeling exposed by the mere suggestion.

Sevila rolled her eyes. "Why are you acting like a wilting flower? There's nothing under there! See!" Darting forward, her movements surprisingly fluid and quick, she ripped off one of Aurel's gauntlets. In the place where a hand and forearm should have been, the air rippled like a mirage tipped with dark fingers that dripped shadow. Immediately, Aurel tried to hide their strange and formless hand beneath the ragged cloak they wore, repulsed by the sight.

Meanwhile, Sevila tossed the gauntlet to the ground where it clattered in a cloud of dust. "Strip," she ordered. "Before someone else sees you preferably."

Silent, Aurel did as instructed. Mounds of bloody cloth fell to the ground, revealing a gaping chasm of a chest — the hint of a shadowy ribcage encasing a carnal scarlet void — and naught else. Trying not to look down at their own nebulous shape, Aurel gathered up the scraps of armour. When Sevila arched an eyebrow, they insisted, "I like the weight. It's comforting."

"Needy *and* tasteless. Whatever am I to do with you?" Sevila sighed. Still she did not press the issue as Aurel had feared. Instead she gestured for them to follow down another dingy street. "Leave the rest. We won't be here long enough for anyone to investigate, and it's not like the local garrison is going to come chasing after us. You saw all two of their members back in that abattoir."

"Couldn't someone — I don't know — summon their souls for questioning? You could ask who they saw!" A pauldron almost slipped to the ground, and Aurel shifted their grip.

"You really don't know anything do you?" Sevila snorted, a derisive sound. "I can only have one contract at a time. That's the Law. And trust me, anyone from these parts who could summon another human soul would have been whistled away into the highest ranks of the priestly College or the imperial army long ago. These people couldn't summon a goat."

As they rounded another corner riddled with cracks along its white-washed façade, the sounds of people mingling grew louder. Together, the two of them came upon a small but bustling marketplace in the town square. Cool and self-possessed, Sevila forged on, passing easily through the colourful swathes of cloth everyone wore, the patterns all bearing a striking geometric similarity. In a futile attempt to hide their formless shadow from sight, Aurel hugged the bundle of armour to their chest as a few people turned to stare. A man at a stall struck his wooden ladle against an enormous metal frying dish brimming with meat over an open flame, and somehow amidst the throng what Aurel found most distressing was the fact that they could not smell the food.

Footsteps slowing, Aurel turned to stare when they saw the spirit of a small bird perched atop a passing woman's shoulder. And there by the stocky bell tower, three children played with a cat's soul before a man rushed forward to scold them, and order the cat away, to which the soul merely stretched, yawned, and lazily flicked its black-ringed tail. The souls of larger animals however, were nowhere to be found.

Sevila stopped at a cloth merchant's stall draped with bold splashes of colour. In the shade of the tent a wizened old woman thumbed a long ivory-capped pipe that trailed threads of blue smoke. She sucked at the pipe, then blew a bolt of smoke in Aurel's direction. "Freshly summoned, I take it?" She addressed Sevila alone.

"Yes." Sevila lied without missing a beat. She wrinkled her nose at a hanging ream of blue and orange wool. "We need something simple, but not drab."

Ducking down to see additional stacks of cloth in the crowded tent, Aurel reached out with one hand to touch the wool, to feel the twilled thread count, only for their fingers to pass right through the fabric like the dispersal of smoke. Aurel jerked back, and their fingers furled once more in a cloudy mist.

The woman ignored Aurel, and instead glared at Sevila. She puffed up her chest and jabbed at Sevila with her pipe. "You'll find nothing but the finest quality here! I even have a bolt of silk all the way from Pala!"

Sevila took the pipe with one hand, while with the other she lowered her veil. Bringing the pipe to her lips, she filled her lungs. As smoke billowed from her nostrils, she smiled, baring cruel, sharp, yellowish teeth. "We're not at the Farosian Bazaar, old woman. Your wares are rough-spun, the stuff of goat-herders."

The pipe passed seamlessly between them as they bickered. Eventually the old woman trundled forward to thrust various bolts of cloth up to Aurel for Sevila's inspection. At one point Aurel tried to weigh in — "I quite like the green" — but the two women ignored any input in favour of continuing to argue. Straightening, Aurel glanced around at other nearby stalls to find everyone else engaged in nearly identical disputes with shop owners.

"Aurel." Sevila tugged at the battered armour they carried, dragging Aurel's attention back around. "Put this junk down. She needs to take your measurements."

Kneeling, Aurel carefully placed the odd assortment of iron scale armour on the ground, and the old woman approached with a length of colourless string tied with knots at precise distances. She stretched her arms out wide, straining to reach the full breadth of Aurel's chest and shoulders.

From the side Sevila gestured at Aurel with the pipe before sticking it between her teeth once more. "Can't you shift your form to something smaller? You're going to cost me a fortune."

"This size feels right somehow," Aurel said, unfolding to their full height once the old lady shooed them away. By accident their head passed directly through the awning, and they stooped back down once more.

Sevila grunted. "You must have been an enormous *somebody* in life." She tapped the whitened ash from the bowl of the pipe and said to the old woman, "We need more seed."

"When you finish your purchase, I'll think about it!" The woman barked in return.

"This is robbery!" Sevila insisted in mock outrage.

In fact, it wasn't until the very end, after Aurel had been fitted with a long-sleeved tunic, hems that brushed their armoured feet, and — they were pleased to note — a green military styled cloak draped over one shoulder, that the two women mentioned price at all. By that point they had somehow already arrived at a common number, and Sevila — moaning about Aurel's height all the while — handed over a large handful of bronze coins that the old woman then painstakingly counted. When the merchant pulled out a knife to cut one of the coins in half, Sevila stayed her hand. "How about another smoke instead?"

As soon as the sale was made, the atmosphere changed completely. The old woman invited Sevila to sit atop a pile of folded patterned wool, and they gossiped like fast friends, swapping the pipe between them. Meanwhile Aurel watched the roiling of the market, fiddling with the armour so that it set in place properly, and listening to the slap of piss-drenched cloth from the fullers at the far end of the square.

"Other strangers like you visited two days ago," the old woman said. "A priest and two guardsmen."

"After all that money I gave you, and still you insult me by comparing me to a priest!" Sevila shook her head, smoke curling around the lip of her cowl. "Are they still here?"

"They left this morning. Headed north after speaking with the town priest." The old woman waved vaguely in a direction over her shoulder to indicate where the priest resided.

Sevila addressed Aurel with a waspish flick of her fingers. "Darling, don't block the stall."

"No, no." The woman motioned for Aurel to stay put. "Show off my wares. It's good business to have something as prestigious as a human soul be seen wearing my clothing."

Suddenly Aurel felt more like a prized mannequin than ever, and they aimed a glower at the two women, who not once paused in exchanging information. Directly opposite the cloth merchant's stall though, the sounds of a mounting argument escalated. Slabs of red-marbled meat were hung on display, and a whole skinned lamb lay stretched out atop the stall's wooden table. A man, dragging a young girl behind him by the arm, shouted furiously at the butcher in charge of the stall, a broad woman wearing a blood-stained leather apron.

"What's all this about?" Sevila uncurled from her place, lithe as a cat.

The old woman craned her neck to see the growing commotion, more people flocking to the butcher's stall and listening to the man's shouting. "I'm not sure. He's a local shepherd. Sells me good wool on occasion."

At that Sevila hummed, thoughtful. She wandered up to Aurel, and leaned against one of the wooden pillars holding the small tent upright. Together, they observed.

"She is sick!" The shepherd yelled, pointing an accusatory finger at the butcher. "My daughter ate your foul meat, and now she speaks in tongues!"

The butcher scowled and shouted back, waving her gore-slicked cleaver. "I slaughter all my stock lawfully! The priest was there!"

"Liar!" The shepherd roared. He thrust his daughter forward, and she wailed a series of mindless babbling, eyes rolling into the back of her head. "Look at what you've done to her! Your meat is bloody! Look! Look! You do not drain it properly! The soul lingers in the flesh you sell, and now my daughter has subsumed it!"

An ugly murmur passed through the watching crowd, and even the old cloth merchant waddled forward with an intense expression. At Aurel's side Sevila stiffened. "I know what that noise means," she murmured. "Come. Quickly."

Pulling her veil up, Sevila slipped behind the line of stalls, followed closely by Aurel's hulking form. They skirted along the very edge of the market. The villagers were all too engrossed in the growing mob to notice. When they escaped down a meandering side alley, Sevila finally slowed her pace. "Blaming the priest! It's as if she wants to be stoned to death."

Flinging her hands up in disgust — Aurel could not tell if it was due to the idea of stoning or simply an intolerance for fools — Sevila stalked from the alley and onto another street, navigating the labyrinthine landscape with practised ease.

"We should go back and help her." Aurel trailed after Sevila, ducking beneath a line of washing that dried in the sun.

"And provide what evidence, exactly?" Sevila shot back, glancing idly into buildings as they passed by.

Stymied yet resolute, Aurel said, "She deserves a trial."

"The nearest magistrate is five day's ride away, if you pack lightly and take few breaks. Out here people tend to avoid that kind of inconvenience, which means that the only other presider over legal affairs would be the priest." Sevila stopped before the only building in town over a single story in height apart from the bell tower. "Ah, this looks like the place."

"Sevila —!" Aurel began, but they were interrupted by a shushing noise from the woman in question.

Standing in front of the entrance, Sevila brandished a finger up at Aurel, expression stern behind her veil. "Don't say anything when we get inside. And while you're at it, divest yourself of that hero complex. It's incredibly dowdy."

Then, without waiting for Aurel to deliver a sufficient retort aside from an offended monosyllable, Sevila opened the door and stepped inside. Hands clenched into fists, Aurel ducked to follow. They straightened once in the building, but had to stoop when their head brushed the ceiling. Even lit with candles at every niche in the walls, the interior was murky. A layer of smoke hung along the ceiling, obscuring Aurel's vision, though through it they could see a number of furnishing cluttering the space, all of them fine in comparison to what they had seen of the rest of the village. Aurel could not feel a shift in temperature, but Sevila muttered, "Close the door already. You're letting the cold out."

As soon as Aurel did so, the room was plunged into near darkness, and the candles flickered in the resultant draft. Sevila did not bother with discretion — somehow Aurel doubted she ever did — and instead she strode boldly across the room and into another. There a man in plain black robes sat at a desk. Before him a platter of food was piled high, and a pitcher of wine stood to the side. The only adornment he wore was a simple gold chain of office draped low over his shoulders, identifying him as a priest.

Upon noticing his new arrivals, he did a double take, startled. Quickly he finished chewing the bite he had taken before saying around the mouthful, "Who are you?'

Pulling her veil down, Sevila moved forward and sat on the edge of the desk, knocking a few loose pages to the floor in the process.

"What on earth are you —?" The priest started in outrage. When Sevila reached over to pick up the platter and begin eating his food, he spluttered, "You can't just —! Guards! *Guards!*"

"They're not coming" Sevila mumbled as she shoved fingerfuls of food into her mouth, expertly not dropping a single crumb of bread or sliver of poultry. "I'm assuming you haven't seen them since this morning, when they accompanied your guests out."

He stared at her, incredulous, until he gathered his wits about him and growled. "I don't need them to condemn you."

Rather than reply to that threat, Sevila picked up the pitcher of wine. She swished what remained of it in the bottom then drained it dry, tipping her head back. Then, she tossed it aside, and it clattered to the ground, rolling across the floor. "Aurel, see if you can find more wine. I imagine there's plenty around here."

As Aurel stepped into the room and crouched down to open a low cupboard, the priest seemed to notice the spirit's presence for the first time. His eyes went very wide and flicked between the two. Clearing his throat, his voice carried a sudden wary note. "What exactly do you want?"

Sevila studied the priest as she continued eating, and beneath her unblinking, inscrutable stare he shifted in his seat. Finally, she said, "Your guests — who were they?"

Opening another cupboard, Aurel happened upon a dusty gourd wrapped in silk, and they uncapped the top, trying to smell its contents only to realise they couldn't. Aurel crossed over to the desk and handed the gourd to Sevila for inspection. Upon their approach, the priest shrank back fearfully in his seat, gripping the arms of his wooden chair tight. "Another member of the College," he said. "I'm visited every year for routine record keeping. I showed them my tabulations and manuscripts, and they left. Nothing out of the ordinary."

Sevila sniffed at the gourd's contents, and her face brightened. "Lapedion Red!" She did not bother pouring a cup, instead taking a swig directly from the gourd itself. "What else have you been hiding from me?"

The priest's gaze darted nervously from Sevila to Aurel and back again. "Nothing! That's everything!"

With a doubtful hum Sevila cleared away the rest of what remained on the platter, speaking between mouthfuls. "I find it hard to believe that they were so interested in your records, yet found absolutely nothing wrong with your glaring malpractice." She dropped the cleaned platter to the table where it clanged loudly, making the priest flinch. "Drunk by midday. Uninterested in local politics. I'm the gambling sort, and I'd wager you slur your way through blessings at the butchery. How do you think the people will react when they discover the meat they consume is unlawful because of you?"

The priest's hands and jowls trembled. A fine sheen of sweat speckled his brow. "I can —" he had to pause to swallow past the sudden dryness in his throat. "I can show you my records and books. All of them."

Smiling, Sevila slid from her perch on the table, and used the priest's robes to wipe her hands clean. "I'd like that."

He scraped his chair back and stood, hurrying away so as to put as much distance between himself and Sevila as possible. With every other step, the priest glanced nervously over his shoulder to find Sevila and Aurel haunting his footsteps. Leading them up a set of creaking wooden steps, he stopped once they reached the second floor. It was itself a single room crammed with manuscripts and scrolls, spare inkwells and loose rolls of paper. Work slates covered in wax were scratched with writings in progress, and rare parchment was hoarded carefully in one corner.

Sevila wandered through the stacks, pulling out sections of papyrus here and a dusty manuscript there, seemingly at random. Her eyes scanned the documents rapidly, but nothing she read managed to catch her interest, for she soon tossed them to the floor with careless abandon. Spare pages fluttered and rumpled. Heavy manuscripts thumped against the floorboards. The priest winced at every discarded work. Curious, Aurel walked to the section nearest them and pulled down a scroll. The parchment unfurled in their hands, and they handled it with care so as to not rip the page with their gauntlets. A soft relieved pleasure flooded them when they picked out the words without any trouble. Somehow in the midst of all this chaos, it was comforting to know that they could at least read.

Across the room Sevila slammed shut a tome between her hands, the pages of which erupted in a plume of dust, and it, too, she threw to the ground. "Did they take anything?"

"An old scroll passed down by my predecessor," The priest answered hastily. He wiped at his forehead with the sleeve of his long robes. "I don't know what it read. It was written in a foreign tongue I've never encountered."

At that Sevila muttered under her breath, nearly inaudible as she rustled through more scrolls. "Well, we know something of what they're after at least." Then, giving up on her search, Sevila approached the priest. He was not a tall man, but still Sevila had to tip her face back to meet his gaze. When she spoke, her voice was low and dangerous, "This is everything?"

He nodded furiously. "Everything."

"Excellent." With one hand, she fixed her veil back in place, while with the other she clasped the priest by his upper arm. He winced from the contact, and even though most of her face was covered Aurel could see the cold smile that lit up her golden eyes. She murmured, "Keep up the good work."

Upon releasing him, Sevila gestured for Aurel to follow her downstairs. The priest scurried aside to give Aurel a wide berth, but as Aurel took the first step down, the priest hissed, "I don't know what the nature of your contract is —" he lowered his voice so that Sevila could not hear, "—but there is something deeply *wrong* with your Mistress. Be wary, spirit."

Aurel fixed him with a hard look, but before they could press for details Sevila called their name from the bottom of the stairs. Reluctant to leave without answers, Aurel nonetheless turned away and descended after her. Together the two of them left as quickly as they had arrived, though not before Sevila snagged the gourd of wine from the priest's desk. When Aurel gave her a reproachful look, she brushed it off with a nonchalant shrug. "Fine wine is wasted on that charlatan. He deserves only pigswill."

Outside the sun was creeping westward. Aurel looked up at it, then in the direction of the marketplace. "We still have time. We can expose the priest, and save that woman."

"What?" Sevila appeared taken aback by the idea, as though the thought had never even occurred to her. "No, no. If we want to catch up with your killers, we need to leave for the next town immediately, and I still need to pack my things in the taverna. Besides, she's probably already dead by now."

"You don't know that," Aurel growled, and the fingers of their gauntlets curled into fists.

Raising her eyebrows, Sevila cocked her head, an inquisitive stance. For a brief moment she considered them, drumming her fingers against the neck of the gourd, until she said, "Ugh. Fine. I'll pack. You go to the market. When you find that I'm right — which of course you will — meet me there." She pointed down the road towards a line of three camels roped to a post dug into the sandy earth. Not bothering to waste time on a snappish reply, Aurel turned and stormed away, ignoring Sevila's voice calling after them, "And don't take too long!"

Strides lengthening, Aurel rounded a corner. They darted down an alleyway, trying to recall the route they had taken from the town square. They clanked hollowly with every step. The edges of the green cloak fluttered in their wake, and their head trailed droplets of shadow like dark banners. The sounds of the market were muted, and Aurel feared they had taken a wrong turn. At the very end of the alleyway however, could be seen the colourful tents and stalls arrayed in the town square. Hopeful, Aurel trotted forward. People there continued to shop, though they murmured solemnly to one another — a far cry from the boisterous haggling Aurel had witnessed not long ago. Winding their way through the crowd, Aurel stopped.

The butcher's stall stood empty. The meat that had once hung on display was now trampled along the dusty ground. Streaks of blood painted the dirt, and the earth was disturbed as though something heavy had been dragged away.

"Have you lost your Mistress, spirit?"

Whirling around, Aurel saw the old cloth merchant attending her stall. She still sucked away at the pipe, gazing curiously up at them.

"No," Aurel answered. "I was just leaving."

Aurel spared the butcher's stall one last look, then walked away. Slowly the shock sank in, heavy as a stone. The complete numbness to physical sensation remained new, unwieldy, and juxtaposed to this backlash of regret, it made the emotion that much more abrupt and all-enveloping. As Aurel trudged from the market and towards where Sevila had told them to meet, the outside world seemed to fade to a blank nothing, all at once insensate yet tumbled with feeling.

Already Sevila was waiting for them at the rendezvous point, mounted atop a rust-coloured camel, perched among her numerous saddlebags that she had slung across the pack animal. A leather-tasselled riding crop was stuck beneath one of her knees. She was eating a fig. Her teeth split the flesh and the rows of glistening, pink, pearl-like seeds. When she saw Aurel approaching, her dark eyebrows rose. "Are you finished?" she asked.

Dazed, Aurel did not answer. She studied them with an oddly distant curiosity, as though trying and failing to gauge their expression. Then with a shrug, Sevila stuffed what remained of the fig into her mouth, flicking the stem aside and pulling up her veil. "In that case, let's get a move on."

Aurel began to untether one of the other camels from the post. The camel balked, pulling back its upper lip to spit in Aurel's direction. With a reflexive flinch, Aurel stepped away.

Sevila stared at them. "What are you doing?"

"Aren't —?" Aurel stuttered, suddenly unsure. They pointed at the other two mounts. "Aren't one of these for me?"

A rough snort of laughter escaped Sevila, and she shook her head. "Certainly not! Why would I waste more money on something as trivial as that?" She gestured at Aurel with her tasselled riding crop. "What need have you of a camel, when you could walk across the desert without ever feeling the hot sands whipping your face, the merest touch of thirst or hunger? You could travel the breadth of the earth without resting, without eating, without ever tiring." Again, she laughed, a cruel bark of a sound. "Don't ever forget what you are."

"And what exactly am I?" Aurel looked down at their hands, their cold unfeeling gauntlets.

"You're dead, of course."

At that, she jerked her camel around by its lead and urged it into motion, snapping her crop against its flank. Aurel watched, glowing eyes taking in the landscape beyond — the wind cresting along a line of dunes, broken only by a vast and crumbling monument that once might have carried water, but which had long since been whittled away by time to a skeletal reflection of its former glory. A faceless imperial horseman carved from paint-stripped stone raised its arm to the sky to guide travellers towards the capital, but its hand had long since cracked and fallen, so that colossal fingers sat half buried among the wind-lashed dunes, pointing at nothing.

Aurel followed, and together the two of them departed across the withering sands.

Chapter 2

They made the trip to the next town in four days and an evening, a hard pace achieved by no pauses apart from what the camel required. Sevila dozed while riding, chin nodding against her chest as the camel's paces gently rocked her body back and forth. Any misstep in the wrong direction, and she snapped awake with a tug on the lead to straighten the camel's course, only to fall asleep again almost immediately. Through it all Aurel walked, and though they knew instinctively fatigue would never come, they still expected the weariness to creep forward. While Sevila shivered in her sleep against the chilly desert night air, Aurel felt nothing, and tipped their head back to observe the star-strewn sky.

When they arrived, it was nearing night once more, though the sun still scorched the land, lowering itself on a lavender horizon. This town proved to be considerably larger than the last. Aurel's armoured feet scraped along paved roads, leading to the centre of the town where a small stone fortress squatted, surrounded by a short series of vendors.

"At last! I'm famished!" Sevila tied her camel up at the courtyard's entrance, and marched straight for the food stalls.

Hauling her bags over their shoulders, Aurel grumbled, "How can you still be hungry? You eat half your own weight every day."

She brushed off the comment with an airy, "How quickly you forget the pangs of hunger without a body! Some of still have taste, you know. And I'm not just talking about food."

As they trailed behind her, Aurel eyed her form with a critical glance. Thin as a blade, gaunt, she did not walk so much as prowl like an animal, lithe and dangerous, always on the hunt for quarry. Aurel shifted the saddlebags with ease, and they clanked heavily. "What do you even keep in here?"

"Tools for summoning, and the like." Sevila answered vaguely. The two of them reached the market vendors, still populated at this advanced hour in the hopes of a last-minute sale. "Clothes. Spare coin. Jewels. Ingots."

"No weapon of any sort?" Aurel gave the fine yet durable clothes she wore a quick once-over for any signs of a knife strapped to her body. "You travel alone. What if someone attacks you?"

"Then I make them regret it." She stopped at a vendor selling boiled goat sausages along with loaves of freshly baked bread.

Aurel watched her haggle quickly with the vendor and purchase two whole loaves and a handful of meat. One of the loaves and most of the sausages she handed to Aurel to stow away in the bags for later. The other she tore open with her hands, crammed the meat artlessly inside, and heaped a pungent fish sauce upon it, which — judging by its foul colour — Aurel was fortunate they could not smell. When they wandered to a nearby well in front of the fortress, where many of the town's inhabitants gathered for fresh water and gossip, Aurel finally asked the question that had been eating at them for nearly two days. "Back in the other town you mentioned something about knowing what the people who killed me were after. What did you mean?"

Hands full of food, Sevila struggled to tug her veil down with her shoulder before tearing into the food ravenously. Her cheek bulged as she chewed. "Whoever they are, they don't know what they're doing. Your soul severing was sloppy at best." She explained in a near unintelligible mumble. "I reckon they're searching for instructions."

"Is it not very common?" Aurel stepped out of the way of a woman swaddled in bright robes trying to get at the well with her grandchildren, both of whom pointed openly at Aurel, and only stopped when their grandmother scolded them for their rudeness.

Sevila almost choked with laughter at the question. Struggling to swallow a large bite, she coughed, eyes watering. "Common? No, no, darling. Not at all. Summoning and contracting a human soul is rare, and powerful, and dangerous, but not illegal — simply reserved for those of the highest order of society. On the other hand, soul severing is, in fact, one of the Three Taboos. Best not mention it to anyone." She leaned forward and said with conspiratorial glee, "You're an abomination unto the laws of nature."

She went back to her meal, and Aurel stared at her in shocked silence. All at once Aurel noticed the fascination with which the villagers regarded them, the awe painted openly upon their faces as they filled their amphorae at the well, as they muttered excitedly behind their veils and headscarves about the new visitors. Even though they weren't hostile, Aurel remembered all too clearly the events of the last market they had witnessed.

Lowering their voice, Aurel said to Sevila, "You must know, though? You seem to know what you're talking about."

Sevila's chewing slowed, and she had a cryptic look about her as she finished her food. "I know how to sever a soul from the body, which is by itself enough to warrant my execution," she admitted, careful so that her words did not travel. "But I have yet to discover how to join the two together once more. As far as I'm aware, nobody alive is privy to that forbidden knowledge."

"And me?" Aurel pressed, unable to keep their anxious tone at bay. "What about my body? What about our contract?"

"So long as we find your body alive and relatively intact, I should be able to figure out a way to accomplish this feat." She reached up in order to pat their shoulder in a patronising manner, rings clicking against the hard iron of Aurel's pauldron. "All the more reason to track down your killers and your body, dear." Suddenly she snapped her fingers and announced. "Now, I require something to drink. Wait here for me, won't you?"

Aurel watched her saunter off in search of wine, or so they presumed. They had yet to see Sevila drink a drop of honest water, even while they traversed the harsh desert clime. It was a mystery how she survived.

With a sigh Aurel trudged to the nearby bulwark of the fortress clutched with vines, and leaned against it if for no other reason than to avoid the townsfolk's scrutiny. Idly they plucked a pale-throated flower from the vine, and twirled it between their fingers. Nearby a child toddled past, gripping his mother's long tunic. He gazed up at Aurel with an expression bordering on caution and uncertainty. For a moment the two considered each other, until Aurel knelt down to offer the flower.

At once the child's face was suffused with horror, and when he burst into tears his mother was quick to whirl around in search of the culprit. She found Aurel, stunned, massive, and holding out a tiny white flower. Immediately the woman gathered her son under one arm, and fled to the safety of the crowded well, leaving Aurel kneeling upon the cobblestones, alone.

By the time Sevila returned with a sweating wineskin slung over one shoulder, Aurel was standing but still clutching the blossom, and staring over at the villagers. She looked questioningly between Aurel and the people surrounding the well. Her lips were stained burgundy with recent drink. "I was only gone a moment. What could you possibly have done in that time?"

"I think -" Aurel had no throat with which to choke, but their voice came out sounding strangled. "I think I had a child in life. She was almost too heavy to hold, but I clung to her fast. I remember them dragging her from my arms."

In the fog that shrouded any recollection before the abattoir, that lonely memory bled bold and viscous as amber sap. Aurel's gauntlet tightened into a fist and, realising what they'd done, they looked down to find the flower crushed to a green pulp.

For a moment Sevila just stared at Aurel blankly, then she reached around to take a swig from the wineskin. "Well, that's depressing." Slinging the skin over her shoulder once more, Sevila squinted around through the late afternoon sunlight glancing across the square. She craned her neck to try looking down a far street. "I hope this shithole town has a taverna. I am not sleeping outside again to be eaten alive by insects."

As if in answer, the barred iron door of the fortress gave a deep groan. It opened, pushed by four guardsmen in chain mail, to reveal two people. They were well dressed, though upon closer inspection their clothes were rather conservative in comparison to the rich gold embroidery of Sevila's garb. A man and a woman, they stepped into the square. When a few people still lingering near the well called out to them, they waved in greeting.

"Magistrate!" one of the villagers shouted, balancing a full amphora on his hip. "When are you going to answer my petition about bringing chariot races to the town!"

Cupping her hands around her mouth, the woman yelled back, "When you lodge it on time instead of sleeping off your drink!"

The other villagers jeered good-naturedly at that response. Shaking her head with a rueful grin, the magistrate turned to address Aurel and Sevila. "I'd heard rumours of more visitors arriving not long ago. Welcome."

"News travels fast." Sevila remarked, accepting the greetings with a shallow dip of her head. "I take it you don't receive many visitors here."

The magistrate laughed lightly, returning the nod with a deeper one of her own. "No, though I do hope this latest trend continues. Gods know we could use the trade." At her side, the man also bowed his head, and the magistrate placed her hand fondly on his arm. "My husband and I would be honoured to host you for however long you plan to stay."

Sevila's voice went silky. "We would be delighted. Wouldn't we, Aurel?"

Surprised at being addressed at all, Aurel's response was automatic. "Of course."

The magistrate held out her arm to gesture for Aurel and Sevila to follow them inside. "Please."

With only a cursory glance to check that Aurel had all her luggage, Sevila walked forward, falling into line behind the magistrate and her husband, who politely asked, "What might we call you?"

"Peinatokos," Sevila answered, supplying what Aurel guessed was her surname, for the magistrate's husband furrowed his brow.

"That is not a clan I'm familiar with." He plucked contemplatively at his greying beard. As the four of them stepped inside, the guards shut the heavy doors behind them, shutting off the view of the square and the villagers beginning to disperse for the evening.

"We're not very large." Sevila turned over her hands in an imploring gesture. "Tragedy reduced the clan to only me."

"Our condolences, Lady Peinatokina," the magistrate murmured, and her husband shook his cloth-wrapped head in sorrow. "We should not pry."

"Not at all," Sevila assured them.

Smoky torches lined the stone hallways, interspersed with faded tapestries. Once the patterned rugs lining the floor must have been costly and fine, but the jaw of time had chewed them up and left them threadbare. Silently Aurel thanked the architects who had lifted the ceilings and capped every doorway with a steep arch. Still, Aurel towered over their hosts.

"What of heirs of your own?" Sevila asked as they rounded a corner.

An odd pause followed that question, which the magistrate's husband rushed to fill too quickly. "We have not been so fortunate, I'm afraid."

Abruptly the magistrate changed the topic as she pushed open a door to admit them into a respectable banquet hall that was — Aurel noticed from the armoured stands lining the perimeter — actually a repurposed armoury. "More fortunately we had the cook make too much food this evening. I'll have a platter brought out for you, Lady Peinatokina."

Though Sevila had already eaten just moments ago, she pulled down her veil to reveal a smile that glinted with hunger. "That sounds wonderful."

While Sevila strode over to situate herself upon a cushion at the low table, placing the wineskin on the floor at her side, and the magistrate disappeared through another door to the kitchens, her husband turned to Aurel. "Would you like me to show you to your quarters so you can put your bags down, spirit?"

Aurel bowed their head. "Thank you."

"Not at all." The magistrate's husband smiled, revealing a gold-capped tooth bright against his sun-darkened skin. Aurel cast a look at Sevila, but she ignored them in favour of drinking from her wineskin, and so with a shrug Aurel left.

Deeper into the fortress they delved. From the outside the crenelated walls had not seemed so large, but the fortified building hid a labyrinth entombed beneath the earth's surface.

"This was once an imperial outpost," the magistrate's husband explained when he saw Aurel studying a side hallway they passed. "Two hundred years ago it sheltered a cohort. Now we have but a handful of garrison troops at most, and more space than we know what to do with." He pointed towards a sealed off section of hallway. "The western half we converted into a public bath."

"That's -" Aurel was going to say *admirable,* but froze. Through a door to their right could be seen a room wholly dedicated to books, at least twice as many as those the priest in the other town had cultivated.

Puzzled at Aurel's sudden absence by his side, the magistrate's husband turned to find Aurel a few steps back. "I see you've found our library." He re-joined Aurel with a guilty sort of smile. "When we moved here not long ago, we couldn't bear to abandon our private collection. Some of these were passed down from my grandfather's father. I can't boast a collection as vast as the Twin Libraries of Faros, but I'm proud of it nonetheless."

"It looks like a wonderful collection," Aurel admitted truthfully.

"Would you like to browse?" The magistrate's husband gestured for Aurel to enter. "You can borrow as many as you like during your stay."

"Oh, I couldn't possibly impose," Aurel said, hovering in the doorway even as they gazed longingly at the many bound tomes and leather-cased scrolls.

"I insist!" The magistrate's husband looked like he was about to clasp Aurel's gauntleted forearm in a comradely fashion, only to hesitate and stifle the flash of fear across his features at his near transgression. He recovered quickly, plastering a fearful smile on his face before continuing. "They so rarely have the opportunity to be read, especially by one of your calibre."

Puzzled by his reaction, Aurel nonetheless wandered inside. Their battered hobnail boots clacked against the brief stint of granite before meeting carpet once more, and they perused a shelf for titles. Nothing in terms of content looked familiar, though of the two prevalent languages Aurel could understand both without trouble.

"Your previous visitors—" Aurel began, running a fingertip along the spine of a worn manuscript, "—did they show an interest in your collection as well?"

"Yes, they did." The magistrate's husband gestured towards the writings sadly. "Though nothing I had impressed them. Not even my rare copy of Quintel's uncensored poems from exile!"

"That's a shame." Aurel tried to sound commiserating, even if they had no earthly idea who that poet was.

Aurel pulled two books from the shelf—the musings of an Emperor, and a treatise on natural philosophy, each in a different tongue—and returned to the hallway. As the magistrate's husband continued leading Aurel to their quarters, he peered over at their selections.

"Ah, Emperor Proban! An excellent philosopher but a poor general. Not at all like our current Regent, who could probably stand to take a leaf from this work." When Aurel merely blinked at him in silence, the magistrate's husband mistook their confusion for quiet ire. He stammered, "Not that the Lord Regent isn't perfectly legitimate! I just meant—! Well, you know how it is." Nervously he cleared his throat and stopped before another door. "These are your quarters. I must check in with my wife. If you'll excuse me."

Back down the corridor the magistrate's husband fled. Aurel watched him go until he disappeared around a corner, then with a shrug they shifted the books in their hands and the bags over their shoulders to open the door. They had to stoop to reach the low handle, and once inside they kicked the door shut behind them. Carefully Aurel placed Sevila's bags in a corner, and straightened.

The room was neither particularly large nor small. Sparsely decorated, it had only basic amenities: a pitcher and bowl bearing water, a small bronze dish polished to a reflective shine and propped upon the narrow writing desk, an uncomfortable looking chair, and a rug before the low-slung sleeping sofa. Eyeing the spindliness of the chair's legs, Aurel instead sat on one corner of the sofa, so as to sprawl their feet and lean against the wall. Upon the sill of the only niche along the wall behind them, Aurel placed one of the books before flipping to the first page of the other.

Reading came rapidly. They thumbed through the Emperor Proban's words in search of any flashes of familiarity or insight, and while the act of reading itself was soothing, Aurel discovered no new memories. Proban wrote of philosophers and grand libraries at length, and only of military matters very grudgingly. While not a long work, Aurel finished it quickly and with a sense of dissatisfaction, as it ended with an unfulfilling abruptness. The scribe made a note at the back, explaining that Emperor Proban was killed by his guardsmen and usurped by the captain of the capital city garrison before he could complete his memoir.

Aurel placed the book aside, and picked up the other. No sooner had they read the first few pages than the door opened, and Sevila stumbled in, clutching her now half-empty wineskin. Glancing up, Aurel turned a page. "How was the food?"

"Flavourless yet plenty." Sevila shut the door, and dropped the wineskin to the floor where it sloshed. She sighed. "The baths are shut as well, and don't open until tomorrow afternoon. Looks like I'll have to wait for a proper soak until we reach Lapedion. By the Abyss, it's dark in here!"

Aurel hadn't even realised. The ink had stood out against the parchment clear as day to their eyes. Shuffling over to the writing table, Sevila scratched around blindly in the dark. A few sparks accompanied a chipping sound, and a candle leapt to life in her hands.

"That's better." She began burrowing through her saddlebags, pulling out a long pale tunic and draping it over the curved back of the chair. Then without preamble she began to strip. Immediately Aurel jerked the book up so that they could see nothing but the pages, and kept reading with an adamant disregard.

The room was filled with the gentle rustle of silk, followed by the huff of Sevila blowing out the candle.

Crossing the room, she clambered onto the sofa and sprawled across it, unceremoniously propping her bare feet in Aurel's lap. She yawned, nudging the book in Aurel's hand with her toes. "What are you reading?"

"Philosophy." Aurel pushed her feet away.

With a grunt Sevila shuffled a pillow under her head, long dark hair bound loosely at the nape of her neck, and curled up on her half of the sofa like a cat. "I should have expected something so dull. Perhaps in life you were a scholar." Yawning again, she mumbled against the rough cotton sheets. "Did you learn anything from that nag's husband?"

Aurel flipped a page. "Nothing we didn't already know. I admire their hospitality however."

Sevila's derisive snort sounded muffled. "They must have angered someone in Pala to be stationed all the way out here. And no heir either! Their family has been sentenced to obscurity. It's the worst possible fate for their lot."

Her voice trailed off the longer she continued speaking until she dissolved into silence. Painstakingly not rustling the pages in order to let Sevila sleep uninterrupted, Aurel continued reading. Over the course of the next hour or two they learned two things: that the natural world would bend reality in order to honour the sanctity of a contract, and that Sevila kicked in her sleep. The philosopher's dialogue attempted to find the limit of a contract, while Sevila's foot repeatedly tried to pass through Aurel's armour. In the end neither were very successful.

While Aurel remained incapable of feeling a chill, they could not shake a shivering sense of dread. *'The only limit we know of—'* the philosopher wrote in a precise overly-inflected language, *'—is in a contract's interpretation. The more complex the creature, then naturally the more complex the bargain. My youngest daughter, for instance, foolishly offered the spirit of a mangy dog a thimbleful of her blood if it would get her out of practising the lyre. Alas, the spirit bit off three of her fingers, and she never played the lyre again.'*

Aurel glanced at Sevila, who slept deeply and yet fitfully, who in slumber appeared very small and fragile. Deception, Aurel already knew from even so short a time accompanying her, was one of Sevila's most outstanding qualities. And with increasing horror Aurel understood the full depth of agreeing to do for her any one thing.

Abruptly Aurel stood. Sevila merely rolled over and did not wake. Grabbing the memoirs of Emperor Proban, Aurel crept from the room. They closed the door as softly as they could manage, but the iron-ringed handle clanged against the stone doorway. At some point earlier in the night, a guardsman had travelled the halls and quenched all but the torches at each corner, so that darkness spilled along the corridors. Aurel picked their way back to the library and was relieved to find it uninhabited.

They placed the two books back where they had found them, and stepped back, scanning titles. Most were poets, great playwrights, imperial historians of varying stripes. An enormous codex of laws and edicts sat untouched on a bottom shelf like a mandatory set piece for any politician worth their salt. Finally, Aurel stumbled upon mention of summoning and contracting, but when they unfurled the vellum scroll in question, it was to find that the diagrams were a complex jumble punctuated with graphically detailed notes on how to best slaughter any number of farm animals for specific rituals.

The torches burned low and smoky. After pouring over a heap of different texts, mounded around the floor where they sat, Aurel heard a noise. Gazing at the entrance, Aurel clambered to their feet and wandered over, peering out into the corridor. Partway down the hall, a door clicked against its frame in a draft. Curious, Aurel walked towards it, pulled it open, and saw nothing but an empty stairwell leading down into the belly of the fortress. Aurel was about to shut the door when the sound of urgent voices floated faintly through the gloom.

The passageway was cramped and Aurel had to duck in order to descend the steps. At one point their broad shoulders almost scraped against the narrow walls, and they slowed their pace to avoid detection. Near the bottom, Aurel stopped and looked around a corner.

The large room's original purpose could have been anything from sleeping quarters to emergency food storage, but had long since been refashioned into a jail. The cells were all empty, their bars wounded with rust, except for one at the very opposite end of the room, in front of which the magistrate and her husband argued.

"There isn't enough food!" the magistrate snapped.

"I thought you had the cook prepare enough to feed four!" Her husband's brow furrowed, emphatic in his gestures.

Jerking her hand up to point to the ceiling, the magistrate hissed, "That damn woman ate everything. We only have raw meat now, and we can't risk opening the kitchen without waking the cook."

Head in his hands, the magistrate's husband groaned. "We'll just have to make do with the raw meat, then."

"We can't!" The magistrate gasped. "You know the Law!"

"It's not as if his condition could get any worse!"

"But—!"

"We have to! He's still hungry!"

As they fought, behind the bars something moved. A high keening whine slipped from the prison cell, and in the low torchlight Aurel's glowing eyes widened.

Retreating as quietly as possible, Aurel hurried towards the upper level. They scrambled back to their quarters, and this time did not bother with delicacy. The door slammed open, and Aurel rushed to the sofa. "Sevila!" They pushed at her shoulder and glanced fervently at the door as though expecting their hosts to burst in at any moment. *"Sevila!"*

With a raspy, tired moan Sevila swatted at Aurel's gauntlets. "I'm awake, you idiot. You can stop shaking me."

"The magistrate and her husband! They -!" Aurel wrung their hands, lowering their voice. "They're keeping some kind of — of *creature* in the lower levels!"

Heaving a sigh, Sevila dragged herself upright. "One night. Just one night of decent sleep. Is it too much to ask?" She pinched the bridge of her nose and mumbled, "What did it look like?"

After a moment of awkward hesitation, Aurel admitted, "I'm not sure. They were standing in front of it. It wasn't very large, but I swear: it wasn't human."

Sevila glowered, a look both flat and unimpressed, before swinging her legs over the side of the sofa. "This had better not be a waste of my time," she growled.

Regardless she followed Aurel out into the hallway. Upon reaching the nearest crossroads, Sevila pulled a torch from its sconce, and carried it with her.

"They'll see you," Aurel reminded her, following her down the stairs.

"That's the point." Sevila glared over her shoulder at Aurel lurking anxiously behind her. "And why am I the one going first into a dark, unknown dungeon? No, don't try to justify your cowardice. I'm not awake enough to listen."

Whereas before Aurel had taken great pains to tread unheard and unseen, Sevila stomped down the stairs bearing her torch like a flame-tipped club. Aurel winced at every loud noise, straining to hear the sound of voices. Sevila paused only when the two of them reached the bottom of the stairs, and saw a trail of blood scraped and glistening along the ground. To that Sevila's only response was a thoughtful grunt, and then she was striding into the dungeon, careful to avoid stepping upon any splatter with her bare feet.

At the opposite end of the cavernous room the magistrate's husband had dragged a flensed goat carcass over iron-coloured stone. The cell door was open, and the magistrate's husband was pushing the carcass inside while the magistrate restlessly jangled the gilded chatelaine at her hip.

Without breaking stride Sevila spoke, "Please tell me you're feeding that to a dog. Or a lion. Frankly, I'll accept lion as your answer."

Hearing the intrusion, the magistrate spun around, and her husband dropped the carcass so that its legs slapped wetly to the floor. "You need to leave immediately!" The magistrate ordered, her voice brusque and deepened in pitch.

"I just want to get back to sleep, so make this easier for all of us, won't you—?" Sevila began, but stopped. A few paces away from the cell Sevila froze in her tracks.

With horror Aurel watched as a human hand reached from behind the magistrate's husband, and clawed the carcass further into the cell.

"Is this a waste of your time now?" Aurel asked.

A tense silence reigned. Rather than answer Sevila stared at the two standing in front of her, and the line of her back was rigid. When she spoke, her voice was a hoarse whisper. "I am most definitely not awake enough for this."

The magistrate's husband shakily stood upright, his hands outstretched as though warding off a blow. "It isn't what it seems."

"Isn't it?" With every passing moment Sevila's glare grew more fierce, biting off words between clenched teeth. "Allow me to guess what happened. There's a coup. Your family — like so many others — is upended. Your friends and benefactors are dead. There is only one chance of your name's survival, but you cannot conceive by natural means. You pay only for Healers to inform you that there's nothing to be done, and then you get desperate, so you hunt down the first quack who will say: yes."

When Sevila took a step forward, the magistrate and her husband closed ranks to guard the entrance to the cell. Their expressions were stony, but Sevila's bared teeth gleamed, cold. "What exactly do you think is going to happen? Do you think that thing will escape notice forever? Someone will find out, and when they do, they won't just kill that thing you lock behind bars."

The magistrate's jaw trembled with conviction. "He is not a thing. He is my son," she said, and her husband clasped her hand.

Sevila laughed. "He is a monster." She waved her torch towards the cell behind them, and as dim shadows danced around the magistrate's bulky hems, Aurel caught a glimpse of small feet, heard the sound of tearing flesh. "He will outgrow this sad cage, and — consumed with insatiable hunger — he will devour everything until he is slain. Only then will he know peace." Sevila's words became a vicious snarl, and her golden eyes blazed. "Killing him is a mercy."

The silence that followed that statement was interrupted only by the intermittent crunch of teeth against bone from the cell. For a long moment, nobody spoke. Then Sevila stepped forward to push her way into the cell. "Since you obviously don't have the stones, I'll gladly do the deed."

Fumbling at his belt, the magistrate's husband drew a long dagger from its sheath with a cry. No sooner had the blade gleamed with wicked intent in the torchlight than Aurel moved. One moment Aurel stood a few paces behind Sevila. The next, the air scorched with the stench of sulphur, and Aurel towered over the magistrate's husband. With ease, they snatched his wrist and squeezed. He shouted out in pain, dropping the knife. When it clattered to the floor, Aurel slowly bent down to retrieve it. The magistrate's husband cowered and nursed his hand, his wife's arm around his shoulders. Throughout the entire exchange, Sevila remained still and unflinching, an almost bored expression on her face.

Rising to their full height once more, Aurel caught the first glimpse of the creature beyond. It hunched over the half-eaten carcass on all fours. From the neck down, it had every appearance of a human child, small and lean and hairless. Its bloodied mouth however belonged to a calf. Its face bristled with a dark pelt; its forehead bulged with nascent horns; its bovine eyes held a shrewd glimmer. Upon closer inspection its teeth were sharp, and it moved with a furtiveness that belied a lurking intelligence.

"Aurel." Sevila held her hand out. Temporarily puzzled, Aurel handed her the dagger, handle first. Longer than her forearm, it gleamed in the torchlight. She gave it an expert flourish. Sevila walked into the cell, and the magistrate and her husband shrank away to let her pass.

"I'm not normally one for charity —" Sevila muttered half to herself, "—but you'll thank me for this later."

She threw the torch upon the ground and there it cast a shower of sparks across the stones. The creature shrank away from the glowing embers, nostrils flaring. Quick, a strike like that of a snake coiled upon itself, Sevila darted forward to grab the creature by the scruff of its neck. She planted her knee into its spine, wrenched its head back, and with a fluid practised motion she drew the blade across its exposed throat.

It squealed and twitched as it died. Blood streamed over its chest, and it pawed at Sevila's arm in vain until at last with a warm gurgle it slumped forward to join the carcass on the ground. Straightening, Sevila shook her free hand, scattering drops of red across the ground. When she looked down at her blood-stained tunic, she sighed. "I knew I shouldn't have worn something white. Why does this always happen to me?"

She swooped down to grab the torch from the floor, then — pressing the dagger back into Aurel's hands — she stalked towards the stairs without sparing even a glance at their hosts, who stared after her in abject horror. Nonplussed, Aurel said to them, "I— uh—am very sorry for your loss."

Aurel's words seemed to snap the magistrate from a daze, and she yelled, "Get out!"

Flinching, Aurel hurried after Sevila. Already back in the room, illuminated only by the light through the open door, she was pulling the ruined tunic over her head. "I take it our invitation has been revoked? Here. Use this."

She thrust the tunic into Aurel's hands and jerked her chin at the knife. Slowly, Aurel cleaned the blade and gore-speckled, wire-wrapped handle, carefully not looking at her. "You should have been more gentle with them."

With a snort, Sevila poured water from the pitcher into the basin, and began to splash her arms and hands. Blood paled in the water. "And you should have broken his arm instead of just giving him a bit of bruising. Still," she admitted grudgingly, "I take back my earlier accusation of cowardice."

To that Aurel did not reply, nor did Sevila seem to expect any remark. Using the sofa sheets, she patted herself dry, then dug through her bags for clothes. She pulled out her usual gold and saffron ensemble, and when she shook it a cloud of sand scattered along the floor. Lip curled in distaste, Sevila muttered, "Just my luck finding the only people in a hundred miles that dabble in cross-breeding abominations instead of an honest laundering service."

"Where will we go now?" Aurel asked. They tossed the tunic on the chair, then tucked the dagger into the broad sash that served as their waist. There the handle protruded, ready to be drawn.

"Lapedion." Sevila wrapped her head in pale silk so that her hair was covered, but was unsatisfied with the job, so she unwound it and wrapped it again more tightly. "It's the largest city in the empire this far south, with a decent sized temple to boot. I have no doubt our quarry will be stopping over there for supplies before travelling any further."

"And then?" Aurel pressed as they gathered up Sevila's saddlebags in preparation for their departure.

She put the finishing touches on her outfit — breeches gathered at the knee, heavy gold bracelets circling her wrists, veil draped around her neck and midway down her chest — and pulled up her cowl so that a shadow cast over her face.

"Then," she answered, crossing the room to leave, "I will have a proper bath, a proper meal, a proper lay, and a proper night's sleep."

Chapter 3

Gradually the arid desert gave way to a sloping plateau. Sand no longer slipped beneath Aurel's booted feet, and instead the camel's long legs brushed against the occasional thorny bush. In the west mountains purpled, rocky and steep, along the horizon. Though they could not feel it, Aurel could see that the heat remained. Swaddled in their heavy armour and cloak, Aurel studied the spiny flora, the slow spiral of small many-legged insects around stalks and delicate petals. Far off to the north and east, the land shimmered with heat, blending the smudged horizon with pale colour.

Determined to catch whoever it was they were pursuing, Sevila again slept atop her camel, never once stopping to pitch a tent for seven days and six nights. By the time they began to pass large flocks of hardy sheep, fields of wheat and grapes and citrus fruit beneath the towering aqueduct ruins they had followed through the desert straight as an arrow, Sevila looked haggard. Aurel half expected her to slip from her seat, but she did not err. She had torn through the supply of bread, hard cheese, dried meat, apricots, and dates until nothing remained. Over the top of the bone-clattering veil her eyes gleamed gold, and keen, and hungry.

At last when they saw Lapedion within reach, Sevila's shoulders straightened, and she lifted her head like a sleuth-hound catching the scent of a hunt. A few other travellers could be seen on the road ahead: merchant caravans and farmers mostly, though very few came from the same direction as they. Towards the south

Aurel could now say with some certainty there lay little to interest the likes of anyone but a reluctant tax collector.

"It didn't always used to be this way." Sevila jerked her head at the empty roadless expanse behind them while the camel plodded resolutely onward. "There once was a grand city not far from the town where I found you. One of the many jewels of the empire. A flourishing trade centre with connections to Aegryph and even deeper south to the far-off kingdoms across the sands."

Aurel peered up at her curiously. "What happened?"

"What usually happened in those days." She shrugged, swaying with the camel's steps. "A spiteful god started a war, and another vengeful god took umbrage. They trampled the hillsides to sand, and scoured the earth with their wrath. They're not a problem these days, though."

"I'm assuming they settled the score and went their separate ways at last?" Aurel hazarded a guess.

They expected Sevila to scoff and roll her eyes, but instead she answered gravely. "No. They're all dead. Or at least as dead as gods can be."

A breeze tugged at the long ends of Sevila's cowl, curling the corners around her thighs where she sat. Aurel searched her face, but she remained as inscrutable as ever. "I wasn't aware gods could be killed."

"Gods have a different relationship with things like death and time. They are so wholly focused on their own natures that they simply forget to die, and death passes them right by. You can never truly kill them. You can only eat them." Her tone was aloof, but Sevila refused to meet their gaze, choosing to instead study the road ahead.

Aurel recoiled at the thought. "*What?*"

"Souls cannot be created or destroyed, but they can be subsumed. It is Law." With that offhanded reply, Sevila snapped her riding crop, urging her mount to a faster pace. Craning her neck, she shouted to Aurel, "Do keep up, darling!"

Stumbling, Aurel ran after her.

The city's walls were a stout fortification reinforced by a series of deep trenches dug into the earth at key points along the perimeter. Banners streamed lazily along the walls, a dark royal purple emblazoned with a double-headed eagle, its golden wings outstretched— the imperial crest. Aurel trotted just behind Sevila through the gates, flung open to admit travellers. More than one unfortunate farmer scattered as Sevila passed so as to not be trampled, and Aurel tried apologising as they clanged by in their armour. For their efforts, Aurel received rude gestures and shaken fists.

Once inside, Sevila dismounted and tossed the camel's lead to a boy, who held out his hand for coin before beginning to lead the camel away to tie it up. "Grab my things, won't you?" Sevila said idly to Aurel, already striding off into the bustling street. "Else I'll have to pay the boy extra."

Hurriedly Aurel grabbed the saddlebags and went after Sevila, determined to not get lost in yet another new and foreign environment. Dusty and travel-worn as she was, Sevila blended seamlessly into the mass of people, and Aurel had to search every face at waist-height before finding her with a sense of relief. Here the people only spared Aurel a cursory appraising glance before continuing with their own business. Speckled frequently among them were a number of other souls. On one street alone Aurel counted eight, though the most powerful among them was a bored looking vulture that manned a stall selling brass trinkets, while its master was away running errands. It glowered at potential customers, and pecked viciously at the hands of would-be thieves.

Eventually Sevila stopped at a restaurant on a crowded corner, plopping herself onto a wicker chair at an empty table on the street side, and waving her hand at a serving girl who bore cups of rich tea. The girl seemed uncertain as she placed a steaming teacup on the table in front of Sevila, who was already rattling off an extensive list of orders. Meanwhile, Aurel set the bags down against the tile-bright wall near their table, peeking through the patterned screen to see the bustle of customers and staff inside.

When the girl disappeared into the kitchens, Sevila pulled down her veil and leaned back in her chair with a heavy sigh. "I've been dreaming of this for days."

"I know." Aurel cautiously lowered their bulk onto the chair opposite her. "I heard you muttering about veal in your sleep. You snore, by the way."

"I do not!" Sevila insisted, appalled at the suggestion.

Before Aurel could reply, someone stepped from the restaurant, and approached their table. A large woman — hair wrapped in sweat-stained cotton, and sleeves rolled up to her elbows to reveal skin weathered with small grease burns from the day — crossed her arms, and glared down at Sevila. "Food is for paying customers only," she said. "Finish your tea and go."

Sevila frowned over the top of her cup before placing it delicately back on the table's uneven surface. "I'll pay after the meal, as is customary."

The woman — Aurel assumed she was the owner — sneered, gesturing at Sevila's dirtied finery and bedraggled appearance. "I've seen your kind before. Nobles fleeing the capital without a brass to their name, sneaking away after eating. Go steal scraps from the back like the other gutter vermin!"

Sevila did not move from her seat, but the air around her grew tense and still. Her muscles coiled, and her slitted pupils narrowed to a knife's edge. "I guarantee you have never seen 'my kind' before." She smiled, a cold baring of her teeth. "And I did not travel halfway across the desert to be treated like common scum by some goat-fucking pig."

The woman's face flushed red in a combination of fury and fear, but before she could shout for assistance from guards or nearby customers, Aurel pulled a handful of coin from one of Sevila's bags. The coins spilled through their fingers to rattle against the table top, glinting fat and rich, a combination of brass, and silver, and gold. "My Mistress is hungry and has ample coin," Aurel said, keeping their voice soft and soothing. "Please. There is no need for a quarrel."

Immediately the owner's eyes widened at the sight. Clearing her throat, she mumbled a series of curses as she turned away and stormed off to the safety of the kitchens once more. With a derisive sniff, Sevila turned in her seat to help Aurel gather back up the coins that had tumbled across the table, a few rolling to the ground. "You see now why laundering services are so important? Hmm?" She scooped up a pile of gold, which clacked against her rings. "And you should call me Mistress more often! It has a lovely ring in your voice, dear."

"Not on your life," Aurel replied, stuffing the money back into Sevila's bag. "You'll be lucky if all she does is spit in your food."

"I've had worse," Sevila flicked a coin between clever fingers, and caught it in mid-air. To the side, a street urchin dressed in rags darted forward to snatch up a pale coin that had rolled between the nearby cobblestones. Sevila slammed her foot down atop the coin before he could grab it, and she growled. "I won't bother reporting you to the city guard. I'll just cut off your hands myself."

"Sevila!" Aurel said reproachfully, and handed a coin to the child, who snagged it and darted away into the crowd. After the child was gone, Aurel bent over to retrieve the coin Sevila was jealously guarding, swatting at her ankle. "You really are a mean old bitch when you're hungry."

Mumbling something foul under her breath, Sevila picked up her still steaming tea and sipped at it. Aurel did not know someone could drink tea grumpily, but somehow Sevila managed to pull it off with aplomb.

Soon the serving girl returned with a jug of wine, and then scurried back into the restaurant to return yet again with her hands full of platters and bowls. One was filled with warm water and rose petals, in which Sevila washed her hands before diving into the food with her fingers. Plate after plate, bowls of curried lamb, spiced veal and pork, mounds of flatbread drizzled with oil and studded with olives. Sevila ate continuously; she ate neatly; she ate voraciously. It never failed to fascinate Aurel how much she could pack away without pausing, and they toyed with one of the remaining coins while watching Sevila with a strange and vaguely sickened enthralment.

The coin had been pierced along the edge to show it was pure metal all the way through. The obverse bore the image of a honeybee wreathed in laurels with the year stamped on the bottom. Flicking it over idly, Aurel froze. There, stamped into the gold, was a woman's face turned in profile and surrounded by the letters *IMP. IUST. KOM.* Blinking down at the woman's image, Aurel brought the coin closer to better inspect it.

"I know this woman."

"Hmm?" Sevila's questioning hum echoed within her cup as she downed another mouthful of wine. Leaning over she cocked her head, and squinted at the coin in Aurel's hands. She poured what remained of the wine jug into her cup, and waved her free hand, dismissive. "Of course, you do. That's the late Empress Iustina Severa Komateros. The Lady Augusta. Mother of the Land. Her face has been stamped on imperial currency for the last twenty or thirty years. Everyone in the empire and beyond would recognise her."

"Perhaps you're right," Aurel conceded slowly. The coin caught a slant of sunlight, and Iustina's face sparkled warmly.

"I usually am," Sevila mumbled around a mouthful of bread dipped in a soup of thick red sauce.

Over the course of the meal, the empty dishes stacked up around her until by the end Sevila's side of the table and much of Aurel's, too, had been colonised by an impenetrable fortress of earthenware. At last she tipped back her chair and gave a long, contented groan. When the serving girl came around to take everything away, Sevila slipped her the appropriate amount of coin, and said dryly, "My compliments to the chef." Then she rose, stretched her arms above her head, and announced to her companion. "Time to find the baths."

Aurel stood, scooping up the saddlebags, and gestured for Sevila to lead the way. The late morning had faded into early afternoon, and the few wispy clouds streaking across the sky did little to dampen the sun's rays. Smaller side alleys were strewn with awnings and broad bolts of cloth to shelter the city's inhabitants from the heat, and people walked jagged lines to criss-cross through the shade at all times. The city garrison patrolled in pairs, stopping here and there to chat with city-dwellers or otherwise chase after a thief and drag them away for trial and swift punishment. A dome capped a large building near the city centre, and at its altar people bore offerings for the priest to burn, fragrant smoke blackening a column of air to the heavens. Directly opposite the temple sat the baths, a complex of chambers open to the public.

Out front Sevila paused. "Wait here just a moment."

Puzzled, Aurel did as requested. People milled about and though they jostled one another, they took great pains to not so much as brush up against Aurel. Sevila returned not long later, wrapped in a plain yet fresh sheet, and handed Aurel her dirty clothes.

"What's this for?" Aurel shifted the bags in their arms so as to accommodate the clothes.

"For you to clean," Sevila answered as though it were obvious.

"No." Aurel shook their head. "Not a chance. You'll have to command me."

Mouth wrenching open, Sevila stopped. She pursed her lips, and her eyes narrowed. With an odd sense of triumph Aurel watched her struggle with the notion of wasting a single limitless wish on something as trivial as laundry. Finally, her face relaxed into a silky smile, and her voice turned syrup-sweet. "As you like. While you wait for me then, there's a gift for you in the left pocket of that bag."

Suspicious, Aurel reached into the pocket in question, and pulled out three books — the banned and uncensored volumes of Quintil's poetry from exile. "How did you even manage to steal these from the magistrate without my noticing?"

Sevila feigned offence. "I got those just for you, and that's all you have to say? No: '*Thank you so much, Sevila! You shouldn't have been so thoughtful, Sevila!*'" She mimicked Aurel's deeper tone with dramatic flair.

Aurel gave her a flat stare. "You stole them to sell them, didn't you?"

"Well, obviously, but I see no reason why you can't read them first," Sevila admitted, as shameless and unapologetic as always.

Shaking their head, Aurel sighed deeply, "Fine."

She beamed up at them, and clapped her hands together. "That's the spirit!" she said, turning to walk back into the baths.

"Was that a pun?" Aurel called after her retreating back. "You really are horrible, you know that?"

In answer, she flashed a roguish grin over her shoulder, and vanished inside.

Aurel shoved the volumes back into the bag, and looked around in search of any hint of a laundering service. Seeing none and at a loss for where to find one, Aurel began to wander, making a circuit around the paved city centre. In the middle of the square a massive tetrapylon arch cast its broad shadow over the cobblestones. From Aurel's place along the fringe they could see deep carvings all along the inner walls, detailing battle scenes and a great victory over an enemy hoard mounted on horseback. People milled around at its base, eating food, strolling with a friend or lover. A man stood atop the base of one pillar, and addressed an uninterested crowd, yelling about the gods and their abandonment. Pedestals atop the structure were empty, but once must have held statues that were then chiselled away and carted off for someone else's triumphal monument.

Along the outer fringes in the comfort of the shade merchants hawked their wares, though none attempted to sell Aurel anything even when Aurel paused to browse. At the temple Aurel stopped near the end of the queue where people waited, bearing live fowl or sheep. One noble even led a bull by its nose ring, and the animal stamped its foot as if impatient with the wait, not knowing the slaughter to come. Up ahead Aurel could see the city's chief priest gesturing with his leaf-shaped sacrificial blade for the next in line, the sleeves of his black robes heavy and dripping with blood.

"Are you in line?"

Startled at the sudden question addressed to them, Aurel turned to find a young man standing there. He held a chicken by its legs, and occasionally it would struggle to escape, flapping in a flurry of loose feathers and squawks.

"Apologies. No." Aurel stepped aside, and the man nodded respectfully, warily, before taking his place in the queue. Aurel was about to leave when instead they asked. "What are the offerings supposed to achieve?"

The man's dark brow creased, and he answered with caution. "That depends. Some people come for haruspicy; they cannot summon spirits themselves, so they pay a priest to do so instead. Some come just to be seen — public displays of piety, that kind of thing. Others try to appeal to a god with sacrifice."

"And what are you here for?" Aurel nodded towards the chicken, which had gone limp once more.

In reply, the man gave a sheepish sort of shrug. "A bit of one and two, I suppose. Nobody's been able to contract with a god for years. I remember them as a child. You'd be foolish to waste stock on an attempt now, but many people still do."

Thoughtful, Aurel mused aloud, "And what would you want from a god?"

Suddenly the man paled. He took a trembling step backwards. "Look, I don't know what it is you're after, spirit, but I don't want a contract with you. Do you hear me? No contract!"

People were beginning to stare. A gap formed around the two of them, a bubble of space trapping them together, and the man's eyes darted like those of a cornered animal. Aurel raised their free hand, palm up, and said soothingly, "Please. I am just asking a few questions."

The man brandished the chicken in what would have otherwise been a comical fashion had his face not been suffused with terror. "I will not be tricked!"

When Aurel tried speaking again, he threw the chicken at them, and ran, pushing through the crowd. The chicken hit Aurel square in the chest, and flapped noisily, squawking. Aurel almost dropped Sevila's bags as they snatched at the chicken, finally holding it upside down by the legs as the man had done. Looking around Aurel found that the queue to the temple had moved ahead, but nobody was brave enough to join the line for fear of getting too close. Without a word and with chicken in hand, Aurel ducked away to continue their walk around the square.

People gave Aurel an even wider berth now. Aurel approached no more strangers, until at last they made almost a complete circuit and found a side alley behind the bath complex where fullers lashed cloth against stone basins. Careful so as not to get splashed, Aurel found a middle-aged woman washing a basket of clothes in what they hoped was clean water. The basin she worked in was sudsy, and she scrubbed her laundry with wiry, bare hands.

"Excuse me." Aurel held up the chicken, which clucked aggressively at being swung around. A few feathers drifted to the ground. "Would you wash these clothes in exchange for this chicken?"

The woman's movements slowed but never stopped. She squinted at the clothes, at the chicken, and then at Aurel. "Those clothes specifically?" She pointed, hand dripping with water. "Just those clothes, and that chicken?"

"Yes," Aurel said. "That's all. Please."

The woman leaned back slightly, expression guarded. "What's wrong with them?"

"Nothing! They're just dirty!" Exasperated, Aurel sat down on the edge of the stone basin where she worked. They dropped the bags to the ground, and heaved a sigh.

The woman held out her hand, and when Aurel simply blinked at her in confusion she said, "Are you going to give me the clothes, or not?"

Hurriedly Aurel passed them over. "Thank you," they gasped in relief.

Spreading the fine cloth between her hands, she held them up to an appreciative eye. "Your Mistress is a small woman," she said, plunging the silk into the cold water and kneading it gently. "In the future you should open with, '*my Mistress wants thus-and-such,*' else people will think you are trying to bargain for much greater stakes, spirit."

Sliding down to the cobblestones, Aurel leaned against the short retaining wall of the basin. "Thank you. I'll be sure to remember that."

The chicken tried to make another bold escape, and the woman shook her head as she worked and watched Aurel to struggle to keep hold of the animal without injuring it. Manoeuvring the chicken into one hand, Aurel used the other to pull out a volume of poetry. While Aurel read, the woman dunked Sevila's clothes, then pressed the water from them. Careful not to place them in the sun, she lay the silk out to dry and went back to cleaning her own clothes without further comment. In a companionable silence, she worked and Aurel read, and when the sun began to touch Sevila's clothes the woman rearranged them further in the shade.

Halfway through the second volume, Aurel was beginning to wonder when Sevila might be finished, when they heard a voice. "There you are!"

Scrubbed, soaked and oiled, Sevila walked towards them. The late afternoon light washed over her in warm honeyed tones — the slick curls of her long dark hair, the leonine tilt of her freshly painted eyes and mouth. She wore a simple white cotton tunic and leather sandals. When one of the fullers in the lane slapped dyed cloth against stone, she leapt away from the splatter with a grimace. "Of course, I find you in the most malodorous parts of the damn city."

Rather than reply, Aurel stood, and handed over the chicken to the woman with a bow and a brief, "Thank you."

The woman took the chicken, and waved Aurel away as though they were a fly worrying her meal. Aurel gathered up Sevila's bags and damp clothes, then strode over to meet her. As they turned together to walk back to the main square, Sevila asked, "Where on earth did you get a chicken?"

Slinging the clanking bags over one shoulder, Aurel admitted, "A man threw it at me." They tried to sound nonchalant about the whole affair.

Sevila bit her lower lip to poorly stifle a smirk. "Did that happen to you often in life? Men flinging their cocks at you?"

Aurel did not dignify that with an answer, only glared at her, unimpressed, and still Sevila laughed. Tossing the clothes at her, Aurel grumbled, "That is the last time I ever do your laundering."

Still grinning, Sevila folded the silk between her hands and tucked the bundle beneath one arm. "Last stop for the evening, and then we decide our next course of action tomorrow morning."

She struck out along a side street, ducking into alleys, and climbing gentle sets of stairs that curved around private apartment blocks and low-slung homes. No matter where they went, Sevila seemed to have an inherent instinct for how to best navigate, whether it be labyrinthine cities or the vast undulating dunes of the desert. At one point, turning sideways to allow a few children to scamper by while chasing a small rodent spirit, Aurel remarked, "You must travel often. You've known every city we've visited thus far."

"I'm not the type to settle down, so to speak." She rounded a corner leading out onto a broader street. "Ah, here we are."

The buildings here, while not the most prestigious in appearance, were treated with impeccable upkeep. No brick facing could be seen through the plaster, which had been meticulously painted with black and grey veins to mimic marble. Even the interior was bright and airy, window shutters thrown open to admit a fair breeze. A young man, beautiful and bare-chested, watered plants, while an older woman scratched mathematical figures in a ledger behind a desk. Her eyes were hooded and dark, and she wore no other colour than red — red draped over red. Her fingers clacked with rubies and carnelians bound in blackened iron.

Sevila approached the desk with a swagger and a quick smile. "Constantia, you look as glorious as ever."

Constantia glanced up, saw who it was, grunted an annoyed note, and returned to her work. Not once did she stop her calculations. "What do you want?" Her tone was short, uninflected.

"Is that any way to treat one of your best customers?" Sevila placed a hand at the dip of her collarbone as though taken aback by so rude a greeting.

"My best customers are noble patrons and men of stature. You—" Constantia gestured with her stylus at Sevila's tiny figure, "—are neither of those."

"I pay well!" Sevila shot back, all charm gone, suddenly defensive and surly. "I treat the girls nicely!"

"Congratulations," Constantia drawled. "You meet the bare minimum requirements for a halfway decent person. Now, do you want a room, or did you come here just to harass me?"

With a huff Sevila grumbled and pulled out a small handful of coin from one of the bags slung over Aurel's shoulder. "A nice room. I've had a very long few days, and we'll be staying the night."

For the first time Constantia acknowledged Aurel's presence, her eyebrows raised. "You're going to need more coin if there's two of you."

As if afraid Constantia would make a grab for the coins, Sevila clutched the fistful close. "What about the two for one discount for newly-weds?"

"Newly-weds?" Aurel and Constantia repeated simultaneously with varying degrees of disgust and — on Aurel's part — horror.

Sevila leaned her shoulder against Aurel, and made the outrageous claim, "In life, we were in love. Now we're engaged."

"In a contract!" Aurel shrugged her off, but Sevila persisted.

"Of love!"

"No," Aurel growled, ignoring the way Sevila's sharp elbow dug into the sash at their waist. "The arcane kind."

Constantia fixed Sevila with her most unimpressed stare yet. "Double the price, or you can sleep in the street with the dogs."

Glowering at Aurel as though this were somehow all their fault, Sevila passed over the money, and stomped down a hallway in search of their room. Aurel had to duck down to pass beneath the entrance when Sevila threw open the door. She stormed inside, sandals clacking angrily against her heels. "It wouldn't kill you to play along," she huffed, flinging her clothes against a wall and herself onto the large mattress that awaited her.

"I'm already dead, and I'm not going to lie for your petty gains," Aurel retorted staunchly, setting the bags down in the corner.

Half-buried among a mountain of plush pillows Sevila kicked her sandals to the ground. "Double the price, and for what?" She pointed at Aurel from the low bed, then gestured to the finery all around them — the stuccoed walls, the velvet lined chair in the corner, the complimentary jug of fine wine. "You can't even enjoy these services! You're physically incapable!"

"I'm going to enjoy the peace and quiet when you finally go to sleep," Aurel shot back. They were in the process of digging out the volume of poetry they had been reading, when a knock at the door gave them pause. Straightening, Aurel crossed the room and opened the door. Two young women dressed in nothing but gauzy silk, their ankles bound in gold and silver, waited outside, expectant. "I —uh—" Aurel averted their gaze, looking over the girls' shoulders. "Can I help you?"

From the mattress Sevila waved lazily. "Let them in already, won't you?"

Puzzled, Aurel moved aside so that the two could step in. Peering out the door then back into the room, Aurel said, "Thank you, but I think we have everything we need here."

The girls exchanged fleeting looks before laughing softly. "I've never had a client bring a spirit before," one of them said.

"I have." The other shook her head with a smile, reaching forward to trail her fingers along the edge of Aurel's cloak. "Never a human one though."

With cruel amusement Sevila watched the realisation dawn on Aurel's face. She let loose a bark of laughter, propping herself upright on the pillows. "I'm afraid you won't be getting your peace and quiet for a while yet, darling." Taking off her rings and placing them on the floor beside the mattress, Sevila gestured for the girls to join her.

Still clutching the door handle, Aurel fumbled for a proper response. "I think—" One of the girls knelt over Sevila to kiss her deeply on the mouth, and Aurel looked up at the ceiling. "I think I'll go for a walk."

"Don't feel obliged on my account." Sevila's gaze sharpened with a dark want as the other began to remove Sevila's tunic. "By all means, stay. It doesn't matter to me."

Aurel's only response was to step from the room, and slam the door shut behind them. Through the carved wood they could hear Sevila laughing. Not wanting to hear anything else, Aurel quickened their pace to the exit, seeing the establishment with new eyes now that they knew what it truly was. At the front desk Constantia had pulled out an abacus, and was pushing around the wooden beads with the end of her stylus to calculate more complex sums.

Aurel was about to flee the brothel entirely, when instead they stopped at the exit and, turning, asked. "Is there a curfew I should be aware of?"

"This is a whorehouse. What do you think?" Constantia snorted wryly, and shook her head. She scrawled a figure in her ledger, then tipped the abacus to reset her calculations. "How did a sweet simple thing like you end up in a contract with a Mistress like that?"

"Bad luck? Desperation?" Aurel shrugged in the doorway, their voice small even as their shoulders scraped against the wooden frame.

Constantia's stylus pushed up a bead slowly, and she considered Aurel with a contemplative furrow in her brow. "You might try the guild quarter for entertainment. It's in the south."

"Is there a library?" Aurel's expression was hopeful.

She narrowed her eyes, and tapped the end of her stylus against the ledger. "Only in Faros. All other collections are private, and seeing as you are what you are, I wouldn't recommend randomly knocking on doors at night asking for things. I'm not normally in the business of giving information for free, but take heed, spirit: your Mistress is not what she seems. Run, while you still can."

With that Constantia went back to her sums, expertly flicking the end of her stylus against the abacus.

Thanking her and receiving only a dismissive grunt for their trouble, Aurel left. Their eyes scanned the rooftops for the faintest glow of the setting sun, and they headed as south as the street allowed. No unattended torch sconces were allowed on the buildings for fear of fire hazards, though while walking along Aurel watched two guards stop at a corner to light torches that they then carried with them on patrol. Even as night crept up, sweeping the cobblestones in lilac and myrtle hues, Aurel navigated without trouble. At one point, they rounded a corner, and accidentally frightened a young girl sneaking from an upper story window. Blending easily into the shadows once more, Aurel bit back the urge to apologise, knowing that would only do more harm than good.

The further Aurel ventured south into the bowels of the city, the more people appeared. People stumbled out of tavernae. People drank in doorways, and talked, and yelled, and laughed. People loitered around small food stalls, tearing their teeth into slices of goat cooked on a spit. While walking unseen behind a group of men, Aurel had to dodge around a fight that broke out, when one of the men learned that the other supported the Blues rather than the Greens in the chariot races.

When Aurel at last came upon the guild quarter, it was to a boisterous scene. Groups of people huddled over gambling boards, throwing dice. Another larger group congregated to take bets on some activity Aurel couldn't see. When Aurel peered over the tops of heads, they found a small ring with two chickens engaged in bloody sport. As the chickens ripped into one another with their iron-tipped spurs, the crowd cheered, pressed intensely inward, welter of blood and frenzy. Repulsed, Aurel recognised one of the people in the front as the woman who did Sevila's laundry earlier in the day. Aurel left quickly before they could determine for sure if one of the chickens fighting was also familiar. As they did so, a few guardsmen rushed into the fray, not to break up the gambling, but to crane their necks and take part, just as arrested by sport.

Near the far end of the quarter it was no less crowded, though somewhat more orderly. A wooden stage had been erected, and many sat either on sloping chairs or on the ground itself to watch events unfold. Atop the stage, positioned to one side, a large man with an even larger voice narrated the play in what was — Aurel soon discovered — a comedic retelling of the latest politics.

"Stricken with grief over the death of her son, our beloved Cyrus—!" The narrator was interrupted by a chorus of sorrowful groans from the crowd as on stage a man in a small wooden carving meant to mimic a ship sinking beneath waves made of blue cloth.

"Grief stricken, the Venerable Empress Iustina encloistered herself in her palatial home in the capital with her grandchildren!" A man painted as a woman and wearing an overly-large crown huddled together two identical children over the spot where Cyrus had drowned.

"There she ruled, while on the battlefield General Theodoros led the charge!" A man whose face was obscured by a massive prop helmet swaggered onto stage to cheers and laughter. His only defining characteristic was an enormous phallus that drooped around his knees, which he used to strike enemies down as though it were a sword. The audience crowed with raucous laughter as droves of actors fell to Theodoros' mighty blows.

"But no matter his unmatched prowess, the Helani's numbers never dwindled! On and on the horse-lords advance! They take our land! They kill our soldiers! And what did Iustina do?"

"Nothing!" The crowd roared back in answer. Someone near the front even stood to hurl stale bread at where the Empress still crouched, shielding her grandchildren from external harm. The bread hit the crown squarely, knocking it and the wig beneath from the actor's head, revealing a bald spot at which the crowd jeered.

"All was lost, she believed!" The narrator bellowed to be heard over the din. "Again and again, Theodoros implored her for action until finally he arrived at his wit's end! With his troops, he stormed the capital to secure the empire's future heirs, but in the ensuing chaos Iustina and little Leo perished!"

With one of the children in her arms, Iustina collapsed to the floor by her fallen crown. Just previously the fickle crowd had condemned her, but upon seeing her sprawled with her grandson they let loose a hoarse cry of dismay. Over their bodies the General wept loudly, boldly, openly, falling to his knees. Aurel might have found it compelling if it hadn't been for the actor's fake phallus bulging along the ground.

"Their sacrifice wasn't for naught!" The narrator claimed, lifting his arms in a vain attempt to implore quiet. "Now as Lord Regent, Theodoros took little Zoe under his protection! He vowed to raise her, to train her into an Empress worthy of command! And not only that—!"

Once again, the narrator's voice was swallowed whole by an eruption of joyous noise from the crowd. Emboldened and heedless, they even jostled against Aurel.

"And not only that!" The narrator repeated, forging on. "Not a moment after their deaths, a god reached out to Isidore, High Priest of the Holiest Office! After over two decades of absence, the gods have returned to strike a contract! Following the Imperial funeral in the Golden City, Isidore and Theodoros will travel north with their armies once again! They will reconquer our lost territories and beyond! And when they are finished, we will have an Empress before whom all will tremble!"

In a single surging motion, the audience leapt to its feet, whipped to a frenzy. On stage, a man completely obscured in black priestly robes clasped the arm of the General like a brother, before the two of them took the remaining child from the stage, cradling her grandmother's crown in her arms. Along with the narrator the crowd chanted, "Long life to the Empress! Long life to the Lady Invicta!"

All around Aurel the mass of people thronged. Cups clacked together, and people drank to the girl on stage, to their absent infant Empress and her guardians. Splashed with wine and beer, Aurel struggled to push their way free. Nobody bothered to keep their distance now, and more than once Aurel had to stumble in order to avoid treading on anyone.

Overhead a gibbous moon waxed. Aurel managed to become disentangled only by taking to the outer walls of the district. Slipping away from the clangour and confusion, Aurel fled back to the safety of the brothel, dodging along winding streets and alleys through the faint veneer of moonlight. They were intent on authenticating the play's events, but when at last they returned it was to find Sevila fast asleep. Alone and naked upon the mattress, draped loosely with embroidered sheets, she snored face-first into a pillow, which did little to dampen the noise.

Much to Aurel's dismay, the building had too-thin walls. Grumbling and not bothering to keep their voice down — nothing would rouse Sevila from her slumber short of a bucket of cold water poured over her — Aurel tried to ignore the sounds of neighbouring clients, and pulled the volumes of poetry from the bags in the corner. They sat. They read. They awaited the far-flung dawn.

Chapter 4

Nearing midday Sevila awoke in a rare good mood. Caught in a resin of dappled sunlight through the windows, she stretched upon the bed, and even at full length her feet never reached the edge of the mattress. While she rose and began to pull her clothes on at a leisurely rate, Aurel — seated upon a window sill — stared pointedly out and into the courtyard beyond. They had long since finished reading, and had spent a better part of the morning watching the sun cast the garden courtyard into bold warm colour. A few statues were erected throughout the garden, hiding behind flowering myrtle and thorny vines, all of them presenting titillating scenarios as was befitting the brothel. While Aurel found none of the statues particularly tasteful, they still admired the craftsmanship.

Fixing a ruby-studded gold belt around her narrow waist, cinching her red silks in place, Sevila greeted Aurel cheerily. "A fine morning! Only finer still had you thought to fetch a meal for me."

"I'm not your servant," Aurel said in a bored tone, not moving from their place upon the windowsill. They idly watched a pair of young women who worked at the establishment comb each other's hair in another room across the courtyard, finding comfort in the simple act

"Perhaps not, though you are bound to me." Sevila hummed a dissonant tune as she pinned her hair into a tight bun at the nape of her neck.

"Last I checked, contracts worked both ways." Aurel cocked their shadowy head at her. "Should I start making my own demands of you?"

Her good mood not to be so easily deterred, Sevila snorted, and grinned around a brass hairpin stuck between her teeth. "Someone didn't have a nice night!"

"It was noisy," Aurel admitted, oddly fixated at the way Sevila smoothed back any stray strands of hair from her face. The moment passed as soon as she covered her hair with a tight headwrap, the pale silk covering her ears and brow, and framing her sharply-featured face. "And I ran out of things to do."

Draping her long cowl over the crook of an elbow, Sevila started toward the door. "What about your walk around town?"

"Also noisy." Aurel slouched upright to join Sevila in the hallway.

"I know. It's what I love about this place." Sevila's tone was gleeful. Worldly pleasures were apparently all it required to lift her spirits, and Aurel might have found the sudden shift bearable had she not spoiled it with her usual careless remarks. "A dour old scholar definitely suits you, darling. I hope your body isn't too frail, else it might perish the moment I stick you back in there."

Aurel scowled down at her, but Sevila blithely moved along the hallway as though she had done nothing at all wrong or out of place. Together the two of them walked into the kitchens, where Constantia was engaged in an argument with a delivery boy out back whose price for fresh produce was too dear. She caught sight of Sevila's happy stroll and Aurel's glower, and immediately she waggled a finger at the boy with a few irritable words. "This discussion is far from over!" she snapped, then bustled over to Sevila. "What have I told you about the kitchens!"

"I may not be staff, but I am essentially a permanent fixture in this august establishment, which I think entitles me to a small meal." Sevila reached over to pluck a freshly baked roll from one of the benches, only for Constantia to slap her hand away.

"Your meals are never small." She grabbed Sevila by the upper arm, and herded her back out into the hallway. Sevila went with only mild complaints, and Aurel followed if for no other reason than to be away from a few of the cooks' guarded looks in their direction. Once away from prying ears, Constantia glanced down the halls to check for other potential eavesdroppers before asking, "What is it you really want? And don't waste my time with your bullshit!" she said as Sevila opened her mouth to speak. "If you want something: ask it. No false praises. They bore me."

For a moment, it seemed Sevila would dispute the notion that her praises were false, but in the end she conceded with a shrug. "I require the services of your main business. We're looking for someone, who would have passed through the city not long before us. A priest from the capital — or someone posing as such — and a handful of guards. They might have had a mute companion with them, or perhaps even a suspiciously heavy rug. With feet hanging out the end, if you catch my meaning."

At that Constantia's thickly painted brows rose, and she peered down at Sevila with renewed interest. "Grave robbers?"

"Something like that." Sevila answered dryly, though she refused to divulge any further information.

This time when Constantia looked up at Aurel towering over Sevila's shoulder, her expression held a note of understanding — or at least what she thought of the situation. Briefly Aurel feared she might have gleaned too much, but the brief flare of panic passed when she spoke. "I'm glad at least one of you is pursuing a noble cause. Grave robbing is a plague. People will steal the dead before cremation for their own filthy means with no regard for the family's peace."

Had Aurel a pair of lungs, they would have sighed in relief. Better Constantia think them a vengeful guardian than an abomination.

"Very touching, yes." Sevila brushed the remark away flippantly. "Have you seen them, or not?"

Constantia turned her attention back to Sevila, her face once again hard and unimpressed with her client. In answer, she turned her hand over, palm up, and did not speak until Sevila dropped a few silver coins into her hand. Then she pursed her lips, and inspected the silver before, with a sly rotation of her wrist, the coins vanished. Breathing in deeply, Constantia closed her eyes, and when she opened them again, they briefly bled black at the edges. "Not personally, but my network informs me that a group matching that description arrived just a few hours before you. They visited the temple for supplies, and then continued on their way."

"That's all?" Sevila pressed. "They didn't check any records? Pay any social calls?"

Crossing their arms, Aurel grumbled, "We might have caught them if you hadn't insisted on a bath and laundry."

Sevila shot them a dirty look over her shoulder. When Constantia held out her hand again, Sevila sighed, and gave her another two silver coins which again vanished.

"They headed west into the mountains." Constantia informed them. "On the road to Nicoma, is my guess."

Sevila's reaction was immediate. Whatever good mood she had exhibited before withered up in an instant, and her lip curled in a sneer. "Please tell me you're joking."

"Yes, because I do so enjoy a good prank. You must be mistaking me for my sister." Constantia turned to enter the kitchens once more. "If that's all, I have an outrageous delivery rate to contest."

As soon as the door swung shut behind her, Aurel looked curiously at Sevila. "What's in Nicoma?"

"Now what. *Who,*" Sevila spat. She stomped down the hall back to her room, swinging the cowl from her arms around her head and shoulders, where it draped down her back. "It had to be Nicoma! They couldn't just hop on a ship straight to Faros!"

"Who, then?" Aurel repeated, trailing after her and wincing when she slammed the door open, the handle cracking the paint along the wall.

"The Oracle." Sevila growled, crossing the room to snatch up what remained of her things and stuff them into her saddlebags with no regard for tidiness. "A bitter crone. A mouthpiece for mischief and falsehoods."

"And you don't get along well? Shocking," Aurel remarked.

Sevila's answering glare could have melted iron. Yanking the straps and buckles shut, she threw the saddlebags into Aurel's arms, having to heave at the weight with her whole body. Aurel caught them easily, layers of leather muting the heavy clink of the bags' contents against their armour. As Sevila stormed out of the brothel, she fixed her veil in place, the cloth and bone doing little to shield the afternoon from her foul expression.

"There used to be ten," she muttered as she quickly gathered travel supplies at the market for the journey, and shoved her way to the city gates. "Scattered across the empire in their holy sites, marked for pilgrimage. The other oracles might still exist, but the empire's borders have long since abandoned them. Not that it matters; they cannot prophesy with no gods to give them voice."

Aurel listened, murmuring apologies to anyone that crossed Sevila's ill-tempered path. Once at the gate, Aurel began searching the line of tethered mounts for Sevila's camel, but she stopped to bark at one of the boys in attendance instead. "You there! Bring me a horse!"

"A horse?" Aurel began, puzzled. "But -?"

"A horse is better suited for treacherous rocks."

Sevila waited with hands planted at her hips, tapping one of her rings against the belt and its strings of interlocking chains delicately draped over her silks. When a dusty sorrel mount was led to her, she threw a coin at the boy and snapped her fingers at Aurel, pointing at the bags.

Irritated, Aurel made sure to take extra time lashing the saddlebags into place. The horse was skittish under their hand, shying away at every touch. During their travels so far, the only ones truly discerning of Aurel's nature yet unable to express it seemed to be children and animals. No amount of sweetly whispered words could calm the beast, and even when Aurel tried offering an apple, the horse only snorted at the gift.

Swinging herself into the high-backed saddle with some difficulty due to her height, Sevila grabbed the apple from Aurel, and stuffed it back into one of the bags. "Don't waste good food."

Her feet dangled freely around the horse's stomach, and wrenching on the reins she kicked it into motion. Aurel trotted after her, clanking, dodging around the horse's flicking tail to run at Sevila's side. Around the city walls they went, and when the road forked in twain Sevila urged her mount to the west. In a brooding silence, she maintained a brutal pace, passing by merchants with their train of caravans and pilgrims making their way to Nicoma, until the horse's neck began to lather with sweat. Then she yanked on the reins, and allowed a stiff walk.

Tugging down her veil, already covered in a fine layer of dust from their brief journey, Sevila pulled out the apple from earlier. Scowling at it, she tore a large chunk away, and chewed noisily. The only good Aurel saw in their pace was how the horse was now too tired to care if a disembodied soul walked beside it.

"I saw a play last night." Aurel attempted to conjure some sort of conversation to life.

Used to sitting astride a camel instead, Sevila tried folding one of her legs over the horse's withers, only to be foiled by the bulky saddle horn there. With a grunt of displeasure, she took another bite of apple, and allowed her ankles to dangle. "More propaganda drivel?" She listened to Aurel recount the play's events. When they finished, she laughed coldly. "Half-truths and lies. All of it."

"Do you know any of them? Theodoros? Iustina?" Aurel asked.

"I have it on good authority that nobody ever really *knew* Iustina." Sevila evaded answering outright. With every bite she left deep gouge marks in the fruit's flesh, and she had to pause to pick red-gold skin from her teeth. "To say that she did nothing is ridiculous. I doubt she spent a single day of her life doing nothing. It will be important that the most magnanimous Lord Regent Theodoros present her as such. The fact that the late Empress remained inside the Court for most of her career—" Sevila trailed off and bit savagely into the apple's core. "You can imagine why commoners would believe Theodoros' tales."

Aurel mulled over her words. "And this High Priest? Isidore?"

"Is going to be very disappointed when he finds out he's been deceived by something masquerading as a god." No part of the fruit save the stem was spared, and that Sevila flicked away. "Either that, or the god is a complete fabrication designed to rally support for the College."

"You think the latter." It was not a question, though Aurel's voice was not accusatory.

Licking her fingers, Sevila glanced at Aurel. "I do. And what do you think?"

Mildly surprised at even being asked their opinion, Aurel frowned at the mountains far into the distance. Dark peaks jutted towards the cloudless sky like the ridges of a spine. At the very top, a speckle of snow refused to melt no matter the season.

"I think—" Something in Aurel stirred, a deep and wounded thing that lumbered in its shackles. Aurel struggled to put it to words; the more they fought to pin the dim feeling in place, the more it slipped beyond reach. "I think he must be a pious man to have achieved his rank. Lust for power alone would not have seen him so far."

Sevila gave a thoughtful hum. "Maybe. Though it certainly wouldn't hurt. I know men like Isidore and Theodoros. Hunger for power. Hunger for piety. Hunger for fame, for money, and for retribution. Hunger takes many forms, but in the end, it's all the same." A light breeze carried with it sheets of dust, and Sevila covered the lower half of her face with the veil around her neck. "We have a few days until we reach Nicoma. I suggest we hurry if we ever want to catch up." With that she dug her heels into the horse's flanks, and it broke into a trot.

By the end of the day they reached the base of the mountains. Unlike before, Sevila stopped to camp for the evening. She had no tent packed away, but they found shelter in the ruins of a crumbling outpost that had long since been abandoned. Upon closer inspection, Aurel spied the effaced statue of a god with great curling horns sprouting from its head, and too many sets of arms from its torso, many of which had been broken off with time. Sevila hung her cowl irreverently upon one shorn-off stone wrist as the two of them made camp for the evening.

"Travel through the mountains is always such a pain," Sevila groaned as Aurel gathered the remains of spiky branches and other sparse flora for kindling. "You have to watch the horse at all times, lest it slip and break both your necks. You don't have to worry about such things, but let me tell you: breaking your neck? Not pleasant."

Aurel knelt down to arrange the collection of dense twigs and twisting branches while Sevila sulked, sitting directly on the ground and leaning her back against the base of the deity's statue. Aurel nodded toward it. "What god is that?"

"Who cares?" Arms crossed, Sevila tilted her head back to glare at the many-armed figure over her. "This one lost devotees long ago, anyway. Twenty-odd years the gods have been gone, and this unlucky bastard's shrines go untended for a few centuries even before that. Humans are a fickle lot."

"Must not have been a very good god." Aurel dug out the flint from Sevila's saddlebags to start the fire.

"Now you're learning!" When Aurel forgot they had no breath with which to blow a few sparks to life, Sevila rolled her eyes. "Here. Let me."

She leaned forward, craning her neck down to coax out a few tongues of flame. The fire took to the dry kindling quickly, and soon it blazed and crackled. Tethered nearby, the horse nosed at a few brownish leaves upon a shrub with a desultory air. Aurel watched Sevila through the smoke and shimmer of heat. "What kind of contract would someone seek with a god?"

Sevila shrugged, and her many gold accoutrements lit up briefly, reflecting the fire's hard glow. "How long is a piece of string?"

As if still expecting to feel something — anything — Aurel nudged their iron-shod toe against the fire's base. "Have you ever contracted with a god?"

Sevila bared her teeth at the suggestion, and her eyes gleamed, hard and rich as copper. "I wouldn't give them the satisfaction." Then curling her feet up, she nodded towards the fire. "That will go out soon if you don't do something about it."

It was dismissive, but Aurel only rose to collect more kindling. They did not have to fumble around thorns, and simply gathered branches into their arms that would have given anyone else pause. By the time they returned to the camp not long later, the fire was sputtering on a bed of coals, and Sevila was fast asleep. All through the night Aurel prodded at the flames, keeping them alive. Once they tried to approach the horse for lack of anything to do other than brush its mane. The horse however proved to be poor and timid company.

At the first flossy rays of dawn Sevila awoke, blinking blearily through the dim air. She grumbled as she shuffled off behind a stone wall to relieve herself. When she returned, she yawned and draped the cowl over her head and shoulders in preparation for the journey ahead. As she swung herself into the saddle, fishing around in the bags for a paltry meal of dried meat and bread, she mumbled, "When this is all over, I'm going to lie around in bed for a whole week."

They started up the road leading into the mountains. It was well-worn, slate-shod. Its edges were bordered with wooden railings that gave Aurel little comfort when they peeked over the side. Small alcoves had been hewn into the mountain's face along the road, each niche bearing the idol of some god or another. Each was different, and the further they ventured the less corroded the statues appeared. At one point the two of them even passed a family clustered around one of the statues, and leaving offerings of fresh fruit and lit candles. It were as if the act of worship circled inwards towards the woman who had been touched by the divine.

Another group they passed. Then another. Each greeted Sevila without cheer but with a certain politeness. In turn she ignored them, as though the idea of even being associated with devotees was rancid. When they stopped for the night at a rocky clearing devoted to a campsite, a handful of pilgrims had gathered there as well. Sevila treated them with the same stony silence she had maintained throughout the day unless she was speaking to Aurel — alternatively decrying the oracle, or otherwise regaling Aurel with past conquests in an attempt to cheer herself up, no matter that Aurel scorned her for her less than noble escapades.

All efforts however were in vain, for Sevila tucked her legs up beneath her waist-length cowl to sleep in as foul a mood as ever. She slept fitfully, and Aurel was left to gaze longingly at the nearby fires of the other travellers, wishing to engage them in conversation but fearing to do so. When Sevila awoke, the day was young yet — dawn a rose-coloured suggestion throating over jagged peaks.

Rather than continue on the main road, Sevila nudged her horse directly north on a winding footpath. Overhead the sun seared the sky a blinding cloudless blue. Here in the mountains, the temperature was no less extreme, switching swiftly between hot days and icy evenings. The path beneath them narrowed along the rocky slopes until at one point Aurel pressed against a sheer cliff, and Sevila led the horse on foot after wrapping its head in her cowl to cover its eyes.

Aurel's heel slipped on the lip of rock, and they had to grab at the mountainside so as to not fall. "Are you sure this is the right way?" they asked. Far below the ravine slendered, and at its very base a river ran like a silvery thread.

"It's a shortcut," Sevila claimed, tugging at the horse's reins to encourage it along behind her. "Don't tell me I need to cover your eyes, and string you along as well!"

"I think I prefer knowing what I'm going to walk into," Aurel said, though they turned to shuffle sideways after the horse.

"Good, because I don't have another bridle," Sevila replied. As though to emphasis her point, she yanked at the reins once more, and the horse suddenly rushed forward. With a yelp, she had to scramble along to avoid being trampled, and by the time the animal slowed down she was swearing profusely.

As much as she insisted that this route would shave half a day off their trip, Aurel had their quiet suspicions. The two of them spent an uneasy night on a little ledge hanging over the ravine. All through the starlit hours, Aurel had to listen to Sevila's uneven snoring, and the horse stamping its hooves, sending stones leaping down the mountain.

The next afternoon it began to rain. Clouds swept in from the east like the tide, and unleashed a deluge. The air darkened, while the flinty slopes went grey then black and slick with rainfall. Still using her cowl to blind the horse, Sevila cursed the heavens. With every passing moment, her expression soured further until her face was awash with rivulets, her brows dripped into her eyes, and her clothes were soaked completely through. Aurel of course felt nothing apart from a pleasant increase of weight as their long hems absorbed the rain.

By the time the pathway widened, and everything re-joined the main road, it was still pouring. So close to Nicoma, the main road carried a near constant trail of newcomers flocking to catch any glimpse of the oracle, hear any inspired whisper she might let slip. Most of them huddled under oiled cloaks, the water beading atop and rolling away.

"We should have bought you one of those back in Lapedion." Aurel gestured towards one of the passing strangers, and the man in question hurried along nervously at being noticed by a human soul.

Sevila's nose wrinkled. She removed her cowl from the horse and wrung it between her hands. A steady stream of water bled from the silk, and as she settled it over her own head once more the fabric squelched. "You can almost never accurately predict the weather up here. I'd hoped to be through quickly enough to avoid anything like this but -" With a disdainful sniff, Sevila swung herself into the saddle. "At least I don't look dowdy."

Aurel glanced pointedly at her appearance — the smudged black lines drawn around her eyes, the droop of her saffron silks plastered to her skin. "No. Instead you look miserable."

In response Sevila bared her teeth, then kicked the horse into motion. They made their way up the path towards Nicoma. Built into the cliff side, the small city appeared hard and dour in the rain. No banners to god or empire flew over the tops of buildings carved directly from the rock, and the bold artistry of Lapedion was nowhere to be found. In a city bereft of ornamentation, and filled with the desperate seekers of godly inspiration, Sevila stood apart like a torch. Even utterly drenched, her eyes gleamed bright against the backdrop of stone and rain.

The city of Nicoma had no walls, and its gates no doors. The massive outcropping archway had been whittled away by wind, sand, and rapid rainfall. The only purpose it served was not to keep out invaders — for who would dare invade such a holy site and risk the wrath of gods? — but to mark a threshold. Upon that liminal space, a line was engraved in purest gold, and there every pilgrim stopped to lower their heads, and murmur a prayer of safe passage before crossing into the city. Sevila, on the other hand, did not even bother dismounting; she rode right on by, her horse's hooves clipping the glinting line.

"I've always wanted to try stealing that," Sevila told Aurel, nodding towards the gold, not bothering to keep her voice down. "Just to see the chaos and confusion it would cause, but they guard the damn thing day and night."

Sure enough, no less than six guardsmen could be seen attending the gate, hands resting on the hilts of their swords. Beneath the mesh of chain mail draped from their helms and concealing their faces, dark eyes tracked Sevila with distrust born from her blatant impiety. Meeting their gazes with her own brazen glare, she admitted, "Losing a few limbs would be awfully inconvenient."

"I'm afraid I understand the sentiment all too well," Aurel replied, voice dry.

The corners of Sevila's eyes crinkled as she grinned. "That's why we make such a team, darling."

Aurel was about to tell her that they'd rather get this whole ordeal over with and try to forget that the two of them were ever a team to begin with, when two additional guards marched straight toward them down the main road. "They must have heard your plans of theft," Aurel said, watching with apprehension as the guardsmen approached.

"Nonsense! I've never been arrested for simply talking about a crime!" Sevila ignored the irony of implying that she had in fact been imprisoned before for actual crimes committed. Though somehow the implication did not surprise Aurel in the slightest.

The two guards stopped, and as they addressed them a few other of Nicoma's new visitors looked on with poorly veiled interest. "The Oracle has requested your presence for a private audience at the inner sanctum."

Sevila reined in her horse, and leaned an arm upon the saddle horn to fix the guards with an intensely golden stare through the downpour. "How on earth could the old bat have known I was coming?"

The guards exchanged confused glances. "Not you," one said. Then the other pointed at Aurel. *"Them."*

Sevila reared back in her seat as though the shock and insult of being passed over in favour of Aurel had manifested itself into a physical blow. Aurel was no less shocked. "Does the Oracle know me?" they asked, and an eagerness brimmed in their voice at the prospect of some clue about their lost identity.

A shrug made the other guard's leather and iron reinforced pauldron creak against his chain mail jerkin. "We make no claims as to the Oracle's knowledge, only that she requested an audience with the human soul that would be entering the city around this time."

At that, Sevila's eyes narrowed. She slid from the horse's back, landing on the cobblestones with a small splash. Stepping forward to stand in front of Aurel, she scowled up at the guards. "This soul is bound to me, and I to them in eldritch contract. You'll not take them without me, or I will see this city in ruins before nightfall."

The top of Sevila's head barely reached the guards' shoulders, but the force of her conviction and the slithering hiss of her words was enough to drive them back a step. "Be at peace, Lady," one of them said, and he raised his hand from his sword, palm up. "We did not mean to imply you could not also attend."

"The Oracle is generous," the other added quickly. "She will gladly receive you both."

Sevila's lip curled. "I have neither need nor desire for the Oracle's generosity."

Placing a hand on the peaked cloth of gold at her shoulder, Aurel said gently, "Please." Their voice was deep and soft and many-layered. "Perhaps she can tell us something."

Though she did not soften, Sevila grudgingly ceded with a huff. Shrugging Aurel's hand away, Sevila brandished the horse's reins at one of the guards. "You," she said sternly. "You will stable my mount at the taverna over there. And you." She pointed at the other. "You will lead us to the Oracle."

For a moment, it seemed they would object to being ordered around, but eventually one of them sighed and, water sloughing from his glistening chain mail cowl, he led Sevila's mount aside. The other turned away without further word or gesture, expecting Aurel and Sevila to follow. Through the squat stone dwellings, he led them. Nicoma had no main temple as did Lapedion, but little altars speckled along crossroads, and mausoleums holding the ashes of ancestors long past. Most niches were marked with a simple engraving — masons charging by the letter — but some bore busts with the likeness of the deceased. Many families came to tend to these like the shrines, while others still were driven to the Oracle. The tavernae overflowed with customers, as did a number of buildings with no signs.

When Aurel nudged Sevila inquisitively, she glanced at one of these dwellings and grunted. "Pipe dens," she answered Aurel's unspoken question. "Technically Nicoma's pipe dens are the only legal purveyors of opiates in the empire, though it isn't difficult to find them elsewhere."

Ahead the guard gave a resigned sigh. "Lady, I must ask that you do not admit to criminal activity in my presence. I detest paperwork."

Though Sevila rolled her eyes, she said nothing, and the remainder of their walk went uninterrupted. Deeper in the heart of the mountain they travelled, the city itself carved in an odd somewhat circular wedge that bore into the steep flanks. Overhead there formed an irregularly shaped dome. Eyes widening, Aurel realised that the organic barrel vaulting was in fact the imprint of fingers, as if something colossal had reached in and scooped out handfuls of dense rock like it was made of sand. Not man-made, but god-made.

At the crux of the wedge, a building's façade marked the inner sanctum like a door. The pillars were twisted and rough-hewn. Humans of the empire had come along centuries later and added carvings over the entrance, depicting a woman flooded with floral representations of smoke. Outside a crowd had gathered in the hopes of a glimpse of the Oracle, but all had been barred entry. Rather than lead them directly through the congregation — sure to cause a stir — the guard took them around the side. There a small door hidden by rock sheltered a tunnel that bore into the mountain. Through winding narrow passages, they were led, the curved walls illuminated with torches fed with blue flame that cast an eerie light, and made Sevila's usual bold colouring appear bloodless and wan.

In one turn the corridor opened up to a grand womb-like cloister. The rough-textured walls sloped away into a broad dome. A breath of wind and light rushed down from a shaft drilled through to the mountain's peak, sweeping smoke from coal-bearing braziers into a fitful dance along the ground. Suspended from the ceiling were the remains of past Oracles, embalmed, silk-wrapt and hung in coffins that were murky as glass. Beneath them upon a raised ledge in the centre of the room the Oracle sat, ensconced atop a seat of high bronze, and attended by priests — male and female alike — waving censers that burnt fragrant oils Aurel could not smell.

"To cover up the stench of rotting eggs," Sevila muttered, answering Aurel's unspoken query. "The whole mountain stinks of it."

Where Sevila looked pale and colourless, the Oracle was a vision of vibrant blues, draped in silver threads. Her face and most of her body were obscured by rich bolts of sky-coloured cloth. The backs of her hands and the arches of her feet were dotted with designs in dark ink as if in marriage. The temporary dye would need to be applied and reapplied daily; she was caught in a wedding stasis, perpetually handed up to a god. Her head lifted somewhat at their entry, her attention drawn by unfamiliar footsteps, and as they approached Aurel could see the lower half of her face. The Oracle was not as old as Sevila had made her out to be. When she spoke, her voice was not deep, though just as sombre as Aurel had imagined.

"Approach me, spirit," she said, soft yet commanding. "I knew you would soon follow."

Aurel walked through the ranks of attendants as requested, Sevila bristling at their heels. "You have met with those we seek?" Aurel asked.

The Oracle bowed her head in answer, and the smoke-filled air licked her chin. "They came to me not a day past, searching for answers about this so-called new god."

"And what did you tell them?" Sevila's tone bordered on the edge of an accusation.

Not looking towards her, the Oracle replied, "The truth: there are no new gods."

"Wisdom from an Oracle!" Sevila mocked, though she sounded brittle and thready. "How novel!"

If anything, the Oracle seemed amused rather than angry. A smile pulled at one corner of her mouth. Before Sevila could issue any further retort, Aurel asked, "And what of my body? Did they have it with them? Did you see it?"

With a darkly-painted finger the Oracle pointed at Aurel's feet, and the incense seemed to rise to her touch, curling about her wrists in coils like the slippery backs of serpents. "It stood where you now stand, a tall, silent figure shrouded in black cloth, crown to toe. Whether it had been gagged or simply could not speak, I do not know. Though beneath its robes there clanked iron chains, and it performed tasks only when physically provoked."

At that Sevila hummed, a thoughtful noise. "I had suspected an improper soul severing due to your lack of memory, but this only confirms it."

She spoke so benignly of the taboo, Aurel's head whipped around, trailing droplets of shadow as they fearfully looked for the guard who had led them here. At some point however, he had left the inner sanctum. All those that remained were the attendants, who made no motion, no sound, who gave no indication that they were listening at all.

"Relax, won't you? You're making me jumpy," Sevila snapped, though she still scowled up at the Oracle. "Anything spoken in this chamber is considered sacred nonsense. They've taken a vow of silence."

"Mine is the only voice they serve. Be at peace, spirit," the Oracle reassured Aurel far more effectively than Sevila, who if anything seemed to take offence to that as well.

"I'm not just one of the voices you hear!" Sevila growled. "You can address me directly."

Slowly and for the first time the Oracle's head swung in Sevila's direction. Surely, she could not have seen from beneath the hood pulled down over her eyes, and yet the Oracle gave the distinct impression of looking piercingly, thoroughly at Sevila. "Nearly thirty years since I last saw you, Sevila Peinatokos. I was but a child then, yet you look just as I remember you."

"I've changed outfits since." Sevila's manner was joking, an attempt at being disarming.

Rather than be taken in by her cavalier attitude, the Oracle nodded gravely. "Yes. Even then I knew everything about you was superficial."

Sevila's lip curled in anger. "You know nothing about me."

"Don't I?" Reaching up the Oracle lifted the hood and pulled it back, revealing her face. She was in appearance unremarkable. Above all else she looked tired, drained. Her temples had started to go white, and her unshorn hair was bound in a single thick braid. "Throughout my years of service, the gods have whispered many things to me — your name among them."

"Hollow words," Sevila sneered.

"Hollow words for a hollow woman." The Oracle's eyes were very dark, and shadow coveted her cheeks. "In the end, they howled nothing. And then — silence."

As much as Sevila tried to hide behind hard eyes and bared teeth, Aurel could see the fine tremble at her fingertips. "Is that really their best? Wasting their time with cruel gossip? Babbling torments in your ear even as they are dying, rather than save themselves?"

"Save themselves from what? Or who?" The Oracle laughed. She leaned a forearm onto the low-backed seat to look down at Sevila from her great height. "If I knew who was responsible for this blessed silence these last twenty-six years, I would kiss their feet. For nearly a decade I straddled the line between human and divine, and in all my life I have never known peace like this."

Sevila jaw hardened as she grit her teeth, and though she did not move she gave the impression of stepping back. "All men were at the mercy of the whims of gods, not just you. Straddling the human and divine? Don't insult me. They just enjoyed tormenting you a little more than your kin."

Leaning perilously forward, the Oracle jabbed her hand towards the crystalline coffins twisting overhead by their chains, and her voice echoed along the walls. "The priests burnt my predecessor rather than entomb her, because her body was so mangled after she flung herself from the highest peak." Suddenly her eyes were bright, suffused with veiled smoke. Like ash they burned, and like ash their light was short-lived. As she sank back in her seat, they dimmed once more, and her clenched fists unfurled. The movement revealed her forearms, which were also intricately inked, except through the dye Aurel noticed a mesh of narrow scars from the slash of blades. "Eleven years was enough to lose my sense of self, if not my life."

A thin smile cut across Sevila's features as though in victory. "They'd managed to drive your own name from memory, last we met. I've tracked it down in my travels, you know. What would it be worth to you, I wonder?"

The Oracle went very still upon her perch. Her chest did not rise or fall, and she seemed stricken of breath. "I have nothing to offer. What could you possibly desire from me?"

Sevila's teeth gleamed. Her eyes were golden lamps in a sunless place. She crooked one finger at the Oracle, then pointed to the ground. "I want to see you climb down, crawl across the floor, and kiss my feet."

From the side Aurel could see a few of the attendants flicker their eyes in an exchange of silent glances, their incredulity unexpressed but no less palpable. The Oracle for a moment was unreadable, and then slowly she descended. Rungs branched between the throne's bronze, spindly legs like those of a ladder. Once on the ground she looked much smaller, almost as short as Sevila herself — indeed their appearances were altogether not so different. In another life they may have been sisters. Without hesitation, the Oracle went down on her knees, and began to crawl. The jagged floor scraped her palms. Her long robes dragged, rippling, in her wake.

Aurel was about to object, when they caught sight of Sevila's face. What triumph they had expected to find did not enkindle there. The closer the Oracle drew, the more Sevila's inscrutability sharpened into something different, something cowering, cowardly, spiteful and self-loathing. When at last the Oracle lowered herself through the smoke-swirling air to brush her lips against the silk of Sevila's shoes, Sevila allowed only the briefest contact before tilting the Oracle's chin up with her toes.

"I cannot stand the very sight of you, Sophia," Sevila said, her voice a pained whisper.

A deep-seated shudder travelled through the Oracle, and for a moment she seemed transported at the sound of her long-forgotten name, until she roughly shoved Sevila's foot aside, and pushed herself upright. Standing proudly, she squared her shoulders. "If I ever get word of you entering Nicoma again, I'll have the guards dash you upon the rocks lining the steepest cliff."

Teeth clenched, the muscles in her jaw bunching, Sevila turned and stormed away. The Oracle reached up to draw the hood back over her face, looking at Aurel as she did so. "I understand your misfortune, spirit, but I beg of you for your own sake and the sake of the world: interpret whatever bargain you two have struck very carefully, and be rid of her as soon as you are able."

Bowing their head, Aurel, too, left, and behind them the Oracle made the long climb back to her lonely seat.

Chapter 5

Sevila did not go to the taverna. She headed straight for the nearest pipe den. Outside, the world looked more intensely grey after the stark blues of the inner sanctum, and Aurel squinted through the downpour to see Sevila walking briskly along, her outfit a sudden striking red on an otherwise dismal street. People still thronged outside the sanctum, and more continued to flock from the city entrance. Many would remain in holy vigil until dawn or until hunger drew them elsewhere.

Skirting around them, Aurel hurried after Sevila. They caught up to her just as she shoved the door to one of the dens open violently enough that the handle struck the wall. When Aurel tried speaking to her, she ignored them utterly, and ventured further inside. Aurel had to stoop through the entryway, and they closed the door as gently as they could. Cloth had been pinned along the walls and billowed across the ceiling in an attempt to soften the hard planes of monochromatic stone, but no amount of colourful rugs seemed to be able to brighten the building. A damp seeped in beneath the ill-fitting door and the rectangular holes that had been punched through the walls at set intervals. The holes could not be properly called windows, and they provided minimal ventilation.

Sevila waded through a haze of thick smoke towards a bored-looking man seated behind an iron-wrought cage. With trembling hands, she flung a few coins through the bars, and in turn he slid a number of tokens carved from woodchips shiny from the press of many oiled fingers. His eyes held a jaundiced yellow tinge, and he lazily followed Aurel with his gaze as though not believing Aurel were real at all. Even so he tugged at the cloth wrapping his hair from view, pulling it more firmly over his ears and brow.

Snatching up the tokens, Sevila stomped down the single hallway that extended to her right. Cubicles constructed from wood were shielded from view by thick curtains. Through gaps in the fabric Aurel spied people of all variety — some solitary, some lying across one another in little groups — their faces vacant, their bodies languid. Near the back of the building Sevila ripped back a curtain, and dropped heavily into the soiled single couch waiting for her there. By the time Aurel arrived not a few strides later, she was already preparing a pipe upon a wooden tray that had been left on the floor for just this purpose.

"Is this wise?" Aurel watched her fingers shake so badly that she fumbled with the pipe. "We should be preparing to leave. They can't be far now."

Without looking she poked a token through one of the holes in the wall behind her. Immediately the gap darkened, and someone in the hall that ran parallel to them exchanged it for a bundle of cloth, the contents of which could not have been much larger than a fingernail.

"Some of us still have bodily needs to attend to," Sevila muttered, unwrapping the cloth and placing its contents — a thinly pressed disk — into the pipe's bowl.

"I don't want to see you like this," Aurel said, holding the curtain open, and looking at her with a sense of mingled distaste and pity.

"Then leave!" Sevila snarled. "That's what she told you to do, isn't it?"

Aurel gave no answer, and Sevila seemed not to expect one. They watched her clothes begin to darken their surrounding cushions from carrying in the rain, droplets clinging to the bluffs of her sharp exposed cheeks and jawline, cottoning onto the veil draped around her neck. Then Aurel wrenched the curtain shut, and left Sevila to her earthly vices.

For once Aurel was glad they could not smell anything. Outside the air was fresher in appearance alone, even as it thronged with long sheets of rain that blanketed the buildings just down the road so that they seemed at a great distance. Water unspooled from the eaves. Aurel pushed through the gauze of rainfall, and did the only thing available — they walked. There was not much of Nicoma to explore, yet Aurel travelled its lengths. Mostly they ignored the many unsettled and unsettling stares of visitors, knowing that any kind of engagement with them was sure to be rebuffed.

When Aurel saw a beggar sitting against the side of a building, seeking shelter from the elements beneath a thin shelf of stone, they paused. The man's clothes were threadbare rags, and only a few bronze coins lay at his feet. Digging through the folds in their own clothes, Aurel unearthed a coin that glistened, fat and gold. The Empress Iustina's profile looked to one side with an august slant to her nose and cheeks. She still looked familiar, perhaps even more so now — though Aurel could not say why — and while they wanted to keep it, nevertheless they approached the man with hand outstretched.

The sight of gold made the man's eyes widen beneath bushy brows; a coin like this could feed him for a month. Two, if he were frugal. The moment he saw who — or rather what — offered it however, his expression changed. Like a withering plant he shrank away, then spat at the coin. "No deal!" he barked before Aurel could get a word in edgewise.

Aurel sighed, but did not pull away. "My Mistress has no need of this. Take it."

"I see no Mistress!" The man waved his hand to gesture at the empty air around Aurel. "And I've seen your kind! I know full well what you're capable of!"

He was missing a finger, and the tips of those that remained were yellowish with smoke. The back of his hand bore a brand that Aurel could not read before the man folded his arms. When Aurel tried placing the coin on the ground with the others, the man threw it back. Frustrated, Aurel took the coin, and left. They glowered, and people avoided them even more than before. It wasn't fair — Sevila who had the means and the ability but no desire for altruism, and Aurel, who had the desire to give alms but none would take it from them.

Eventually, with their wander through the city exhausted, Aurel was forced to return to the pipe den. The long rains had slowed to an intermittent drizzle, and the clouds darkened to iron and lavender hues, shielding the new moon from sight. All around the streets began to empty, though a crowd could be heard muttering their prayers at the door of the inner sanctum in the distance. The sound droned on, a sustained hive-like, torch-bearing hum of a vigil.

The pipe den however, had no shortage of customers at this hour. People were crammed inside, waiting in line to pay for a cubicle and tokens. One opened her mouth angrily when Aurel stepped past them all, only to quickly shut it again, and avert her gaze. Down the narrow smoke-strewn passageway, Aurel struggled to remember which cubicle had been rented by Sevila. More than once they pulled back a curtain only to be greeted by the laconic stare of strangers.

At last Aurel found her, and for a moment she seemed not to recognise them. Pipe held loosely in her hand, she sprawled across the sofa in a smoke-drenched haze. Only one lonely token remained on the little tray — the rest presumable she had smoked into oblivion. Coughing, she squinted up at Aurel, her pupils blown into bevelled wedge-shaped slats of glossy black.

"Oh, it's you." Sevila cleared her throat, and waved Aurel away. "Tell that fraud out front I want my money back."

Aurel watched as she lifted the pipe with her other hand and sucked lazily at its end. "No," they answered. "You've consumed nearly everything you bought."

Tilting her head back against a rough-spun cushion, her hair still bound all in damp silk, she exhaled towards the ceiling. A long prehensile plume peeled from her open mouth, drifting around her in a single coil. "This isn't strong enough," she mumbled. "I can still remember all that red. How nice it was. How much I liked it."

The hand bearing the pipe fell limply to the sofa, and Sevila continued to mutter about perverse things, bloody colours, grating sounds and tastes — most of all tastes. She coughed, and the pipe began to slip from her fingers. Aurel stepped forward to gather her cowl, and carefully pluck the pipe up, depositing it back on its tray. "I think you've had enough."

A sound like a low rumble sputtered at the back of her throat. She pointed at the wall. "No. Take some coin, and get me some more."

"I won't sit idly by and watch you kill yourself. You can do that after you get my body back." Gently Aurel slid their hands under Sevila's knees and shoulders. It was not difficult, lifting her from the couch. She weighed far less than the bags with which she travelled.

Her bitter laugh was interrupted by a hacking cough that reached deep into her chest and squeezed her lungs tight. "It would take more than a bit of smoke to kill me."

"You have inhaled more than just a bit of smoke." Aurel shuffled along the hallway sideways so that they would not knock any part of her against the wooden cubicle frames. "You must smell like a tannery."

As Aurel stepped outside into the cold, rain-speckled evening — here the air brittle and thin — Sevila began to shiver uncontrollably. "Smoke. Smoke and fire in the heavens." Her hands, curled up to her chest, shook. "Meat. Raw meat. Flesh stripped from the bone, and the crack of marrow. I need another smoke."

Her ramblings slurred together, grown frantic and limb-trembling. Aurel held her closer, and headed toward the taverna at the gates. "I don't know what you're talking about, but I am sure the only thing you need right now is sleep."

At the taverna, Sevila had gone mostly quiet, only a mumbled word or two comprehensible here and there. Aurel approached someone behind the bar counter who they hoped could direct them to a room. All other customers crowding the common area, seated around the fire pit or candle-lit tables, went completely silent upon Aurel's entry. When Aurel met a few gazes, immediately they all struck up conversation once more, though this time the atmosphere became nervous, tense.

Behind the bar a young man, whose face had not yet found the need for a razor, announced, "We don't want any trouble, spirit."

Before he could continue, Aurel interrupted him. "A guard stabled my Mistress' horse here earlier today. We need a room for the night."

Understanding crossed his features. "Guard failed to mention it was a *human* soul." He sighed, shaking his head. "Though I suppose news of you will bring in more business. Your bags have been put in the last room on the left, but I have to warn you — it doesn't have any lock."

"Thank you."

Aurel turned and picked their way across the teeming common area to the stairs. The noise from below filtered easily through the wooden floorboards, and every step down the hallway creaked. At the room Aurel was able to nudge the door open with their foot, closing it behind them again in the same way. The room itself bore only a single sofa, a rickety chair, and a low-slung table with an unlit candle welded into place by old melted wax. The saddlebags had been thrown into the far corner. Aurel was surprised to see that its contents had not been plundered.

Depositing Sevila upon the chair, which gave a warning groan at the extra weight no matter how slight, Aurel crossed the room to retrieve dry clothes from the saddlebags. A thump sounded behind them, and when Aurel whirled around, they found Sevila trying to claw her way over to the couch.

"Not yet! Not yet!" Aurel rushed over to ward her off, clutching a dry tunic.

"I'm tired," she mumbled, reaching for the mattress.

Aurel grabbed her wrist and held her back. "You'll get everything wet, and then you'll catch your death. Here." They held out the tunic to her. "Change into this."

Basic instructions took longer to process than normal, and Sevila began to strip with heavy motions as though pushing her limbs through water. Decency was pointless — there was very little of her Aurel had not already seen — but it made them feel better to study the floor beside her, keeping hold of a wrist or shoulder only when it seemed she would stagger over. When she had finally pulled the fresh tunic over her head, Aurel guided her onto the sofa. There she spread herself over the sheets, hanging half off, in danger of toppling over the side and onto the floor.

"Move over a bit. That chair will collapse under me, and I refuse to sit on the floor." Aurel prodded at her shoulder until she sluggishly made space for them.

Rather than grumble, Sevila curled up against them, her head propped in Aurel's lap so that her dark hair spilled out like ink. Only a few clumps of it remained bound into the usual tight bun at the base of her neck. Uncertain at first, Aurel began to gently pick out the pins, and place them on the floor. While they worked, Sevila's breathing settled, her shaking slowed then ceased. Softly, she began to snore.

Aurel did not rightly know how long they sat there, combing through the tangles in Sevila's hair while she slept. Aurel only knew that her hair was very lustrous and dark, and that it slipped between the fingers of their gauntlets like black water through a sieve. They carded it smooth. They thought of the girls at Constantia's with unshorn, unbound tresses. Hours later Sevila stirred, and Aurel froze, hand resting atop her head.

"That is awfully spirit-like of you, darling," she murmured, her voice holding a rough edge from her earlier excursions. She swallowed back a series of coughs that rocked her body.

The urge to run their hands through Sevila's hair again welled up in Aurel's cavernous chest. "What do you mean."

"The two most common items exchanged in a contract: blood and hair." Sevila held up two fingers, which bore a fine tremble, though nothing like before.

As if burned Aurel pulled their hands back, appalled. "Why? What would I even do with it?"

"Consume it, obviously."

She said it with such a matter-of-fact air, as though this were something Aurel should already understand innately. Aurel tried to imagine eating human hair, choking down matted strands, and they shuddered at the thought. Not wholly because it disgusted them, but because the thought was somehow terribly appealing. "I have no body. It shouldn't be possible for me to consume anything."

"Try it, then."

The urge to reach out, to pinch strands of black glossy hair between their fingers, and pluck them free, overcame them. Before they could withstand the compulsion, Aurel's hand was in Sevila's hair, stroking it back from her brow. With a sharp hiss, Aurel recoiled, yanking their hand away.

"No," Aurel said, adamant. "This isn't what I want."

The moment passed. Sevila had rolled onto her back to watch them, her face gaunt and tired. "As you like. Consuming these things gives you a glimpse at life once more. Souls crave them, so people take precautions against such urges. They cover their hair. They burn the bodies of their dead. They cannot risk being possessed or eaten."

"I am not some sort of carrion-eater!" Aurel growled, and was surprised to hear an otherworldly echo enter their own voice in anger. They scowled, leaned back, but made no move to stand.

Sevila's gaze was keen and inscrutable as a honed knife. She searched Aurel's formless face with an expression that could not be named. Her stare was broken only when she had to clear the burr of a cough from her throat once more. Rolling back over so that she used Aurel's lap as a cushion, she rasped, "I'd kill a man for a cup of decent wine."

Briefly Aurel considered pushing her away and leaving. They could abandon her here. They could track down their body without her, and bring it back only when they needed her to perform the necessary rituals. Had Aurel retained any memories, they would have done just that. As things stood however, they did not have the knowledge required to navigate this world without her. They were nothing and nobody.

"The priest was right," Aurel told her. "There is something very wrong with you."

Sevila appeared to be dozing, but after a beat she sighed. Without turning over to look at them, she replied, "I was wondering what he said to you back in Avaza."

"Whatever it is you're hiding, you cannot hope to keep it a secret from me forever."

To that she did not immediately respond. Aurel was about to press demands, to wield the contract held, unbreakable, between them like a bludgeon, when at last Sevila said, "Just as you have no body, I have no soul."

Whatever Aurel had been expecting, this was not it. They thought back to their weeks of travel together, to the Oracle's words earlier that very day, even to Sevila's physical appearance. "Did someone take it from you?"

Sevila wheezed, and it took Aurel a moment to realise she was laughing. For a reason that escaped them, she found this amusing. "No. Not at all. I drew out a last breath, and I cut it from my lungs with a bone knife. Then I hid it in a jar where nobody could find it. I had my reasons," she said before Aurel could ask why she would possibly consider doing such a thing. "A life bereft of fulfilment and empathy — trust me, it's better this way."

With a resigned groan, she struggled upright. Sitting on the edge of the couch beside Aurel, Sevila kneaded one shoulder, and rolled her neck to produce a few cracks and pops of cartilage. "The next time you want a cuddle and chat, you might take off your armour, dear."

What small shred of intimacy and trust they had begun to share went up in smoke. Aurel glowered. "You drugged yourself, and lost consciousness."

"All the same." Wobbling somewhat, Sevila pushed herself to her feet. There she stretched, and glanced around the shabby room. "Nicoma's self-proclaimed finest taverna really is a delight to the senses."

"You're the one who chose it," Aurel reminded her, and she — of course — ignored them. When she crossed the room and began rummaging through the saddlebags, Aurel stood. "You should rest before we continue. You need sleep."

"As I stand before you, I will never have enough sleep to feel well-rested. There is no purpose to sleeping or eating other than that it feels good in the moment itself. After that, I derive nothing from it." While she spoke, she tugged a new set of clothes into place of a similar style to her other outfit which still piled on the floor in a damp heap. The fabric of this outfit however was a rich dark red tooled with gold so pale it gleamed silver. The fish scale belt cinched her narrow waist, and finally Aurel understood why she was so thin, why her body could not be sustained by food or drink alone, why it always appeared starved for something greater. Sevila pinned up her hair, wrapped it in ivory silk. "Do not forget what I am."

"And what exactly is that?" Aurel asked. They handed over a few of the pins removed earlier to be tucked away into the saddlebags once more alongside an assortment of cosmetic items and whatever secret treasures Sevila hoarded there.

She flashed them a wry, self-deprecating smile. "A living corpse." Then, stuffing everything into the bags, she fixed a long cowl into place so that its squared edges hung about her forearms. "I think it time for that cup of wine before we track down these bastards, don't you?"

With a sigh, Aurel picked up the saddlebags, slinging them over one shoulder and following Sevila out the door. Downstairs the common area was empty, devoid of even a few dedicated patrons mulling over cups as if to pour themselves in as well. Dawn was hours away still, and the young man had traded places with an older fellow who looked up from the bar to regard Aurel and Sevila's approach with suspicion. Barrel-chested and short, his rough-spun tunic stretched over powerful shoulders, and there was cunning edge to his features. He stopped what he was doing — cleaning the top of a table with a rag — and said, "My son told me someone like you had arrived. We see your lot around these parts more than I'd care to tell."

Pausing in adjusting the veil around her neck, Sevila arched an eyebrow at him. She twitched the veil, and it gave a rattle, bone against bone, bone against cloth. "Is that so?"

He gestured at Sevila's clothes. "Rich nobles looking to lose themselves in the bowl of a pipe. Wasting their money for a week, or fleeing the capital like dogs. Never seen one with a fellow like this, though."

His stare moved to Aurel, who was startled to find open hostility brewing there.

"Trust me, you haven't seen people like us before." Sevila slapped down a few silver coins atop the scarred table top, and though the effects of the pipe were still taking its toll, her expression was hard. "Three days food and a pitcher of wine, or I'll have 'this fellow' make an example of you."

With a sneer, the taverna owner scooped the coins into his hands and made a show of counting each of them, checking their stamps for purity before storming away to gather her order from the kitchens. When he had gone, Aurel leaned down to murmur in Sevila's ear. "That isn't necessary. We could have just left, and bought supplies somewhere else."

Sevila leaned her hip against the table, and shrugged. "And after the night I had, I'd like to be amused."

"If you don't need to eat, then why bother buying food at all?" Aurel prodded at her upper arm, measuring its thinness between thumb and forefinger.

She swatted their hand away, her many rings clacking against Aurel's armoured gauntlet. "It may not satisfy, but it still feels nice."

Aurel cocked their head. They were about to respond, when the taverna owner returned. A cloth sack was thrown atop the counter without a word, and beside it he slammed down a small pitcher of wine and an accompanying cup. He glared as Sevila did exactly as he himself had done before, and looked over every piece of food inside. She even raised the loaves of bread to her nose and sniffed, loud, exaggerated.

"Everything to your liking, Lady?" he mocked, performing a slight bow. As he did so, Aurel noticed a few of his fingers were missing. He had covered the stubs of flesh with strips of leather, and on the back of his wrist there was a brand — the number fourteen etched with old livid scars. It was, Aurel realised, a similar brand to the one they had seen on the beggar in the streets. The only difference was that the taverna owner had numerous other scars criss-crossing the backs of his forearms.

Sevila's eyes darted to his hand and arms. A furrow darkened her brow. She jerked her chin towards him. "The Fourteenth legion? You're a bit old to have served under Theodoros. Or does the army recruit grandfathers these days?"

"I did my time. Sixteen years of service, and for what?" He thumbed at the handle of a short paring knife tucked into his belt.

Its edge still held the remains of whatever vegetable he had been peeling at some point in the day. He tried to loom over Sevila, but she did not retreat from her place. "A hectare of good land west of Pala that I was forced to abandon with my family, because it was overrun by those unshaven horse fuckers. The only reason we were able to afford opening a business in this rat hole of a city is because the Lord Regent reimbursed us. All of us. Everyone who lost their homes to invaders."

"So, I've heard. And with treasury money, no less. How does it feel knowing your good fortune came from the backs of poor taxpayers, and not from the private wealth of the nobility you so despise?" Sevila pulled a jug of wine over, and poured herself a cup. The wine flowed, ocean-dark. She seemed to pay attention only to the way she tilted the jug, but she watched the taverna owner from the corner of her vision. Aurel meanwhile remained poised, gauging the taverna owner's every motion for any sign of violent intent.

A muscle ticked in the man's clenched jaw. His posture did not change, but Aurel was overcome with the urge to step forward beside Sevila, and tower over him. When they did so, the taverna owner glanced at them before keeping his focus solely on Sevila. "The Lord Regent is a man of the people, for the people," he said in a very soft voice. "He has done more for this empire than men of greater name ever did."

A cruel bark of laughter, and Sevila sneered around her cup. "Such as — what? Kill children and grandmothers?"

The taverna owner slammed his fist against the table, making the wooden planks rattle. "Iustina would have watched the empire burn if it meant putting her own family first!"

"Yes." Sevila took a sip of wine, swirling the cup. "And now she has been toppled in favour of a man, who would watch his family burn if it meant preserving this husk of an empire. What a trade!"

Knuckles flashing pale in a tight fist, the taverna owner took a step away. He drew the little knife at his waist, and Aurel — unsure of how exactly to respond — did the same with the dagger acquired from the magistrate's husband. With a hurried chant — ancient words in the archaic tongue — the taverna owner drew the blade across the back of his arm. He smeared his palm with fresh bright blood, then thrust his hand forward, fingers outstretched. From the ground beneath his hand where drops of blood bloomed upon the floorboards, an inky darkness took shape. Shadows gathered and spread like dark fire, coalescing into the form of a beast. Eyes wide, Aurel watched as the taverna owner summoned the spirit of a wolf, lashed together from shadow and blood.

"Heed me, spirit!" The taverna owned held forth his hand, and announced, "Two of my fingers if you drive this woman from the city! A third if you ensure that she suffers!"

At his offer, the wolf swung its head towards Sevila. Its eyes were a dripping carnal red. The floor touched by its skeletal paws pooled with a black ichor. In silence, it regarded Sevila, then turned its attention upon Aurel. In the past, no other souls had ever interacted with them directly. Aurel was accustomed already to being ignored by the living and the dead alike. Now that they had another soul's attention however, Aurel was struck with an alien sensation. The spirit gauged them, and the weight of its stare was an almost palpable thing. Aurel clutched at the dagger, arrested with indecision, as the other spirit measured its odds against them. It felt like oil slicked across the surface of water. Like the jump of a blade across ribs. It found no purchase; it sloughed away sure as a wind through tangled boughs.

It took but a moment, and the wolf spirit rushed into non-existence with a roar absent sound, shadows splashing across the floor, and evaporating into nothing until only a few drops of blood remained, glistening. Both Aurel and the taverna owner gazed at the spot where seconds ago the wolf had stood, shocked at its sudden dissolution.

Sevila on the other hand looked unimpressed, even bored. "It seems the spirit recognises a losing deal when it sees one. Which is more than I can say for you." She waved her free hand at the taverna owner's bloody knife, a dismissive gesture. "Was that really your best? I thought the army preferred to employ soldiers with necromantic abilities of some calibre."

The taverna owner's entire demeanour change in an instant. Whatever sure-footed confidence he had wielded previously fled, and in its place horror dawned. Hand shaking, he pointed the knife between Aurel and Sevila, unsure which one might attack him first. "I've faced my share of souls and their masters on the battlefield, but you -!" In his retreat, he stumbled against a bench that clipped his heel. He only just caught himself in time to stagger back a few more steps. "Get out! Whatever pact you two have struck, I want no part of it! *Get out!*"

"What did you think we were doing? So dramatic! And for what?" Rolling her eyes, Sevila drained her cup and then tossed it to the floor where it tumbled towards the taverna owner's boots, trailing dregs as it went. "Your wine tastes like piss, by the way."

She scooped up the bag of food supplies and started towards the door. When Aurel did not follow, she stopped and nudged one of their shoulders. The sound of plate scraping against chain mail brought their attention back, and with a start Aurel tucked the dagger away before departing with her, leaving the taverna owner pointing his knife at the closed door behind them.

The rain had stopped altogether, though the sky was still sheathed in iron-coloured cloud. Sevila rounded the building in search of the stables, already digging through the bag for food. As she tore into one of the loaves of bread, she said, "I can't stand that kind of bravado posturing as high-mindedness. Soldiers follow whoever pays and whoever wins. That's all they care about. Ask any number of emperors and empresses who have been killed off by power-hungry generals!"

Still shaken by the encounter, Aurel was relieved that Nicoma at this early hour was all but empty. No guards could be seen patrolling apart from a few resting their eyes while standing at the city entrance, and in the distance could be heard the monotonous drone of the pious at the door of the Oracle's inner sanctum. "We could have been in serious trouble, and all you want to talk about is moral grandstanding?"

"That is rich, coming from you," Sevila countered. She had found the stable's entrance, and unlocked the latch that held a chest-high wooden gate shut. Swinging it open so that Aurel had to dodge around it or be struck, she wandered inside. "On the chance that I'd use the full power of our contract, the spirit knew it was outmatched. I wouldn't have, of course. Ours is a pact too valuable to waste on the likes of a washed-up veteran."

"And if the soul had taken the wager regardless? What then?" Aurel located the horse in one of the pens alongside a handful of other pack animals. Lifting the saddlebags Aurel placed them over the horse's back and strapped them into place, while the horse tried to shy away from their presence.

Sevila meanwhile pulled the leather bridle over the horse's ears, urging the bit between its teeth. "Then we would have been driven from the city, obviously. Which, when you think about it, is what we were doing anyway."

Movements slowing, Aurel blinked at Sevila as she struggled to heave herself into the saddle. Aurel moved behind her, and lifted her by the waist so that she could swing one leg over the horse's back. "I suppose," Aurel conceded. "Though he did offer for you to suffer."

With a derisive snort Sevila tied the bag of food to the saddle horn. Manoeuvring the reins with one hand and the last of the loaf in the other, she spoke around a mouthful of food. "I am a living corpse devoid of soul and fulfilment. My life is suffering."

"Now who is being dramatic?"

Sevila pretended not to hear, and kicked the horse into motion. With a rueful shake of their head, Aurel followed her into the misty morning and out of Nicoma.

Chapter 6

In Chalos the people lined up for a public stoning. The sounds of a flourishing market could be heard not far off, and a humidity clung to every surface, making skin gleam. The fine heat of the day settled in the sky with a haze. The sea salted the air and bronzed the shore with sediment. White-capped waves extended along the coastline. Ships masts crowded the harbour. And along the outer wall of the city barracks, a man, weeping, had his hands and feet bound in preparation for his execution.

Sevila made a wide circle around the crowd — eager for blood — herself only eager for whatever wares the market beyond could offer. Aurel on the other hand paused to look on in alarm. As a priest dressed in black read out the man's crimes to those in attendance, Aurel tapped at a woman's shoulder. She turned to face them. She was young, far too young Aurel would have thought to be witnessing something like this, and when she saw what it was that addressed her, she drew the cowl over her ears to cover the hint of hair at her temples.

"Excuse me," Aurel began, smoothing their voice to a low soothing burr. "My Mistress did not hear properly. What is this man's crime?"

Frowning, the young woman nevertheless answered, "He has been found guilty of stealing a body, and attempting to bribe a Healer to put another's soul into it."

When Sevila heard what Aurel was asking, she quickly turned around. Striding over, she grabbed Aurel's arm, and tugged. "What do you think you're doing?" She hissed, hauling Aurel away from the young woman, who watched them go with a guarded sort of curiosity. "Now is not the time or the place!"

"Whatever this man did, surely, he can be dealt with more dignity," Aurel tried insisting, but Sevila cut them off in a hushed tone.

"You listen to me." She yanked at the strap crossing Aurel's chest, holding their pauldron in place. "Do you want to get your body back? Hmm?"

With a scowl Aurel pushed Sevila's hand away, but remained bent over so the two could speak, unheard. "I don't see how that's relevant."

"Look around you. Pay attention." She gestured towards the crowd, many of whom hefted handfuls of rocks, others jeering loudly as the convict began to sob. "What do you think will happen if you interfere? This isn't a backwater like Avaza with no population to speak of. If you try to stop this verdict, then there will be a riot. We won't be able to buy passage on a ship to Faros, and we will lose even more ground. By the time the city dies down, the trail will go cold, and your body will be long gone."

Aurel straightened, and for a moment they only surveyed the barracks, the people thronging for blood, their voices an ugly murmur tinged with fear more than with rage. Fear of taboos being broken, of silent gods turning their faces away, of the empire and its citizens continuing to rot into a bleak and unspoken future. "If what you and the Oracle have said is true, then killing this man won't solve anything."

"I would prefer if you don't include me in the same breath as that useless old bat." Shaking her head in exasperation, Sevila started off once more in the direction of the market. "And how can you expect society to adjust that quickly?"

"People are more adaptable than you give them credit for." Aurel followed her only reluctantly, glancing back at the crowd but not intervening like they might have wished. This may not have been Avaza, but Aurel felt just as powerless as they had back then. They shouldered the saddlebags and forged onward.

"And you give them too much. The Three Taboos exist for a reason, you know, else there would be a lot more things like us wandering about." Sevila replied. She waved towards Aurel over her shoulder, and her fingers glinted gold in the harsh light. "I'm beginning to see why you were murdered. Might I suggest you pick fewer battles? Especially when they might get me involved?"

Now that Aurel knew what she truly was, watching Sevila interact with others — even when she did not seem to — revealed her very nature. People who spoke to her seemed vaguely discomfited by her presence, though if asked they could not pinpoint exactly why. Those like Constantia back in Lapedion might have claimed they merely found Sevila to be reprehensible, and that was source enough for their dislike of her. Now as Aurel trailed after her towards the harbour, people parted for Sevila without conscious thought, as though their first instinct was to shrink away from the wrongness of her. Though Aurel supposed people did the same with them; a human soul was a rare and powerful enough sight to give most strangers pause.

For most of their travel from Nicoma, sunlight had parted the rains and accompanied the two of them throughout the days climbing down the steep mountain slopes, but a combination of early morning mist and Sevila's insistence on taking shortcuts had proven to be a step too far. The rocky path slicked with fog, the horse's hooves had slipped, sending the animal sliding and crashing down the ridge. Aurel was able to recover the bags including the majority of their contents, but the horse had broken two of its legs. Sevila had put it out of its misery, and Aurel had been burdened with the responsibility of being the replacement pack mule for the remainder of the trip.

Upon reaching the base of the mountains, the two of them had followed the river to the sea. Any number of barges bearing supplies skimmed across the surface of the water, but Sevila had flat refused to step foot on a boat regardless of how much time it might have saved them, and without a mount their pace had slowed considerably. Even without full rest and food, it took them a full three days to arrive. Here among the city and its inhabitants, Sevila's finery once again appeared dull with dust from the journey. Beneath the patina of grime however, her wealth was enough to catch the eye of a potential thief or two, though none were bold enough to try stealing from her with Aurel's hulking form striding at her side. If that failed to dissuade them, a single cold glance from Sevila sent them sloping away in search of another target.

"What I want to know—" Sevila began, pulling down her veil to allow the fresh breeze to cool her skin "—is how on earth we are still behind? How could a toddling priest, two guards thicker than pigshit, and a mindless body always keep one step ahead of us?"

"Perhaps they took a barge," Aurel answered, their tone dry.

Sevila shot them a dirty look over her shoulder. "We've been over this before. I get ill if I even stand on a wet rag, let alone a boat. It is bad enough that we'll be travelling by sea to Faros — a testament to my dedication to you, one might say!"

"A testament to the unbreakable law of a contract, more likely." Aurel shifted the saddlebags so that they settled more securely in place across their shoulders.

It came as something of a relief that they did not need to fear stepping on passers-by, since nobody drew near enough. Only once on their way to the market did someone fail to notice Aurel and Sevila's approach, and the boy in question scrambled to get out of their way when his older cousin motioned for him to move. The closer the two of them drew to the harbour however, the busier the city grew. People thronged on all sides until only a small bubble existed around Aurel and Sevila, and eventually that too faded away. Soon enough the two of them walked with slowed steps while the mass of people flowed around them like water parting around the sleek profile of a ship's prow.

Rather than gather supplies for the trip, as Aurel had expected, Sevila only stopped at a stall for what was in her case a light snack. Rows upon rows of fish bared their silvered bellies — split and emptied — upon lines and racks, in fresh mounds that were slippery with scales. The voracity with which Sevila ate never became any less fascinating, and even though Aurel knew what she was, they watched Sevila wolf down a clam and fish stew served in a loaf of bread that also acted as a bowl. As she began to tear into the bowl, passing by a number of other stalls, Aurel asked, "Aren't you going to need something to eat on the leg to Faros?"

At that Sevila groaned softly around a mouthful. "Don't remind me. And — no. I won't be able to keep down anything solid as soon as we are out to sea."

Up ahead the tall skeletal masts were circled with white-winged gulls. Avian cries, and the creak of timber, and the slap of waves against painted hulls filled the air. Sevila did not hasten towards the fleet of ships tethered to their docks, and by the time they arrived she had polished off her meal. Together the two walked along the brimming harbour, and while Sevila surveyed ships with a critical eye, Aurel — who had no knowledge of what deemed something seaworthy outside of the obvious category of *'it floats'* — admired the bold colours applied to the hulls. The ships gazed back with their painted sidelong glances, their hulls barnacle-bearded and sprouting a fringe of oars.

"I have never seen Chalos like this before. Not even when Basilius moved the capital to Pala," Sevila muttered. She frowned at the crowds clamouring for the attention of the ships' crews. Many of them were accompanied by children. Almost all of them carried heavy-laden packs, or otherwise drew carts burdened with all their worldly possessions — fine silks, small statues bearing the likeness of revered ancestors, hoards of coin in unearthed urns.

"Refugees." Aurel said aloud as they passed a haggard family that wore too many layers of clothing rather than carry them in sacks that were already overflowing with heirlooms. "The horselords must have pushed further south than we thought."

Sevila hummed in agreement. "This makes things difficult. We look too similar to them, too desperate. Whereas our priest friend —"

"—Could have requisitioned a vessel without trouble," Aurel finished for her.

"You have touched the boil with a needle. What we need is something to set us apart from the crowd." She gestured for Aurel to lean down. "I need something from my bags."

Swinging the bags around, Aurel placed them at Sevila's feet. She opened one, peered down into it with a cocked head, then closed it and opened the other. Each was large enough that when she burrowed into it, bent over double, her arms were buried up to the shoulder in deep red cloth. A clinking and a clanging as she rummaged through their contents, mumbling to herself — "Now where did I put it -?" — until at last she made a triumphant noise, announcing she had found whatever it was she sought. When she straightened, she held in her arms a plan ungilded box fastened with a simple brass lock in the shape of a beetle that could be opened with the flick of a switch.

"What does it hold?" Aurel gathered the bags up once more, curious as to what they had been carting around this whole time.

"You will find out soon enough, my dear." Sevila tried tucking the box under one arm, but when it turned out to be too large, she grumbled, and continued cradling it to her chest. "This partnership of ours is proving to be very expensive."

"When it's costly, suddenly we are partners. But when you want something, you're my Mistress." Aurel tugged Sevila's cowl down so that it covered her eyes. "Pick one. You cannot have both."

Spluttering and indignant, her hands full, Sevila rearranged her cowl with a few graceless tosses of her head. "In all my years, I have never known a soul to be so overbearing!"

"Not even your own?"

Aurel had meant it to be teasing, but Sevila went very still, poised like a snake to strike. Something cold and hard glittered darkly in her eyes, and her pupils were thin as the edge of a knife. When she spoke, her voice held a dangerous, silky lilt. "Mine is, I think, exceptional in many regards."

With that she started off towards the nearest ship, and perhaps it was Aurel's imagination but people seemed to get out of her way more quickly than before. Mulling over her words, Aurel followed. While there was no real queue to speak of, a few members of the crowd swore vehemently when Sevila moved ahead of them. There, standing at the water's edge, the ship's captain argued with a woman.

"Your coin is no good," he told her, pushing a bag back into her hands, heavy with the jangle of silver. "It's Proban minted."

"The quality is fine!" she insisted, trying to shove the bag over while her family — four children of varying age — watched nearby. "Please! My children -!"

The ship's captain sighed, and ran a hand over his dark clean-shaven head. He had forsaken a headwrap and instead wore only a fine stubble of hair across his scalp and jaw. "If I gave passage to every mother with a sob story, my boat would sink beneath the waves from the weight. I would drown in the tears you refugees have spilled on my shoulder." He regarded the woman with a tired look and recited a line he must have repeated a dozen times that day alone. "The only coin I'll accept is pre-Proban or stamped by the Komateros clan."

In reply, the woman spat in his face, then grabbed one of her children by the hand and stormed off towards the market. For a moment, the ship's captain made no move, until he raised his hand and wiped his cheek and nose. His fingers lingered around his face to rub at his jawline, working the lower jaw back and forth with a grimace.

"I was wondering why your face was so clean," Sevila said with a small laugh as she approached him. "Now I know."

Arching an eyebrow, the ship's captain gave Sevila a quick once over. He brushed his hand against the baggy trousers that bunched at the ankle above his bare feet. "And you should also know my terms of payment. Passage for one is thirty gold or seven hundred equivalent silver *of good quality.*"

"Passage for two," Aurel corrected him. They did not notice Sevila was elbowing them in the stomach for mentioning extra fees to be paid.

Both of his eyebrows rose at being addressed by a human soul, and his expression grew more guarded when he took in the sight of Sevila and Aurel together, who he had previously not considered part of the same party. "Souls do not pay passage across water. It is tradition."

Clearing her throat, Sevila held up the box in her arms. "I have something far better than gold."

"If I had coin for every time I heard that today, I could buy myself a name of worth and—" As he spoke, he trailed off and his eyes widened. Sevila had unlocked the box and opened it to reveal pale blocks of pure cut salt set in a velvet. One of the blocks had shattered into multiple pieces due to the fall at Nicoma, each section as wide again as Aurel's hand and thick as two thumbs.

When the ship's captain reached for the box, Sevila snapped it shut. "Half a block for passage to Faros. And I want a nice place to sleep."

He crossed his arms, and his skin was sheathed from wrist to elbow in a shark-toothed pattern of tattoos. "A whole block. Then we can talk sleeping quarters."

"Half a block." Sevila had a flinty set to her narrow jaw. She jerked her chin towards the goods sequestered away in her arms. "You can have one of the broken pieces."

His laugh was soft, deep, incredulous. "You come to me first, yet you insult me with your offer!"

Sevila shrugged. "I have to start my negotiations somewhere. It might as well be with the cheapest looking option."

He grinned at her, his teeth yellowish and pale against his dark face. "Three quarters of a block, and I enjoy the pleasure of your company during the trip."

Unamused, Sevila replied, "Three quarters of a block, and you never speak to me again."

Far from taken aback, the ship's captain ceded with grace and a world-weary sigh. He leaned back, rubbing once more at his jaw. "You drive a hard bargain, Lady -"

"Peinatokos," Sevila supplied. With a nod of her head, she continued. "And my associate: Aurel."

He glanced only perfunctorily at Aurel before fixing his attention back upon Sevila. "Lady Peinatokina, welcome aboard. You can have one of the swinging cots below deck."

In return Sevila offered no smile. She simply opened the box and allowed him to select two broken pieces of salt, which he balanced in his square-fingered hands as though weighing the heft of rare jewels. Closing the box, Sevila motioned for the bags and stored the box away once more. She tucked it among the other nameless valuables with great care, and as Aurel followed her past the ship's captain, she grumbled, "That ill-footed horse managed to kill itself *and* break the salt I'd acquired in Aegryph! All that travel across the desert for naught!"

The plank that sloped from the docs to the ship shuddered beneath their feet, and Aurel looked over their shoulder to find the ship's captain flooded with offers from onlookers in the crowd, who had watched Sevila buy her way on board. "You refused his proposition. I'm surprised, to be perfectly honest. You don't strike me as they type to deny yourself pleasures wheresoever they may come, and he is decent enough looking. Is it fear of pregnancy that drove your decision?"

At that Sevila snorted, a graceless sound. "No. A matter of taste." Her footsteps were light, near noiseless along the wooden planks. "Even if I had a soul, I am incapable of child-bearing. Very fortunately, too, I should think."

"While I do not always agree with you, I think in this case—" Aurel let the sentence go unfinished, and was pleased when Sevila's only reply was a huff of wry laughter. "You mentioned Aegryph?"

She hummed a wordless note. "The kingdom across the southern sands. Why else do you think I stumbled across you? Did you think I was travelling through Avaza for the scenery? Perhaps for the thriving culture?"

It was of course a rhetorical question, and Aurel gave no answer where one was not expected. Together they stepped aboard the galley, and were greeted with general disinterest. Like the ship's captain, the crew all went about their business bare-footed. Some shielded their heads with wraps of tattered yet colourful cloth. Others had adopted the captain's completely clean-shaven approach. All had beards that were either non-existent or kept carefully trimmed short. The only person aboard the ship bearing facial hair of any real length was what appeared to be a fellow passenger: a hatchet-faced man wearing pale robes with a large lacquered box strapped to his back. A long red veil stitched with bone — not unlike Sevila's —obscured his face and trailed down to his knees as though someone had taken a brush and painted a streak of oxblood down his chest. Aurel spotted a few stray wisps of greying beard beneath the veil, their gaze honed at the sight of it. Beside him were a huddle of refugees and two other men, one of whom had skin cast in a sickly pallor.

Aurel was about to ask Sevila about the other passengers, but when they glanced over it was to see that she had a similar grey tinge about her. Before Aurel could ask if she was alright, she sprinted for the railing, and was violently ill over the edge of the deck into the water below. Beneath them the ship rocked gently among the waves, yet even that minimal movement was enough to send Sevila heaving again. Awkward but wanting to offer comfort in some small capacity, Aurel crept forward, and patted her on the back.

Straightening, Sevila wiped her mouth with the back of her hand. "Six whole days of this."

"Will you be able to manage that?" Aurel continued patting her back with one hand as softly as they were able, until Sevila waved their concern away.

"Yes, but at what cost?" She swallowed against the dryness in her throat, then made a face. "Don't answer that. We save three days by avoiding a journey on land."

Aurel considered that information. "Which means we are already two days behind, assuming our quarry went by barge from Nicoma."

Sevila shot Aurel a sour look. "Always the optimist, aren't you?"

"I value honesty above all else."

"Your values are depressing me." With an unsteady gait Sevila pushed away from the railing, and stumbled towards an opening that led to the cabin below deck. "Now, I am going to find myself some wine to vomit back up. If you need me, don't bother me. If you must insist on bothering me regardless, I will be the miserable bastard in a cot for the next week."

Aurel blinked after her as she clambered down a ladder into the lower decks, and vanished from sight. Her absence was a glaring silence filled with the wary gazes of others. In her presence Aurel resented Sevila — her manners, her pettiness, her crude, sly, spiteful nature — but faced by the world, alone, they dreaded the dearth of her. Anger came roaring at them, vivid as colour, broad and sweeping as the sky. Quick, brief, and brilliant it boiled, the raw frustration at the thought of being dependent on someone as loathsome as Sevila Peinatokos. Dimly through the anger Aurel wondered if this was what it meant to feel something, if this was as close to physical sensation they would ever come until they were once more reunited with a body.

Faced with the stark notion that day might never come, Aurel forced through to a simulacrum of calm, and strode over to the other passengers. All conversation that had been present died the moment the group caught wind of Aurel's approach. For a long moment, the only sound was the creak of sailors' footsteps and the muted slap of rope accompanied by a gull's solitary cries, until the man in white cleared his throat.

"Can we help you, spirit?" he questioned, and as he did so he stroked at his bright crimson veil, which flared down his chest.

Aurel's height meant they could not help but tower over the others, and they smoothed their voice, smothered any ember or spark of ire. "No. My Mistress is ill and has retired."

"Ah. Right." Nodding, the man in white pulled the lacquered box around his shoulders, and sat it upon the deck. He unlocked one of the many compartments, and when he pulled back the lid, he revealed a collection of vials, satchels, and ceramic jars all clinking together. With practised hands he unstoppered various vials, adding a pinch here and a dollop there to a jar that he then handed over to Aurel. "Mix a thimbleful of this with her drink. It should ease her stomach."

Aurel gazed, puzzled, down at the little jar in their hand, its glass dyed a murky green from its contents. "You are a Healer."

The Healer regarded Aurel with a slow, plodding confusion. "Yes," he said. "Was this not what you wanted?"

Tilting the jar made sunlight glance off its squared sides. Aurel tucked it away into the sash wrapped around their waist beside the wire-handled dagger there. "Thank you. Though it was not my intent, I am grateful. How much will it cost?"

"Half a silver coin will suffice," the Healer said, already locking away his wares.

As Aurel began to sift through the bags over their shoulder for coin, one of the other passengers stepped forward, a refugee woman in once fine clothing that now were tattered at the hems and encrusted with dust. "Could you have a look at my boy?" she said to the Healer. She dragged the child around, and placed her hand atop his head, her fingers vanishing into his uncut curls. "He has had a cough for days."

Aurel watched as the Healer gestured the young boy closer, felt around his neck, and asked for the boy to cough. The sound rattled in his small chest the way rain echoed through a cave — dull and wet.

"I can make you a tincture," the Healer told her while still frowning at the boy. "Though it may not clear his lungs before infection sets in. Or for an extra ten silver I can summon a spirit to cure him immediately."

"I—" The refugee woman gathered her son back towards her, raking her hands through his hair in a fit of nerves, over and over again. "I don't have that kind of money. Not after travelling all the way to Faros from the horselords. They burned our house and dug up all the gold I had saved beneath the flower gardens."

From the bag Aurel pulled up a fistful of coins that glinted, silver and gold. "Will this suffice?"

Both the Healer and the refugee woman stared. She opened her mouth, pulled her boy close, but said nothing. Her son coughed into his hands, hacking against a wet obstruction in his chest. The Healer gauged first her reaction then Aurel's as he reached out to take the coin, his movements measured and unhurried. "This is easily enough for me to treat everyone aboard this ship for the duration of the trip."

With a nod Aurel told him, "Then do so."

A dull murmuring passed between members of the passengers gathered, and by this point Aurel had attracted the attention of sailors, whose steps slowed as they passed by, their dark eyes curious. When the Healer began to open his pack once more in order to treat those that were clustering close around him and Aurel, the ship's captain strode onto the deck from land. He was followed closely by a broad-chested sailor carrying all the money, goods, and sundry with which passengers had paid their way. While the sailor went about putting all of the items away, the ship's captain halted in his tracks with a frown at Aurel surrounded by people. Striding forward, he called out, "Where is your Mistress? What have you offered to these people?"

Before Aurel could speak however, the Healer answered in their defence, "I have been paid most generously to treat your clients and your crew, a task which I accepted of my own will and upon my own head, should it come to that."

Rubbing at his jaw, the ship's captain squinted between Aurel and the Healer. "I trust you know what you're doing."

The Healer gave a bow of his head. "Human souls are beyond my power if not my ken. You worry like an old buzzard, Captain. And you should pay me a visit as well, when you are able," he added when the ship's captain gave a wince upon rubbing to hard at his jawline. "I'll be able to take care of that bad tooth of yours."

With a grunt, the ship's captain began to turn away. As he did so, he gave Aurel a wary glance, quick enough that Aurel might have imagined it. His tongued poked the skin of his cheek as he tested the teeth at the back of his mouth. He made a show of administering duties to nearby sailors, who ignored him, and continued working while their captain feigned disinterest in the crowd.

A gap was made by the passengers around Aurel and the Healer, just large enough for him to have drawn a circle upon the deck in thickened blood from a stoppered jar. His brown fingers were dripped in red to the knuckle. With careful contemplation and furrowed brows, he wrote out symbols, and letters, and words in a ritual far more complex than Aurel had seen before. As the refugee woman shuffled her son forward however, a man who had been watching among those gathered shouldered his way to the front.

"The boy can wait! My brother needs help now!" He supported nearly the full weight of his brother at his side. The two were near identical — the slope of their brows, their heights, their loam-black hair — except that the brother's skin held a sickly pallor. He was gaunt and thin, and his mouth had flaked away from exposure to the elements and lack of water. His arm had been wrapped in discoloured cloth.

"You will wait your turn like everyone else!" The refugee woman began, but the strength in her voice faded, when the man unwrapped his brother's arm. The brother was missing a hand; the stump that remained cut off at the wrist, revealing jagged spears of bone encrusted with pus. Up to the elbow burgundy veins of colour had spread, as though the forearm had been splashed with putrid wine.

At once the refugee woman recoiled, pulling her son a step back, and clapping a hand over her nose. Through the mangled mess Aurel could see the hint of a number branded into the flesh of his wrist. Meanwhile the Healer leaned forward on his knees to more closely inspect the wound without drawing too near. Almost immediately he sat back on his haunches, hands planted on his thighs. "Your brother is beyond my help. The infection has poisoned his blood. It would require a human soul to heal his injury."

The man's face contorted into a rictus snarl. "You're only saying that because he is a deserter! There is a human soul standing right there!" He jabbed a finger at Aurel, who raised their hands as if to ward off a blow.

"I can't -!" Aurel tried to say, but the Healer came to their rescue once more.

"This spirit is already engaged in a contract. Unless you want to ask their Mistress for a favour, I doubt you will get anything from them." The Healer rolled up his long-sleeved tunic as he spoke. "All I can do is lessen his pain before he dies."

When the man gave Aurel a pleading desperate look, his eyes shining with unshed tears as he clutched his brother around his too-narrow waist, Aurel shook their head. "I cannot in good faith even suggest you ask her; she is not the kind of woman to grant favours to those in need."

"Surely—!" the man started, but Aurel cut him off before he could speak another word.

"I am sorry to be so blunt, but she would sooner spit in your face and laugh than order me to save your brother."

The brother sagged, limp and half-dead where he stood, and the man's face hardened as he fought against the tremble at his chin and lower lip. "Can't you inhabit him?" he gasped, swallowing back tears like bitter bile. "You can have his body! Please! I just want him to live!"

Shocked silence followed that statement. The crowd surrounding the Healer retreated a few more steps, and all of the sailors pretending not to listen stopped to stare. Everyone — even the young boy — gaped at him as though he had lit himself on fire: with disgust, with horror, with pity. Desperate, the man shambled forward to push his brother into Aurel's arms despite the Healer's vehement protests, and Aurel dropped Sevila's bags to catch him before he fell.

"Enough of this!" the Healer hissed, jumping forward to grab the man, and try hauling him back.

Flinging the Healer's hands away, the man yelled, and his face was shining with tears now; they caught in the stubble of his rough jaw. "Any chance, any chance at all, and I'll take it! My brother served his time for citizenship, and when he tried to leave, those fanatics of Theodoros did this to him! They mutilate him! They withhold his pay! Half his life to the army — I will save what's left of it!"

"Don't be a fool!" the Healer snapped back, his eyes very dark over the top of his veil. "That would not save him! It would kill him! And then the body would continue to rot around this foreign soul until the flesh slipped from its bones!"

Aurel held the brother upright while the two fought. Up close his skin held a sour oily sheen. His breathing was rattling and thready against Aurel's chest, and with his remaining hand he fumbled at the sash around Aurel's waist in a vain attempt to hold himself upright. His fingers trembled, weak and yellowish at the tips. During the journey to Chalos his hair had grown until it curled beneath his ears. Without thinking, Aurel reached up to brush it back from where strands stuck to his sweat-slicked brow. Aurel curled their fingers at the back of his head, gripping his hair tight, gauntlets scratching at the nape of his neck.

Aurel could do it. Here a body before them like a skin of water dangling and sweating within grasp of one parched and dying of thirst. The periphery of Aurel's vision blurred, and the people standing aboard the ship became something less. Bodies

hung like fruit from the parabolic limbs of trees. All of them —
bodies with the potential to be inhabited, and this one offered to
Aurel as if served up on a platter of pale gold. Head tipped back,
the brother's face was lit with an unearthly light. Aurel could see
the trace of individual bone and sinew, the structures peeled back,
split open, laid bare.

"Stop! Stop this!"

Slowly Aurel tore their gaze away, and swung their head
around. The Healer was heaving all of his weight against one of
Aurel's arms, while two sailors hauled at the other, straining
against Aurel as though at an iron statue. The ship's captain was
shouting at three of his crew, who were dragging the man away,
whose face was half-smeared with fresh blood. The ship's
captain's knuckles dripped. The other passengers had crossed the
ship as far as they could go without disembarking, and the young
boy was clutching at his mother's legs, crying, and pointing at
Aurel, "Its eyes! I don't like its eyes!"

Aurel dropped the brother, and he collapsed to the deck
with a wordless groan of pain. Turning their hands palm up, Aurel
stepped away. The Healer rushed to check on the brother's
condition, and the two sailors released Aurel as though afraid
prolonged contact would transmit a plague.

"Forgive me!" Aurel's voice stuttered, clogged and choked.
"Is he alright—?"

When Aurel made a motion to peer over the Healer's
shoulder, the ship's captain turned to point an imperious finger and
glare at them. "You have caused enough trouble! Stay away from
him!"

"I didn't mean to! You must believe me!"

Drawing close, the ship's captain lowered his voice though
his scowl remained fierce. "Your Mistress has paid her way, and I
cannot refuse a spirit passage, but I beg that for the rest of the trip
you remain out of sight."

The Healer was packing the brother's wound with a viscous
paste, and wrapping it with pale gauze. The man who had pushed
his brother in Aurel's arms was being gagged by the two sailors
that dragged him off to be chained up in the brig. A few other crew

members offered tepid words of consolation to the other passengers.

Already retreating, Aurel nodded. "Yes. Yes, of course." Though any apology they offered was ignored. Their hobnail boots slapped against the deck, heavy and unwieldy. The armour shuddered at Aurel's arms and shoulders, and they gathered up the saddlebags before fleeing after Sevila to languish in the bowels of the ship.

Chapter 7

"If I find out you have wasted my hard-earned gold on senseless altruism, I'll put you back in your body and immediately kill you again," Sevila rasped from her place on the cot. Beneath them the ship rocked gently, and Sevila flushed a few shades of colour in rapid succession before emptying her stomach into the red and black clay-fired pot clutched between her knees.

"You have never owned anything hard-earned in your life, unless you stole it from someone else who earned it," Aurel replied. They sat on the floor of the galley, back against the rounded, rough-hewn planks that formed the hull. In their hands they held a wineskin, which they had pried from Sevila's fingers in order to water it down and add the Healer's tincture to the mix.

Sevila groaned into the mouth of the pot. The noise echoed. "You would harangue a sick woman?"

"If that woman were you? Absolutely."

"Heartless!" Sevila accused them.

"Quite literally." Aurel held out the wineskin to her. She shook her head, but Aurel pressed it into her hands, insistent yet soft. "The medicine has helped you these last few days, hasn't it?"

Making a face and sticking her tongue out, Sevila took the wineskin. "It makes the wine taste bitter."

"More so than your vomit?"

In answer, she lifted the neck to her lips and, hesitant, tilted the bladder back to take a sip. Her chest heaved at the intrusion, but she swallowed the wine down, even managing another sip before lowering it with a grimace. Sevila's was only one cot among rows of five all crammed together under the deck, yet for the five nights nobody had dared to occupy the cots on either side of her. Every day when the crew came down to rotate through their sleeping schedule, they would eye Aurel askance, and avoid both of them as though exposure would cause their skin to rupture with boils.

The latch above the ladder opened, and a broad blade of light struck through the air. One such crewmember, a pock-faced young man cowled in bright colours, clambered down only to skirt around the edges of the cots to retrieve something from his bag. He avoided looking at Sevila and Aurel, and after he had retrieved what he sought — a spare knife to cut through rigging — he scampered back above deck once more. His bare feet slipped on the top rung in his haste to escape and, cursing, he hauled himself to the surface.

In the shadow of the ship's belly, Sevila's eyes shone, sickly bright. Even hollow-cheeked and sallow-skinned, her gaze was as keen as ever. Still she said nothing. She only sighed and curled up on her cot, holding the wineskin to her chest as the medicine slowly began to take effect. Her breathing deepened, but her feet were too still; asleep, she would have been kicking and twitching like a hound dreaming of killing hares. On the second day of the trip Sevila had forsaken her headwrap, and now her lustrous dark hair fanned out on the cot; its ends tangled.

Aurel clenched their fists. The gauntlets creaked, plate and mail against leather. Sevila's hair needed combing, washing, trimming, eating. "Sevila?"

From the cot, she grunted. "Hmm?"

"Why did you name me Aurel?"

A pause. A silence. Then Sevila propped herself up on one elbow to aim a curious look at them over her shoulder. "What brought this on, darling?"

In the old imperial tongue — the language of texts, of law and scholars — it meant 'golden.' It conjured images of shining, bright, valuable things, of riches, of purity, highly-sought after items: veined amber and stitched raw silk. Not of dying brothers with no need of their broken bodies, or of Aurel's own reflection wavering in a pail of freshwater: a black, formless ink face suspended over dead men's armour.

"I'm not sure it suits me, is all."

Sevila's legs rustled against the rough-spun sheets. When she placed the wineskin on the floor, its contents sloshed, then were still. She leaned over from her place on the cot, and tilted Aurel's face up with her fingers. Her hand sank briefly into the substance of Aurel's cheek, like dipping her fingertips into a dark and viscous cloud. Aurel could not feel the touch, but her sudden nearness startled. Aurel tilted their shoulders back in an attempt to move away, but was stopped by the hull.

"Listen to me." Sevila's voice was low and intense, her eyes mesmerising, unblinking as a serpent's. "When mortals look at you, they see the manifestation of their subconscious fears, but when I look at you I see a bright light. To the soulless, you are a beacon."

Aurel stared up at her. When she moved away, they remained fixed in place, arrested by her bout of unforeseen sincerity. "When you went below deck, I almost -" Aurel glanced down, and fiddled with the straps of their gauntlets. "I could have done something terrible."

Propping herself back upon the cot, Sevila reached for the wineskin. With each sip, some of her usual colouring was restored. "Of course, you could have. Do you think people regard you with fear because you are powerless?"

"I'd rather they not regard me with fear at all." Aurel could not keep the bitterness from creeping into their words. In all their encounters so far, not once had they felt anything but powerless, and yet everyone they had come across looked at them as though they were death enfleshed.

Aurel looked up to find Sevila watching them with an expression akin to pity. On her however, it appeared to be a mingling of ridicule, a close cousin of contempt, yet when she spoke her voice held a gentle burr. "They understand you for what you are, innately if not explicitly. The sooner you accept it as well, the easier it becomes."

"I think illness makes you sentimental," Aurel told her.

She grimaced and took another swig of wine. "You're right. I'm too feeble to fight off such flights of fancy like I normally would."

"It's nice."

With a snort Sevila scoffed, "I am not nice."

Beneath them the ship gave a mighty groan, its tar-sealed hull creaking. Dimly Aurel could hear the chatter of people above deck and beyond, pierced with the cry of red-winged gulls. More steps than usual hammered against the decking over their heads, and Aurel could just make out the muted slap of rope, thick slabs of it lashing the ship into place.

Sevila's head was cocked as she listened, too. "We're here. Finally."

"How can you tell?" Aurel watched her stand, wobbling to her feet as the floor rolled among the smooth waves.

Regaining her uncertain footing, Sevila tapped the side of her slender nose with one ring-studded finger by way of explanation. "I have a nose for these things. And we arrived not a moment too soon. Another hour on this wretched boat and I'd go mad."

She pulled one of the saddlebags from behind her low-slung cot, and began to dress herself properly. Her red silks were rumpled but otherwise clean enough, and in the low light their borders gleamed with gold, broad and pale. When she was finished, Aurel gathered up the bags, balancing their bulk over one shoulder before following her up the ladder and to the deck above.

For the first time in six days, sunlight struck them. Aurel straightened to their full height to look around, while Sevila blinked in the harsh glare. Behind the ship, reinforced stone pillars towered above the water's surface upon the tips of a crescent-shaped harbour, and between these giants a colossal chain was strung through the water. A mechanism ground away with a rumble like thunder, lifting the chain into place, and blocking off access to a fleet of merchant ships for inspection. All around the peninsula walls ran their course, thicker than ten men lying toe to crown, and tall enough to shield the horizon from sight. Aurel's eyes followed the path of the walls until they vanished behind the city. Faros sprawled from the horns of its harbour, jealously guarding a narrow stripe of the sea between two points of land, the Lunar Straits the key to the city's financial and strategic strength. A constant flood of ships such as theirs streamed into and out of Faros, and the city bulged against its concentric rings of walls. Upon the highest of the three hills a massive domed temple shone in the sunlight, capped all in purest flashing bronze.

While Aurel marvelled at the new sight, Sevila instead squinted around the ship. She shielded her eyes with the flat of her hand, and upon seeing the other passengers she lifted her veil to hide her face. Through the bone-stitched cloth she murmured, "What did you actually do while I was out of action?"

All of the passengers — the refugees, the children, the Healer — congregated on the other side of the deck and shuffled further away still as soon as Aurel had emerged. Aurel pried their gaze from Faros, and turned to find the ship's captain directing two members of his crew, who dragged along the man in chains from the brig.

"Nothing!" Aurel insisted.

Two other sailors followed, carrying the brother's dead body draped in white cloth. Sevila's eyebrows rose and her expression was near indiscernible behind the veil.

"Right," she said.

"He was going to die regardless! Ask the Healer!" Aurel pointed towards the Healer across the ship.

With a sigh Sevila shook her head, reaching up to pinch the bridge of her nose. "So much for keeping a low profile. Word of us is going to spread through Faros like wildfire. I really can't take you anywhere, can I?"

Aurel gaped at her in disbelief. "Do you ever hear yourself speak?"

"Whatever do you mean?"

Aurel began ticking off names on the fingers of one gauntlet. "Avasa. Issoi. Lapedion. Nicoma. We haven't been able to visit a single city where you refrained from picking a fight, or where you haven't been immediately reviled by one of its inhabitants!"

"I'd hardly call Issoi and Avasa *'cities,'*" Sevila countered lamely.

"All the same. And now you want to keep a low profile here? What is wrong this time?" Aurel squinted at her. "You have enemies here, don't you?"

"What? No! Not exactly!" Crossing her arms, Sevila lifted her chin. "The people here hold a grudge to the grave. That can hardly be considered my fault!"

"And beyond the grave, knowing you," Aurel grumbled.

"Slander!" Sevila held up a finger. "I'll have you know that I have only been the cause of one revenant!" She paused, then raised another finger after some consideration. "Alright. *Two*. But he deserved it!"

Squinting at her, Aurel asked. "Do I want to know what a revenant is?"

Sevila gave a dismissive little wave of one hand as she spoke. "Revenants are the souls of people who refuse to pass on to the Abyss. They are so consumed with vengeance that death escapes them, or some such rubbish."

Aurel leaned back as it dawned on them. "Is that why you told Constantia my body had been stolen by grave robbers? So that she would think I was a vengeful spirit seeking justice before passing on to the next realm?"

"First of all, I did not tell Constantia that. I just let her believe an assumption that she made all on her own. Second of all—" Sevila leaned forward and lowered her voice, "—if you want to be named an abomination, and driven from the bosom of civilisation with nary a chance at finding your body, by all means keep yelling at me for everyone to hear."

Jerking around so quickly that their head turned almost completely over their shoulder in a motion that would have snapped their neck if they had a spine, Aurel checked to see if anyone had overheard the conversation. The ship's captain was shouting instructions at a sailor climbing up the netting that stretched along one mast. A small group of crewmembers lowered a plank to the docks below with a slap of wood against stone, and the other passengers had begun to mill about in preparation for their departure. Meanwhile, Sevila took Aurel's abrupt silence as an opportunity to slip around them, and head over to the queue forming by the ramp. Enough people were watching that Aurel refrained from grabbing Sevila's long cowl, and hauling her back. Instead, glowering, Aurel followed, towering over her, while she pretended to not notice their long shadow cast across her footsteps.

Rather than wait her turn, Sevila pushed right to the front of the queue. With Aurel beside her, looming and menacing, nobody voiced their complaints to her directly, though most shot Sevila ugly glances, and many whispered snide comments to one another. It was to a litany of curses and misgivings that the two of them disembarked at Faros. At the base of the planks that bridged between the dock and the ship, two guards stood in wait, but they only raised a curious eyebrow at Aurel before grabbing the man in chains who followed immediately behind, flanked by sailors. The guards tugged at the fetters binding thick bars of iron at his neck and wrists. Still walking, Aurel watched as the guards questioned him, and as he in turn answered, pointing after Aurel and Sevila.

"Try to look a little less threatening," Sevila murmured, picking up the pace and tugging down her cowl to better hide her eyes.

In response Aurel hunched their shoulders and stooped, bags clanging across their back. "This is just how I look all the time."

"Yes. That is the problem."

"Next time we travel by sea," Aurel grumbled, "remind me not to give you medicine, and let you suffer instead."

"Oh, fine! Thank you for taking such good care of me during the trip!" She shot an exasperated glance at Aurel around the brim of her cowl as she walked. "Is that what you wanted to hear?"

"You are a child." Aurel continued to lumber close at her heels, bent over in a failed attempt to reduce their height somewhat. "How old are you, really?"

"Old enough," came her cryptic reply.

Weaving a path through hoards of stevedores, dockworkers and immigrants seeking a safe haven from the war with the Helani, the two of them made their way to the eastern gate. Broad avenues of paved stone swept up the hills of Faros, splintering off into narrow winding streets. The city stacked upon itself over the years, its many generations evident in the buildings themselves — the bottom layers nearest the ground a dark brick and marble gradient that paled up, up towards the sky. Fresh applications of plaster wore coats of new paint on some buildings, where others still remained bare-faced and weathered. An army of guards patrolled the streets. More guards than Aurel had seen in any cities previously visited. Their pointed helms were festooned with yellow cloth that draped around their necks and their scale-clad shoulders. As best she could Sevila ducked behind groups of other travellers that swarmed the streets from the harbour entrance, bringing her hand up to touch her veil again and again, as though to reassure herself that she was completely covered.

At one point, she dodged down a side street to avoid a squad of guards marching by in neat militant lines, two abreast. The crowd parted before them, and their helms cast an iron-bright sparkle in the hot mid-morning sun. A slow ocean breeze lifted their mantles so that they streamed like amber-coloured standards, and upon the guards' backs was emblazoned not the imperial eagle, but a rampant bull wreathed in black laurels. Sevila pressed herself against a crumbling brick wall until the guards passed, at which point she darted back into the main avenue, blending into the crowd with a seamless ease.

Aurel slouched in her wake. "Where are we going? That old temple on the hill?"

The temple itself towered on the skyline above the other buildings. Sevila blinked at it in confusion, then snorted. "*Old?* That thing was built — what? — forty years ago? Maybe fifty? It's one of the younger buildings in Faros. No, no. If our quarry seeks occult knowledge, there's no better place to find it than the twin libraries of Faros. But first: food."

"Are you capable of thinking with anything other than your stomach?" Aurel muttered, trailing after Sevila as she turned down another broad avenue and came upon a thriving square.

"I require something that doesn't involve the horrible oats you forced me to eat back on the ship," Sevila said, approaching the very first food stall in sight, a dingy little shop dug into the basement of an apartment block.

"Because it was the only meal you could keep down!" Aurel reminded her.

"Have I not thanked you enough for that?"

"No."

"Oh." Stymied, Sevila paused in front of the shop. A short stone bench had been erected for customers, and she dropped down upon it, looking contemplative. Her eyes narrowed, and she studied Aurel with that odd curiosity of hers. Then with a shrug she said, "I'm afraid I don't know what to do about that, then."

As if that statement settled the matter, she craned her neck back on the bench to address to shop owner, who leaned his elbows upon the wooden railing to take her order. Cured meats dangled from hooks on the low ceiling alongside strings of spices and sundry: bay leaves and dried twisted ginger root, bulbous garlic and bristling peppers, an assortment of knives with worn handles. Through the back of the shop could be seen a triangular stone pillar in the centre of a lawn capped with a heavy conical slab, where the owners milled their own flour.

Three other customers were filed along the opposite end of the bench, bearing platters of food. One of them nudged the other with his elbow, and jerked his head in Aurel's direction. All three of them wore blue strips of cloth tied around their upper arms, or blue sashes binding the tunics at their waists. When Aurel stepped over the bench to side beside Sevila, one of them spat at Aurel's feet.

Sevila paused in the act of ordering to lean around Aurel's bulky form and see who else sat along the bench. Her eyebrows rose.

"Never mind," she told the shop owner as she rose to her feet, her voice cold. "We're leaving."

Puzzled, Aurel was led away from the food stall, and the glares of the three other customers burned after them. Before Aurel could ask, Sevila grumbled, "You had to wear green, of all colours."

"I like green," Aurel replied. They glanced back at the three wearing blue. "People haven't taken a liking to me in most places either."

"This time, it has nothing to do with you being a soul, and everything to do with politics." Sevila walked further along the square, passing the stalls that faced the open crowd in congregation before a tall rounded monument with archways that stretched down a long avenue. The arches were lined with painted statues in different athletic poses, and in the largest arch above the main entrance there rode a statue in a chariot pulled by four horses, cast all in bronze. "While we're here, we should really buy you a different coloured — oh no."

She halted so abruptly in her tracks that Aurel bumped into her. Frozen in place, her eyes widened. Aurel's head swivelled around, and they scanned over the heads of the crowd. "What is it? What's wrong?"

Whirling around, Sevila dove behind Aurel. She cowered in their shadow, clutching the green half-cape, and hissing, "Hide me!"

"What? Why?"

"Sevila Peinatokos!"

A voice roared through the din. Across the square a woman flanked by four guardsmen strode towards them. At a distance, she appeared to be just another guard herself — broad-shouldered, tall, and helmed — but as she drew closer minute differences became apparent. Her armour glinted far more richly with scales and chain mail, layered over leather and hardy padded cotton. A touch of gold adorned her bracers, and threaded through the mantle draped around her neck, marking her a station above the normal cut. Her dark-skinned face bore a jagged pink scar that ran from above one eyebrow down to her squared jaw, which was set in a hard line, teeth clenched, rage a living, seething thing in her black gaze.

Reaching around their back, Aurel dragged Sevila into view. Sevila forced a strained smile into place as she tugged down her veil. "Cosmas Thorakis Komaterina! How lovely to see you again!"

Cosmas stopped in front of them, and the four guards awaited her command. A sword hilt jutted above one of her shoulders, and another was strapped to her waist. She jabbed her finger in Sevila's direction, and announced, "You are under arrest!"

Sevila spluttered and backed away, only to bump into Aurel. "What for? I haven't done anything yet!"

"I told you I didn't want to see you in my city again! With you, it is only a matter of time before catastrophe strikes, and I cannot have that. Especially now. Things are tenuous enough without you wreaking havoc." Cosmas motioned to the guards, a sharp gesture of her gloved hand, and one of them stepped forward with shackles.

Eyes darting furiously about, but only finding the crowd packed in on all sides like a bulwark — everyone staring at the commotion — Sevila looked up at Aurel, and beseeched, "Do something!"

Aurel shrugged, nonchalant, and adjusted the saddlebags over their shoulder. "I could. If you commanded me to."

"Why, you ungrateful—!"

Sevila swore — colourfully and loudly — as the guard clapped her wrists in iron. Meanwhile Cosmas stepped forward, straightening her back to loom over Sevila. "You have no idea how long I've been wanting to do this," she said, her voice a hushed victorious murmur.

Sevila flashed a grin that looked more like a sneer. "Careful. Your mother liked to strap me up in chains, too."

Fury painted Cosmas' face in bold hues, and she reared back to deliver a blow with her closed fist. A dull smack rang out, and Sevila staggered a few steps to the side, clutching her cheek. Blood poured from her cracked nose. When she tried to stem the flow, she pressed down too hard and hissed in pain.

Eyes flinty, Cosmas wiped the blood from her leather glove on the edge of her tunic. "Alexios," she barked at the guard who had bound Sevila in manacles, "Take her to a cell. I will be there shortly."

"What about the spirit?" Alexios asked. His nose pressed against the bridge that flared down from the cap of his helm.

Cosmas studied Aurel for a brief moment, then spoke about them as though they weren't present at all. "Take them as well. She hasn't ordered them to get rid of us, which means she won't ever. We may not know the nature of their contract, but they have struck a deal with Sevila; that makes them untrustworthy by default."

Without another word Cosmas stormed away, trailed by two of her city guardsmen. The other remained behind to herd Aurel along, while Alexios pulled on the chain that dangled from the manacles at Sevila's wrists.

"Cosmas!" Sevila shouted after her even as she was yanked in the opposite direction. Flecks of blood melded with the burgundy dye of her clothes. "I demand to speak with a lawyer! It is my right as a citizen of the empire! *Cosmas!*"

Cosmas marched away, not looking back, and the crowd swallowed her up. The guard beside Aurel toyed with the spare set of manacles at his belt, but made no move to bind Aurel in any way. Instead he brought up the rear of the group, and kept a watchful eye. Aurel turned to Sevila. "Do you have any friends to speak of?"

Sevila spat out a tooth at the back of Alexios' head, when he yanked on her chains too hard for her liking. Then she smiled at Aurel, showing a dark bloody gap in her teeth. "You're the only friend I need."

Aurel actually laughed, a sound full, and warm, and echoing. "You think we're friends?"

"Of course! Is this not how it works?" She gestured to the guardsmen, then between herself and Aurel, as though to imply that getting arrested together was the mark of a true bonding experience.

"No," Aurel said. "And I am still not helping you out of this mess without an explicit command."

"All the potential in the world, and yet this is somehow the most useless contract I have ever been engaged in!" Sevila snapped. Then with a wordless snarl she rattled at her chains until Alexios stopped pulling at her.

The city's inhabitants parted quickly, when stared down by stone-faced guardsmen who weren't afraid to bark at any that stood in their path. Soon Aurel and Sevila were led into a gated barracks.

There the courtyard teemed with ranks, drilling and diligent, whole squads of guards housed against one of Faros' outermost walls, in what once would have been outside the city's borders. Above the gates flew banners — the imperial-crested eagle on a field of dark purple, a rampant sable bull on a field of gold, and a single flag of plain green that had been unceremoniously draped over the ramparts.

Down into the barracks they were taken, and where Alexios shoved Sevila into a dank cell, he held the iron-banded door open for Aurel, his expression wary. Before Aurel could pass however, the guard trailing behind took Sevila's bags from them, straining under the weight of their contents. As soon as the two of them were inside, Alexios twisted a key, and the door locked with a series of heavy metal clicks. The sound of his footsteps and those of his fellow guardsman faded, and Sevila shouted after them, "Damned mealy-faced son of a goat!" She kicked the base of the door, which clanged against the thick bars on either side, then turned to Aurel. "You see? These people and their grudges! They're unreasonable!"

Aurel sat on a worn bench tethered to the wall by rusted iron bars. The bench creaked beneath them, and gingerly they rose back to their feet before it could collapse. "And I'm sure Cosmas' hatred of you is entirely unfounded."

"Bah!" Sevila waved with both of her hands, her wrists still shackled together. "You sleep with one person's mother, she runs off to get a divorce, and suddenly you are a pariah!"

"You ruined her parents' marriage?"

Sawing her wrists back and forth in their bonds, Sevila glared. "I do not have sex with people without consent. Cosmas' mother ruined her own marriage. And it was years ago! Decades even!"

With a growl Sevila reached up beneath her cowl and silk headwrap to fiddle at her hair. She pulled two pins free, and after bending one edge with her teeth into a tiny hook, she worked them at the lock between her hands. A few expert twists, and the chains clattered to the ground.

"There!" she exclaimed. One of the bands landed directly atop her foot, and she cursed, leaping away. Walking over to the door with an exaggerated limp, she muttered, "And since you refuse to help me, I'll just do everything myself."

Crossing their arms over their chest, Aurel watched her reach around the door, her skinny arms slipping through the bars with ease. "Tell me: how do you intend to sneak out of here, unnoticed? This place is a fortress!"

One arm jammed through the bars up to the shoulder, Sevila shrugged. "I've faced worse odds."

"Somehow, I don't find that reassuring," Aurel replied.

Sevila pawed at the other side of the door, tongue poking out of the corner of her mouth as she searched for the keyhole by touch alone. When she found it at last, her face screwed up in concentration. The headwrap—loosened from her previous fiddling—slid down her brow, and she had to push it back up again with her free hand. Her fingers fumbled at the makeshift lock picks, followed by a gentle clinking of metal against stone. Swearing under her breath, Sevila squatted down to scoop the hairpins up from the ground.

"This sure would be easy if I had intangible limbs!" she grumbled at Aurel over her shoulder.

Before Aurel could fire back a snide remark of their own, the door to the dungeon entrance slammed open at the far end of the hall. With a yelp, Sevila pulled her arm back, making a dive for the discarded manacles, and clamping herself in the unlocked irons. The jangle of armour, the strike of leather-soled shoes over damp stone, and Cosmas strode into view, one hand resting on the pommel of the sword slung around her waist, wrist sloped, fingers gloved and sculpted. She arched a brow at the glint of slender hairpins on the ground at her feet, but made no comment about them. Cosmas stood just out of reach, a practised distance should prisoners attempt to grab her from within their cage.

"What is your purpose in Faros?" she asked, hooking a thumb through one of the belt straps that hung low at her hip. Her hand other remained on the sword pommel, poised upon the edge of movement.

Rather than answer straight away, Sevila approached the bars to study their captor with narrowed eyes. "You're even more uptight than usual, Cosmas. Last time it took you two days to track me down, but now you're stalking the streets within the hour. Whatever is the matter?"

Jaw clenching, Cosmas glowered. "In case you have been living in a desert hovel for the last few years, we are a hair's breadth from civil war, and I am currently the only thing keeping this city from devouring itself."

"Funny you should mention the desert; we just came from there. Proof enough that I have done nothing wrong!" Sevila held up her shackled hands. "So, you can release me now, thank you."

Cosmas lifted her chin, and her hand clenched into a fist around the hilt of her sword. "There is always something with you. You're an ill omen. You will have to forgive me if I keep my scepticism close."

"Forgiveness not extended!" In a fit of pique Sevila slammed her chains against the bars. Cosmas did not flinch, only continued to glower at her in stony silence. Smiling, all oil and charm once more, Sevila held her hands up in an imploring gesture. "How long have we known each other?"

"Too long," Cosmas retorted.

"That question was rhetorical, but anyway—" Sevila brushed Cosmas' glare aside with very little effect. "Surely we can reach an understanding. What is it you really want? There must be some small service I can provide. Come now." Her voice went silky. Her golden eyes seemed almost to glow. "Let's make a deal."

Cosmas squinted between Sevila and Aurel, who hung back, refraining from joining the conversation. She leaned back on her heels, gathered a deep contemplative breath, fingers flexing around her sword, then said, "No."

Sevila's face crumbled into incredulous disarray. "No? What do you mean: *no?*"

"No," Cosmas restated. Then without another word she whirled around, a smart abrupt about-face, and marched away.

With a breathy laugh, Sevila shook her head. "Don't worry," she told Aurel, who had taken an abortive step forward.

"This is her idea of humour. She'll stop at the door, and turn back. You'll see!"

Cosmas kept walking, and with every cell she passed, Sevila grew increasingly fidgety. The chains hanging down to her knees clanked as she shuffled her weight from foot to foot. She craned her neck to watch as the distance between them spread wider. When Cosmas threw open the far door to leave, Sevila cracked.

"Alright, alright! You've made your point!" Sighing, Sevila rested her forehead against the cool iron bars. "The truth is, I am helping this poor spirit reclaim that which it has lost."

Cosmas paused in the archway. Only the slope of her broad scarred cheek was visible around the bold yellow cloth that shielded her neck. She arched an eyebrow, and the scar stretched upwards. "From anyone else, that would sound philanthropic, but since this is you we are talking about—"

"It's true! For once I am not lying!" Sevila's voice echoed through the damp, empty, narrow chamber.

At last Aurel stepped forward so that they stood beside Sevila. "She made a deal with me. I will vouch for her on this alone. Her end of the bargain is to get back my body, and for her I would do—"

Before Aurel could finish, Sevila let loose a harsh hiss, rounding on Aurel for nearly revealing their contract with such specificity. Aurel shooed her away. "You want her to believe us, don't you?"

"You just don't tell other people the exact nature of a contract! That sort of information is worth its weight in gold!" Sevila growled, and though her words were hushed, they carried along the stone walls.

Keen-eyed, Cosmas listened in on their bickering. She opened the door a little wider, and addressed someone waiting outside. "Alexios, come with me."

When Cosmas and Alexios began to make their way back towards the cell, Sevila abandoned the façade of being chained. She flung the shackles aside, and jabbed a finger against Aurel's chest. "Now look at what you've done!"

"*Me?*"

"Yes, you!"

"Are you two finished?" Cosmas came to a halt before their cell door. Hands clasped behind her back, she nodded at Alexios. "Watch them. Accompany them, no matter where they go. If they do anything even remotely out of line with the law, lock them up, and inform me at once. If they attempt to leave the city, let them, and then inform me at once. If they attempt to enter any civic buildings, bar them. If they attempt to make contact with any civic entities — apart from myself — bar them. Send me twice-daily reports on their movements, courier by spirit if necessary."

Alexios bowed his head in acceptance and understanding. He stepped forward to unlock the cell, and the door groaned as it swung open. Flakes of rust squeaked against their hinges. Sevila darted forward to pick up her hairpins, and Cosmas' hand flew to the hilt that jutted over one shoulder, ready to strike Sevila down at the slightest movement. Slowly raising her hands, Sevila straightened, and backed away from Cosmas' dangerous, dark-eyed scowl.

Cosmas lowered her arm. She gave Sevila and Aurel a taut smile. "Enjoy your stay in Faros. I hope your business here is concluded with all haste."

Chapter 8

The grand markets of Faros stretched as far as the eye could see. Spices piled up in mounds that reached the waist. Bolts of rich cloth adorned the shops in more colours than there were stars in the mountain sky, or grains of sand in the southern desert slopes. A merchant's young daughter sat atop a hillock of slender red peppers, playing with their greenish stems, while beside her women spread a garden of fresh rose petals across pale cloth with their dark hands. In the centre of the vast bazaar there stood a statue atop a squat triumphal pillar, a beardless youth of an emperor with his arm outstretched, and a conquest trampled under heel. Broad streamers of red and ochre yellow were strung over him from rooftop to surrounding rooftop, creating a striped canopy of shade over the market stalls. The buildings shone in the afternoon sun, cream and white with native stone unearthed from quarries to the east.

"This is a shambles." Sevila stalked the stalls like an angry jungle cat, her movements lithe, her downturned mouth hidden behind her veil.

Aurel followed, trailed in turn by the ever vigilant, ever silent Alexios. "All this for access to a few scrolls and manuscripts?" Aurel asked. In passing they admired a display of intricately woven carpets, and they almost reached out to drag their fingers across the fine texture, only to jerk their arm back when the soul of a dour raven guarding the stall crowed, and spread its shadowy wings.

"You mean the largest collection of literature and artefacts in the known world, which also happens to be wholly owned by the Komateros clan? Yes. All this fuss." Sevila paused to pour over a basket of figs and dates, pomegranates with their seeds split and glistening wine-dark, dusty grapes clustered on the vine and curled around stark citrus fruits. "We need signed and sealed permission granted by the City Prefect in order to access one of the libraries in particular: the exclusive, jealously-guarded private collection. I'd hoped to bribe our way in, but with Cosmas breathing down our necks —" She broke off her sentence to shoo away the stand's spirit guardian, a coiled serpent that snapped its shadowy fangs at her when she thumbed at the rind of a citron.

While Sevila exchanged silver and copper with the serpent for a bundle of various fruits, Aurel idly picked up a gold-fleshed apple, turning it over for inspection. "Then why don't we just ask this Prefect?"

"Because we aren't allowed near public officials, but mostly because he and Cosmas are related. They're cousins." Sevila said. She plucked a grape from the stand, and popped it into her mouth without paying for it. The snake hissed at her for her indiscretion, and Sevila hissed back, unfazed. At that, the snake jerked back, slumping down to hide from view.

Aurel blinked, then slowly placed the apple down. "Just how large is this family?"

"Very large, very rich, and very powerful." Sevila pushed ahead through the market with her wares clutched in one hand. "How else do you think Iustina became empress in the first place?"

"I—" Aurel trailed off in thought. "I had assumed she was born into the position."

With a snort, Sevila dug through the fruit for an apple of her own. "There hasn't been a stable dynasty since the Valerians. Iustina's husband was a popular general — not all that different from Theodoros if you ask me, but don't tell Cosmas that. Killed one or two supposed *'tyrants'* in his day, but he himself was only of middling name. He was proclaimed by his soldiers because of his marriage into the Komateros clan."

"But he did have an army," Aurel pointed out. "That must count for something."

With a hum, Sevila tugged down her veil, took a bite, and smiled while chewing a mouthful of apple. "And who do you think paid for that army?"

"Ah." Aurel's glowing eyes squinted. "So, you mean to tell me you slept with Iustina's sister?"

"Cousin! I slept with her cousin!" Sevila corrected. She took another large and vicious bite. "Cosmas is a distant niece to our beloved late empress. They're like flies, this family: prolific breeders! We must have tripped on half a dozen of them on the docks of Faros alone. You!" Sevila stopped and pointed an accusatory finger at Alexios. "I would wager you're related to Cosmas, too. Well? Aren't you?"

Alexios glowered. His silence was answer enough.

Sevila flashed Aurel a triumphant grin over her shoulder, and continued onwards through the marketplace. Aurel was about to laugh, when instead they paused. Leaning down, they inspected Sevila's face closely. Puzzled, Sevila craned her neck away from them. "What is it?"

"Your tooth." Aurel pointed. "It's in your mouth."

"Of course, it is. Where else would my teeth be?" She bared them, then slapped Aurel's hand away from her face. "Now, onto more important matters: our new pet." Lowering her voice, Sevila glanced over her shoulder at Alexios before whispering to Aurel, "We need to dispose of him."

"I'm not killing him, if that's what you are implying."

"Heavens, no!" She feigned shock, clutching the half-eaten apple to her chest. "In broad daylight like this? What do you take me for?"

"Exactly what you are," Aurel replied, their tone dry. "A snake of a human being."

"What is it with everyone taking my rhetorical questions so literally these days?" Sevila muttered under her breath. She gestured Aurel to follow her, and together they strolled by the loudest shops so as not to be overheard. "We just need to lose him for a few hours."

"Cosmas will be irritated," Aurel warned, but Sevila scoffed.

"Cosmas is always irritated. We might as well finish our business here and then be out of her dreadful helmet hair for good." As they ambled by a shop hawking little wooden chariots and green flags, Sevila's gaze brightened. "And I've just had the perfect idea."

She pushed to the front of the queue, ignoring the exclamations of irritation in her wake, and slapped down a few coppers. "That one, there," she told the merchant, pointing at a green length of cloth with tasselled ends. When the merchant gave it to her and scraped up her money in exchange, Sevila stuck the apple core between her teeth in order to tie the band around her upper arm. With a crisp crunch, she bit the core in half and chewed as she worked.

"I thought the point was to not display any political inclinations." Aurel dragged her out of the line, and finished tying the band into place for her.

Sevila hummed something wordless around the last of the apple. Finishing it, she spat the lone stem away, and pulled out a pomegranate from the small cloth bag tucked into her gold belt. "Today we are staunch Greens supporters. Cut us and we bleed Imperial gold. Isn't that right, Alexios?"

Alexios, who hovered just out of reach nearby, made no reply. Instead he clutched the hilt of his sword, which dangled from his hip by a green sash of his very own.

"That means: yes." Sevila tilted her head back to squint at the position of the sun in the sky, as Aurel put the finishing touches on the band around her upper arm. "If we hurry we can make it."

Quick footed, she started off away from the market, back in the direction of the docks to the west. In one hand she palmed the pomegranate, digging her nails into the rind and splitting it directly down the middle, revealing a belly of gleaming ruby entrails. Aurel had to lengthen their stride to match her pace.

"Make what?" they asked.

"The race!"

The three made their way across the city. Neither carts nor pack animals could be seen roaming the streets, carrying goods. The only mode of transport Aurel could see apart from walking was to be a noble or person of some wealth, who could afford a litter born aloft by servants in short tunics shorn at the knee. One such litter passed them upon a street. It bounced along as four servants trotted by, and through the silken flutter of drapes Aurel spied a patrician nose and two figures reclining in dark robes. A heaviness pushed against the maw of Aurel's chest, like a great stone caving inwards.

"Was that—?" Aurel stopped in the middle of the street, trying to track the litter even as the crowded street swallowed the carrier, and hid it from view.

Sevila tugged them along by their cloak. "Do stop gawping, darling. It makes you look even more out of place than normal."

Now the litter had well and truly vanished, and not even Aurel's height could see over the sea of heads spreading out before them. The weight faded as swiftly as it had arrived, draining away, until once again Aurel could feel nothing — not the sea-salted breeze, not the smells of the city, not the acrid lick of new paint rouging the cheeks and lips of twin statues flanking the far avenue. Aurel shook the memory free with a rattle of their armour, and allowed Sevila to steer them towards the hippodrome.

Rather than approach the main gate flooded with people streaming from the square to see the upcoming race, Sevila walked along at a clipped pace to the fleet of merchants scattered around the hippodrome's circumference, each hawking their wares of blue and green. In a beshadowed enclave furthest from the main square, a woman sat tending a stall. The light seemed to shy from her shop, pooling around the edges, but never leaking through so that she stood, guarding a counter barren of wares but for a ledger that stood starkly beside her, large and scrawled with a cramped neat hand. Upon their approach, she looked up from her cup of wine with a bored expression which only grew more lacklustre when she saw Sevila.

"Oh, it's you." She drained her cup and reached down for a wineskin, pouring herself another before tucking the skin out of sight once more. "What do you want?"

"Constantina, you are looking positively sunny this afternoon!" Sevila greeted her, leaning her elbows atop the counter. Alexios hung back with crossed arms to watch at a respectful distance, his expression puzzled as he looked at the stall. Aurel meanwhile hovered beside Sevila, peering into the shop. Even their glowing eyes could not pierce the murk that hung there, thick as a shroud. They could only catch a glimpse of shapes, vague outlines here and there: bundles of fragrant dried flowers and rare herbs, rough wedges of quartz suspended from the ceiling, a table bearing something that dripped red onto the floor, a butcher's cleaver stuck into a wooden frame.

Not a daub of blood could be seen on Constantina's clothes; the dark cloth, black on black, hid any hint of crimson, but for the flakes of dried blood beneath the pale crescents of her fingernails. Rings gleamed darkly on her fingers, onyx and purpled jasper, and her hooded eyes looked familiar. She rapped her fingers rhythmically against the table, and said, "My sister said to expect you, but I did not think you would arrive so soon. How unfortunate."

"The speed and accuracy with which you three communicate never fails to astound me." Sevila handed over a sliver of pomegranate bristling with burgundy seeds. "Tell me: how do you do it?"

Constantina's eyes darted to the offering, but rather than take it, she sipped at her cup of wine. Her lips and teeth were stained a rusty claret. "What do you want?" she repeated.

With a shrug, Sevila tucked the fruit into the small bag hanging at her waist. "We're looking for a priest and his retinue."

"Ah, yes. Your grave robbers. Constantia told me about them." Constantina traced the rim of her cup, her knuckles gnarled and round as the knots of an oak tree, a sharp contrast to her youthful face. "I have seen them."

Sevila's eyes glittered keenly. "Where are they?"

In answer, Constantina gave her hand a sly turn of the wrist so that she held her palm up. With a sigh, Sevila fished for some coins and dropped two silvers into Constantina's hands. In an exact mimicry of her sister, Constantina's eyebrows rose, and she levelled a look at Sevila, who grumbled, and passed over one more coin. "You and your siblings are going to bankrupt me."

Closing her fist around the silver, Constantina turned her hand over, and flexed her fingers. The coins vanished. Her eyes bled black at the edges. She answered, "The priest is accompanied by two guards and a tall figure draped all in black like a College Acolyte. They are here in the city. Tread carefully."

"Can you give me any more information?" Sevila pressed. "What do they look like?"

Once more Constantina held out her hand, but when Sevila reached for more coin Constantina grabbed her by the wrist. "Not like that. I want something else. These." She tapped at the tips of Sevila's fingers. "These will do."

Sevila grinned, showing a seedy gleam of her teeth. "If it was my fingers you wanted, you need only ask."

"Don't be vulgar." With a flourish Constantina produced a curved knife with a jewelled hilt. A black pearl the size of a quail's egg glittered green and blue upon the dagger in the shadows of her merchant stand. Sevila's eyes widened, and she tried to snatch her hand back but Constantina's grip tightened around her wrist.

"Stop squirming," Constantina chided with a crease of her brows. "You're worse than a cat getting a bath."

Then she began to carefully trim Sevila's fingernails. Sevila sagged in relief. "You could have just said this was what you wanted!"

Shaving the nail from Sevila's thumb, and moving along to the next finger, Constantina's face remained stolid. "And miss the opportunity to torture you? Where's the fun in that?" One of Sevila's fingernails almost spun off the countertop, and Constantina paused to brush it into a pile with the others. "Besides, you should keep them shorter. Your female admirers would appreciate your affections more."

"I think they prefer my other many charms."

"Is that so?"

Using her free hand, Sevila brushed her fingers against the soft sensitive underside of Constantina's wrist. "I could show you — ow!"

A bright bold drop of blood bloomed from Sevila's skin, and caught against the blade, painting a narrow vein along the metal. Sevila snatched her hand back to inspect the small cut with a frown.

"How clumsy of me," Constantina murmured. Rather than wipe the droplet of blood free, she brought the knife's edge to her mouth, and licked the blade clean. Her tongue smeared with red. Once more her eyes went black all around the edges, and she blinked. Musing, she lowered the knife and licked the backs of her teeth, a furrow in her brow. "There is power here, yet you taste—" the tip of Constantina's tongue peeked briefly against her lower lip. "—*empty*."

Shaking her head as though ridding herself of a sudden bout of dizziness, Constantina sheathed her knife, and began scooping up the small pile of clipped fingernails, brushing them into one hand, and depositing them in a little stoppered jar of coloured glass. Sevila watched her with a guarded expression, pressing thumb and forefinger together to staunch the strangely sluggish flow of blood from her finger.

"Answers," Sevila said, all charm gone. "Now."

Sliding back a hidden panel in the wall beside her, Constantina placed the jar among a rack of many that lined the cupboard to her right, crowded together in jumbled rows, then ran her fingers along the jars as though counting each one, her gaze long and distant as the night's sky. Within could be heard the skittering of live specimens scratching at their cages. "The priest guards his face very carefully, and wears no indication of office apart from his robes. His guards on the other hand are happy to turn their cloaks to suit their every whim. They wear College colours one day and city colours the next. Now they masquerade under the banner of the Komateros clan, but who can say how long that will last?" She breathed in deeply and closed the panel, turning away to take a heady draught of wine and clear her head. When she turned her attention back to Sevila she wore a frown. "I've already said too much."

"I like that about you. Don't tell the others, but—" Sevila leaned forward to murmur low in Constantina's ear, "—you're my favourite of the siblings."

One of Constantina's eyebrows rose, and she tilted her head to give Sevila a sidelong glance. "Even with the knife?"

"*Especially* with the knife."

"Constantius will be heartbroken to hear, I'm sure. He does so enjoy chasing you out of our shops with bared blade." Constantina said, her voice dull, and she dipped her fingers into her cup to flick a few droplets of wine at Sevila, who spluttered and reared back. "Now, go. Your company is always so tiresome. You're a burden on the soul."

At that Aurel stifled a laugh, their eyes squinting in their version of a smile. Sevila glowered, but pulled out a few more coins. "I'm not finished yet."

"I have no more information to give." Constantina drummed her fingers along the base of her cup, and the sound rang out, wooden and dull. "None that you'd want, that is."

When Sevila slapped down a fistful of gold coins, Constantina blinked, and she sat up straighter. "I'd like to place a bet." Sevila nodded towards the ledger behind Constantina. "A victory for the Blues. By at least a length."

Constantina gave a puzzled look at Aurel's cloak and the band of green tied around Sevila's upper arm, but only said, "The pools favour the Greens this race."

"The pools don't know shit, and I never make a wager I can't win." Sevila pushed the coins across the table, metal scraping against the scarred wooden countertop. "Blues by a length."

Reaching forward without another word, Constantina pulled the coins towards her. They fell from her edge of the counter, tipping over her lap, but there was no sound of gold falling as they vanished from sight. Then she turned to amend the ledger behind her with a bit of charcoal, the strokes of her handwriting tight, tidy, and unembellished. When Constantina rounded back on Sevila, she pulled a wooden token from beneath the countertop, and handed it over, its surface scorched with a black brand. "Good fortune. And may you find peace, spirit." The latter she directed at Aurel.

Inspecting the token closely for something in particular — Aurel could not tell what, for the token itself seemed very plain and very bare but for the single mark branded upon its surface —

Sevila gave the token to Aurel and turned away without another word. Constantina's gaze moved to Aurel with a keen and invasive kind of curiosity. Unsettled by her scrutiny, Aurel tucked the token away, and quickly followed after Sevila.

Alexios rejoined them, falling into step beside Aurel to ask, "What was that about?"

Aurel glanced down at him. "What do you mean?"

"That." He jabbed his finger back towards Constantina's stall.

When Aurel looked over their shoulder, they did a double take, staring. Behind them, Constantina's stall stood empty, no more than a dilapidated awning shading a bench cluttered with broken clay pots.

"Who were you talking to?" Alexios pressed, and beneath the ridge of his helm his eyes had narrowed with suspicion.

Before Aurel could answer, Sevila called out, "Keep up, you two!"

Offering a shrug, Aurel quickened their pace to walk behind Sevila, while Alexios trailed behind.

A small crowd had gathered in the square nearby to hear the bellows of a crier, still dressed as he was in a travelling cloak dusty from a trip on horseback. He gestured to those in attendance and those passing by with the broad practised gestures of an orator.

"News from Pala!" he shouted in a booming voice that echoed across the square, catching the interest of many who paused to listen, and some who only leant half an ear as they continued on their way. "The capital remains secure! Our illustrious Lord Regent's forces have kept the Helani invaders at bay, rebuffing attack after attack! The Lord Regent and our young Empress will arrive with the High Priest, Isidore, later this week as planned with the bodies of the late Iustina Severa Komaterina and Leo Phokas Komateros. Their funerary rites will be presided over by Isidore with all gravity and ritual! All citizens are invited to attend, and free bread given to those who honour the imperial dead! Long life to the Lady Invicta!"

Members of the growing crowd wearing green cried out in return, "Long life to the Lady Invicta!"

Those on the fringes of the crowd wearing blue muttered and murmured, and one of them shouted in response, "Long life to the Lord Regent!" Others wearing blue picked up the cry, and added their voices to the fray.

An ugly rumble seethed, fermenting and spreading. They volleyed insults back and forth, then a stone struck Alexios on the back of his helm. As he bared his iron blade, the Blues supporters around him shrank away. When more guardsmen marched over from across the square, the crowd scattered, a desultory disbandment accompanied by rude gestures and feet kicking up dust at one another. Alexios grabbed hold of Sevila's arm, and steered her from the mass excitement despite her squawk of protest, keeping a tight grip on her even as she squirmed until they were well away from the crowd.

"Unhand me!" Sevila wrenched herself from his grasp, curling her lip.

Alexios aimed a hard look at her, lowering his hand to instead grasp the hilt of his sword. "Much as I dislike your presence, I will not see you injured under my watch. And you, spirit!" He jabbed a finger in Aurel's direction, who flinched at being addressed with such vitriol. "Shouldn't you have a care for the bodily safety of your Mistress?"

"I—!" Aurel began, at a loss for words.

Sevila planted fists on her hips, and chose to launch into Aurel as well, though her eyes fairly glittered with mirth at Aurel's obvious discomfort. "Yes! 'Have a care' for my person, why don't you!"

"Assuming you are in fact a person," Aurel shot back. "I have my doubts."

She flashed a teasing grin at Aurel's simmering glower, and made her way to the entrance of the hippodrome, flocking with the others that streamed in from all parts of the city to witness the race. Shaking their head, Aurel trailed after her, ignoring the strange look Alexios gave the two of them. As they all shuffled along through the darkened archway and up the many flights of stairs that opened onto the stadium seats, Alexios leaned forward to murmur so Sevila could not overhear, "I would not trust that woman to tell me the colour of the sky, yet you two are—" Alexios grimaced "—

friendly. It is a most unusual relationship between spirit and Master."

Aurel lurched away in shock and disgust, nearly careening directly into Sevila who gave them an arch look before turning her attention elsewhere. Rounding on the guard, Aurel growled, "We are not friends!"

Alexios' bushy brows drew down together, and he glanced incredulously between Aurel and Sevila. "As you say."

"We're not!" Aurel insisted. They fell into a sullen silence after that, refusing to trade another word with the man. This arrangement seemed to suit Alexios fine, for he returned to alternatively scanning the crowd, and watching his wards like a hawk watches field mice, until the three of them exited onto the stands in search of seating.

People filled every seat in four tiers, winding round and round the stadium which stretched far along and wide enough for ten chariots to ride abreast down the dust-combed arena. Down the centre of the arena ran a long thin barrier that carried twin monuments, obelisks carried away from Aegryph with strange pictographs carved along their lengths. Food vendors dispensed handheld rotisserie delights to those in the crowd with the money to pay. Aurel frowned when Sevila passed one such vendor by without purchasing anything for herself, sparing only a passing hungry glance at the wares before moving along. She slipped through gaps in the crowd, Aurel shadowing the void in her wake, while Alexios battled with supporters of various colours, shouldering his way through, while his two wards managed to slither along unheeded with uncanny easy.

As if taking pity on the poor man, Sevila paused to wait for him at the end of one aisle, which straddled a firm unspoken line between Greens and Blues. Members of opposing factions exchanged glares, some silent, some speaking loudly and derisively of their own upcoming victory. Down below the charioteers themselves had yet to appear. Servants swept up roses into swollen linen sacks, waiting to drop a fountain of pink and silver-fleshed petals onto the victor.

When Alexios caught up with them, Sevila was rummaging through her small bag of fruit. She held out one hand in a deferential gesture to the guard. "After you."

He looked at her hand, then her face, squinting as if he could scour her fathomless expression for a hint of her ploy. When no great revelation came over him, he shrugged, and scooted by to take a seat. As he did so, Sevila casually tangled up his feet with one of her own, and Alexios tripped right into a group of avid Blues supporters. Aurel darted forward to steady him, but the damage was done.

Three Blues supporters leapt to their feet to throw Alexios from their section of the stands, one reaching for the hilt of a dagger strapped low at his hip. In mock outrage, Sevila wielded a bruised peach, flinging it at one of the assailants. "Cowardly dogs!" she spat, digging out three more pieces of over-ripe fruit, and passing them out to nearby Greens supporters who jumped to the defence of their supposed brethren. "Why wait for a race? We'll best you here and now! Long life to the Lady Invicta!"

The cry was taken up, and fruit was hurled. Aurel did not feel so much as hear the squelch of something striking their broad shoulders in the fray. Staggering beneath the press of bodies on all sides, Alexios was quickly overwhelmed, gripping his sword but unwilling to draw it and risk sending the crowd into a frenzy at the scent of blood.

Through the din and tussle, Aurel heard Sevila hiss under her breath, "This way! Quickly!" They ducked away as inconspicuously as they could manage, and it was only due to the sheer number of assailants blocking Alexios' view that allowed Aurel to sneak off without being spotted. Every shout had Aurel on edge, hunching their shoulders and peering around to see if they had been spotted only to find that nobody was following. Still they hunkered down at Sevila's side until the two of them emerged from the hippodrome alone.

"That went better than I'd hoped," Sevila glanced around, seeking her bearings, then gave a lofty wave of one hand. "The public library is just a short walk. We should be able to slip in, poke around the collection, and return before Alexios notices exactly where we've gone off to."

"He'll ask questions." Aurel straightened. Their armour creaked, and they reached forward to brush off a bit of rotten fruit that stuck to Sevila's back.

"Thank you, darling. And yes. We'll just lie, and claim that we escaped the kerfuffle, and went to wait for him at the nearest taverna."

"Hmm." Aurel made a noise voicing their incredulity. "And you really think that will work?"

"Only if we're quick enough." Sevila turned down a street, continuing along.

In this part of the city, the most impressive buildings of Faros were jammed up alongside the most downtrodden. Fading brick façades crumbled beside gleaming marble structures. Altars bore their offerings like diminutive treasures alongside a common whorehouse, where two women and a young man plied their wares in the shadow of an archway. Aurel turned their gaze aside respectfully, while Sevila aimed an openly admiring glance at the women, who laughed at the odd pair passing them by.

"You, my dear companion, need to work on your charms. They leave much to be desired," Sevila said as she guided them around another corner into a narrow alleyway.

Aurel gave her a sour look. "The day I start catering to your desires is the day the sun rises in the west."

"Stranger things have happened, I'm sure." Her steps slowed, and she paused at the entrance to a courtyard beside a towering granite building with branching pillars that staggered in tiers of three high. The wooden gate was somewhat ajar. Footsteps within brushed along the dusty ground. Sevila frowned, and approached the gate to peer through the gap. "Nothing can be easy, can it?"

Had they raised up on their toes Aurel could have glanced over the top of the gate, but instead they bent over double in a half crouch to look over Sevila's shoulder. Two city guards wearing yellow cloaks emblazoned with a black bull stood watch over the courtyard, faces obscured by their veiled helms. Their voices were muted through distance and cloth; they spoke in low tones to one another.

"They shouldn't be here," Sevila muttered under her breath as if affronted by their presence. "Why would anyone need to guard the servant's entrance to the hypocaust?"

"How were you expecting me to fit into the hypocaust in the first place?" Aurel asked.

"Neither of us are going anywhere unless we do something about those two inconveniences." Stepping away from the gate, Sevila rubbed at her chin thoughtfully. After a moment she announced, "I have a plan, but you're not going to like it."

Aurel heaved a weary sigh. "Just tell me."

She told them. As predicted, Aurel did not like it.

"Just remember: be charming!" Sevila hissed as she prodded Aurel forward, keeping herself tucked from sight.

Grumbling quietly, Aurel pushed through the gate. Immediately the guards went tense and quiet, glaring at Aurel from beneath the bridge of their helms, eyes suspicious around the battered bits of metal that shielded their noses. Aurel tried to smile, but whatever effect it had on their face made the guards grab at the hilts of their swords.

Dropping that expression — Aurel was afraid to know what it actually looked like — Aurel approached, hands clasped before them in what they hoped was a pleading gesture. "Peace!" Aurel began. "I bear neither weapons nor ill-will towards you. I simply request that you let me slip by. I must see to the tending of this hypocaust so that my Mistress' reading room can be heated without delay. I hope you can understand my plight. My Mistress is of a great and noble name, but that is where her virtues end."

The act of lying twisted knots in Aurel's chest. At least they could sprinkle a few acerbic truths through this farce. The guards' grips around their swords relaxed only somewhat, and their stances remained tense, so Aurel pressed on with vim. "In truth, she is a vile creature. I would not be bound to her but for necessity's sake. Yet for all her faults, my Mistress is a woman of means — I would ensure that you are richly compensated for your discretion."

At that, Aurel opened their hands to reveal fat gold coins cupped in their palms, a small fortune that most soldiers would only see throughout the course of their entire careers. The guards lowered their swords, and made a jerky motion forward, an abortive half-lunge for the gold offered to them.

"Stop that woman!"

The bellow of a familiar voice made Aurel jump, and the coins scattered about the ground, bouncing every which way. Startled, all three of them turned to see Sevila scamper through the gate, a furious Alexios hot on her heels.

"Change of plans!" Sevila announced to the courtyard. "We remain charming, but this time we grovel!" Behind her Alexios made a grab for Sevila's cowl. She only just escaped his grasp with a yelp. "We grovel *a lot!*"

Slamming the gate shut behind him, Alexios took a menacing step forward, his face a dark thundercloud, his armour smeared with dust and rotten fruit, a cut blooming on his lower lip from his scuffle in the hippodrome. "There's no escaping this time," he growled. Pointing to the other guards, he ordered, "Seize them! We are to take them back to the barracks! Cosmas will want to question them."

The two guards exchanged a silent look, expressions inscrutable behind their veils. Their hands rested on the hilts of their swords. They did not move.

"I said seize them at once!" Alexios glanced between them, puzzled and irate, stepping forward to further enclose Aurel and Sevila between the three wearing Cosmas' colours. "Why are you standing watch here? State your names and ranks!"

At once the two guards leapt forward, a flurry of sudden motion in a snapping of yellow cloaks. Swords drawn from their sheaths, one of them closed the space between himself and Alexios, driving his blade into the scale-stitched leather armour shielding Alexios' gut. Aurel had only enough time to blink in shock before springing into action, and catching the guard's sword arm in a futile attempt to pull him away. Clutching his abdomen, Alexios fell to his knees, coughing up blood. The sword slid free with a glistening sound.

Aurel yanked the guard around, holding him fast. "Sevila, you need to—!"

Behind them — a sickening crunch. Iron-hewn gristle and bone. Releasing the guard who had killed Alexios, Aurel whirled about to find that the other had hacked his sword clean into Sevila's head. Her skull was cloven nearly in two, parted from crown to jaw. With a heave of effort, the guard ripped his sword free, and turned to find Aurel's hands around his throat.

The world was a blood-dimmed tide. Aurel lifted the guard into the air as if he weighed no more than a bag of half-rotten fruit. His boots swung above the ground, toes scraping the air, and he clawed at Aurel's gauntlets. Aurel throttled the gasp from him, then tossed him away. Sword clattering to the ground, the guard's body went flying, crashing into a pillar and crumpling at its base with a raspy groan. As he stirred on the ground, pushing himself upright once more, Aurel advanced. Before they had taken two paces, a sword burst from Aurel's chest, slipping through layers of cloth and leather. When nothing happened, the other guard's hands trembled around the hilt. Turning slowly, Aurel yanked the sword out and cast it aside. The guard stumbled back a few steps at the haunting glow of Aurel's eyes, the vacant glare like two flames captured in living shadow.

Aurel moved with an eerie grace, all shadow-smooth and liquid-quick. Darting forward they tore off the guard's helm, and placed a hand over his head, holding him in place. The guard grappled with Aurel's arm, slamming his fists against the unyielding metal gauntlet, kicking at their iron-clad legs. When Aurel squeezed, the guard began to scream. Blackness welled up in his throat like a final breath, dripping from his nose, stemming from his eyes in tines of dark and clotted steam. He thrashed, his voice rising to a tinny shriek, the pressure building in his chest and expelling outward.

Aurel reached beyond him, into him, drawing something murky and vital from his lungs like a tangled skein. He was soft as cooked meat. He slipped right off the smoke-blackened bone. A tarnished cloud gathered above him, and began to take shape — a nascent face of ink. Over the guard's shoulder Aurel caught sight of Sevila's body and froze. They dropped the guard to the ground, where he crumpled in a heap, the blackness retracting back into his chest to fill the vacuum there — alive but pale and shaking.

There on the ground, Sevila's body convulsed like a fish being flayed alive. Movements sharp and jerky, her joints spasmed, fingers furling and unfurling, until finally she went perfectly pristinely still. Then with a shuddering inhalation she pushed herself into a crouch. Her head still bore a crooked cloven wedge, which lanced from crown to halfway down the bridge of her sloped nose, but even as they watched Aurel could see the glistening red matter stemming over itself, bone and skin and sinew lacing together like the wild growth of ivy-clutched walls. Half her face was obscured with a curtain of blood, but one of her eyes opened wide and burned a fierce and fiery gold, her expression barren and reptilian.

With a wordless animal snarl Sevila launched herself at the guard between herself and Aurel. His movements sluggish and panicked, he jerked his sword up in a wild slash from the ground that caught Sevila full across the shoulder. She stumbled but hardly slowed at all, a wicked gash blooming across her skin then knitting shut once more before their very eyes. No longer concerned with Aurel, the guard scrambled away from Sevila as she continued her advance. The next swipe of his sword she caught between both hands, the blade digging into her palms, and dripping red down the nicks and groves in the iron. Eyes burning and molten, she wrenched the sword from his grasp, and drove it into the gap of armour at his neck. Blood fountained from the arteries there. The guard collapsed forward, grasping in vain at his throat with both hands, staunching the flow, and still crimson sprayed across Sevila's legs and leather-bound feet, her rich silks darkening to a redder hue.

Her cowl and headwrap lay trampled with blood and dust. Her hair was an unruly sprawl, strands escaping from their bun, and sticking to the bluffs of her sharp cheeks. Sevila breathed heavily, wincing as her wounds healed themselves fully shut, the sound interrupted only by a mortal gurgle from the guard clawing at her feet, and then by a hoarse cry a few paces away. The other guard struggled to right himself by the pillar, one of his legs twisted at a sickening angle that refused to hold his weight. A clarity returned to Sevila's eyes, losing a tinge of their wild lustre.

Hefting the sword in her blood-slicked hands, she marched over to the remaining guard, and hacked at him with heavy unwieldy swings until he moved no more. Her breathing now ragged, she threw the sword atop the corpse. When she turned back to Aurel, her tongue ran along the splatter of blood across the side of her mouth. She raised her hands to wipe her face, only to grimace at the gore there.

"I'll need another laundering service at this rate," she grumbled, leaning down to wipe herself clean as best she could with a relatively unstained edge of the guard's cloak.

Aurel watched her with a weak sense of awe, their eyes tracing over the fresh skin of her face, where the wicked wound had bloomed not long before. "You're alive."

"No." Sevila said. "I'm dead. I've always been dead." She glanced down at the guards at their feet. "You nearly killed one of them without me."

Aurel stepped away from the guard's glassy accusatory eyes. "I didn't mean to. That's not what I wanted!"

"And what did you want? What did you hope to achieve?" Using her toe, Sevila prodded at the guard in question, tilting his body up to better inspect her handiwork. Her own clothes hung ragged about her skinny frame, slashed and grisly, revealing only smooth skin beneath.

"I—! I don't know. I was angry. I wanted retribution. For killing you. For killing *me.*" Aurel's voice wobbled, and they closed their eyes, shutting off the world around them, feeling nothing but the weight of emotion heavy in their cavernous chest.

"Well, well!" Sevila's smile, like all her smiles, seemed more like a feral baring of fangs. "It seems you have teeth after all."

Aurel shook their head. "I don't even know what I did."

"From what I can tell—" Sevila let the guard's body slump back down in a small cloud of dust, "—you tried removing his soul."

"I would have severed it?" Aurel said, eyes going wide in horror.

"Of course not. Don't be ridiculous. That requires a ritual days in the making. You merely would have—" she made a shooing motion with her hands, scattering a few drops of blood along the ground, "—pushed it along. As surely as driving a blade into his heart. Except this was in pursuit of possessing his body." Sevila cocked her head at Aurel, looking between them and the body in question. "Do you still want it? You can have it, if you like. Our little party would be far less conspicuous during our travels, though after a while you would begin to smell something terrible. Eventually we would have to procure a new one for you."

"No!" Aurel flinched back. The very thought of inhabiting a body — however alluring — made them feel vaguely ill. The sensation of want overwhelmed them, a hard lump of hot iron driving Aurel forward a step until they stopped in their tracks, staring down at the empty vessel before them. "No." They repeated, softer this time. "The only body I want is my own."

Sevila shrugged. "Suit yourself." She glanced about. "And where is our dour friend?"

"I am afraid he did not make it." Aurel stepped aside so Sevila could see beyond them. Her eyes widened at the sight of Alexios lying on the ground, his armour slashed, his stomach opened, a bit of darkened bowel bloodying the earth. "We will need to take his body back to the barracks for proper funerary rites. Cosmas will want to see to it."

"Oh, no," Sevila breathed. "Oh, this is quite unideal. Cosmas is going to be furious." She turned her gaze to Aurel and she looked pale. "We may have a problem: I don't think I'm capable of this much grovelling."

Chapter 9

"It wasn't my fault."

Dust and excrement gathered in the corners of the prison cell. The sound of rats scurrying beyond the walls was interrupted by the scrapes and clangs of guardsmen training in the courtyard outside. Aurel could hear their grunts and the yelling of the drill sergeant through the walls. After being discovered by a passing citizen, Aurel and Sevila had been descended upon by flocks of guards, and dragged back to the barracks. Now — looking a fright and drenched in dried blood — Sevila stood behind bars imploring a flinty-eyed Cosmas, while Aurel watched from the side-lines with crossed arms.

"Three men are dead, all of them wearing my colours, and that is all you have to say for yourself?" Cosmas barked. She had not bothered remaining out of reach; this time she had joined them in the cell to loom over Sevila, fists clenched as though she were a hair's breadth from throttling Sevila then and there.

A pause followed as Sevila scratched at her chin as though deep in contemplation, before she announced, "Yes."

Cosmas inhaled a breath so sharply it came out as a hiss. "Tell me why I shouldn't have you hung by the neck in front of a crowd baying for your blood?"

"I would like to answer that — I really would — but I have a very important question of my own." Clearing her throat, and adopting a sombre tone and expression, Sevila asked, "Who won the race?"

In a flurry of iron, Cosmas drew the short sword over her shoulder, and pressed it against Sevila's neck, driving her back and pinning Sevila against the wall with her free hand. "Alexios, my kinsman, is dead," Cosmas growled. "Theodoros arrives tomorrow for the public funeral of my Empress, the head of my clan, and her grandson. And here you stand, making jokes at the expense of the deceased." Her blade drew a line of red high against Sevila's neck just beneath her chin, which bobbed in a shaky swallow.

"I—I told—!" Sevila choked on words, unable to speak past the pressure of Cosmas' hand around her throat. When Cosmas loosened her grip somewhat, Sevila gasped out to Aurel, "I told you they were related!"

In disgust, Cosmas shoved at her so that Sevila's shoulders jammed against the stone wall. She stepped back, and raised her sword to chest height so that its tip hovered over Sevila's heart, iron whispering over bloodied and tattered silks. "I could kill you now, and not a soul on this earth or beyond would mourn your passing."

"If you did that, then how would you solve the mystery of your dead kinsmen?" Sevila tried to push the blade away with two fingers, but Cosmas only brought it back. Cosmas' dark eyes burned with such intensity that Sevila shifted her weight from foot to foot, clearing her throat with an uncomfortable grimace.

"Is this your idea of grovelling?" Aurel asked Sevila over Cosmas' armoured shoulder. "Because you're very bad at it."

"Not helpful!" Sevila barked. She prodded at the sword once more, but this time Cosmas flicked the blade so that it nicked Sevila's fingers. "Ow!" With a wince, Sevila stuck the wounded side of her fingers in her mouth, lapping up the drop of bright blood that welled up sluggishly from her skin.

Cosmas gestured with her short sword towards the rips in Sevila's clothing. "What happened? Start talking."

Glaring over her knuckles, Sevila pulled her hand away, hiding it behind her back before Cosmas could notice how quickly, how unnaturally the wound had sealed itself over. "We were attacked by two men masquerading as members of your guard. You should really tighten your security, by the way. I saw at least four different ways to break in and out of your barracks when you dragged us in here. Absolutely appalling, to be honest."

Cosmas lowered her sword but did not sheathe it. Her gloves creaked as she tightened her grip around the ornate hilt. "And you expect me to believe this? To believe that you acted in self-defence? That Alexios conveniently died protecting you? That you escaped from this supposedly harrowing ordeal entirely unscathed?"

"Well, when you put it like that—" Sevila trailed off weakly.

"Where are your wounds? Hmm?" Cosmas lifted aside a piece of Sevila's tattered silks with the tip of her sword, as if actually touching her made Cosmas' skin crawl. "Did this spirit heal you? If so, why are they still here? They would have left by now, once the terms of their contract was complete, untethered from this world."

Now it was Aurel's turn to quail beneath the force of Cosmas' ire, for she turned her narrowed gaze upon them. Aurel warded off her glare, raising their hands as if in surrender. "I didn't—"

"No, you didn't," Cosmas said flatly, turning her attention back to Sevila. "And I ask again: where are your wounds?"

"I'm so glad you asked, because — Hey! *Hey!*" To very little effect, Sevila tried squirming away from Cosmas, who grabbed up Sevila's wrist, and turned her hand over to inspect her fingers. Tracing the smooth, unmarked skin there with her gloved thumb, Cosmas raised an inquisitive eyebrow at her. Sevila snatched her hand away with a wordless hiss.

Cosmas let her go, her lip curling with disgust. "I always knew there was something wrong with you, Sevila. Even when I was a young girl. I just could never explain why. Until now."

Baring her teeth, looking like a cornered animal in the shadow of the prison wall, Sevila snapped, "And what exactly is it you think you know?"

"I served my years leading the eastern armies. On the battlefield, men will plumb the depths of desperation to stay alive." Cosmas looked Sevila up and down. "I've seen my fair share of failed abominations, but they were never powerful enough to sever themselves completely. Not like you."

Sevila sneered right back, giving no ground. "Yet it took you this long to figure it out. Your powers of observation are admirable, Cosmas. I can see why you did so well in the military."

One of Cosmas' eyebrows lifted in a cold, unamused expression. "Still with the jokes, when by Law I should be turning you over to the priestly College for immediate eradication."

"And why haven't you?" Sevila asked, seeming entirely unconcerned at the prospect.

Rather than answer, Cosmas's eyes flicked to Aurel. "You, spirit. Who were you in life?"

Straightening, Aurel replied, "Sevila named me Aurel. I know nothing of who I was before I—"

When Aurel cut off before they could finish, seeing Sevila shaking her head furiously in the corner, Cosmas sighed, and sheathed her short sword over her shoulder in a fluid, practised motion. She rubbed at her temple beneath the yellow-dyed cowl of her helm, which glinted in the low light. Above all else she appeared tired. "If you do not tell me, then I cannot help you."

"Oh, so you'll help them, but you threaten me with the priestly College?" Sevila groused. She scuffed one of her heels against a loose stone in the floor, sulky.

Cosmas only spared Sevila a dirty look over one shoulder. "From what I can tell, their association with you is through sheer necessity alone, and for that they deserve my pity if nothing else."

"I—I didn't—" Aurel fumbled for a response, torn between the two watching them. Finally, Aurel said in a panicked rush, "I was murdered and my body stolen. Please — I don't want to be handed over to the priestly College. I just want my body back."

Cosmas' expression hardly changed — an imperceptible softening around the eyes and mouth — but her voice did not sound unkind when she said, "I can understand the sentiment."

With an indignant squawk, Sevila stepped forward. "So, they get a pass for being an abomination?"

The dull tone returned to Cosmas' voice, but she did not look over at Sevila when she said, "As far as I'm concerned, they are the victim of a most terrible crime. Justice must be met."

Aurel stared at her with something akin to awe. "Thank you. You are the first person I've encountered on my travels who has taken that view."

With a stiff nod, Cosmas said, "Anything less would be shirking my duties."

"How touching," Sevila drawled. Then she planted her hands on her hips. "And perhaps I'm just as deserving of your staunch heroism! How do you know I wasn't murdered, and my soul wasn't severed against my will?"

Eyebrows rising in an incredulous look, Cosmas asked, "Were you?"

"She wasn't," Aurel answered.

"I suspected as much." Cosmas crossed her arms, and cocked her head. "Then why did you do it? Simple cowardice?"

Glaring at them both, Sevila grumbled, "That's personal."

Cosmas glanced over to Aurel for further explanation, but Aurel merely shrugged. Shaking her head, Cosmas said, "Fortunately for you, Sevila, your story checks out. Two of the dead men who wore my colours also bore the mark of the Fourteenth."

"I hate to say, '*I told you so*', but—"

"—You'll do it gladly anyway," Cosmas cut her off.

"Well, obviously." Sevila grumbled. "But that doesn't mean you have to ruin my fun."

When Cosmas aimed a ferocious glower at her, Sevila simply blinked innocently until Cosmas said to Aurel, "Tell me about your killers."

Before Aurel could answer, Sevila did so. "One killer. Someone masquerading as a priest has the body in the guise of a College acolyte. The two dead soldiers wearing your colours under false pretences were accompanying them, and had colours for each city they visited."

Cosmas squinted, suspicious. "And you got this information where?"

"I have my sources," Sevila answered with a vague gesture of her hand.

With an unimpressed grunt, Cosmas said, "The Constantine Siblings." She gripped the hilt of the longsword at her hip, and rubbed her thumb across the round pommel, a habitual fiddling. "Damn black-market ring leaders."

"Why, Cosmas! I hope you have evidence for such strong accusations!" Sevila said, feigning outrage on the behalf of her informants.

Glowering at her, Cosmas continued. "I don't understand why the College changed its tune so abruptly. Isidore has always served the empire's best interests. He would not have turned against Iustina without cause. Theodoros must have swayed him somehow."

"Perhaps with this god of his," Aurel supplied with a shrug.

Cosmas looked at Aurel sharply. "What god?"

"There is no god," Sevila sneered.

"You're sure about this?" Cosmas pressed. "The re-emergence of a god could change the course of—"

"There. Is. No. God." Sevila repeated, her face growing dark, and her voice low.

Closing her eyes and shaking her head, Cosmas reached up to remove her cowled helmet. Her short dark hair stuck to her brow, slicked with sweat at the temples. When she raked fingers through her hair, dark strands stuck up at odd angles. After a moment, she said, "I may know who took your body, though I cannot say for sure."

Both Aurel and Sevila straightened. Taking a small step forward, Aurel asked, "Who?"

"Yes, and how have you come to this conclusion?" Sevila countered with far more scepticism.

In lieu of an immediate reply, Cosmas studied the two of them, pinning them each in place with an expression both thoughtful and guarded, weighing her options just as she weighed her helm between her hands. Finally, she announced, "Before we discuss any details, I want to make one thing clear. If you cooperate—" now she glared at Sevila, "—I will ensure any present charges of murder or other transgressions are dropped. Should you break the law in the future however, I will hound you to the ends of the earth. Is that clear?"

Rolling her eyes, Sevila waved her hands as if shooing away a flurry of flies. "Yes, yes. What is it that you want?"

A pause followed the question before Cosmas answered, "Zoe."

Sevila laughed. "Impossible! Not with Theodoros as her guardian."

"Theodoros is *not* her guardian," Cosmas growled.

"Ah, yes. According to the law, that designation should have fallen to you, shouldn't it?" Sevila scoffed, tossing back her head in a dismissive manner even with blood clumping the side of her face, and matting her hair. "Too bad the coup ruined that as well."

"That—" Cosmas began, sighing, "—is not quite right either."

Blinking away a look of fleeting shock, Sevila asked, "You mean to tell me Iustina transferred guardianship outside the family? To whom?"

With a grimace Cosmas answered, "The Lady Aelia Glabaina, the woman who I believe murdered your spirit friend here."

"Theodoros' dowdy old aunt?" Sevila wrinkled her nose. "You must be joking."

"Trust you to describe a gifted clan leader as old and dowdy." Shifting her helm, Cosmas tucked it beneath one arm in a leisurely fashion. "Clan Glabas may not be as vast and powerful as some, but they aren't without means. Last I checked, Aelia had close ties with the College. She was a scholar of some repute, and Iustina had employed her services for reasons unknown to me; in the final year of Iustina's life, they could often be seen together. And what's more — nobody has seen her since the coup."

Looking pensive, Sevila ran her thumb over the gold bands of her rings on one hand. "Iustina never would have passed over your head without cause. Who was this Lady Glabaina sleeping with?"

"Not every alliance begins and ends with sexual relations," Cosmas snapped.

"Most of history would disagree with you."

"Perhaps," Aurel interrupted before the conversation dissolved into physical blows. "Perhaps she and Iustina were friends."

At that both Cosmas and Sevila stared at Aurel incredulously. "Iustina did not have friends," Cosmas said. "She had allies. Though I suppose Aelia was as close as anyone came."

"Tenuous allies, at best," Sevila added with a huff of laughter. "Apparently she even distrusted her own family."

Glowering at the insinuation, Cosmas said through grit teeth, "Everything she did was for family."

"And look how that worked out for her." Pretending to ignore Cosmas' heated glare, Sevila pressed, "In any case, what are we supposed to do with this information, hmm? What exactly does this 'cooperation' entail?"

Cosmas placed her helm back in place, tugging the cowl around her neck. "Attend the Court of Gold and the Imperial funeral as my guests. Find the Lady Glabaina, and bring her to me. If you're lucky, she'll still have the body with her, and I'll be able to confront Theodoros with every advantage on my side."

"Easier said than done," Sevila sighed.

Cosmas wore her usual intense expression. "I want Theodoros' power crippled on all sides. With the cities under my control, his clan in ruins, and Zoe reunited with her family, he will fall without question."

"But not without a fight," Sevila pointed out, picking at her fingernails in a disinterested fashion. "He'll ravage the countryside for ways to pay his soldiers and ruin your supply chain — as well as the people's faith in your cause — in the process. I sincerely hope your legendary military prowess hasn't rusted away during your years of leisure counting coin in Faros."

The snideness of Sevila's remark made Cosmas' face darken. "By any means, I will see it done. An empire is at stake."

Sevila snorted. "No, it's not. A little girl is at stake."

"Yes. And to me and my family, she is worth an empire." Cosmas leaned over Sevila, and glowered. "Do not cross me, Sevila. Not this time."

"I thought you said I was untrustworthy?" Sevila said, her tone arch, her expression dismissive, even as she watched Cosmas over her fingernails with the keenness of a snake eyeing a mouse.

If Cosmas was perturbed by Sevila's scrutiny, she did not show it. "You are. But at this moment I trust Theodoros even less."

"Your faith in me is touching." Rolling her eyes, Sevila placed a theatrical hand over her heart. "Very well, then. You have my word."

"I want more than your word—" Cosmas began.

"Such a shame then that I am already engaged in a contract," Sevila sighed with a melodrama that conveyed her distinct lack of remorse.

"—Which is why I'm confiscating your belongings and withholding access to the libraries."

"*What?*"

Cosmas gave Sevila a joyless smile. "Just until our joint venture is complete. Then you can have everything you require to leave. With any luck, I'll never see your face again in this lifetime."

"I at least need access to my money. Unless you're willing to fund our stay here?" Sevila countered slyly, and when Cosmas shot her a hard look, Sevila grinned. "I thought not."

With a grunt, Cosmas conceded, "I'll inform my men you are allowed to gather money from your supplies." Then she nodded towards Aurel. "And don't forget to dress properly for the funerary rites this evening."

Aurel glanced down at their armour. "What's wrong with what I'm wearing?"

"Everything," Sevila said. She craned her neck, and lifted herself up on her toes to peer out the small barred window in the cell. "Hopefully we'll have enough time to visit the markets. You can't be caught dead wearing that in the Court of Gold."

"I am dead," Aurel pointed out.

Sevila shrugged them off with an exasperated roll of her eyes. "It's just an expression. Didn't we have a talk about taking me literally?"

Striding towards the cell door, Cosmas pushed it open. Even unlocked, Aurel and Sevila would have had to go through her and an entire barracks to escape. She held the heavy door aside, and stood on the threshold. "Come to the palace district on the twentieth hour. The Court meets then to oversee all necessary rites before the funeral tomorrow."

"Will your mother be there?" Sevila asked.

Very slowly Cosmas turned, and her face could have been carved from stone. "If you so much as look in her direction, I will cut off your fingers, and you'll never pleasure another woman again."

"You're so unimaginative," Sevila drawled in reply. Before Cosmas could storm away however, Sevila held out her hand. "Wait, wait! You still haven't told me who won the race!"

Going tense, Cosmas gathered herself to her full height — taller than an average man, and taller still in her peaked helm — and said through grit teeth, "The Blues by a length." Then, without another word, she strode off, letting the heavy iron-banded door slam shut behind her.

Sevila crossed over to haul the door open. The hinges creaked and groaned. "That's both good news and bad news."

Following after her, Aurel pulled the door open with far more ease, letting Sevila walk beneath their arm and into the narrow damp walkway between cells. "What's the good news?"

"The good news is: I've just won a great deal of money. The bad news is: this city is most certainly going to riot, and we can't leave." She started off down the corridor towards the exit, running a hand through her blood-caked hair with a grimace. "The other bad news is: the public baths are closed today, and I'll have to make myself presentable with a bucket and a rag."

Aurel let the door shut with a clang. "I'm sure you'll look fine."

"Why, aren't you sweet, darling!"

ᛉ

Atop the hill across from the colossal domed temple of wisdom, the Komateros palace sprawled. Light flooded the marble archways, illuminating the silhouettes of guards stationed at every corner like a fortress. No less than twenty of Cosmas' men flanked the front entrance alone, turning aside any who did not bear a name of worth or a writ of admittance. When Aurel and Sevila drew up to the gate, Sevila did not pull a piece of parchment from a fold in her clothes — as many others did. She simply gave a guard her name, and he stood aside to let them pass up the walkway towards the main hall.

"How did you know that would work?" Aurel muttered, straightening their new court clothes — long robes all in gleaming white — and fidgeted with the mask in their hands.

"I didn't." Resplendent in her own finery, gold-trimmed silks dyed to the hue of a desert sunset, Sevila snapped her ring-bright fingers at Aurel. "And put on your mask. You can't be seen on the premises without it."

Waving the mask at her, Aurel said, "It doesn't have any straps to hold it in place."

With an exasperated roll of her eyes, she sighed, "You don't need them. Honestly, you are a disaster."

Before they could cross the threshold into the main entrance, Sevila pulled Aurel aside, tugging them into a dim corner by the edge of their white robes. She gestured for them to bend down and hand the mask over to her. Crouching so she could reach their face, Aurel closed their eyes as Sevila fixed the mask in place.

"Why don't you have a mask?" Aurel asked.

"Only the dead wear masks to funerary rites," Sevila replied. "And seeing as I can't have everyone knowing I'm actually dead, that rule only applies to spirits." There followed a pause, then she said, "You can stand up now."

Straightening, Aurel blinked down at her. The edges of their vision were boxed in by the lines of carved ivory, the mask smooth and simple with only a red painted crescent on their brow, the crescent turned on its side so that its points were directed up like curved horns. Aurel's presence crowned the mask like streamers of black smoke or ink that wafted through the air. "How does it look?"

"Very gloomy and sepulchral. It suits you," Sevila said with a satisfied nod before gesturing for Aurel to follow. "Come along. We're already well past fashionably late."

The moment they entered the main hall, Aurel's footsteps slowed. High above and far beyond the ceiling stretched overhead, great vaults brightened by coal-fed braziers, and covered with gold-painted mosaics, in which gods and men intermingled. Pillars cut twin swathes through the space, dividing the crowded room filled with vast numbers of family members all gathered together in their finest reds and bold saffrons and not a thread of white. A number of people paused in their conversation to stare as Sevila and Aurel passed by, and — feeling self-conscious beside an elegant Sevila, who batted not a single eyelash at the sudden attention — Aurel tugged at their own white hems in the hopes that the action would somehow transform their robes into something that even faintly resembled dignity.

Sevila made straight for a long table bearing gem-studded goblets, expensive coloured glass, and pitchers of wine. "Find the Lady Glabaina, she said! It'll be easy, she said!" Pouring herself a glass of honeyed wine to the brim, Sevila grumbled and glared at all the guests. "I've never seen so many Komateros family members in one place. This looks like one of my pipe nightmares."

"I hate to agree with you, but in this case, I'll make an exception." Aurel looked around at the many people aiming queer looks and whispers behind veiled hands in their direction. Back at the market, Aurel had been reluctant to allow Sevila to buy them a mask. Now, they hunched their shoulders, and wished she'd bought them a larger one.

Nearby a man stepped through the crowd, his features familiar and dark, like all of those congregated here. Opening his arms wide, he greeted them with a polite smile, "A woman accompanied by a human soul! You must be The Lady Peinatokina and her ward. My esteemed cousin has told me about you."

"That cannot bode well," Sevila muttered around the lip of her glass.

Rather than be puzzled by her comment, he chuckled, and held out his hand to take one of Sevila's, bowing over her knuckles. "Petros Thorakis Komaterinos. City Prefect." Straightening, he released her hand. "Cosmas has told me not to let you anywhere near public buildings during your visit in Faros as her guest. Whatever have you done? I've never seen her so surly!"

"A great number of things, I imagine," Aurel replied dryly, ignoring Sevila's glare.

Petros' dark eyes sparkled with glee. "Well, I must thank you. Most days her ire is directed at me, and I've noticed a distinct lack of it since your arrival."

Eyebrows rising, Sevila sipped at her wine and murmured, "I think we'll get along just fine, Petros."

With a grin, he gestured towards Aurel. "You clearly have no military or collegiate allegiance, Lady Peinatokina, and yet you manage to summon and bind a human soul. What is your secret?"

Lifting one shoulder in a sly shrug, Sevila evaded rather than answer directly. "I learned a few tricks from my siblings."

Aurel looked down at her in surprise. "I didn't know you had brothers and sisters."

"Half-brothers and half-sisters," Sevila clarified, taking a sip of wine. "There is a lot you don't know about me. Not that you'd have any occasion to meet them; they're gone. All of them."

"What happened?" Petros asked, the morbid curiosity plain on his face.

Sevila's lips pursed, and for a moment it appeared she would not answer, but then she said, "Some years ago they travelled through the desert, when in the night they were descended upon by an unfortunate creature." She swirled the contents of her cup, meeting the man's horrified eyes with her own stalwart stare, her voice level and hypnotic in its sheer indifference. "It tore them apart and ate them. Not necessarily in that order."

Any trace of mirth vanished, and Petros blanched. He swallowed thickly. "That's horrific."

"Yes. It was." If Sevila was upset by the memory, she did not show it; her expression remained as inscrutable as ever.

"You were there?" Aurel asked, meeting her gaze unflinchingly — unlike the nobleman who now peered into his own wine rather than hold Sevila's sharp-edged eyes.

"But of course."

"And the creature?" Petros pressed, daring to search her face for any sign of grief. He found none.

"Dead." Sevila gave a wave of her free hand, her elbows trailing their shawl of heavy silk. "I returned to that place, and ensured it would never harm another again."

At that Aurel shot her a suspicious look, which she ignored. "How very courageous of you," Aurel murmured.

Hearing Aurel's mocking tone, she aimed a warning glare at them over the brim of her cup. Before she could fire back what would doubtless be a waspish retort, Petros sighed, "And now you are the last of your line. A pity. A great pity, my dear lady. Surely you will be seeking a marriage? Children are of utmost importance at such a vital time in your precarious lineage."

Aurel had to smother a laugh at the look of sheer horror on Sevila's face. Biting back a derisive sneer, she said by way of blunt explanation, "That would accomplish very little. I am barren."

"Oh, but you could adopt! They may not be your blood, but they would be recognised by society. Your line need not end so cruelly." Petros' face lit up, and he waved over a servant to refill his cup. As more wine flowed, he continued speaking, more animated than ever. "As a matter of fact, my son is widowed with two children. You must allow me to introduce you. He's here tonight."

Petros even looked around as if he were about to pull someone from the crowd, and foist him upon Sevila right then and there. Aurel crossed their arms, and narrowed their eyes in silent laughter behind their mask at the way Sevila's jaw set, the way she glanced furtively about for a means of escape. She reached out, and put her hand on Petros' arm, giving it a none too gentle squeeze, while she smiled at him, all syrup sweet. "You're very kind, but unless you have a widowed daughter, I very much doubt such an arrangement would suit."

He paused, eyes widening in shock and understanding, before he rubbed thoughtfully at his stubbled jaw. "No, though I do believe the Lady Eudokaina's daughter might be better suited to your—ah—particular tastes. She, too, has struggled these past few years to find a halfway decent match. Shall I make the proper introductions?"

A slow smile spread across Sevila's face, and she tightened her hold on his arm, earning a wince. "That would be lovely."

His own smile was one of relief when she finally let him go, and he started off through the crowd. Sevila started after him, but she got no more than two steps when Aurel held her back with a hand on her shoulder. "You're not seriously considering this? A union with some unfortunate girl?" they asked, lowering their voice. "Tell me you jest."

She rolled her eyes. "Don't be ridiculous. The only thing I plan to do is enjoy myself for an evening."

"We're supposed to be looking for the Lady Glabaina," Aurel hissed.

Wagging her fingers towards Aurel's face, Sevila countered, "You have eyes, don't you? Go mingle. Maybe you'll even enjoy yourself for once."

Reluctant, Aurel released her, though not before parting with a warning, "Just make sure this one isn't too closely related to Cosmas. We don't need that kind of conflict of interest, now of all times."

"Darling, we're well beyond that now. Everyone in this room apart from us is somehow closely related to Cosmas." Glancing Aurel up and down, she added thoughtfully, "And even you might be."

"What?" Aurel blinked. "Sevila, what do you—? *Sevila!*" Aurel began, but already Sevila was on her way, weaving through the crowd after Petros for an introduction to the Lady Eudokaina's daughter.

Now, abandoned and alone in a crowd of unknown people, Aurel shuffled their feet. The pale silk wrappings around what passed for their feet collected grime across the patterned marble floor, spotting with droplets of spilled wine, white cloth blooming with claret. After a moment of gathering their courage in their hands, Aurel approached a group of three nobles — two women and a man, nursing their glass of wine — but the moment Aurel stepped too near, making their intentions to join the conversation clear, all three blanched, and mumbled excuses to be elsewhere before dispersing into the crowd.

Shoulders sagging, Aurel tried again to similar effect. Finally, after the third time this happened, they placed a firm hand on the shoulder of a young nobleman, whose back was turned, and asked softly, "Do you know where I might find the host?"

The young nobleman pointed a trembling finger towards the other side of the room, breathing a sigh of relief when Aurel released him, and turned to stride away with a murmur of thanks. Making their way across the room, Aurel passed through the congregation with ease, the crowd parting before them. High above the ceiling glittered with gold through a cluttering of smoke that dimmed the air. Approaching an empty seat at the head of the hallway, Aurel peered over the heads of the crowd in search of Cosmas. Two guards in black and gold, bearing Cosmas' personal seal of a rampant bull, their faces hidden behind their cowls, flanked the throne-like curule chair that stood atop a low-slung dais beneath a canopy of rich velvets festooned with garlands of drooping white flowers.

When Aurel took a step too close to the empty seat, both guards grabbed the hilts of their swords in warning. Aurel stopped, raising their hands, which bled thick black smoke into the air around their robes. "Have you seen Cosmas?"

The guards exchanged unreadable looks beneath their helms, before one of them jerked his head towards a door to the side, leading onto a balcony. Aurel offered a shallow bow, and walked beneath the broad archway and onto the balcony.

There, Cosmas stood with her back facing the hall. She, too, had discarded her usual armour in favour of coral red silks that in the dim light appeared a dusky rose, though she still wore a military-style cloak that draped around her shoulders and down her back despite the warm air, heavy with humidity. As though she sensed a change in the air at Aurel's presence, Cosmas turned abruptly, her scowl softening somewhat when she saw who it was that disturbed her.

Hesitant, Aurel tried to smile as best as they were able, but Cosmas shuddered at the sight. "Don't do that."

Immediately, Aurel stopped. "I apologise."

"It's fine. It's just—" Cosmas fixed them with a piercing glance. "You don't know what you look like half the time, do you?"

Crossing the balcony to stand beside her at the balustrade, Aurel shook their head.

With a wordless grunt, Cosmas said. "Good. Keep it that way."

Cosmas looked out over the city. She leaned her forearms on the stone railing, and her profile caught the light from the nearby braziers lining the walls. She had removed her ornate headwrap, and now she fiddled with the cloth between her fingers so that the ends of the gold-trimmed silk dangled over the balustrade. In the shadows, she looked more tired than ever. She chewed at her lower lip, worrying it between her teeth. "Ever since learning of the coup, I haven't had a moment to myself. The rest of my family look to me to restore the rightful order of things, and all I can think about is a decent night's sleep."

Watching her run a hand through her short hair, Aurel said, "I could leave you alone, if you'd prefer."

"No. Stay," Cosmas sighed. "Your presence is unnerving at the best of times, but that does not mean you yourself are unwanted."

"I'm sorry. I was not aware—" Aurel made an abortive motion to grasp Cosmas' shoulder, to lend some small measure of comfort, only to clench their fist and lower their arm once more. "Sevila never mentioned anything about my presence being a discomfort."

Gathering the cloth headwrap between her hands, she folded it carefully. "I doubt she feels it. I doubt she feels anything, being what she is."

Aurel searched Cosmas' face with a puzzled frown, eyes glowing brightly through the mask, the light drifting through the dark night air. "You pity her?"

With a derisive bark of laughter, Cosmas scoffed, "I fear her. I fear what she is, and what she is both capable and incapable of." Cosmas glanced at Aurel, her expression guarded. "I fear you as well."

Taken aback, Aurel said, *"Me?"*

Cosmas hummed in wordless confirmation, running her thumb over the folded fabric in her hands.

"But I haven't done anything!" Aurel insisted.

"It's not what you've done. It's what you can do. What you might do." Tilting her chin up, Cosmas' gaze swept the skyline to the horned harbour, where ships lay anchored beyond the chain. Even from here, Aurel could hear the distant clanging as the chain was lifted to admit merchant vessels. "You are leashed to a woman without soul in a contract about which I have very little information. She could order you to do anything."

A chill gripped the chasm of Aurel's chest in a phantom ache. For once, they took Sevila's advice, and said nothing further about the nature of their contract.

While Cosmas looked out across the city rooftops, Aurel could see her watching them out of the corner of her eye, gauging any reaction. "To say nothing of your own state. You could be anybody."

Trying to appear nonchalant, Aurel shrugged. "Sevila reckons I was a nobody."

"Does she? Or did she just say that to make you feel worthless? To make you feel further indebted to her?" The corners of Cosmas' mouth turned down, and she straightened, turning away from the city to face Aurel with nothing but sincerity written across her face. "People do not get murdered, their souls severed, and their bodies stolen because they are worthless."

"And do you—? Do you think that I'm—?"

Before Aurel could ask the question that hung heavy and unspoken between them, Cosmas shook her head. "I pray that you are not. I wouldn't wish your fate upon anyone, least of all my own blood."

"Is that the only reason why you're helping me? Because of who I might be?" Aurel whispered. The disappointment stung, burrowing deep as a barbed arrowhead.

Cosmas stared at them, aghast. "Is this what you think of me? That I would only help you on the off chance that you might be my kin?"

"I—I'm not sure," Aurel said weakly. "I don't know you well enough, Cosmas."

For so many weeks they had grown accustomed to Sevila's wounded pouting, that when faced with the real disappointment in Cosmas' eyes, panic flared in Aurel's chest like a tar-pit fire. She smiled at them in a sad, self-deprecating way. "I suppose that's fair."

When her attention turned to brooding over the city, an awkward silence fell between them, Aurel watched her. Even now she seemed poised on the precipice of motion, tense and coiled and ready to fling herself into action at a moment's notice. The exact opposite of Sevila in every regard, who languished, utterly at ease. The stone railing was too low for Aurel to lean their elbows upon as Cosmas did, but they leaned their hands against it nevertheless, hunching over at her level to ask in a low voice, "If they had killed Zoe as well, would you have become—?"

"I don't want to—" Cosmas interrupted, her voice hoarse, only to stop herself, and inhale a deep steadying breath. "I don't want to think about it."

This time Aurel did not hesitate to place a comforting hand on Cosmas' shoulder. "I can imagine an empire under you."

"I can't."

She came off as flinty and unyielding, but she did not push Aurel away. Aurel gave a reassuring squeeze before lowering their hand, and Cosmas gave a grateful shiver when they released her. "If Iustina placed you in charge of Faros, then she must have trusted you greatly," Aurel said "And from what you and Sevila have said, she did not give her trust so easily."

Rather than be appeased, Cosmas spat bitterly, "Yes. She put me in charge of Faros and the Komateros clan so that I could squabble with money-lenders and guilds like a glorified merchant, when I should have stayed in Pala and—" She grit her teeth, and furiously shook her headwrap out, undoing all her careful folding in order to tie it round her head once more. "If I'd been there, Theodoros would never have dared raise arms against Iustina and Leo. I would have removed his hands first."

"You cannot blame yourself for what happened."

"I don't! I blame Theodoros and his lot! They did this!" Cosmas tugged hard at the cloth in her hands, growling when it came loose. She snatched it from her head, and started again.

"May I?" Aurel asked, gesturing to the headwrap.

Jaw tense, Cosmas relented with a nod. Careful so as not to actually touch her and cause any more discomfort, Aurel took the silk, and wrapped it around her brow. The action came with ease, like a ship gliding over smooth waters, as if Aurel had done this countless times before. Tuck here. Pull there. When they finished — it took but a few moments in which the silence between them was broken only by the sounds from the nearby door and windows, lamplight and conversation slipping out into the night — Aurel stepped away.

Looking up, Cosmas studied Aurel with a sombre gaze before announcing, "I will aid you in whatever way I can, as I would do for anyone in your position."

"Even Theodoros?" Aurel tried to sound wry, but the effect was timid instead.

Cosmas drew herself up, shoulders square, eyes hard yet earnest. "Even Theodoros."

With a careful pensive look, Aurel murmured, "I believe you."

At that, Cosmas nodded briskly as though she had expected nothing less. Then she jerked her head towards the door. "I should return. People will be wondering where I am. You may join me, or remain out here if you wish."

Aurel started to smile, but stopped. Instead they merely nodded. "Thank you, but I think I will retire for the evening."

"As you like." She bowed her head and let them be.

Chapter 10

By the time Sevila stumbled into the room Cosmas had arranged for them at the palace, night was giving way to the creeping dawn. Her clothes were rumpled, and she carried her headwrap and cowl in her hands. Her long dark hair looked finger-worn and slightly damp with sweat at the temples. Seated in the windowsill, Aurel looked up from one of the scrolls they had taken from the shelves in the room. They greeted her, and received only a weary grunt in reply, before she all but flung herself onto the large bed against the far wall without undressing. Soon her snores rasped throughout the room.

Unperturbed by her actions, Aurel unfurled the scroll further, moving slowly so as not to clank and wake Sevila, though they were convinced she could sleep through a frontal assault on the palace itself. As soon as Aurel had returned to the room earlier the previous evening after leaving Cosmas, they had discarded their white robes, and donned their armour and green military style cloak with a sense of relief. Now the robes lay on the floor, neatly folded beneath the matching mask. With every passing moment, the sky brightened, little by little, and the city roused itself from an uneasy slumber. By dawn the crowds had started gathering, streaming in from all parts of the city and beyond, filling the air with a restless hum until the fortifications of Faros trembled like the pitted walls of a hive. Glancing up from their reading, Aurel could see the people building a pyre in the forum at the centre of the city, stacking the kindling twice as tall as the height of a man.

As the sun at last peeked over the horizon, a loud persistent knocking rapped against the door. On the bed, Sevila groaned and rolled over but did not rise. With a sigh, Aurel stood and crossed the room, opening the door to find Cosmas there, fully dressed in her guard captain regalia as if prepared for a battle rather than a public funeral. Today however, her suit of armour was tinted a sombre black, small links of plate mail glinting in the early morning light like scales of dark articulated glass. With her sculpted features, she looked like a basalt statue of the warlike god-kings of Aegryph given flesh.

She only nodded at Aurel in greeting before announcing, "Theodoros is on his way with the bodies. Where is Sevila?"

In answer, Aurel stood to one side, and opened the door wider so Cosmas could see Sevila curled up beneath the fine cotton sheets. Expression stony, Cosmas crossed the room and grabbed the sheets. She ripped them from the bed, flinging them to the floor, then grabbed hold of Sevila's ankles and hauled her halfway off the feather-stuffed mattress. "Get up!" she barked. "I didn't release you from prison so you could laze about while there's work to be done."

Grumbling and pushing herself upright, her legs hanging over the side of the bed so that her heels dragged against the floor, Sevila rubbed at the dark shadows beneath her eyes. "It's called sleep, Cosmas. Even the soulless enjoy it. You might try it yourself sometime."

"I remember sleep. Waste of time," Cosmas replied, her tone dry. With a swipe of her foot against Sevila's ankles, she ordered, "Be ready, and downstairs in the main hall in a quarter of an hour. The final preparations will begin shortly."

Aurel held the door open for her as she left, and she gave a brisk nod of thanks before marching from the room. In disgust, Sevila ran a hand through her sleep-tangled hair, and said, "What an awful woman."

"I like her." Aurel shut the door softly yet firmly in Cosmas' wake.

"No accounting for taste." She stood with a great groan and production, knuckling at the small of her back and stretching with a yawn. Then, she frowned at Aurel. "You're not expecting to wear that to the funeral, are you? Where are the robes I bought you yesterday? I seem to remember paying an extravagant sum for them."

Not bothering to answer, Aurel began stripping off their armour, and piling it in a corner. By the time they had draped the white robes over their shadowy figure—fussing at the way the folds carried their dagger, and hung across the breadth of their shoulders—Sevila had changed into an outfit of ebony cloth so clustered with gold thread it appeared to be cloth-of-gold stitched with black. Aurel gestured at her with the mask. "What was it you said about extravagant sums of money?"

With a dismissive sniff, Sevila said, "This is for a good cause."

"Which is to — what? Make you look magnificent in every sense of the word?"

She shot them a roguish grin. "Can you think of a better cause?"

A huff of rueful laughter escaped Aurel at that, and they held open the door once more. Together the two of them started down a marble arched corridor festooned with tapestries and lavish paintings, no finger-width of the walls left uncovered. Colourful statues of past emperors and empresses and other important Komateros clan members lined the archways. Peering around one of them, Aurel spied a courtyard far below, across which several liveried servants scurried from room to room. Sevila stifled another yawn behind her hand.

"You had a late night," Aurel remarked. "Did you accomplish anything useful, or was it all for naught?"

The effect of Sevila's glare was lessened somewhat by her haggard appearance. "And what did you do after I left? Vanish into some dismal corner and read dusty old books?"

Aurel fiddled with their mask rather than answer. Drawing some of the loose cloth around her shoulders over her head like a hood, Sevila hummed a self-satisfied note. "That's what I thought."

As they descended sets of broad spiralling staircases, the number of guards roaming the palace increased the closer they drew to their destination. In the main hall itself, where so many people had congregated just the night before, Cosmas paced in front of the empty curule chair. Her footsteps echoed, an unyielding clack of leather and iron rebounding along the gold-sheathed vaulted ceiling. Now, instead of guests, guards lined the walls, stoic and unmoving. They had exchanged their customary yellow-dyed cloaks for those of purest black, yet over their shoulders Aurel could spot Cosmas' personal emblem emblazoned in gold across their backs.

As Aurel and Sevila entered the hall and approached, Sevila called out to her, "Are you ever going to give in and take that seat?"

Cosmas whirled around in a smart about-face at the sound with a flinty expression. She gave the throne-like chair an uneasy glance. "It's not for me."

Gesturing to the empty room that sprawled around them, Sevila drawled, "How silly of me! It must be for all these other deserving family members lining up to take it! You there!" she barked at one of the nearby guards. "Standing all day must be exhausting! Why don't you take a seat?"

The guard did not even seem to register that Sevila had spoken to him, and for that Sevila grunted in disappointment. "I see all your kin are just as humourless as you are, Cosmas. Or do you drill good cheer right out of them at the barracks?"

"Now is not the time for your little quips and games," Cosmas snapped, and struck up her pacing once more. She prowled before the steps leading to the throne-like chair with a gaze intense enough to strip the mosaic tiles from a nearby pillar.

"You always say that," Sevila replied with a flutter of her eyelashes that made the furrow between Cosmas' brows deepen.

In the distance Aurel could hear the sound of many feet marching in unison. They cocked their head. "Someone is coming."

"Theodoros," Cosmas said grimly. She stopped her pacing with an abrupt halt, hands behind her back, shoulders straight, drawing herself up to her full height with a deep breath. Jerking her head, she commanded, "Stay behind me and say nothing.

Especially you." She fixed Sevila with a brook-no-nonsense stare. "This situation is tenuous enough with your meddling."

"If you're that worried about it, then you could have left me in bed," Sevila muttered even as she dropped back a few steps to stand behind Cosmas. She lifted a veil of filmy black silk in the place of her usual bone-stitched shroud to cover much of her face.

Clearing her throat, Cosmas glanced surreptitiously at Aurel before lifting her chin and turning to face the tall entryway at the far end of the hall. "Your presence here adds a certain gravity to the proceedings."

Sevila's kohl-rimmed eyes narrowed as she looked between Cosmas and Aurel. "Ah, I see. You didn't necessarily want me here at all."

Puzzled, Aurel blinked. "What do you—? Oh. *Oh.* You wanted me." They fidgeted with the mask in their hands, unsure of what to do with this information — how useless they felt, how utterly out of their depth.

With an apologetic grimace, Cosmas said, "Both of you carry your own weight, I assure you."

"Some of us more than others apparently," Sevila grumbled under her breath. Before Cosmas could retort in her own defence however, the entryway at the end of the hall darkened with the appearance of a long train of people.

When Aurel took a step back to stand beside Sevila so that the two of them flanked Cosmas on either side, Sevila tugged at their white robes. They looked down at her in silent question, and she hissed, "Your mask."

Fumbling with the mask, Aurel placed it over their face. Wisps of inky shadow curled around the carved ivory. They straightened just as the entourage arrived.

Theodoros walked at the head of the procession. Like Cosmas, he wore blackened armour, but the military-style cloak swept from his shoulders in a field of oiled blue fabric, and in the place of a helm he had donned a matching blue headwrap. His dark eyes flicked to Sevila then to Aurel, and he paused at the threshold for a brief moment before overcoming his surprise and forging onward, pushing into the hallway. He was followed by two stretchers bearing bodies swathed in purest white, carried by ceremonial lictors, and led by a priest all in black. Beyond them, no less than twenty-five soldiers marched, two-abreast, their faces obscured behind helms draped with chain mail cowls. All of them were tall and broad-shouldered, and at their sides walked the summoned spirits of wild boars with great curling tusks that bled shadow.

If Cosmas' expression had been flinty before, now it was downright thunderous. "You dare bring soldiers armed with contracts into my city, Theodoros?"

"No soldiers." He waved towards his retinue. "These are members of my honour guard."

Where Cosmas spoke in a voice commanding and powerful, Theodoros spoke softly, his tone measured and surprisingly cultured. From what Aurel had heard during their travels so far, their impression of the general who had staged a coup was a far cry from the man who stood before them now. He and Cosmas were of a similar age, with only the beginnings of grey streaks in his short-trimmed beard evidence that he might have a few years on her. The closer he drew, crossing the hall, the more apparent it became that he was even fractionally shorter than Cosmas, though his dark gaze was no less intense. He took note of his surroundings with a shrewdness that belied his false front of gentility and calm.

"I was not aware the High Priest of the College counted himself among your honour guard," Cosmas retorted. "Though I should have expected nothing less from you, Isidore, after the events of these last few fortnights."

As Theodoros stopped a good few paces away from her, the high priest in question — Isidore — stepped forward to stand beside him. Whatever extravagance from a man in such a position Aurel had been expecting was met instead with someone whose only statement of office was a simple gold chain that hung heavy across his chest and shoulders. Isidore's eyes were concealed behind a long cowl folded flat across his cheeks and nose, obscuring his vision entirely. Regardless he moved with ease, and his head swung to face Cosmas when she spoke, as though his eyes could pierce the dark cloth. Placing his hand over his heart, Isidore offered a shallow bow, no more than a tilt of his head in her direction. "Such a shame we must meet again under such inauspicious circumstances, Cosmas. I have never had anything less than the greatest respect for you and your family."

Cosmas' gaze hardened, and though her voice remained level, Aurel could see that she clenched her hands into fists behind her back. Her fingers trembled. "You respect me so much you murder my kin?"

Theodoros remained unfazed by her accusations. "Situations change. This is a matter larger than us. You just don't see it."

"I don't want your excuses!" Cosmas sneered.

"But you'll settle for our heads?" Isidore countered dryly, waving towards Sevila and Aurel with a hand that smoked with the viscosity of black ink — spirit made flesh. He turned his face first Sevila and then Aurel, his attention lingering over each of them in turn. Though Aurel could not see his eyes, they could feel the weight of his scrutiny all the same, piercing as a skinning knife. The moment he turned away, Aurel darted a questioning glance at Sevila, but her brow was furrowed in concentration, and she did not look their way.

"Won't you introduce us to your friends?" Theodoros pressed, though he did not take his eyes off Cosmas.

"No," Cosmas answered, blunt. "Where is Zoe?"

"With her legal guardian and my troops, camped just outside the city walls," Theodoros said.

"So, you'll kill her brother and grandmother, but you won't let her bury them?" Cosmas growled, her voice slipping on a low dangerous note in her chest. "Your love for my family shows its true skin more and more, Theodoros."

"She will make her appearance at the public pyre before her people," Isidore assured Cosmas, though his words only made a tense muscle tick at her cheek. Sevila stiffened, drawing in a sharp hiss of breath at his declaration, but otherwise she remained silent, ignoring Aurel's look in her direction.

Gritting her teeth, Cosmas asked, "I would see the Lady Glabaina."

In reply, Theodoros swept his hand to his forehead in a bow. "Aelia has asked that I send her regards and make every apology on her behalf. She will be accompanying Zoe to the funeral, but she will be unable to stay for long. Currently, my esteemed aunt is suffering from a grave condition, and we are working tirelessly to see her through to a swift recovery."

Cosmas revealed her teeth in a joyless smile. "I shall sacrifice a sleek heifer for the Lady Glabaina's improvement. Otherwise you'll be forced to hand the young princess back over to her rightful family."

Theodoros' expression gave every appearance of composure but for minute details — how stiffly he stood, how brittle his gaze became at the implication that his most prized and hard-won asset in a civil war might be wrested from his grasp by a question of mere legality. He smiled, a tense draw of his mouth that quickly vanished once more.

Stepping aside, Isidore gestured for the lictors to come forward. "May I present to you the bodies? I trust you'll find them in pristine condition."

As the lictors bore the two litters closer, Cosmas tore her gaze away from Theodoros. She and Isidore both moved forward until they stood across from one another over the white-shrouded bodies. He waited for her terse nod of approval before reaching down with one hand — his human hand this time — and one by one pulled the cloth aside, careful so as not to touch their flesh with his own. Upon seeing the bodies unwrapped, Aurel felt a distinct chill race through them.

Leo could not have been more than nine years of age, and embodied everything Aurel had expected — his cheeks round, his shoulders narrow and naked beneath the shroud. On the other hand, Iustina looked both nothing and everything like her image stamped on imperial currency. Her untethered hair was struck through with greys, and her aquiline nose cast a regal shadow across her long narrow face. She appeared unnaturally still, as if the most unusual aspect of her lying on this litter was not that she was dead, but that she was motionless. Motion became her; Aurel was half convinced she would rise up at any moment, and begin delivering orders in a cool clipped tone.

With a heady swallow, Cosmas turned her head aside and breathed deeply. "You -" she began with a rasp, but had to clear her throat free of a burr. Her jaw clenched, and she rounded on both Theodoros and Isidore with an expression Aurel could not see from this angle, but which had Theodoros' honour guard go tense in unison. "Get out. Take your men and leave."

Rather than object, both Isidore and Theodoros offered their shallow bows before turning and making a measured retreat, neither hastening nor lagging behind, while the honour guard and summoned spirits trailed after them. Their footsteps echoed throughout the grand hallway, fading the further away they drew. Cosmas glowered at the lictors fiercely until they placed the litters and the bodies they carried on the ground, and followed suit, fleeing after their masters.

Cosmas remained silent until they had left. Then, she inhaled sharply and straightened. "Gather the troops and send word to our armies in the east," she ordered hoarsely to the room at large. "I want them ready to march by tomorrow."

Two of the guards lining the walls stepped forward and bowed before hurrying off carry out her commands. Pulling down her veil, Sevila stepped forward. "Well, I think that went very well!"

Lip curling into a sneer, Cosmas said, "After this is over, I'm going to crush them."

"We all deal with grief differently," Sevila drawled. "Some of us drink ourselves into oblivion. Others raise armies to trample our foes into the dust. To each their own."

Aurel began to remove their mask, but stopped when Cosmas shot them a dark look, her eyes darting to the bodies lying nearby. "How far away are your troops?"

"I have enough men here to protect the city from attack and withstand any potential siege for a decade," Cosmas answered, then added with a grimace, "But the bulk of my armies are at least a week away."

"In other words," Sevila said, "Plenty of time for Theodoros and Isidore to scurry back to Pala and seize every advantage, forcing us to go to them. Cosmas, why didn't you have your armies prepped beforehand? I've never taken you for a slouch."

Running her thumb along the pommel of her sword, Cosmas said, "If I'd brought my troops down any sooner, Theodoros never would have agreed to this public funeral in the first place, and my kin would go unburied."

With a hum of acknowledgement, Sevila sent a sidelong glance towards the bodies. Then she pantomimed grabbing hold of one of Aurel's hands — her fingers passing through the shadowy impression of theirs as if grasping at smoke. "We'll leave you in peace for now."

If anything, Cosmas appeared grateful at the suggestion. She let loose a weary sigh. "I still expect you to attend the funeral at my side. Don't be late."

"Perish the thought," Sevila said.

As Cosmas turned back to the white-shrouded bodies, Sevila jerked her head at Aurel, and the two of them retreated to a nearby archway, far enough away for Aurel to duck their head and mumble quietly, "The bodies—They still look—"

"—Warm?" Sevila finished for them. Her eyes narrowed and she tapped at her chin and mouth with her slender fingers. "Completely unscathed? Tampered with? I couldn't agree more."

"I was going to say 'empty'," Aurel corrected. "Like I could push on their chests and their ribs would sink inwards."

Eyeing Aurel askance, Sevila responded with a thoughtful hum. "If you possessed either of them, their bodies would immediately begin to rot around you. Theirs was not a pleasant fate. Improperly done — not unlike yourself. My bet is Theodoros and Isidore were trying to control them by putting another's soul inside. Pity that sort of thing is impossible. Idiots."

"One of those could be mine," Aurel murmured, glancing back towards the corpses with a gaze that could only be described as hungry.

"Oh, yes." Sevila pulled up her veil so that only her eyes could be seen, glinting like molten coins. "Come along, darling. We're leaving."

"Leaving?" Aurel repeated with an incredulous hiss. "They are going to burn those bodies! We have to stop them!"

"Even if we did, even if we somehow managed to steal two imperial bodies from beneath the noses of an entire city populace, what do you think would happen? Hmm?" Sevila turned to stride away, gesturing for Aurel to follow with a crook of her finger. "I can't put you back in them. Not yet. We need that manuscript."

Aurel said in a hushed hurried tone, "By the time we find the Lady Glabaina and gain access to the libraries, it will be too late! These bodies will have been reduced to ash!"

"Under normal circumstances, you would be correct, but today — today I have acquired sealed permission from the City Prefect to grant entry to both libraries." With a smug grin that showed around the crinkled corners of her eyes, Sevila pulled out a slip of folded parchment, and gave it a triumphant wave. "And here you thought my dalliance last night was just for pleasure!"

Aurel had never been so glad to see Sevila's thieving ways come to fruition. "I stand corrected."

Sevila playfully prodded Aurel's chest with the parchment. "And don't you forget it."

Outside, even atop the palatial hill Aurel could hear the rumble of the streets, growing louder the further the two of them descended. The city was a roiling mess of people gathered in the main square, surrounded by guardsmen on all sides. Slipping through the back alleys, Sevila and Aurel passed unnoticed through the streets. Along one shaded corner, Aurel spied three men and a woman wearing green cloaks over their black mourning clothes kicking another man unconscious. Their lips peeled back in rictus snarls, they spat on him. Through their legs, his blue cloak grew dusty and bloodied with every strike of their feet.

Even as Aurel stepped forward, Sevila tugged at their white robes with an angry hiss, "Leave them."

Reluctant, Aurel continued onwards, peering over their shoulder as the man in blue spat a mouthful of blood onto the cobblestones, his face already swelling up with bruising, a wicked gash forming above his eye.

Further up ahead, the libraries loomed, twin structures of gleaming white and grey granite. Unlike the last time the two had attempted to enter, Sevila led them straight towards the main doors, gates of heavy iron three times as tall as a man, their façades emblazoned with fanciful scrollwork and imagery. Even on a day like this, four of Cosmas' men guarded the entrance, leaning upon their spears, and keeping a wary eye upon the street. As soon as Aurel and Sevila began climbing the steps to the entrance, all four of them stiffened, gripping their weapons.

Before they could even ask, Sevila produced the piece of expensive parchment bearing Petros' seal, and stamped in imperial purple wax. "Calm down, won't you?"

She pushed the parchment into the nearest guard's hands, and beneath his black and gold cowl his eyes narrowed as he scanned the writing. He squinted at the two of them over the piece of parchment. "You've chosen an odd time to peruse the stacks. Aren't you attending the funeral?"

"Aren't you?" Sevila countered. She pointed to the position of the sun, still low above the horizon. "Besides, we have time."

With an annoyed grunt, the guard handed the parchment back to her but did not stand aside. "Be quick about it."

Snatching the parchment from his hands, Sevila refused to step around him, and instead brushed their shoulders together so that he was forced to stagger back a step. The other three guards lowered their spears, but froze when Aurel loomed at Sevila's side. The early morning light slanted over Aurel's shoulders, catching the pale cloth draped across their massive form. Across the steps Aurel cast a shadow that fumed, eyes blazing like the noonday sun beneath the pale mask marked with blood.

The guards stood aside and let them pass.

"You don't have to goad them," Aurel grumbled as the doors groaned shut behind them, enclosing the both of them in the dry, dark hush of the library.

"Where's the fun in that?"

The library was suspended in a resin of dim quiet. Silence cottoned to the tall ceilings arching overhead and to the many rows of books and scrolls interspersed with a rare lamp, whose flame was contained by glass jars upended over them. Dimly Aurel could hear the commotion outside from passing crowds of people flooding towards the funeral, while in here it already felt like a tomb. No other patrons were in sight, nor watchful librarians peering down their long noses at potential misconduct. The dark-washed wooden floors creaked beneath Aurel's bulk, where Sevila walked ahead with footsteps light and agile as a desert cat's. When Aurel glanced along the ground, they saw shiny swathes in the dust, like animal tracks through a mist-clung forest glade.

Sevila led them up various flights of stairs, passing through a maze-like warren of dusty shelves that extend high up towards the towering ceiling. Along each row a ladder was perched at an angle, leaning against the shelves, their rungs sagging from years of wear.

Peering down yet another narrow passageway of shelves, Aurel asked, "Do you even know where it will be?"

Sevila shrugged but did not stop walking. "No idea."

"How very comforting."

When they reached the third floor — about halfway up the tower-like structure — they stopped at the top of the stairs. A few paces away there stood a man in dusky grey robes, slender and tall, his hair greying at the temple like wings of white arching over his ears. He looked up, and the board tied around his neck by a length of thin rope swung against his chest. His title had been carved on the board, naming him a resident library attendant.

"There you are!" Sevila sighed with exasperation, already approaching. "We've been looking all over for the likes of you!"

Stooping, the attendant bowed. "Apologies. Most of us have taken the day off. It is, after all, a day of public grief."

"A day of widespread uselessness, you mean." Sevila gestured towards a nearby row of tomes and scrolls. "We're looking for a manuscript or scroll of some kind about the Helani. It will have been transliterated in their language for the most part."

Rather than seem bemused, the attendant nodded sagely. "Ah, yes. You're looking for the work of Nikephoros Lector. How strange."

"Strange?" Aurel pressed. "Why do you say that?"

His eyes widening at being directly addressed by a human soul, he glanced at Aurel then continued speaking to Sevila, clearing a stammer from his voice. "A courier arrived a few months ago with that particular work. I thought he was lying, what with his tales of the public burning of Lector's work in Pala, but he had the paperwork from Empress Iustina herself."

Slowly Sevila lowered her black veil. "Has anyone else looked at this work?"

"Just the once." With a gesture for them to follow, the attendant led them further along. "A priest and his acolyte arrived yesterday asking for it. Wanted to take it away as well, but I'm not allowed to let it leave the library."

Aurel and Sevila exchanged knowing glances behind the attendant's back. "And they just left without it?" Sevila asked, incredulous.

With a rueful chuckle, the attendant said, "I know this place may look empty today, but normally it is crawling with people like me. Not to mention more guards than you could shake a stick at. They were allowed to take notes. Here you are." He stopped near a low table carrying a lamp, and pointed them down an aisle. "You'll find it on the bottom left corner beside the treatise of the mountain gods that carved Nicoma from the rock. You can't miss it."

When Sevila reached out to lift the glass bell jar above the lamp, the attendant twitched. "Ah—!" He began with an abortive step forward, glancing fearfully at Aurel then back at Sevila. "I must ask that you not take a flame into the stacks themselves. For safety reasons, you understand?"

"Oh, I understand." Looking him dead in the eye, Sevila picked up the lamp, and placed the glass container back down. She smiled sweetly, her sharp teeth glinting in the low flickering light. "But you can fuck off."

He made a strangled sound in the back of his throat as Sevila turned and started down the aisle away from him. The attendant looked to Aurel in a pleading manner, but Aurel merely shrugged, and followed after Sevila. He watched the two of them go, and hovered where he'd left them, keeping a watchful eye as Sevila handed the lamp to Aurel, and leaned over to run her finger along the spines of manuscripts clustered together along the shelf.

She tapped her fingertip against one leather-bound spine, and pulled the manuscript out, grunting at its weight as it fell open in her arms. Squinting down at the cramped writing, she jerked her head at Aurel. "Bring that closer, won't you?"

Holding the lamp out carefully, Aurel stood just behind her while Sevila shuffled through the pages. They cocked their head over her shoulder, bending down to read, but they understood only phrases here and there. Much of the text had been written in a tongue completely foreign to them, though the letters themselves were recognisable.

"When did you learn the Helani tongue?" Aurel asked.

"I picked a bit of it up during my travels," Sevila murmured in enigmatic reply. Her gaze roved slowly over the pages before she flipped to another filled with meticulous diagrams and sketches of typical Helani garb — lavishly detailed scabbards, tightly arched bows fired from horseback, and skull-like headgear that covered the eyes. She turned the page again, seeking restlessly for something else. "They are a strange people. I'm amazed they let this Nikephoros Lector get away with writing this. They think the written word is sacred. I've seen them behead a man for less."

As she turned another page, she trailed off, going quiet. With a frown, Aurel tried to read it as well, but the complex charts and figures labelled in Helanic might as well have been complete gibberish. "What is it?"

She did not immediately reply. Her mouth and throat worked, opening as if to speak but shutting again to swallow down the words. Abruptly, Sevila slammed the manuscript shut, and stared down at its embossed cover. Her eyes had gone wide, her slitted pupils narrow as a knife's edge. She trembled all over.

"Are you alright?" Aurel asked, concerned.

When they placed a gentle hand on her shoulder, Sevila jerked as if she'd been struck. She held the manuscript away from her body as if suddenly afraid it would rear up and bite her. Without looking at Aurel, she shoved the book into their arms, and stalked back down the aisle.

"Sevila—?" Aurel trailed after her, balancing the book in one hand and the lamp in the other.

At the end of the row, the attendant stood patiently, hands behind his back. When he saw Sevila striding towards him, he took a hesitant step back. "Did you—? Did you find everything you needed—?"

Before he could finish speaking, Sevila grabbed hold of his upper arms, and slammed his back against nearby a shelf, knocking the breath out of him. A few scrolls rattled and fell onto the floor with a clatter, bouncing against the table that had once held the lamp. "This is the only copy?" she demanded, her voice rough and hoarse. "And you're the only one here who knows of it?"

"What are you—!" The attendant yelled, but cut off with a cry when her fingernails dug painfully into his arms. He started to struggle against her hold, but her face had gone blank and cold and wild. Beneath her reptilian stare, the attendant froze as if hypnotised.

"Answer me," she hissed.

"Yes!" he yelped when she shook him.

Her voice remained hushed and dangerous. "You're sure? And don't lie to me," she rasped, and her eyes flashed golden. "Think very carefully. Is this the last copy?"

"I—? I think—?" He swallowed thickly. "As far as I'm aware—?"

Sevila bared her teeth, an ugly gesture that transformed her face into something alien. "Not good enough."

In a movement swift as an adder's, she seized his head between both hands and slammed it down atop the table and its bell jar. The glass shattered beneath the force of the blow. Shards impaled his cheeks and jaw. He howled, clutching at his face and staggering away. When he tripped over his own feet and stumbled to the ground, Sevila calmly bent down and picked up a shard of jagged glass long as her forearm. A fine tremour ran along her fingers, and she gripped the glass so tightly blood dripped from her fist. She stalked after him. She did not seem to need to blink. She watched him scramble away from her with the fixedness of a great serpent.

Horror rooted Aurel to the spot. They stared, unable to move, as Sevila drove her heel against the attendant's shoulder, pinning him firmly in place as she knelt over him. He struggled against her, pushing frantically at her leg, her arms. When he struck blindly across her cheek, her head snapped to the side, and an animal snarl slipped from her throat. She raised her arm overhead; the slant of glass glinted as she plunged it into the side of his neck. A spray of blood darkened her black mourning robes, and when she stood, breathing raggedly, the fabric hung heavy around her knees and ankles.

The long splinter of glass broke in two as she flung it to the floor in disgust. She did not bother wiping her hands clean. When she walked back towards Aurel, her clothes faintly dripped, leaving a trail of glistening splotches in her wake. Sevila did not ask for the manuscript; she simply took it from Aurel's hands, and held it above the lamp.

Feeling numb, Aurel jerked away, but already the tall flame of the lamp had caught the corners of the manuscript, crackling to life. Aurel lurched forward to snatch the manuscript from her and frantically stamp it out, but before they could do so Sevila tossed it onto a nearby shelf filled with loose scrolls.

"What are you doing?" Aurel shouted. Dropping the lamp to the floor, they raced towards the fire, trying to put it out with their bare shadowy hands, only for them to pass straight through the flames and their robes to singe black at the edges. "Sevila! Stop this!"

Instead, she kicked the lamp and it rolled along the floor, trailing a line of oil that shimmered and burned. Her eyes caught the rising light until her face was suffused with it. Grabbing handfuls of scrolls and books from the shelves, she cast them towards the lamp, feeding the fire with a frenetic kind of fury. When Aurel reached out to stop her, she fixed them with a look so venomous they did not dare touch her.

"We're leaving." Sevila said, her voice hollow.

As she turned away, the fire began to spread, catching along the rolls of parchment, the stacks of books all lined evenly together, dry bits of parchment and vellum curling and blackening. On the floor, the attendant weltered in a pool of his own blood amidst shards of glass, while all around him the library was engulfed in a roar of flame.

Chapter 11

Smoke twisted like a black thread along the skyline. It rose from the squat tower of the library, a reed-thin tendril blotting the vast expanse of cloudless blue, while in the distance the ships hung their masts in the harbour with dark sails in honour of the Imperial funeral. Nobody paid the smoke a passing glance as Sevila stormed down the steps of the library, back the way they had entered not long before, followed closely by Aurel who, despite their long-legged stride, struggled to keep up. Already the four guards standing at attention at the front entrance of the library had been reduced to two, their numbers dwindling as more and more people flooded towards the centre of the city, towards the pyres waiting to be lit.

The flames had not yet cracked open the stone roof of the library, and neither of the remaining guards spared Sevila and Aurel more than a curious look.

Panic lancing through their chest, Aurel fixed the mask more firmly in place over their face, a nervous gesture. They jogged a few paces to catch up to Sevila, grabbing her by the shoulder and spinning her around as soon as they had rounded a corner down the street and were firmly out of sight.

"Where do you think you're going?" Aurel asked sharply. They cast a furtive glance towards the main street to ensure that they were alone.

"To make damn well sure they burn those bodies," Sevila growled. She tried to shrug off Aurel's grip, but the ink-black impression of their fingers only dug more firmly into her shoulder. She glared, and the look was deadly enough to strip flesh from bone. "Don't touch me."

"You can't!" Aurel snapped, but released her nonetheless. "You can't just burn them!"

"Watch me," Sevila snarled.

"No," Aurel said, and their voice grew dark. It shadowed the air around them. "You *can't*. You and I — we have a contract."

"Yes, to find your body." Sevila snapped. "Congratulations! I've found it for you! And now you get to watch me scatter its ashes in the sea!"

Aurel loomed over her, their eyes glowing bright and intense. When they spoke they sounded hollow, like an echo of words across blackened stone. "That was not the contract. You agreed to 'get my body back,' not 'find' it." Aurel towered, dark and shapeless as an oncoming storm. "You will honour our contract."

Sevila stared. She seemed to go cold and rigid all over — tense and still as a statue — and all around them a crushing nameless weight pressed in on all sides, squeezing. The silence tensed like a muscle, like a clenched fist. Her teeth ground together. Her face flickered with fury, with fear. The pressure built until a vein throbbed at her temple, until blood pooled at the corners of her mouth and trickled from her nose, until finally she gasped out, "Fuck!"

With the word came a shaky exhalation and a rush of blood dribbling down her chin. She hunched over, cradling her chest with one hand, and wiping her chin with the other. "Fuck!" she repeated, louder this time. She kicked at a loose cobblestone on the paved ground for good measure, stubbing her toe, and shouting, *"Fuck!"*

"Are you done?" Aurel glowered, crossing their arms.

"Damn you! And damn your contract!" Sevila spat. Redness stained her mouth, slicking her bared teeth. Some of the earlier wildness had returned to her now, this time tinged with desperation.

"What did you expect?" Aurel fired back, refusing to step down — not on this. Never on this. "You may be a heartless, soulless bastard, but not even you can break a contract."

"What I *expected* was to find a corpse! What I *expected—!*" she snarled with a choppy gesture towards the centre of town, "— wasn't this! And then I expected that you would — well — move on, so to speak!"

At that, Aurel gave her a level look. "You were going to abandon me the moment our contract was completed, weren't you?"

"I wasn't—!" Sevila floundered. She swallowed, and licked what remained of the blood from her teeth before admitting waspishly, "Alright, yes! But only after I had kept my end of the bargain!"

"Unbelievable," Aurel muttered under their breath with a shake of their masked head.

"As much as I appreciate your moral grandstanding," she sneered, "now is not the time. If we can't burn your body, then we need to steal them both back before those idiots, Theodoros and Isidore, do something they'll regret."

Sevila made to whirl around and stomp off once more towards where the funeral was due to take place shortly, but before she could get more than a step away, Aurel stopped her with a firm hand on her shoulder. She tensed, muscles coiled like a serpent curling upon itself to strike. When she looked over her shoulder at Aurel, her pupils had narrowed to knife slits. "What," she said, her voice soft and deadly, "did I say about touching me, darling?"

Aurel released her, but took a step closer, near enough that their long white robes brushed up against her shins. "That manuscript," Aurel began in a low tone. "What did it say?"

Sevila inhaled so sharply it sounded like a hiss. "Nothing."

"Bullshit." Aurel ignored her narrowed eyes, and pressed, "Over the course of our brief acquaintance, I have seen many sides of you, Sevila. But this fear — real fear — is new on you. And whatever you may think of me, we are partners, you and I. We need to work together. So, tell me."

Thoughtfully, Sevila tongued the inside of her cheek, weighing Aurel with her eyes, and for a moment it seemed she would not answer. Then, she sighed, and rubbed at her brow. "Necromancy, as you may have discovered, is all about balance. It is an exercise in equal exchange. Souls cannot be created or destroyed. Contracts must be kept. Tit for tat. Severing a soul from its body is one thing, but merging them is something else entirely." She paused to twist the rings around her fingers, and it was the nearest she came to wringing her hands. Biting her lower lip, she scowled at the glints of carnelian and gold over her knuckles. Aurel said nothing, waiting for her to continue. "I never knew exactly how to do it, but in theory I'd always assumed a soul could only ever be reunited with its own body. Theodoros and Isidore — well, their schemes never struck me as anything but flights of fancy. Pursuits in futility."

"And now you think otherwise," Aurel finished for her, their words slow. They frowned in puzzlement, their eyes shining through the dark slits of their ivory-carved mask. "This Helani text detailed how it could be done, and now you think Theodoros and Isidore can achieve whatever it is they're doing?"

Sevila chewed at her lower lip, then nodded sharply. "Yes."

"What aren't you telling me?" Aurel asked, suspicious.

"A severed soul can still only be merged with a body that has been severed, not just any old body. But this is—" Throwing her hands into the air, Sevila groaned in frustration. "We don't have time for all of this! Listen." She pointed at Aurel, fixing them with an intense, unblinking stare. "I will tell you everything you want to know after we snatch two dead bodies from under the noses of an angry mob and the empire's most powerful individuals. Satisfied?"

The sounds of the city clustered together in one area, leaving them surrounded by a false calm. No barking of dogs. No murmur of voices. No foot traffic thronging through the main thoroughfares. Just a distant roar in the forum a few streets down, like the rumble of thunder bearing the threat of rain. Behind them the library began to burn. Sighing, Aurel straightened their shoulders, and stepped away.

"No, but it will have to do for now." Resigned, Aurel gestured towards the main road with a wave of their hand. "Lead the way."

She swept by Aurel, not needing another invitation to take matters into her own hands. As they strode onto the main street leading towards the square, the harsh sunlight slanted across their backs, and shadows lengthened at their feet. From the library tower, smoke drifted over the rooftops, a single plume growing in size like an augury sign.

After a moment of trailing along beside Sevila in silence, Aurel muttered, "You didn't have to kill that man, and burn down the whole library, you know."

Sevila bared her teeth in an unpleasant, unsettling smile. "My dear, you have no earthly idea how wrong you are. I would follow in the Helani's footsteps and destroy every scrap of writing I could find, if it meant safeguarding the world against what abhorrent secrets I just read. Stitching together different bodies and different souls? Words fail me."

Aurel stared at her. "Is that what you think you're doing? Safeguarding the world? Like some kind of hero?"

She shot Aurel an offended look and hissed, "You take that back!"

With a shrug, Aurel said, "Suit yourself."

"*Some kind of hero!*" Sevila repeated, mimicking Aurel's deeper voice with aplomb as she stomped down the street. "How dare you! I've never been so insulted in my entire life!"

The closer they drew to the centre of Faros, the louder the noise became, a great thrumming chant, like the drone of a hive. Rats scurried along the drainage ditches beside the walls of buildings. A conical fountain filtered water down its brick facing, and from it a cat crouched to drink. Every corner they rounded, Aurel tensed in anticipation, expecting the worst. The avenues broadened beneath their feet, the buildings grew tall on either side, and Sevila led them unerringly onward until at last, they turned onto the forum.

All across the sprawling open space the crowd swarmed. People clustered and pressed and roiled around the enormous central pyre, and those that could not force their way to the front of the mass instead clambered atop the surrounding building steps and pillars to better see. The mountain of sticks that had been erected, awaiting the bodies, divided the crowd into two colours — one side in green, the other in blue, both baying like hounds lashed forward on a bloody hunt; the sound like a wave and the two sides meeting like the clash of two seas.

Sevila craned her neck before giving up, and tugging at Aurel's white robes. "Pick me up."

Wordlessly, Aurel did as requested. Placing their hands around the narrow of Sevila's waist, they lifted her onto one shoulder with ease, and there she perched. She squinted through the glare of the sun, which rose steadily towards its peak, and shielded her eyes with the flat of her hand over her brow.

"There!" Sevila pointed clear across the forum, where a line of guards — Cosmas' own men and Theodoros' so-called honour guard — drove the crowd back in a wedge formation. Behind them Aurel could just make out the figures of Cosmas and Theodoros slowly walking behind the litter-bearers that carried the two shrouded bodies.

"How are we supposed to get all the way over there?" Aurel peered around the forum, bristling with people, seeking a route but finding none.

Slipping from Aurel's shoulder, Sevila landed on the ground with a feline grace. Then, she shuffled in behind them, and prodded at their robes. "Just start walking. Go!"

Hesitant, Aurel stepped forward. The first few people that saw them did a double take, and fell over themselves to scramble out of Aurel's way. "Excuse me," Aurel grimaced as a man tripped and nearly dragged another down to the ground in his haste to move. "Sorry!"

Whenever Aurel's footsteps would falter, when they would stop so as not to run into anyone, Sevila would hiss directly behind them, "Keep going! For fuck's sake!"

The more densely packed the crowd became, the slower Aurel's movements grew. Behind them, Sevila crouched in Aurel's shadow, clinging to their robes and shuffling in their wake, while up ahead the pyre loomed, ever taller, stretching towards the sky. The two of them pressed onwards, and less than a stone's throw away, Cosmas and Theodoros mounted the steps to the pyre, leading the procession of imperial bodies. Bearing a lit torch, Isidore followed and with his other hand he led a little girl — no more than ten years of age. She walked with unwieldy steps beneath the bulky ceremonial silks she wore, her hair long and dark, her eyes large and black and fixed on the bodies carried just ahead of her, strategically positioned so that Cosmas could not easily turn to grab her.

The moment the crowd saw both her and Theodoros, the forum erupted into a wailing clangour. Despite Aurel's size, despite the aura of unease they unconsciously exuded, they were forced to a standstill as all around them the crowd seethed. People reached their hands out towards the pyre, straining to touch her, to catch even the barest glimpse of her. Through a mad forest of grasping hands and faces streaming with tears, Aurel could see Zoe flinch back from the uproar, and the chanting rose to a fervent pitch — cries for The Lord Regent and The Lady Invicta.

Over the din and the vast boiling throng, Aurel's gaze slid right across a figure — a tall woman with a broad-shouldered stride — walking just behind Zoe, clad in the dark robes of a College acolyte. Something tightened in Aurel's chest, searing hot and bright and unrelenting. They froze, staring. The woman's face was concealed in shadow beneath the black cowl, but Aurel could see the hint of dark skin, dark eyes in a lined faced, and iron-threaded hair. She moved heavily, her robes swinging with weight, as though her wrists were clapped in chains that trailed down to her knees.

"There she is," Aurel whispered, sounding breathless. They could not bear even the idea of tearing their eyes away from her.

"Yes," Sevila murmured. "The Lady Aelia Glabaina."

Aurel turned to look at her in confusion. "No. My body."

Sevila jerked as if physically struck. "That—?" she pointed, her tone incredulous. "—is your body? Not—?"

When her finger moved towards the shroud-wrapt body of the late Empress Iustina, Aurel shook their head.

"Well, shit," Sevila muttered.

On the raised pyre platform, Theodoros lifted his hands for silence. Instead the Blues thundered their approval, cheering while the Greens bellowed their loathing from the opposite side. Theodoros' grave expression grew strained, and beside him Cosmas gripped the hilt of her sword, her shoulders tense, her gaze darting to and fro. She sent constant glances towards Zoe, but could not edge around the pyre towards her, forced to stand on Theodoros' other side with the eyes of all the city upon her.

"We need to get up there." Sevila frowned at the pyre, then at the teeming mass of bodies that separated them from it. Aurel had to hunch over to hear her over the clamour. "We need to grab Aelia, and run."

"Run where?"

"Anywhere but here."

The bodies of Iustina and Leo were mounted atop the pyre, side by side. A member of the Blues crowd threw a hand-fashioned laurel crown at Theodoros' feet. On the platform, both Theodoros and Cosmas went very still, staring at the crown as though it were a snake.

"Autokrator!" the Blues began to yell. *"Autokrator!"*

Hearing the cries of the opposition, the Greens went wild. A howl of outrage rose up from the forum, and the crowd whipped itself into a frenzy.

"No," Sevila hissed under her breath. "No no no no no!"

Without waiting for Aurel, she began shoving her way forward. "Get out of the way!" she snarled to everyone yet nobody in particular. A few people recoiled when she pushed them, as if repulsed by her touch, but most ignored her. She caught an elbow to the side of her cheek, and her head snapped back.

"Sevila!" Aurel darted forward, grabbing the man who had hit her, and lifting him from the ground with one hand as though he weighed nothing at all. Tossing him aside, Aurel straightened Sevila with a hand on her shoulder.

She shook them off with a growl. "I'm fine! Now, get us up there!"

Above them, Isidore stepped forward, and — together with Zoe — touched the tip of the torch to the base of the pyre. The oil-soaked wood caught the flame and cast it about, and in a roar the fire spread, climbing towards the bodies and clawing the air. Through the haze of sparks and heat, Aurel could see their body — Aelia, they said under their breath, over and over like a prayer. Aelia Glabas. Aelia. *Aelia.* As if the name made her more real, less out-of-reach. Taking hold of Sevila's wrist, and dragging her along,

Aurel shouldered their way through the crowd, wading through the sea of people teeming all around them, a city gone mad in its collective grief.

Theodoros was shouting something at Isidore, battling his way back towards the steps while people from the crowd seized his ankles. He had to yank himself free, stumbling back, and nearly falling into the fire. Cosmas snatched at his arm before he could plummet into flame. Her face was alight with anger, and she snarled something that made him go pale. Yanking his arm free, Theodoros fled, Isidore well ahead of him. The honour guard parted a path through the crowd, closing ranks behind them and protecting the group from view — Theodoros, Isidore, Zoe, and Aelia vanishing behind them.

Cosmas gestured sharply, yelling orders to her own men, who attempted to give chase but the crowd closed in, swarming. She caught sight of Aurel and Sevila, struggling against the tide. Face darkening, Cosmas barked something at two of her guardsmen, and drew her sword. All three of them approached, shoving aside people until Cosmas was near enough to grab Sevila's other wrist, and yank.

"This way!" Cosmas jerked her head in the opposite direction of where Theodoros and the others had left.

"But—!" Aurel began to object at the same time Sevila shouted, "Cosmas, not now!"

"Yes, now!" Cosmas tightened her grip on her sword, which glinted in the harsh sunlight. Behind her the pyre blazed so that she appeared wreathed in flame. Fire glinted from the scales of her black armour. "Come with me, or you'll get torn limb from limb by a mob! Your choice!"

Swearing loudly, Sevila allowed herself to be pulled along from their goal. Aurel followed, but did not release her until the three of them were surrounded by a wall of Cosmas' men. A dozen armoured guards jostled their shoulders together, steadily marching their way from the forum and towards the barracks. Aurel stood a head above even the tallest of them, and peered back as they rounded a corner. Behind them, the mob turned upon itself, tearing burning clubs from the pyre's base. Smoke streamed from the pyre, and in the distance flames rolled down from the library tower, spreading to adjacent buildings.

Three streets down, the barracks rose above the other surrounding structures. Cosmas sheathed her sword as their party passed through the gates, which swung shut behind them with a laboured groan, pushed closed by four guards on either side of the doors. As soon as they were through, Cosmas gestured towards the parapets, where two more men cranked a wheel affixed to the ground. In a clatter of chains, they lowered a series of three thick heavy bars into place, locking the gates from within, while outside the mob seethed, slamming their fists against the banded iron exterior. Some even attempted to scale the walls, and Aurel could see guards along the battlements flinging rocks to knock them loose before they could climb too high. Despite this, the guards never drew the bows slung across their back, though a few of them ran their fingers along the fletched arrows that bristled in their quivers in anticipation of a fight.

"Congratulations, Cosmas. You're now in charge of a city possessed with its own furore," Sevila drawled. She jerked her arm away from Aurel, and wiped the blood from her face, patting pale dust from the hems of her rich silk attire. Motes glittered in the sunlight and she waved them away with an irritable scowl, coughing. "And you let those idiots abscond with Aelia and your beloved Zoe, too. Well done!"

Rounding on her, Cosmas seized the front of Sevila's robes. "What did you do?"

"Me?" Sevila pushed at Cosmas' gauntlets in outrage with very little effect; she might as well have been shoving with all her might against the iron-barred gates that loomed above them. "Nothing! This isn't my fault!"

Cosmas loosened her hold on Sevila's black mourning robes, but did not release her. "Enough with the bullshit, Sevila! It was you! Somehow, it always comes back to you!"

"Even I don't have the power to control every nuance in the political landscape of this shithole empire!" Sevila snapped. "This city was always going to turn on itself! I didn't do anything to precipitate this!"

"She burned down the library," Aurel answered instead. "And she murdered one of its attendants."

"You what!" Cosmas growled. Her hands tightened around a fistful of black silk, strangling the fabric rather than throttling Sevila.

"Aurel!" Sevila glared at them, aghast.

Crossing their arms, Aurel met her gaze head-on, glower for glower. "I think it time you explain yourself. Well past time, in fact."

"I'm not—!" Sevila began.

Before she could splutter more than a few syllables, Aurel cut her off. "You promised. Back at the library." They stepped forward and hunched over, lowering their voice so that it could be heard by Cosmas and Sevila alone. "Need I remind you about our little discussion earlier? About contracts and keeping them?"

A noise escaped Sevila then like a strangled snarl, the sound an animal made when its leg was caught in a snare, and it tried to chew itself free. For a moment, she struggled against Cosmas' hold on her, her movements jerky and involuntary, an internal thrashing that showed across her face as her lip curled in a rictus sneer. Finally, she relented with an angry huff of air through her nose.

"I'm not doing it here!" Sevila gestured around towards all of Cosmas' guardsmen, pretending not to watch the scene unfolding before them. Then she added quickly, "And I'm not doing it in a prison cell, either!"

"You'll be lucky if a cell is all I put you in." Cosmas let go of Sevila, only to turn her around by the shoulder, and shove her towards the barracks that towered at the centre of the square.

"There's no need to push. Where else am I supposed to go? Back out there?" Sevila jerked a thumb over her shoulder towards the walls and the city encircling them. In the distance smoke curled from the rooftops as flames licked along the buildings that the mob had set alight to match the funeral pyre. "You couldn't pay me to face down that mindless horde."

"They're not mindless. They're angry and grieving. Which is something I can sympathise with." Cosmas pushed at Sevila again, just to irritate her, earning a fierce scowl. "Now, move!"

Cosmas guided them onwards, and as the three of them crossed the yard towards the squat fortress, guardsmen would stop and salute to their Captain. For the most part Cosmas ignored them, walking briskly enough that her military cloak flared and snapped at her heels. Many of the guards shot Aurel quick nervous glances as they passed, and Aurel yearned for the weight of the armour they had left behind at their rooms in the palace.

Through the front door and up the steep stone steps that curled in a tight spiral pattern all the way to the top floor, Cosmas led them, occasionally giving Sevila a gruff nudge for good measure. Each time this happened, Sevila's shoulders drew more and more tense, and while her face remained cool and impassive, her eyes gleamed with a dangerous edge. At this point, Aurel reached forward and tapped Cosmas' shoulder. When Cosmas frowned at them, Aurel simply shook their head in warning. The furrow in Cosmas' brow deepened, but she stopped nonetheless.

On the top floor at the end of the hall, two guards flanked the door to Cosmas' personal office. The moment they stepped inside, it was apparent that she spent more time here at work than she did in the luxurious halls of her family's palatial home located just a hill away. A plate of simple bread, cured meats, dried fruits, and a hard rind of cheese sat on her desk atop stacks of leather-bound notes, scraps of vellum, and wax tablets set in wooden frames. Along one wall stood a rack of spare weapons — notched swords and whetstones — beside a frame holding her usual armour and yellow-dyed cloak. In a corner behind the desk there squatted a cot rumpled with bedsheets. Unlit lamps hung by chains from the low-slung ceiling. Aurel had to stoop to walk.

Cosmas slammed the door shut once the three of them were inside, and jammed a bar down to lock the door in place. Then she gripped the hilt of the sword at her hip, remaining in front of the door as though she suspected they would make a run for it at any moment. "What else have you been keeping from me? What other ruinous, earth-splitting secrets could one woman possible have?"

Shooting both Cosmas and Aurel a sour, guarded look, Sevila crossed the room to perch herself on the edge of the writing desk. In the process, she purposefully knocked over a stack of notes to the floor, brushing aside a few more as she pulled the plate of food into her lap. "Your bread is stale," Sevila said around a mouthful.

In answer, Cosmas unsheathed her sword halfway, baring iron.

Sevila lifted one eyebrow, and gestured with a chunk of salted meat that she then stuck into her mouth, mumbling, "Is that supposed to impress me?"

Reaching over, Aurel placed a hand over Cosmas'. Their touch was soft, but still Cosmas flinched away from them as if the swirls of ink-dark shadow that formed into fingers had burned her. With an apologetic sigh, Aurel withdrew their hand. Regardless, Cosmas' frown lessened somewhat, and she sheathed her sword.

"Thank you," Aurel murmured before turning to Sevila, who watched the interaction with an air of smug satisfaction. Immediately, Aurel scowled at her. "Stop smiling. You still owe me an explanation."

Something indecipherable flickered in Sevila's eyes. She held Aurel's steady gaze for a long moment before finally looking away. She leaned over Cosmas desk, and began digging through drawers. "Of course, you don't have any wine. You can't be normal and have a vice like everyone else." When both Cosmas and Aurel glared, she rolled her eyes. "I, for one, like to get good and drunk before I start telling tales of personal drama."

"Something has you scared," Aurel stepped forward to yank the plate away from her. She glared but did not lunge or snatch the food back. Tossing it aside onto the desk once more, Aurel continued, "Theodoros and Isidore want my body for another soul, and now they have the knowledge and the means to accomplish it. But that can't be it. You wouldn't be afraid of a human soul; you're not afraid of me. Were you wrong? Have they found a god?"

Mouth pursing to a narrow line, Sevila said, "No. Well — yes. Technically speaking."

Cosmas clenched her teeth, and tilted her head back to look heavenward as though praying for strength. "You can never just speak plainly, can you?"

Sevila did not answer. She was meeting Aurel's gaze with an unreadable stare of her own, her fists going white and bloodless in her lap while one foot swung, drumming her heel against the desk in a nervous tick. She did not seem to need to blink.

Aurel cocked their head, and their mask scraped against the ceiling. Stooping down once more, Aurel said, "It's yours, isn't it? But that wouldn't make any sense unless you were a—?" It dawned on them. "You're a god."

Sevila's golden eyes flashed, and she tilted her chin up, shoulders straightening. "Only half god. Trust me, it's plenty."

"You told me all the gods were as good as dead! Or was that a lie as well?" Aurel accused, stepping forward.

Brow darkening, Sevila snapped, "Haven't you been listening to anything I've said? I am dead! I've been dead for years! From the moment I cut that thing from my chest! And good riddance!"

Cosmas had gone quiet at her side of the room, her eyes wide, her hands holding a fine tremble as she clutched the ornate hilt at her hip as though it were a lifeline. "What god?" she asked, her voice hoarse. "What god are you?"

"Does it matter?" Sevila asked.

"What god?" Cosmas repeated, more firmly this time.

Shrugging as though against an uncomfortable snag of cloth across her skin, Sevila pretended to find the cleaning of her nails fascinating as she answered, "I am, or rather I was the demigod of hunger and famine, the tutelary deity of serpents and travellers. My father was a human nobody from Aegryph. My mother was a primordial goddess of chaos, mischief, and crossroads. Some of her more charming hobbies involved giving bad directions to wanderers, bargaining for souls on moonless nights, turning her mortal lovers into eternally faithful hounds, and starting wars between nations just to watch their cities burn."

"Last night at the gathering, you said your siblings were—" Aurel had no lungs, but they made a noise like the low hiss of air. "You killed them. All of them. You ate them."

Sevila bared her teeth. "Of course, I did, darling. I ate and hoarded everything. Hunger was my purpose. Do you mind?" She pointed to the plate of food that Aurel had tossed onto the desk. Without waiting for an answer, she picked up the last heel of bread and tore off a mouthful. As she chewed, she said, "It would be such a waste."

From the side, Aurel heard a clunk of two objects colliding, and when they turned it was to find that Cosmas had backed up against the door. Her scabbard hung from her waist at an awkward angle, the sword hilt jutting forward from when it had hit the wall. "You're the reason why they're all gone. All of the gods — you subsumed them. You—" Cosmas looked like she was going to be sick. She put a shaking hand over her mouth.

"And you wonder why I keep my secrets," Sevila sneered, polishing off what remained of the food. She gestured at Cosmas with the plate. "You're taking it better than others. Most people either prostrate themselves before me, or try to rope me down to a pyre for public burning, or worse."

Slowly, Cosmas gathered herself, lowering her hands to her side, swallowing past the dryness in her throat. "This is all your fault. If not for you, Isidore never would have gone into the desert hunting for lost gods. The Helani never would have pushed so far south. Theodoros never would have had the opportunity to overthrow his Empress, and murder her in cold—!"

"My fault!" Sevila repeated. "I didn't do anything other than what was necessary to survive! I refuse to apologise for that! You have no idea what it's like! Don't you dare—!"

Raising their hands in a soothing gesture, Aurel stepped between the two of them, and said, "This may not be your fault, but it is — ultimately — your responsibility, Sevila."

"You're taking her side?" Cosmas reared back to stare at Aurel in utter incredulity. "You, of all people—!"

"I'm not—!" Aurel began, but Cosmas cut them off.

"Her very existence defies the rightful laws of nature! Every aspect of it, no less!" Cosmas spat. She turned her thunderous gaze upon Sevila. "What you are, your state of living — if you can even call it that — is worth than death. At least a corpse is fed upon by other creatures, and fulfils the cycle of things. Aurel, I can understand; this fate was thrust upon them most unjustly. But you—!" Cosmas jabbed an accusing finger at Sevila, whose face had darkened, whose eyes had gone very gold, very bright. "You are an abomination of your own making!"

"And what was I supposed to do?" Sevila snarled, her voice dropping to a low raspy note in her chest. She clutched the plate in a white-knuckled grasp. "What was I to do when hunger consumed everything? When I lost all sense of self, all notion of the world beyond the borders of my own appetites? The hunger embodied in me could drain the very breath from those who stood in my presence, a thirst never slaked, only heightened the more I ate. Hunger fed with hunger. All life existed only to be victuals for my urges. By making myself an abomination, I saved this wretched world and all the worlds beyond it! And for what!"

On any given day, Sevila was a woman small and slight of build. Now however, her presence filled a space larger than herself until she seemed to loom. Looking at her felt like looking at a mountain in the distance, larger than anything in her surroundings, a being poured out and scattered like a flash of oil, like a torrent of fire, like an object of nature wearing a painted mask in a cheap caricature of humanity. Her words teemed with a deep and fathomless weight. "Do not speak to me of life and living! What I was before this — before I became what you see now — that was not living. Even then, I was already dead. Of all the options available to me, this—!" She gestured to herself. "—this was the best I could manage! And yet, after all that, I still feel it sometimes: famine like a phantom pain. Now when I eat, I may not be fulfilled but for once I am *full,* and I can stop."

She flung the empty plate to the floor, where it clattered at Cosmas' feet. Cosmas flinched, but did not step away. Standing, Sevila moved with an eerie grace, the cowl draped across her head never fluttering despite the quickness of her motions. Her eyes shone, over-bright, and the muscles, the sinew, and bone shifted beneath, too loose. She wore human skin like she might wear ill-fitting clothes. Aurel looked at Sevila as though seeing her for the first time, when they'd lifted their head, lost and abandoned in a desert village, to see a silhouette with burning eyes standing in the doorway, shrouded in a slant of sunlight. How unearthly she had been from the very start. How fitting that she had been the one to find them.

When she spoke again, her voice had not lost its uncanny timbre. She seemed to speak from great cavernous depths. She pointed to the ground, and the stones there nearly trembled with the burden. "You should be thanking me. You should be on your knees, kissing my feet. You should be building another great temple in my name, trumpeting my glory, begging for my mercy." Sevila gestured towards the window, where the Temple of Wisdom could be seen in the distance amidst braids of cinder and smoke rising up through the air. "You think sixty years of civil war ended overnight because Iustina's father was an outstanding tactician and general? Because he wasn't. I know. I was there. He struck a deal with me, traded bodies for his victory, leading men to their deaths like fodder to appease my hunger. Your all-important, all-powerful family owes its throne to me."

Cosmas' face had gone slack with shock. Her mouth worked, but no words came out. The silence stretched like a palpable thing, like a body of water or a length of ragged cloth.

"And now Theodoros and Isidore have a god soul on their side." Aurel said softly.

"We need—" Cosmas began, finding her voice though it sounded scratchy. "We need to understand the nature of their contract so we can plan accordingly."

"Finally, a useful comment," Sevila sneered. "I know my soul — I know it well — which means that with me, you have the best chance you'll ever get at surviving the coming storm." Sevila raised her veil so that the lower half of her face was covered, the gold embroidery thick and glinting in the fading afternoon light streaming through the open windows. She spoke calmly, rationally, but the tips of her fingers trembled so finely Aurel might have missed it if they hadn't been looking for any hint of unease. "In the event that my soul found another host, and was able to not simply possess it, but truly inhabit it, I've already thought of an elaborate plan. It goes something like this. Step one: Run."

Chapter 12

The city began to burn in earnest. Rolling flames, and rolling cries, and rooftops rushing down to their ruin. Buildings caved in upon themselves, leaving husks of marble with tinderbox filling. Through the window of Cosmas' office, ensconced upon its guard tower, they could see the wheeling smoke that smote the sky, the sun's rays filtering darkly through, and inside a tense silence — poised on the cliffside of eruption — reigned.

Of the three gathered there, only Cosmas breathed. Sevila's chest remained eerily still, every muscle taut, as though under normal circumstances she had to force herself to maintain human airs, but now she had forgotten. She had discarded her guises; behind her the sun dimmed, and the city consumed itself in flame.

Following Sevila's announcement, Cosmas said in a voice hoarse but unwavering in her convictions, "That's not going to happen."

Sevila shrugged. "Take my advice or leave it. It makes no difference to me. Personally, I'll be on the first ship out of here once this riot has settled down."

"We burned the bodies. Theodoros and Isidore don't have anything, and for all we know they could still be in the city," Cosmas insisted. "I've already ordered my men to shut down every door, gate, and secret passage to and from Faros. Nobody is leaving without my say so. Especially not you."

Sevila scoffed with a rueful chuckle, as though she found the entire situation amusing, "You can't keep me here."

"No," Cosmas agreed, then she tilted her head towards Aurel. "But they can."

To that Sevila could make no snappish reply. Her eyes narrowed at Cosmas, who — for all her brave front — swallowed, and tried to force her hands to stop shaking by curling them into fists.

"You're wrong about one thing," Aurel said. "They still have my body — Aelia Glabas."

"And if we'd been allowed access to the library sooner, we might have been able to foil their plans entirely," Sevila snapped at Cosmas, whose eyes had gone wide. "But, no! You had to rope us into this civil war nonsense!"

"The empire—" Cosmas began, her voice trembling somewhat.

Sevila looked at her with an unblinking gaze. The skin of Sevila's face seemed suspended from animation, too smooth, too still. When she took a step forward, Cosmas shrank away from her as though afraid to be touched.

"Do you know what your empire means to me?" Sevila said softly, dangerously. "Fuck all."

Aurel put a gentle hand on Sevila's shoulder. Beneath their touch, she stiffened but did not shrug them away. "We still have a chance to take my body back before Theodoros and Isidore leave the city," Aurel murmured. They squeezed her shoulder before removing their hand. "This is our window of opportunity."

Sevila glared up at them. "Less of a window and more a crack in the wall. A very small chink in proverbial armour. I don't like our chances."

"We've travelled all this way together. We can't give up now."

"I'm not planning on giving up. I'm planning on surviving." Sevila corrected. "If you — both of you — had any sense, you'd do the same."

"There is more to this situation than you realise," Cosmas added. "I alone control over half of the empire's wealth and armed forces. Theodoros needs to secure his position back at Pala if he wants to make this fight last. Even if he and Isidore escape, I can hound them in their retreat all the way back to the capital. By the time they arrive, their resources will be drained, their men exhausted, and their bridges burned with all members of the nobility — especially once word gets out that we have proof he murdered his own kin."

"You keep talking about resources and money and men as if they mean something!" Sevila said. "Theodoros only has to fight long enough for Isidore to complete the ritual that puts my soul in the body of Aelia Glabas! That's it! Everybody loses!"

Shaking her head, Cosmas replied, "Surely, having a body would make it more vulnerable. Maybe the trick is actually to wait until Isidore completes the ritual, and then we kill it."

Sevila's mouth wrenched open to deliver a scathing retort, but she paused. She turned the thought over in her head. Her brows furrowed, and she drew in a deep breath before shaking herself as if from sleep. Then she muttered faintly to herself, "I can't believe I'm even entertaining this idea."

Appalled, Aurel burst out, "You can't kill my body! I need that!"

"I thought you were the self-sacrificing sort," Sevila drawled.

"I—!" Aurel couldn't summon a reply.

"I sympathise with you, my friend," Cosmas sighed. "But in this case, we must look at the bigger picture."

Yanking her veil back down, Sevila fluttered her hand as if fanning herself. "Cosmas, are you actually agreeing with me? I feel faint!"

Cosmas glowered, and looked like she'd just bitten into a lemon.

Staring between the two of them, Aurel mumbled, "I don't believe this."

"I know, right!" Sevila's mouth curved into a lopsided grin, but quickly faded when she saw the expression on Aurel's face. "Darling, what's wrong?"

The hems of Aurel's white robes trembled. The walls did not close in so much as empty out, and the world was a vast barren space. Looking down at their hands, the ink-black wisps hinting at finger bones, Aurel watched as their lack of flesh and blood dwindled into the air like dark fire. Through the pale cloth of their robes, Aurel could see the dull crimson light from their chest, a hushed glow. The words tumbled forth, and Aurel heard them as though from a great distance. "For years the empire has had my service, my patience, my life, and loyalty. But this is—" Their voice cracked like a naked shin-bone against rock. Aurel clenched their hands and when they lifted their head, their eyes burned. "This is too much. You cannot have this as well. This is the only thing that is unquestionably mine. You must find another way."

"Aurel—" Sevila began, her smile turning placating.

When she reached out to soothe, to place her hands over their own, Aurel lurched forward, and seized her by the wrists. Her bones felt like nothing beneath the strength of Aurel's grip. They could squeeze and snap her in two. Their voice shook with the force of raw feeling that seared in their chest. "You must find another way. We have a contract. You can't—! You have to—!"

Sevila did not try to wrestle her way free, she did not move away at all. Her hands remained slack in Aurel's grasp, and she gazed up at them, her brow furrowed, searching Aurel's face.

"Aurel," she started again, and though her voice held a warm velvet burr, her expression remained cold and unreadable, "I never promised to get your body back *alive.*"

Aurel tightened their grip. "Don't do this, Sevila. Please—" they choked. "I'm begging you. This is all I have left."

Sevila drew closer, and Aurel could not find the strength to hold her away, to keep her at arm's length as she said, "I know it may seem dismal now, but in time you'll find that this existence is not as bleak as it seems."

Mutely, Aurel shook their head. Their hold weakened, and Sevila pried her hands free. She did not blink, yet the skin of her wrists mottled and peeled, reddened with blisters from the severity of Aurel's touch. Aurel tried hiding their face in their hands, but Sevila tugged lightly at the sleeves of their robes.

"Now, now. Enough of that," she murmured. Reaching up — her wrists already starting to heal over with fresh skin — she cupped Aurel's face between her palms as if holding smoke between her fingers. "Know that I don't say this lightly, but — If

I could find another way, I would. Also, whatever it is you're doing with your face: stop it. It makes me feel awful."

From the side, Cosmas cleared her throat. "If we're lucky, it will never come to that. We don't even know where Sevila's soul is, let alone — wait. You don't think they brought it *here,* do you?" Cosmas asked, looking horrified at the very thought.

Sevila laughed, an ugly sound. "Trust me, if it were here, you would already know."

"What can we do against something like that?" Aurel mumbled. "They have a god soul. What do we have?"

"We have you, darling. Aren't we lucky!" Patting Aurel's cheeks one last time, and sending up little wisps of cloudy ink. Sevila smiled at them, revealing teeth. Aurel saw Cosmas stiffen, gripping the hilt of her sword.

Aurel gave her a flat look. "I was hoping you would reveal some hidden power you still retained, being that you are half god."

With a derisive sniff, Sevila said, "Which just shows how little you actually know about gods. Without a soul I retain very little of my former self. And even with a frail human body like yours, my soul would be a force to be reckoned with. More vulnerable than in my own body, surely, but powerful all the same."

"I still have the larger army," Cosmas reminded them.

"Yes, and it's a week's march away. How convenient," Sevila sneered.

"So," Aurel said, asking the question nobody else seemed to want to touch, "what do we do now?"

Rubbing at her eyes, Cosmas sighed, "We wait."

"Wait?" Sevila repeated. "No, no, no. We can't just sit around, while Isidore and Theodoros run amok! We must act quickly!"

"What would you have me do?" The dark circles beneath Cosmas' eyes had, if anything, only grown more pronounced as the day went on. As she leaned her back against the door, she looked more tired than ever. "I already have my men patrolling the gates, and the chain lifted in the harbour. There's no way Theodoros and Isidore will get out without my knowledge."

Sevila's voice slipped to a low note. "You need to do whatever it takes! Put this city to the sword, if you must! I don't care!"

"But I do." Some of Cosmas' backbone returned in full force. Her shoulders had slumped, but her jaw remained set at a bullish angle, her eyes black and hard as river stone slate. "The last time an emperor turned his soldiers loose on his own people, the capital burned for three straight days. He had to repent in front of a crowd by crawling on his hands and knees to kiss the High Priest's feet on the steps of the great Temple of Three in the capital. I won't make that same mistake."

"Crawl, then!" Sevila snapped. "After which, you can slip a sword between his ribs, when nobody's looking! Or make a point of it, and kill Isidore in front of everyone. Who cares?"

Cosmas stared at her in utter shock. "Sometimes I hear words come out of your mouth, and I—" Shaking her head, she growled, "I won't kill Isidore. And I won't allow him to be killed by you, either."

Sevila gaped. *"What?"*

Straightening her shoulders, Cosmas said, "He holds the most sacred office of this empire. It is illegal to kill him."

"Fuck your laws!" Sevila hissed. "He cannot be allowed to live! He knows too much!"

Her expression going stony, Cosmas spoke evenly, as if reciting a long-memorised text, "It is my duty to ensure the peace and prosperity of this empire, and to secure the rights of its people. That includes Isidore."

"The man is scum!" Sevila's voice rose to a shout. "Worse! He is dangerous scum! He betrayed your family, plotted against your great aunt and your nephew, murdered them in cold blood — all of this to serve the whims of my soul! All of this because he believes that I am this empire's saviour! Look at me, Cosmas." Sevila pointed to herself, to her slitted snake eyes, which gleamed a rich molten gold, like floating dross trapped in a crucible. "Do I seem like hero material to you?"

"Is this another one of your rhetorical questions? Or do you actually expect an answer this time?" Cosmas replied dryly.

"Isidore lives. I will make sure he does not spread his knowledge, or harm any other person. The only way he dies is of natural causes."

Hands clenched, the muscles of Sevila's jaw leapt as she ground her teeth. "And what of Theodoros?"

At that, Cosmas smiled. "Oh, you can kill him in whatever manner pleases you. There is no sacred protection that shrouds one who holds the title of Lord Regent."

From the side, Aurel made a noise as if to speak, but stopped when both Cosmas and Sevila turned to look at them.

"Not you, too," Sevila groaned. "What, then? What is it?"

"Well, Theodoros is my blood—" Aurel began.

"He murdered you," both Cosmas and Sevila said in unison, their gazes alternatively blunt and incredulous.

"Yes," Aurel said, their voice weak and uncertain. "Yes, he did. But I would like to — I mean — I just want to know why, before we make him a pincushion for arrows."

Rolling her eyes, Sevila turned to exchange a glance with Cosmas. Something unseen and unspoken passed between them, before Cosmas shrugged. Then, with a few muttered obscenities under her breath, Sevila said, "Alright, fine. But I make no promises. If keeping him alive jeopardises the mission somehow, I'm killing him. Answers, or no answers. Agreed?"

Aurel nodded. "Agreed."

"Wonderful." Sighing, Sevila looked down at the empty plate she had thrown earlier to the floor. "I don't suppose this barracks has a convenient wine cellar located beneath the prison cells? We might be here a while."

For a moment, Cosmas merely pursed her lips, but then she relented. Turning, she lifted the latch barring the door. "I'll ask one of my men to bring you something. In the meantime, I must see to the city, and minimise as much damage as possible." She started to open the door, then she stopped. Hesitating, Aurel watched her mull over something, her brows furrowed in nervous thought, before she said over her shoulder, "Please, just — don't cause any more trouble. Stay here."

"Are we your prisoners again?" Sevila drawled, crossing her arms as she leaned her hip against the edge of Cosmas' desk.

Meanwhile, Aurel bent over to begin retrieving the notes and tablets she had knocked over when they first entered.

"No," Cosmas said. She studied Sevila and Aurel with a faintly bemused expression on her face. "I don't know what you are."

ᛪ

The robes were too loose on Aurel's form, too light. Feeling like they would dissipate into a black mist at any moment, Aurel opened the door through which Cosmas had passed hours ago. Behind them, Sevila sat in the windowsill overlooking the barracks, perched in the arched opening with one foot tucked up beneath her, hawk-like. In her lap, she cradled a platter of food, picking idly at it while she watched the empire's richest city smoulder. The air had thickened into a fire-riddled haze, and the cries of the angry mob had died down to a low simmer in the distance — or perhaps that was the crash of waves against the harbour. Sevila had to squint, and every now and then she would cough, but Aurel felt no difference.

"Where do you think you're going?" Sevila asked without looking over. She tore a leg of roast fowl from the gold-skinned carcass, picked neatly, thoroughly clean. Her fingers glistened with fatty oils and yellowed slicks of cardamom and saffron.

Hand on the door frame, Aurel paused. "I want armour. I feel uncomfortable. Do you want more to eat? I can get it for you on my way back from the requisitions officer."

As she fixed her teeth into the fowl's thigh, Sevila glanced over at them, her eyes sweeping over Aurel's ivory mask. Chewing, her brow furrowed in contemplation, she eventually sighed, "I always want more."

"Alright. Then I'll—"

"You misunderstand me." Sevila cut them off. Placing the stripped bone into the fowl's rib cage, she licked her fingers clean, her tongue a dart of movement, silver and pink. For a moment Aurel could have sworn it was twin-tined like a snake's. "What I meant was: no. But thank you."

Before Aurel could respond, the sound of boots marching along stone echoed down the long hallways leading to the office. Ducking down, they peered through the door to see Cosmas heading their way. She had exchanged her black-fired ceremonial armour for her more practical everyday wear — all but her helm, which she had discarded somewhere along the way. As she drew closer, Aurel's eyes widened. A gash sliced along Cosmas upper lip, parallel to the long scar that ran from brow to jaw, and bruising was already beginning to form, swelling the dark skin of her cheek.

Aurel stood back to allow her entry. "Is everything alright?"

Pausing at the threshold, Cosmas blinked up at them. "What?"

In answer, Aurel pointed to her recent injuries. She tongued at the wound at her lip with a wince. Then, running a hand through her dishevelled hair, she waved Aurel's concern aside. "Don't worry about me. What's important is I've managed to rally the city guilds to work together with my men, and contain most of the burning. There's still fighting near the palatial district, but it's starting to die down for the most part." Jerking her hand in a sharp gesture, Cosmas continued, "Come. Theodoros and Isidore have been spotted heading towards the western gate. My men will hold them for as long as they can, but we need to go. Immediately."

Sevila placed the platter on the windowsill, and stood. Crossing over to Cosmas' spare rack of armour in the corner, she cleaned her hands on the cloak there before lifting the dark veil to cover the lower half of her face. Her gold-stitched hems were caked with red. As she spoke, her eyes seemed to alight with intensity. "Lead the way, then."

With a brisk nod, Cosmas turned, and strode back the way she had come. Aurel held the door open for Sevila, and the two of them followed, matching Cosmas' clipped pace. When they approached the barracks gate, Cosmas barked orders left and right. Twenty guardsmen fell into line behind them, and the gate ahead groaned open. Through them, their party marched, two abreast, led by Cosmas, her cloak streaming like a gold-embroidered banner in her wake.

Any citizens that crossed their path through the city alternatively ignored them entirely, or scrambled out of their way.

Aurel raised their gaze to the smoking palatial hill, then to the library tower, which continued to blaze like a marital torch. Cosmas' men had erected barriers along the fire-blackened streets, turning away citizens who sought to risk their lives by entering their homes. Down one alleyway, people ferried buckets and pumps filled with water in an attempt to salvage what they could. Down another, guardsmen battled with unruly gangs of Blues and Greens, forcing them apart, prying them off one another.

Beneath one set of gated walls, their group passed. Then another. Then, at last, the final layer of Faros' defensive walls rose above them, and at the gate leading to the western road towards Pala, a small crowd had gathered. Theodoros' honour guard stood in formation before their charges between Cosmas' men along the walls and those overseeing the gates. All had souls summoned at their sides, a sentry of wild boars and jackals.

"In the name of your rightful empress, I demand that you open these gates, and let us pass!" Theodoros ordered. Zoe stood by his side, and whenever she would try to take a step away, he would tighten his grip on her hand, and pull her closer, as though afraid she would be snatched from him at any moment.

Lifting her voice, Cosmas called out, "You're not going anywhere."

Upon hearing her, Theodoros whirled about. He pulled Zoe behind him, shielding her from Cosmas, but still the little girl peered around the edge of Theodoros' cloak. Ash smudged her royal finery from their flight through the city, but apart from her expression of wide-eyed unease, she appeared unharmed. Half of the honour guard turned as well to face the new influx of enemies, though the other half continued to watch the men along the walls.

Now, surrounded on both sides, Theodoros' usual calm expression began to slip. His dark eyes roved ceaselessly, seeking a way out, concocting some stratagem that could allow him to slip away, unscathed. On the other hand, Isidore clasped his hands together, unruffled and composed; he looked like he could have been giving an audience to his constituents. And at his side, Aelia Glabas stood, swathed in dark robes. The cowl had fallen back across her shoulders, revealing her lined face, her greying hair and broad, stooped shoulders. No emotion, no comprehension crossed her features. She stared blankly on, her eyes black and vacant. A ropey pink scar peaked along her throat and collarbone, descending down her chest beneath the robes, evidence of Isidore's fumbling attempt to sever her soul.

Coming to stop a short distance away, Cosmas held up a clenched fist over her shoulder, calling for a silent halt. Her guards answered with a stamp of their boots. When she gestured with her hand, all twenty of them drew knives tucked into the belts of their armour, and sliced open the backs of their forearms, narrow cuts that smeared blood across their palms. In unison, they summoned spirits to their sides, ink-black hounds and rams with great curling horns lashed to their heads by blood and sinew.

"Give over Aelia and Zoe," Cosmas said and her voice held a calm surety even as the men on both sides of the encounter shifted their grips on their weapons. The air was filled with the stench of wood smoke, the sound of fires crackling down to embers, and the creak of scale armour against leather.

"That is the last thing I intend to do." Theodoros had not yet drawn his weapon, though his hand was wrapped around the hilt of the sword that hung from his hip. "I have already sacrificed too much."

"Then cut your losses," Cosmas snapped. "This can only end badly if you insist on fighting a losing battle."

"No more battles need be lost. Not with a god soul on our side," Isidore said, and though he spoke softly, his words carried themselves across the courtyard.

Cosmas' face darkened with disgust. "That thing you've pledged yourself to, it is an abomination, the essence of ruin and starvation. Surely, you must see that it cannot be bargained with. No matter how powerful you are, Isidore, you are but a man."

"I know what this soul is. What's more — I know my place," Isidore replied. "I would be failing this empire if I did not seek out contracts with the divine. Only through godly intervention can we succeed against the rising tide from the west. The horselords will not be stopped by soldiers alone."

"You disguise your lust for power as some sort of patriotic duty, but I know you! Both of you!" She fixed both Theodoros and

Isidore with a hard glare. "This was a gamble, a reach beyond your stations to the detriment of everyone, not just my family! Your blindness to the truth will reap consequences that extend across every city, every person, every lowly creature that walks or crawls the earth!" By the end, Cosmas sounded wounded and pleading. She removed her hand from the hilt of her sword, and extended it towards them, imploring. "We can still stop this abomination from latching onto the mortal realm once more. There is still time."

Isidore said nothing, nor made any movement that he had even heard her speak. Meanwhile, Theodoros' smile appeared strained. "You don't want me to work together with you. After what I've done, you'd sooner disband the Fourteenth, and put my head on a spike outside the capital for all to see."

Cosmas lowered her arm. "Needs must. If you cooperate now, I will guarantee your safety."

"You'll what?" Sevila growled from the side. "What happened to *'You can do anything you like to him, Sevila!'*"

Theodoros glanced at Sevila, and his brows furrowed into an inscrutable expression, when he saw Aurel beside her. "Even if I agreed," he continued speaking to Cosmas, "exile is the best you could offer me. I will not shame my name in such a way."

"Oh, you're well beyond that, dear," Sevila drawled.

Squinting at her, Theodoros asked, "And who are you?"

Sevila's lip curled in an unpleasant smile, revealing her sharp teeth. "I'm the one who's going to eat you alive. And not in the good way."

"I came here to bury an Empress, not subject myself to idle threats," Theodoros said through grit teeth.

In reply, Sevila snorted derisively. "You wouldn't have had to do either, had you not killed her in the first place. Believe me, this is the very last thing I want to be wasting my time with, yet here we all are. So, are we going to keep squabbling? Or can we move on?"

Theodoros blinked. Meanwhile, Cosmas closed her eyes, and pursed her lips in a pained wince, like someone waiting for the fall of an axe. Isidore's headwrap obscured much of his upper face, but his mouth was downturned in distaste.

Isidore stepped forward. Surrounded on all sides by Theodoros' honour guard and Cosmas' men, he appeared slender as a reed and just as easily broken, but he moved with a surety that belied any physical frailty. The hems of Isidore's black robes shifted as though in a breeze, stirring to life of their own accord. Beneath his feet, the paved road began to darken, stones enblackening themselves with ink the seeped outwards in a slow creeping wave. The veil of his headwrap fluttered about his face, and through the folds of black cloth his eyes stared straight ahead, filmed over with a milky white blindness. His mouth moved, and a low murmuring chant winged through the air around him.

He stretched forth his inhuman hand, and from the earth beneath it pulled the darkness to life.

"Theodoros," he said in a voice far too calm and even, given that every soldier surrounding him had just reached for their weapons. "Would you kindly take the little lady, and retreat?"

Cosmas hissed through her teeth. Sevila made a sound under her breath caught between a hum and a grunt, something that sounded both impressed and troubled.

Unable to tear their gaze away from the sight of the thing taking shape before them, Aurel asked, "What? What is he summoning?"

"A human soul." Sevila looked at Aurel, her expression grim. "You're about to find out why people fear you."

Meanwhile, Cosmas was torn between glaring at Sevila as though this were all her fault, and alternatively shooting Isidore agitated glances.

Rolling her eyes, Sevila simply shrugged. "Alright. In this instance, I may have exacerbated matters."

"Yes," Cosmas snarled. "Yes, you may have."

The soul reared up through the earth and stone, clawing its way through to the air above like a man clinging to the edge of a cliff, feet dangling, scrambling for purchase in loose slate and gravel. It pushed itself to a crouch, a figure of skeletal shadow. As Isidore's droning chant rose to a frenzied pitch, the spirit gained substance before their eyes, shrouding itself in a black and liquid smoke until it hunched upon the ground in a bulk of darkness. Through the swirling mass, the shape of ribs could still be seen, like a cage shielding a chest that burned with a crimson carnal light.

Aurel stared, but the spirit took no notice yet of anything outside of itself. Slight of build, it would be dwarfed by standing in Aurel's presence, yet when it opened its glowing eyes, every soldier inhaled a sharp breath, and took a wary half-step back — even unshakable Cosmas, whose hand tightened around the hilt of her sword.

The soul turned its face up towards its Master, waiting for instruction, waiting to accept or refuse whatever bargain he could offer, and the entire city seemed to hold its breath.

With a wave of his hand towards Cosmas and her men, Isidore said simply, "We need time to retreat. Kill them."

The human spirit did not even bow its head or give any indication that it had accepted the command. One moment it was still, and the next it moved, slipping through the air like a drift of smoke. Swift as the wind, it appeared before the first of Cosmas' guardsmen. He stumbled back, shouting orders at the spirit of a hound he had summoned, but with a gesture the human soul dismissed the hound, which vanished in a wail of mist, dark and thick as oxblood. The guard fumbled for the sword at his hip, but no sooner had he unsheathed it than the human spirit grabbed him by the shoulders and pulled. His torso wrenched into two pieces like a split pomegranate. The human soul tossed each halve aside, then turned to the next guardsman, while off in the distance, the library of Faros thundered to the earth in a fiery collapse.

Panic reigned. Cosmas men along the walls struck bargains with the souls they had conjured, ordering them to attack while they fled the scene. Those on the ground did not bother with even that; they threw down their weapons and bolted in every direction, any direction, so long as it was away. The lesser spirits that stood in the human soul's path were dissipated into a whirl of grisly ash until all that remained was Aurel. They looked on in horror and disgust as the other human spirit tore apart men as easily as rinds of fruit, peeling back skin to reveal twitching ruby flesh, discarding segments left and right like they were rotten. It descended upon those men that tried to flee, clamping its hand around their faces, and pushing their souls from their mouths until their bodies slumped to the ground, drained greyed carcasses that gaped, slack-jawed, towards the heavens.

Taking a shaking step back from the carnage, Aurel said, "What are we going to do?"

"Hmm?" Sevila blinked up at Aurel before scoffing with a wave of her hand. "Nothing, obviously. We're already dead. What is it going to do? Kill us some more?"

"But what about them?" Aurel yelled, and they gestured towards Cosmas and her guards.

"Oh! Right. That." Clearing her throat, Sevila raised her voice. "Cosmas, I promise to cry and give a stirring eulogy at your funeral, after which I will comfort any number of your attractive female relatives."

Cosmas drew her sword and growled, "Make yourselves useful, and grab Zoe and Aelia before it's too late!"

She drew the sword at her hip just enough to cut the side of her hand and draw blood. With a few drops, she sketched a symbol on her palm, and summoned the spirit of a massive bull. It tossed its horned head, and pawed at the stones beneath its feet, taller at the withers than Cosmas herself, large enough that even the human spirit paused to narrow its eyes. Whatever bargain Cosmas struck with it, Aurel could not hear over the screams of men dying and scrambling over one another in their haste to escape.

Aurel did not wait for instruction from Sevila. They turned their attention upon Isidore and Theodoros, who were already on the move. Isidore had instructed Aelia to open the gates, and both she and Theodoros's honour guard strained at the mechanical levers that operated the gates with a series of great chains. The doors had opened only a sliver from their efforts, just enough for them to pass through two at a time.

Aurel looked between Aelia and Zoe. One well past her prime, the other too young to be witnessing this type of slaughter. The discarded arm of a dead man lay a few strides from where Zoe stood at Theodoros' side. She eyed it with inscrutable impassivity.

Seeing Aurel approach, the honour guard closed ranks, though beneath the chain mail cowls that swung from their helms, Aurel could see their gazes flicker with nascent terror. The tips of their drawn swords trembled. Aurel stopped before them, and said softly, "Step aside, please."

The men exchanged nervous glances, torn between their duty and the carnage of another human soul all around them. Faced with polite requests, they grew baffled. Some slowly lowered their swords. Others gripped their weapons tighter, but backed away, as if Aurel would strike out at any moment. Behind them, Isidore had already grabbed Aelia's arm, and was leading her through the gap in the gates, hurrying her along. Aurel watched the pair slip away with an ache in their chest.

There was still time. They could —

Shaking their head, Aurel's voice hardened. "Step aside," they repeated. "I won't say it again."

Whatever change the men heard in Aurel's tone or saw in Aurel's demeanour had them all flinging their weapons down, and stepping away with raised hands.

"Thank you," Aurel murmured.

Theodoros was urging Zoe along, trying to get her to follow without picking her up and bodily hauling her away, but she had dug her heels in and was spitting invectives at him, kicking at his armoured shins, and trying to yank her wrist free. Moving swiftly, Aurel loomed over him. They placed a hand on Theodoros' shoulder, and squeezed until they heard rather than felt the armour beneath crumple as though it were made of parchment. With a pained cry, Theodoros jerked away, and in the process released Zoe's hand so suddenly she fell.

Aurel stepped between the two of them, and shoved Theodoros back so that he stumbled a few paces, clutching at his shoulder with a grimace. When he stared up at Aurel, who towered in all their wraith-like glory, fear brimmed in his eyes. Looking at him now made an acidic rage boil in Aurel's chest. He squeezed his eyes shut as if waiting for a mortal blow to land, and he all but cowered.

"Shame on you, Theo," Aurel snarled.

His eyes blinking open, he stared in blank shock. His gaze flicked down to Aurel's side, where Zoe had latched her hands into the long hems of Aurel's robes. He made an abortive motion, as if to reach for her, but Aurel growled, "Don't."

Swallowing thickly, still clutching his shoulder, Theodoros turned, and fled through the gate, followed quickly by his men.

Aurel glanced at Zoe, who was still glaring after him, her eyes full of dark ire. Hesitant, Aurel bent down to gently take one of Zoe's hands in their own, unfurling her fingers from the fabric of their robes. She jerked as if slapped, but did not pull away.

When Aurel turned back, afraid that Cosmas would have already been torn to pieces, they saw Sevila standing between Cosmas and the human spirit. The bull that Cosmas had summoned was gone, and Cosmas cradled her ribs, panting and injured but alive. Sevila's usual grin had returned, and she was speaking softly to the spirit, gesturing with her hands in that way Aurel knew so well — bargaining, beguiling, coaxing. The human spirit tried to touch her, reaching out, but her smile turned into a baring of teeth, and the soul flinched back as though burned. Cosmas was watching her with wide eyes, and as Aurel approached, leading Zoe cautiously forward, they heard Sevila say, "...already gone. Be on your way, or I'll have my friend deal with you instead."

She jerked her head towards Aurel, and the human spirit turned its attention upon them. Its glowing eyes scraped like the drag of an arrowhead over bare skin. Its crimson-bright chest seemed to constrict, a light pulsing in quiet thought. The two weighed one another, and Aurel could feel the push of another soul's contract against their own, a weight that wavered beneath the iron-clad bargain they had struck with Sevila in a desert abattoir.

Then, bowing in defeat, the spirit vanished in a night-dark mist.

Sevila's shoulders drooped, and she tipped her head back, breathing a deep sigh of relief. When she turned however, her brows drew down into a fierce scowl. "Why is there a child with you, instead of your body?"

The moment Sevila's gaze fell upon her, Zoe glared right back, yet her fist tightened in Aurel's long white robes. Aurel placed a gentle protective hand atop her head, and answered, "Isidore already knows how to sever the soul from the body. If I had taken it back here, he would have escaped, and have simply done the same again to achieve his ends. At least this way, no one else need suffer my fate."

Pinching the bridge of her nose, Sevila squeezed her eyes shut and growled, "Or you could have just killed him! Problem solved!"

"Cosmas said—"

"Oh, fuck what Cosmas said!" Sevila snapped. Aiming her glare at the woman in question, Sevila sneered, "You can thank me for saving your life any time now, by the way."

Cosmas ignored her. Instead, she straightened, wincing when the motion pulled at her injured ribs, and limped over to Aurel. There, she fell to her knees and wrapped Zoe in a hug, pulling her close. Aurel stepped away to give them space. Only after she had all but crushed Zoe to her chest despite her injuries, Cosmas pulled back. "They didn't hurt you, did they?"

Zoe shook her head even as Cosmas inspected her for the slightest scratch, the merest hint of a bruise. "No. I'm—" She bit at her lower lip to keep it from trembling. "I'm fine, Auntie."

"No, you're not." Cosmas smoothed back stray strands of hair that hung darkly across Zoe's forehead in order to press a kiss to her brow. She gave Zoe a watery smile, and cupped the girl's cheeks with both hands. "But you will be."

From the side-lines, Sevila grumbled, "You're welcome!"

א

The sun slipped down towards the horizon, dyeing the flame-hazed air a rich umber scarlet, and rather than head back to the palace, Cosmas led them to the barracks. Along the way, Zoe had begun to stumble over rubble that lined the streets, and Cosmas swept her up into her arms with a grunt of pain. Somewhere along the walk back, Zoe dozed, her head limp and lolling on Cosmas' cloak-draped shoulder. By the time they entered the barracks, she was fast asleep. When one of Cosmas' guardsmen tried to relieve his captain and heal her wounds, Cosmas tightened her grip, and scowled so fiercely that her men gave her a wide berth.

Once inside, Aurel began to follow Sevila down a separate hallway, but Cosmas stopped with one foot on the stairs leading up to her tower office. "Aurel, I would speak with you a moment. Can you join me upstairs while I put her to bed?" She jerked her head towards Zoe, asleep in her arms.

Aurel gave Sevila a silent, questioning look. In return, she studied Aurel with an odd expression, her face veiled and unfathomable, before shrugging and heading off without a word. Aurel watched her go, then turned to follow Cosmas up the stairs. Her breathing grew more laboured with every step upwards, and she struggled with Zoe's weight, but Aurel made no motion to help when the gesture would only be rebuffed. They waited in the hallway outside her office, while Cosmas carefully placed Zoe atop the cot behind her desk, draping the girl's small figure with sheets of warm linen. Softly, Cosmas closed the door, and joined Aurel in the hall, leaving Zoe safely sequestered inside.

"You should get that looked at." Aurel gestured towards Cosmas' ribs, but she waved them away.

"I'll be fine. It's more important I handle this first."

"As you like," Aurel said slowly. They waited for Cosmas to speak, but she instead ran a hand through her hair before grimacing when the cut on her hand slicked her hair with blood.

"Thank you," Cosmas said after a long, grave pause, during which she searched Aurel's face with a stern expression of her own. "I will never be able to repay this debt to you. Zoe is the core of my family and of this empire. One day, she will become a greater leader than I could ever have hoped to be, and her name will be whispered by generations to come."

"I hope to be able to witness it myself." Aurel smiled, but quickly stopped when Cosmas flinched at the sight.

Offering a taut, tired smile of her own, Cosmas said, "I will make sure of it."

The smile faded, and she looked pained. When she winced, Aurel touched her gently by the shoulder, and ducked their head to better see her face. "Are you alright?"

With a nod, Cosmas replied, "Yes. I just—" Straightening, she met Aurel's gaze, her own hard and steady and dark. "What I

said about you before, about Aelia Glabas being implicit in
Theodoros' schemes —"

"It's fine—"

"No, it's not." Cosmas interrupted them. "And I'm sorry. I
do not know what Aelia was to Iustina — friend or ally — but if
you were anything then like you are now, I can understand why
Iustina would entrust Zoe into your care. I cannot claim to have
known you in life, but I am proud to have known you in death."

Aurel shuffled beneath the weight of Cosmas' sincerity.
"Thank you," they murmured. "For what it's worth, I wish I could
have known you then."

This time when Cosmas smiled, her whole face seemed to
relax. "Me too."

"You should seek out one of your army Healers," Aurel
reminded her. "And then rest."

With a huff of wry laughter, Cosmas nodded. "Yes, yes.
Alright. And you should prepare for tomorrow."

"Why? What's happening tomorrow."

Cosmas turned, and opened the door to her office once
more. The fading sunlight along the horizon slanted through the
opposite window and seemed to cast her face in soft rose-tinted
hues, a contrast to her dark and sharply-angled jawline. Her eyes
had gone hard and unyielding once more. "Tomorrow, we march
to the capital."

The door shut behind her, leaving Aurel alone. Walking
away, they strode the halls, hesitant and seeking out any sign of
Sevila. Their trip to the barracks' stark, militant kitchens bore no
sign of her, though a number of cooks who had gathered round,
already preparing breakfast for the next day, froze upon seeing
Aurel darkening their doorway.

"Can you please see that a Healer is sent to Cosmas? She
was recently injured," Aurel said.

None replied, until finally one of the cooks lowered her
knife and nodded warily.

"Thank you." Bowing their head, Aurel backed away and
continued the search for Sevila. They drifted down corridors both
empty and bustling with guardsmen. They ducked beneath arched

doorways, and peered through windows onto the vast grounds below. They even searched the cells in which they had been detained upon first arriving in Faros.

It was not until Aurel wandered down several flights of curving staircases into the bowels of the barracks' storage rooms, that they found her. When Aurel walked into the dimly lit stock room, it was to see Sevila rustling through her confiscated travel bags. She had changed into new clothes styled for travel, the fabric a changeant silk so dark they rippled black and burgundy when she moved. She jumped when Aurel spoke behind her, "What are you doing? Do you need help?"

Startled, she whirled around. Her expression could not be described as guilty — Sevila, as far as Aurel could tell, never felt anything as mundane as guilt — but she twitched as if caught doing something wrong.

"There you are, darling!" She offered Aurel her most stunning smile. "I was just packing to leave. Won't you carry these for me?"

"I thought we weren't leaving until the morning," Aurel said slowly. They stepped forward regardless, but paused in the act of picking up one of the saddlebags, which clinked, heavy with coin and riches. "But you're not talking about marching to Pala, are you?"

"Oh, no, no. That's a suicide mission. I've killed myself enough for one lifetime, thank you." Sevila laughed, but it sounded forced.

"So—? What? You were just going to run?"

"Yes," Sevila replied firmly, but she would not meet Aurel's gaze. Instead she pretended to busy herself with fixing the long, gold-trimmed cowl over her head.

"And if I hadn't come down here just now?" Aurel pressed. "You would have left me behind as well?"

Evading the question, Sevila flashed her teeth in what was supposed to come off as sweet and endearing, but which on her only appeared thorny and cunning. "Well, you're more than welcome to join me, of course. I'd miss your gloomy presence about the place."

"You'd miss my—?" Aurel couldn't even repeat her words. They felt as if the wind had been knocked right out of them; their chest seized with an ache. Aghast, Aurel inspected the feeling like turning over a bolt of cloth in their hands, a rich, bruised pang. It hooked into them, a barbed thing. Aurel watched Sevila strap the saddlebags shut, and as she fiddled with the brass buckles Aurel shook their head. "What about my body?"

"What about it?" Sevila snapped, shifting from wiles to severity in an instant. Then she closed her eyes. When she opened them and spoke again, her voice was smooth and honeyed. She smiled, revealing sharp teeth. "I'll get you a new body. A better body. Wouldn't you like that, darling?" She positively purred, her eyes bright and hypnotic. "You saw what your body was like: old and decrepit. If I put you back in there, you'll be dead — properly dead — in five years. Maybe less. This way however, I can get you whatever body you want. Young. Virile. Boy. Girl. Both. Neither. Take your pick. I'll do it. Sever their souls, and put you in there instead. Anyone you like."

"No," Aurel said, but it sounded faint. The temptation to accept her offer writhed, it bristled, and flailed. They could walk away with a new body, a fresh start into the vast unknown with Sevila at their side. As if she could smell Aurel's hesitation, Sevila stepped closer. She brushed her hands along Aurel's white robes, smoothing wrinkles in the fabric.

"Come now." Sevila turned her most cloying smile upon them. "It can still meet the requirements of the contract. After all, contracts are all about interpretation." She ran her fingers along Aurel's robes, dragging her hand along the dark cage-like ribs beneath, the whisper of a touch. "I'll get you a body back. Contract met. It just depends on you — what you want."

"No," Aurel repeated, their voice stronger this time.

Sevila's whole face was transformed. From canny to angry in an instant. "Why must you always cleave to your damn morals! Be selfish for once! Even in death, you haven't changed a mote!"

Aurel reeled. "You—? You knew me when I was alive?"

"Certainly." Sevila slanted her eyes towards them in a sly look. "I met Aelia Glabas in Aegryph maybe a month before your death. We had a wonderful time, if I recall."

"You're lying," Aurel said, their voice dull and flat.

With a snort, Sevila replied, "Of course, I'm lying. You were as much of a bore then as you are now, but our paths did cross."

Aurel huffed a note of dark and rueful laughter. "That's really all you think of me, isn't it?"

Sevila blinked at them. "What do you mean?"

Aurel curled their fingers, and mourned the lack of weight, of their gauntlets, and of the hint of sensation when watching the interconnected links tick together and bend like scales. "Nothing. Never mind."

Sighing, Sevila rolled her eyes, "Don't play coy. Just tell me. We're well past all that rubbish now."

"Are we? Because every indication you've given me says otherwise!" Aurel could hear their own voice rising, but could do nothing to stop it. "You were going to run away at the very first opportunity! You were going to leave me! You're still planning on leaving as soon as this conversation is over!"

"I invited you to come with me, didn't I?" Sevila snapped. "What else do you want from me?"

"I don't know!" Aurel admitted, feeling the roar of exasperation burning in their chest. "You're insufferable! You're cruel, selfish, vain, greedy, irresponsible!" They began counting adjectives on their fingers, and as they continued reeling off descriptions, Sevila's eyes widened, to which Aurel retorted, "Oh, don't look so stunned!"

"Well!" Sevila tried to sound lofty, but the effect was ruined by the slightly breathless quality of her voice. Instead of her usual hauteur, she sounded winded. "If that's how you really feel, then by all means—!"

"Can you shut up for even a moment?" Aurel interrupted. They stepped forward to loom over her, and Sevila made an abortive motion to lean away in surprise. "I'm trying to tell you that in spite of all of these things and to my own detriment — by the abyss, but I doubt my sanity sometimes! — that I suppose I still like you! You, your arrogance, all of it!"

Sevila stared at them. She went very still as if she hadn't heard properly. "You—? What?"

"We're friends!" Aurel said. "Whether we like it, or not!"

Sevila scrambled for something to say before finally blurting out, "What am I supposed to do with this information?"

Grasping the air rather than throttling sense into her, Aurel shouted, "It just is what it is! You don't have to do anything with it!"

"Why?"

"Because people don't always need a utility for their emotions! Emotions just exist!"

"No, I mean — why do you like me?" Sevila asked the question as though it were an accusation. "People don't like me!"

"Oh, yes. I'm sure they hang people for less," Aurel replied, their voice dry.

Sevila continued to study them as though they had sprouted a second head, as though she had opened a book, and encountered gibberish. Shrugging against the keen edge of her stare, Aurel burst out, "I don't know! You've seen me at my worst, my lowest points. Despite everything, I knew that you couldn't leave me, that — through every and any adversity — at least I knew you would be there. At least I wouldn't be alone. And now—!"

Choking on the words, Aurel gestured weakly to her packed saddlebags, her travel clothes, her face scrunched up in vexed puzzlement.

"Come with me then!" Sevila exclaimed. She looked like she couldn't believe what she was saying. "If you're so sure you like—" She couldn't even say it. Instead, she faltered and eventually ground out, "Then come with me."

Aurel shook their head. "I can't do that. You know I can't."

"No, I don't!" she snapped. "I don't understand! It isn't logical! It isn't—!" Gathering herself with a deep breath, Sevila continued in a note of feigned calm. Still, her voice trembled somewhat, like the ripple of water beneath the surface. "I am going. That much is certain. The rest I leave to you."

She turned away, hauling the saddlebags over her narrow shoulders. Beneath their weight she teetered, but did not topple. With a grunt, she straightened and gave Aurel an imploring glance.

Aurel threw the only argument they had left, their words a faint whisper. "We have a contract."

Like the flicker of a candle in a brief yet sudden draft, something akin to sympathy crossed Sevila's face. On her, it looked unnatural, an outlandish dance of emotion animating her features with warmth and colour, before it was inevitably snuffed out.

She smiled weakly at them. "You never implied a time frame, dear. As long as it happens eventually, I will have fulfilled my end of the bargain, but that — I'm afraid — is entirely up to me."

And, without another word, she left.

Chapter 13

They sat on the steps of the barracks and watched the guards patrol until night washed over the land in a dark wave. Cloaks drifted like banners atop the parapets, a ripple of dyed wool that gleamed softly in a fistful of torchlight. Smoke blotted out the sky, and the birds had fled from the nooks and eaves of buildings so that the city hung, suspended in an eerie stillness. No stars. No motion. No sound.

The guardsmen gave Aurel a wide berth, pretending not to see the human soul crouched upon the threshold of the barracks, shrouded in white mourning robes like a minor liminal deity. At some point during the night Aurel had taken off the ivory-carved mask, and cradled it between their hands. They traced its smooth-featured lines, chasing the sensation of touch with the tips of their ink-dark fingers across the surface of pale bone. When the edges of the sky began to fade to a pale rosy pink, Aurel stood and wandered to the kitchens as if in the hope that they would find Sevila there, rummaging through the expansive barracks pantry. They left the funerary mask behind, balanced upon the lip of a stone step warped by the tread of time.

Pushing open the door to the kitchens and ducking beneath the arched beams of the doorway, Aurel stepped inside and froze. A small figure ducked behind one of the counters and was rummaging through a cupboard in search of food. For a fleet-footed moment, Aurel almost believed it was Sevila — she had just stepped out for a stint; she had retrieved some supplies from the fire-torn city and returned; she had never left at all — but the moment passed, gripping them with lance-bright hope before fading to swift disappointment as Zoe Komateros straightened from her crouch.

Clutching a loaf of old bread, the girl went very still when she saw Aurel looming in the doorway. A hawkish stillness, her eyes dark and narrowed, every muscle tensed, ready to react at the slightest indication of movement. The instant Aurel stepped forward, Zoe snatched up a knife from a wooden block atop the countertop, backing away and aiming the point towards Aurel until the island workbench stretched between the two of them.

Aurel raised their hands. "It's me! Remember me? From yesterday? At the gates?"

Slowly, recognition dawned on Zoe's face, but her brows remained furrowed, her small body coiled like a spring. Her eyes darted quickly around. She did not lower the knife.

"I am a friend of your Aunt Cosmas," Aurel continued, not moving. "But I can leave if you want? I mean — if I make you uncomfortable."

Zoe opened her mouth to speak, though she paused. She tongued the inside of her cheek in a gesture reminiscent of Cosmas — it must have been a family tick. Then she scowled.

Unsure how to proceed, Aurel pointed towards the bread. "Are you hungry? I can—uh—make you something?"

Mouth twisting to one side, the tip of the knife lowered, and Zoe nodded mutely.

Gesturing towards the table, Aurel stammered, "Why—ah—why don't you sit down, and I'll try to —"

Before they could even finish their offer, Zoe had seated herself upon one of the chairs, and glanced around the kitchen, feigning boredom when really she scoured corners and doorways for a means of escape. She set the bread atop the workbench, but kept the knife clutched, carefully concealed, in her lap. Aurel could see it in the tensed hunch of her narrow shoulders and the dart of her eyes, even as she propped an elbow on the table top, and set her chin upon her free hand.

Floundering for what to do, Aurel began to pull down the simplest of ingredients they could find, olive oil poured into a dipping dish, sprinkled with salt. The moment they touched a long knife on the workbench however, Zoe stiffened, and watched them with narrowed eyes. Slowly, Aurel waggled the knife and gestured with it towards the bread. She relaxed in increments, and only when Aurel began cutting thick slices, the bread parting beneath the serrated edge.

As the silence stretched between them, Aurel dared to ask, "Did any of the guards see you? Shouldn't they have told you to go back to bed?"

Zoe stared at them, and Aurel never could have imagined that a look from a child could have made them feel so foolish and insignificant. When finally Zoe spoke, her voice came out like tempered iron. "The guards do whatever I tell them," she said, as though that were obvious.

"Right," Aurel croaked. "Right. Of course."

The silence returned with a vengeance. Zoe seemed perfectly content to let it fill the space between them, folding outwards like a long length of cloth. She did not hasten to close the distance with wasteful sounds or words, and Aurel doubted her age until she began to fidget in her seat, swinging her legs, and drumming her heels against the legs of her rough-hewn wooden stool. She had always been an impatient child.

The thought struck Aurel like a blow to the chest. They paused, lowering the knife, and staring at Zoe until she frowned back, wary.

"What?" she asked, her tone accusing.

Shaking their head, Aurel arranged the bread before her like an offering. "It's nothing."

Zoe leaned back somewhat, watching them with an expression of disbelief and stark anger. On other children, anger would have suited poorly, but on Zoe it fit like her hand-tailored mourning gown. Other children had grandmothers and fathers and brothers. Zoe Komateros had wrath.

"I hate lies," she snapped, snatching up a piece of bread without so much as a *thank you*. "Don't lie to me."

Aurel blinked. They watched as Zoe dipped the bread into olive oil, and tore chunks off with her straight, even teeth, still gripping the knife in her lap with a white-knuckled grasp. At last Aurel admitted, "I remember you. I remember trying to protect you. I remember them taking you from me. "

Zoe's movements slowed. Her face scrunched up in puzzlement. "Who are you?"

"I am — or — I *was* Aelia Glabas."

Zoe twitched as if stung, and for a moment she studied Aurel with fresh interest, suddenly drinking in the sight of them — their glowing eyes, their gentle composure, the ash-darkened hems of their robes. "What happened?" she asked.

Aurel rolled their broad shoulders in a shrug. "They killed me. Theodoros and Isidore."

"Oh." Zoe's voice did not soften. Her expression remained guarded, though she chewed with a thoughtful look in her eyes. She daubed at the small plate of oil with a fresh slice of bread. "I'm glad."

Now, Aurel stared at her. "What?"

She made a face, and mumbled around a mouthful. "Back in the camp, you wouldn't talk to me. Theo and Isidore told me you were sick, and that I shouldn't bother you, but I snuck into your tent one night, and you acted like you couldn't see me. I thought you had helped them— " Zoe stopped. Her jaw tightened, and her dark eyes burned. With a deep breath, she pushed the plate of oil away from her, and threw down her bread, announcing, "I'm not hungry any more."

Panic branched through Aurel's chest when Zoe pushed back her chair from the workbench, preparing to leave. "Wait—!"

Zoe's eyebrows rose, but she stopped after hopping down to the floor. From this height, her head barely reached past Aurel's waist, and yet Aurel felt small, reduced to begging for scraps of human contact from a child they could only barely remember.

"I'm sorry," Aurel blurted out. "I'm sorry that I'm not more like Cosmas. I'm sorry I couldn't protect you and your family."

Whatever absolution Aurel hoped to gain, Zoe did not give. She merely blinked up at them, her eyes large and dark and owlish, her hair a tangled briary mess in need of brushing, her round cheek smudged with ash.

"OK," Zoe said, simple and no-nonsense. Her face gave away nothing, but her stomach gave a loud rumble of complaint. Cheeks going pink, she lifted her chin in a pale mimicry of hauteur, as if trying on her grandmother's clothes. The airs, despite her grave demeanour, made her age suddenly that much more apparent.

The tension between them broke, fraying like a cut rope. "Are you sure you're not hungry any more?" Aurel asked.

She glowered, but now instead of fierce and proud, it came off as a sullen pout. Still, she did not make a move towards the door and, defensive, she mumbled, "The bread was stale."

Already Aurel was turning to search through the cupboards higher off the ground that she had not been able to previously reach, finding soft goats cheese and spices. "There should be something else around here."

Peeling back the stopper of a large clay urn, half as tall as a man, they alighted upon a trove of dried fruits. Zoe had to rise up on her toes to peer over the top from where she stood across the room, and when she saw what was buried inside, she wrinkled her nose. "I don't like dates."

"They're figs," Aurel corrected, pulling out a handful for her. "It's either this or stale bread, cheese, and the fish sauce I found."

Scrunching up her face, Zoe shook her head as she scooted back atop her seat. "No. Find something else."

Aurel placed the fruit on the bench. "Normally I might be inclined to take you to the market for something to eat, but we can't do that right now. And the cooks have already prepared the morning meals for the guardsmen. We can go to the storage rooms below, but I— "

The words died in the air. Even the thought of descending back into the storage rooms, where just a few hours before Sevila had left them, needled — a phantom pain just on the edge of physical sensation.

"I'm not going back down there," Aurel finished, voice growing faint. When Zoe gave no indication of giving ground, Aurel crossed their arms, and drew up to their full height. "I'm not one of your guards or citizens. Not any more." Aurel pointed to the fruit on the bench in front of her. "Now, eat."

Rather than obey immediately, Zoe raised her eyebrows, and leaned back in her seat. She fiddled with the knife in her lap, less threatening than it was an absent-minded gesture. Something cunning flickered across her face, and when she leaned forward once more, she bracketed the fruit with her elbows, meeting Aurel's gaze with her own unwavering stare. "Let's make a deal."

Aurel jerked. "A—? A what?"

"A deal," Zoe repeated. She cocked her head. "You're a spirit. Spirits like deals, right?"

With a rueful shake of their head, Aurel chuckled. "You're going to be a dangerous Empress one day."

"Yes."

Her eyes gleamed, and in the low light they appeared almost black. In that moment, the years unfurled, a canvas sail inked with a legion of possibilities. Aurel could have sworn they saw the future on her face, on the sharpness that would hollow her cheeks, and the bridge that would curve her nose. How like and manifestly unlike Iustina she would be. How shrewd. How proud. How full of righteous fury. How tempered by fight and fire. What was it Cosmas had said? That Zoe Komateros would be a great leader — the Lady Invicta, the unconquerable — that she would bear a name whispered through the centuries. Looking at her now, Aurel could not tell — would the generations to come speak of her with reverence or fear?

Wary, Aurel asked, "What sort of deal?"

"I'll eat these—" Zoe pointed her finger at the figs with as much disdain as she could muster, which was a lot for a girl of ten or so years, "— if you don't tell Cosmas I left her room to come down here."

"I thought you didn't like lying?"

At that, Zoe seemed to deflate somewhat. Her mouth twisted to one side in a guilty way. "This is different."

"Is it, now?"

She stuck out her jaw, lifting her chin. "Yes."

"You do realise that your Auntie's guardsmen will tell her that they saw you."

"Not if I order them not to."

"And you'll be able to track down all of them before she wakes, will you?"

Zoe faltered. She went quiet and frowned down at the wooden bench top, scarred with long blade marks. Somewhere along the duration of their conversation, Zoe had placed the knife she'd been holding on the bench and, seeing it there now, she snatched it up again and glared defensively up at Aurel. "I don't want her to worry about me."

"I won't tell her, unless she asks. Then, I won't lie to her," Aurel said, and when Zoe opened her mouth, Aurel held up a hand for silence. "Cosmas will worry about you regardless. It's what she does, and she's very good at what she does."

With an annoyed grunt, Zoe nonetheless stuck out her hand for them to shake.

Aurel waved her away. "No deal. I'll do it because you asked me to."

The wariness returned to Zoe's eyes, but she retracted her hand. "Grandmother always said souls never did anything unless they could get something out of you. That's why you should work with the living, not the dead."

"Your grandmother was a remarkable woman, but in this case, I'm an exception."

Sighing, Zoe plucked at one of the dried figs, twirling it by its stem.

"You don't actually have to eat it," Aurel pointed out.

"Yes, but I should." Zoe stuck the fig into her mouth and chewed. After she swallowed, she made a face. Still, she reached for another.

Smiling, Aurel leaned forward, and reached across the table to pat her gently on the head. She allowed the contact, but gave a reflexive flinch at being touched.

Aurel pulled back immediately. "Sorry."

Scooping up the last of the dried figs, Zoe shrugged, and said, "It's fine." She hopped down from her seat once more, tucked the knife into a fold of her clothes, and brushed her hands off in a startlingly officious manner. Even bedraggled and war-tossed, she managed to appear more dignified than Aurel could ever dream of looking. She pierced Aurel with a dark, unreadable glance. "Thank you."

"Anytime."

"No, I mean for earlier. At the gate."

Aurel smiled and repeated, "Anytime."

She returned the smile, and the softness transformed her face into something young again, in which she resembled herself more than ever. Aurel could almost recall memories of her from before — before the start of this mess. Zoe carefree and laughing off a scolding from her wet-nurse for playing in the mud, and dirtying her finest court clothes. Mischief sparkling in her eyes as she wrestled a treat from her twin brother, and held it aloft so that he couldn't reach it.

Then the smile faded, and she left without a backward glance. Alone once more in her absence, the empty space of the kitchen threatened to swallow them whole. Two slices of uneaten bread slouched atop the table alongside a drizzle of oil in an earthenware bowl. Outside, the dawn was a rosy suggestion throating violet and pink along the horizon, and the moon hung in its descent. It would be hours yet before Cosmas awoke, before Aurel could grow distracted with the urgency of a long march and the promise of battle. Even that would be better than this — the empty silence that would remain their constant companion for countless years to come.

With swift and silent steps, Aurel stormed from the barracks. A set of four guards did not even try to question them as Aurel asked for the gate to be opened. Nothing waited for them in the city but rubble and scorched earth, but the smouldering wreckage of the library in the distance drew them onward.

All along the streets of the main quarter from the barracks to the hippodrome, the surrounding buildings stretched in a fire-blackened swathe, as if an inexpert painter had let his brush drift in a lazy scrawl across the city. The remains of a basilica still bristled with coals, and when Aurel peered through an archway gilded with the dying flames, they saw the floor melted with coins, spots of bright metal twisted into marble. Many of the walls of shops had been vandalised, broken into, painted over with rude symbols and words of anger— Blues and Greens attacking each other's places of trade and assembly. All except the lone stall in the shadow of the hippodrome.

The awning was propped up, open for business, and there in the darkness of her shop sat Constantina, wearing all black, and writing in her sprawling book of tabulations. The steady movement of her stylus never wavered as Aurel approached, and Constantina did not look up, when she said, "I thought I'd see the likes of you round these parts sometime soon."

"Did you?" Hesitant, Aurel leaned their forearms atop the stall's counter, and clasped their hands.

"Mm-hmm." Constantina finished an entry into her tabulations, wiped her abacus clear, and only then did she set down her stylus. The tips of her fingers were smudged with ink, and the rings of polish onyx glittered when she moved her hands. "Do you have the token?"

"The token?" Aurel repeated.

Constantina studied Aurel with a small frown. "The token. To collect your Mistress' winnings from the race. Surely, that's why you are here? I've never known Sevila to walk away from a bag of gold."

Lifting their hands in a helpless shrug, Aurel was about to answer that Sevila gave them no token, when they stopped. They pulled out the wooden token, studying the scorched mark on its face before handing it over to Constantina.

Swiping up the token, she reached with her spare hand beneath the counter, and drew out a bag of gold large as a clenched fist. She tossed the bag at them. It hit Aurel in the chest, and they only just caught it before it could fall to the ground, spilling coins in all directions. Aurel stared down at it, then at Constantina, who had returned to her tabulations, her ceaseless hand scratching neat lines along her book.

When Aurel made no motion to leave, Constantina raised her eyebrows, and glanced up at them. "What?" she asked with a sigh.

"I'd like to buy some information," Aurel began. They hesitated for a moment before saying, "About the nature of a contract."

Constantina's reply was dry as she finished a line of her work. She dipped her stylus in an inkwell; the nib glistened, wet-black, against the pages of her book. "I hope you understand that sort of information is expensive."

"I know," Aurel said. "I'm willing to pay, whatever the price."

Writing another line, Constantina said, "You're going to need to be more specific. Who holds the contract?"

"Theodoros Glabas."

The scratching of her stylus stopped. Ink blotted the parchment. For a brief shocked moment, Constantina blinked up at Aurel before collecting her wits. Her face smoothed itself of any telling expression, and her eyes narrowed. With careful, feigned indifference, Constantina set her stylus down, and wiped her ink-stained fingertips clean on the edges of her black robes. When she spoke, her voice remained light and airy, but her dark eyes grew keen as a knife's blade. "And who — or rather what — is the soul with which he has contracted?"

Aurel did not answer immediately. "Can you do it?" they pressed. She looked insulted at the question, but Aurel refused to back down. "I won't give you this information unless you can deliver."

Constantina sat hunched at her stall, a middle-aged woman with a lined face, and beneath her headwrap a few wisps of silver-streaked hair escaped. Despite her outward appearance, when she lifted her chin, and fixed them with a piercing stare, Aurel had to suppress the urge to flinch back from her. "My siblings and I, we don't trade unless the exchange is fair. Call it a family policy."

"Right," Aurel croaked. Fiddling with the drawstrings on the bag of gold, they answered, "He has formed a pact with the disembodied soul of the demigod of hunger."

Constantina drew in a sharp breath. Wordlessly, she held out one hand, turning her wrist to reveal her palm. Aurel stared at her empty hand before fumbling at the bag, and dropping a few gold coins into her care. When she kept her hand held out, Aurel passed over a few more coins, then a few more, until they counted the clink of gold spilling onto her palm, one by one. When nearly half of the bag had been emptied, when gold began to spill from her palm and clatter on the counter top, when Aurel had emptied the bag entirely, still Constantina's gnarled fingers remained open.

"I have nothing else," Aurel said, placing the empty bag on the table.

Constantina's stare did not waver. "Yes, you do."

Puzzled, Aurel patted down their clothes. They paused when their pale robes swung with something heavy, and fished through the folds to retrieve the dagger they had taken from the magistrate's husband, an instrument used to kill a half-breed monstrosity not unlike that which they hunted now. Hesitant, Aurel placed the dagger atop the table as well. "This is everything."

The polished onyx rings at her knuckles glinted darkly. Constantina turned her hand over, and both the dagger and the coins vanished. Her eyes bled black at the edges, spilling over with an ink-dark haze. She sat there, motionless, for so long that Aurel glanced around, and fiddled with the empty leather bag of gold. They almost reached out to touch her, but as Aurel's hand drew close to her wrist, a dry wind rustled the awning of the shop, tugging at their pale robes. Aurel snatched their hand back.

Constantina blinked, and slumped back in her seat. She rubbed at her eyes, her face screwing up with a wince.

"Are you alright?" Aurel asked.

"Yes." Sighing, she looked up at Aurel with eyes that appeared tired but otherwise wholly normal. She muttered, "I should have asked for more."

Aurel started to insist they could give her more, but Constantina waved them away, her scowl irritable. "The deal is done. In exchange for a body, Theodoros Glabas has been granted the ability to keep out any and all foreign invaders."

Aurel's movements slowed as they tucked the empty bag of gold into a fold of their robes. "Not all attackers? Just foreign invaders, specifically?"

Rather than repeat herself, Constantina raised one eyebrow, and picked up her stylus. Once more, she dipped its tip in ink and began to write in her ledger. From this angle, Aurel should have been able to read the script even upside down, but the combination of symbols and numbers jumbled together into an incomprehensible babble of code. The ink gleamed wetly on the page, caught in a slant of blue-tinged moonlight through a gap in the awning, and though the wood-grain of the table was illuminated, the light could not touch the darkness that shrouded the rest of her stall from prying eyes. She did not need to dismiss them to make it known that the conversation between them was over.

Stepping back, Aurel bowed their head. "Thank you."

With a thoughtful hum, Constantina watched from beneath hooded eyes as Aurel turned to stride away. They had taken no more than three steps, when she called out, "I recommend you stop by the harbour on your way back. I hear the view of the water is lovely, even on a day like this."

Aurel paused, glanced over their shoulder, then froze. The shop stood abandoned, a charred ruin slumped in the shadow of the towering hippodrome. A breeze curled skeins of ash along the cobblestones, and a shiver raced through them. Shrugging against the skitter of unease, Aurel continued on their way, skirting along the edges of the main square where Iustina and Leo's bodies had been burned. As Aurel reached the intersection leading to the barracks however, they stopped. Though empty, the bag of gold weighed heavy in the folds of their robes.

They peered down the abandoned street towards the barracks, then towards the harbour. Flocks of gulls winged over the far-off jewel-toned sea. Shaking their head with a rueful laugh, unable to shake the feeling of eyes upon them, Aurel turned away from the barracks, and walked towards the ocean.

They found her sitting with her legs dangling over the side of a stone pier, skimming her soles along the waves, and flinging pieces of bread at a congregation of ducks and seagulls. The birds flocked to her, squawking and flapping their wings whenever she tore a hunk of bread from the loaf. She aimed to hit them, and watch them fight over her scraps. The hunch of her shoulders was sulky. She had thrown down her saddlebags, and tugged off her cowl. Her cloth-of-gold headwrap glinted in the moonlight like the glassy wink of brightness across the water.

The docks creaked with empty ships roped into place, stationary yet bobbing on a breeze. Across the harbour the great chain was strung, patrolled both inside and out by Cosmas' guardsmen, bearing sails dyed in stripes of imperial purple, rich and dark as the sea depths. Standing not off, Aurel hesitated to approach. They drank in the sight of her, irrevocably insistently here.

Sevila did not look around, when she announced, "There are no ships leaving. Cosmas hasn't lifted the travel ban, yet."

Aurel replied with a careful tilt of their head, stepping closer. "As you like."

Over her shoulder, Sevila shot them a sharp look and snapped, "It's true!"

"I'm not arguing," Aurel said calmly, sitting down beside her.

"I'd prefer it if you were," she grumbled. She tore off another piece of bread, and cast it viciously at a troupe of ducklings, which dodged across the surface of the water before descending upon the food amidst the cries of hungry gulls. Then with a sigh, Sevila admitted, "It didn't feel right. Leaving you, I mean. It didn't feel good."

"And you only ever do things because they feel good."

She nodded sharply. When Aurel held out one hand to her, she eyed them with suspicion, leaning away somewhat.

Aurel pointed at the loaf of bread. "May I?"

With a soft grunt, Sevila ripped the loaf in half, and passed it over to them. Aurel pulled little pieces off and tossed them towards the birds. The two of them sat in silence for a moment, accompanied by the scrape of painted hulls against stone and the lap of water against wood, until Aurel reached into a fold in their white mourning robes.

"Constantina told me to give you this." They held out the empty bag of gold.

Narrowing her eyes at the offering with a sidelong glance, Sevila took it. She weighed the bag in one hand, bouncing it in her palm. "It feels a bit lighter than it should."

Aurel shrugged. "I needed a bit of information."

With a sour grunt, Sevila chucked the bag into the water as well. "At least tell me the information was worth it."

"I know the nature of Theodoros' contract with your soul."

Sevila blinked. Then she turned her attention back to the birds, murmuring half to herself, "That's useful, I suppose."

Aurel hummed in agreement. The stiff silence settled between them once again, but Aurel only offered the last of the bread to a blue and green-feathered duck that dared to wander too close, rewarding it for its bravery where most of the others shied from Aurel's presence despite the promise of food. Beside them, Sevila feigned disinterest, yet watched Aurel from the corner of her eye. She flicked the toe of her sandal against the water, scattering a few gulls with the sudden movement.

"Not that it means anything to you," Aurel said, "but I'm glad you're still here."

"Don't—!" Sevila took a deep breath and closed her eyes briefly to steady herself. When she spoke again, she muttered, "Don't start with all that again."

"Alright."

Aurel's cool-headed complacency made her bristle. She glared at them and then at the seagulls. "I still don't understand it." With a scowling grumble, Sevila took the last bite of what remained of the bread for herself. "I don't understand you at all."

Bread gone, the birds soon began to lose interest. Most of the ducks paddled away, while a few seagulls perched atop a nearby moored ship, and continued to watch the two of them with hopeful intensity. Aurel brushed aside a few spare crumbs that had collected in their lap, while Sevila all but wrung her hands. The two of them sat close enough that Sevila's fidgeting made their shoulders touch, and she jerked away from the contact as if burned.

"So," Sevila fumbled with her rings, twisting them around her fingers, and refusing to meet Aurel's eye, "this is what it's like."

Aurel turned, frowning. "What do you mean?"

Sevila waved her hand vaguely between the two of them. "Friendship, or — whatever this is."

"I suppose so," Aurel said slowly. "Why? What does it feel like to you?"

Sevila shrugged. "Like many other emotions, it escapes me. It's like—" She frowned, struggling to put the sensation to words, and touching her chest with her fingertips. "It's like a negative space, a hole for something lost, something missing. I don't feel it so much as I notice its absence."

With a hum, Aurel looked down at her and nodded. "For me it's the opposite. Emotion in excess. Sometimes the external world just fades away and there's nothing else."

Sevila gave an exaggerated shudder. "Sounds dreadful. Though I suppose—" she admitted with a grimace, "— I suppose it could only ever be like this. With someone like you. What I mean to say is: a soul."

Voice gentling, Aurel said, "I'm glad it was you who found me."

Again, Sevila stared at them, her face painted with a blank, puzzled disbelief. She seemed too taken aback to speak.

"Perhaps," Aurel began, their voice slow with consideration, "Perhaps your soul is just as desperate for a body as I am. I know what it feels like, being so unanchored, so adrift. Perhaps— "

"Stop." Sevila said. *"Stop."*

She drew a deep shuddering breath, and closed her eyes. When she opened them again, she rounded on Aurel with an intensity glinting gold in her gaze. Her words came out very low, very soft. "You listen to me. If there's one thing in this world that deserves your sympathy even less than I do, it's the soul I cut from my chest. There are abominations, and then there are *Abominations*. Do you understand?"

Aurel shook their head. "No."

Sucking on the backs of her teeth thoughtfully, Sevila took a moment to reply, "When you eat raw flesh, and subsume another's spirit. When you breed with another species. When you tear the soul from the body. These taboos occur in necromancy when the balance tilts, when it becomes precarious, and hangs by a thread. The natural Law of the world reacts by trying to counteract this imbalance, and create symmetry again. We are like wounds, you see? Like a ragged hole torn in fabric, and someone has come along to stitch us up again. In the meantime, we bleed out inconsistencies all around us. People can feel it. Even without realising exactly what we are, somehow they know, because by simply existing around them we alter reality. You— "

And here Sevila paused to swallow. She took a deep breath and continued, "You represent only one of these taboos, and that itself is enough to slowly unravel reality, creating ripples around you while the universe trails along in your wake, trying to heal itself shut once more." Sevila's eyes burned, but her face remained cold as she gestured to herself. "I am all of them, all at once. I am a wound in the flank of the world."

"But your soul— "

"My soul is a pestilence that can never truly be snuffed out. It does not deserve your sympathy. It cannot understand your sympathy. It is a disease." She looked away, and as she gazed out the window to the smouldering city in the distance, the slant of her profile was cast in ghostly moonlight. "At least without a body, it can do no harm. Well— " Sevila corrected herself with a dry, self-deprecating chuckle. "Less harm, in any case."

For a moment Aurel mulled over what she'd said. Then they asked, "And if Theodoros and Isidore are successful? If they manage to reunite your soul with a body once more?"

At that, Sevila shuddered, and for a rare instant Aurel could see the faintest trace of real emotion flicker across her face, like the glimpse of a star streaking across the black night sky, burning itself out in a fiery immolation. "I imagine it would resume what it had started. It would continue to do the only thing it knows."

"Which is what?"

Sevila smiled and her teeth glinted, pale and yellowish and knife-sharp. "Eat."

Chapter 14

In a long snake-like progression, the army marched, three abreast, and their backs loaded down with packs the size of a man. Behind them far into the distance, Faros retreated against the shoreline. Visible even from here, the battlements peaked atop the high walls. Aurel peered over their shoulder down the line of infantry extending towards the city they had left behind, leading to the caravans weighed down with supplies that followed in the army's wake. Cosmas' vast armies to the east may not have been due to arrive in Faros for a few days yet, but in lieu of their arrival she had ripped out every last guardsman she could spare from the city — a formidable force in and of itself — and set them to marching. She had left behind only a small holding force under her cousin, Petros', control with the intent that her army would follow with reinforcements.

She had also left Zoe in his care, along with bodily threats to his person should any harm come to the young empress.

"If anything happens to her— " Cosmas had said astride her sleek black horse, which champed at the bit, and stamped a hoof against the cobblestones beneath the great gates leading west to the capital. "— I'll haunt you from beyond the grave, Petros."

Petros had swallowed, and all but quailed beneath the intensity of her gaze, while Zoe hid a smirk behind her hand from where she stood beside him. In his defence, he had mustered a tremulous smile. "Have a little faith, Cosmas. Iustina wouldn't have instated me as City Prefect unless I had some degree of skill."

"It's not the city I'm worried about." With a sigh, Cosmas had wheeled her mount around, and kicked it to a canter towards the gates.

Now, the gleam of her burnished helm could be seen midway down the line, bowing her head to trade words with the leader of a cohort, who nodded as she gave an emphatic gesture of her hand, expertly handling the reins in her other grip. She rode with an easy grace, carrying the weight of armour, weaponry, and command that belied years of experience. Even her horse bore a mantle of scale armour that draped across its back and partway down its legs, its face clad with iron plates like the rest of the cataphract force that rode at the head of the army.

She had tried encouraging Aurel onto a horse, but the mount she had offered back in Faros had shied from them with a fierce skittishness, eyes rolling in its head, rearing up, and lashing out with hooves whenever Aurel drew too near.

"Don't worry," Aurel had assured her. "The armour is enough."

Indeed, Aurel sighed and rolled their shoulders against the extra weight across their shoulders in relief, anchoring them to the earth as they walked. Cosmas had braved the streets of Faros — still a tangled mesh of unease after the recent riots — and managed to procure Aurel's things from the palace before their departure. Upon receiving them, Aurel had immediately shed their mourning robes in favour of iron scales and the heavy green cloak Sevila had bought for them an age ago.

Now, Sevila fiddled with the reins of her horse, grumbling curses under her breath when she dropped one of the straps of leather, and had to lean precariously over the horse's neck to fish it from where it dragged along the ground. Aurel bent down, and handed it back to her before she could fall flat on her face in the dusty road.

"Thank you," she sighed, and began tying the two ends of the reins together. Her mouth was twisted to a downward slant, and she tucked the reins around the high horn of her saddle with an irritable grunt. Squinting along the ranks of soldiers, Sevila muttered, "It's awful, isn't it? All this fuss. What a waste of time and energy."

Aurel cocked their head, watching her curiously as the two of them continued to move alongside the soldiers as if they were part of Cosmas' army — and in a sense, Aurel supposed they were. "You're the patron god of travellers, aren't you? I would've thought you'd like this."

"In a sense: yes and no." Stretching her arms over her head, Sevila groaned, her face relaxing into a small smile. "It's certainly good to be back on the road."

"Even under such circumstances?" Aurel gestured towards the troops filed neatly around them. Several soldiers behind them fell back another step, giving them a wider berth, afraid to approach, and shooting the two of them nervous glances.

"Any circumstance that allows me to travel is a good circumstance. It's part of what I do, remember? Though — ugh." she cast a faintly disgusted glance over her shoulder towards the soldiers, "It's different. Troop movements are different. Travel is a measure of solitude, of lonely wanderings, of sitting beneath the open sky with no true knowledge of the destination. This is—" She crinkled her nose, and waved her hand towards the surrounding army as if shooing away a cloud of flies. "Logistics and supply chain. Plans heaped upon meticulous plans. This isn't travel. This is war."

She did not wait for Aurel's response. Knuckling along her lower back, she rolled her shoulders and neck with a grimace. Aurel walked near enough that when Sevila removed her cowl, the fabric brushed against Aurel's shoulder. As she began to undo her silk headwrap, Aurel took the cowl and folded it up, the two of them working in tandem. Sevila stuck pins in her mouth, and unbraided her hair. As her fingers combed through dark strands, she mumbled around the pins, "Before I met you in Avaza, I was fleeing some dire circumstances to rival even this. Trust me."

With a wry snort, Aurel said, "Why am I not surprised?"

Sevila's grin turned conspiratorial, and she leaned forward so that Aurel could take the hairpins from her mouth. "Thank you, darling," she said, almost as an aside before continuing. "I was in Aegryph. Not far from where I first met you, actually."

"What happened?"

She laughed. "Oh, you know me. I travelled around. I indulged myself a bit too much, and got in a spot of trouble. They found out what I was — and not just the soulless part, mind you." Smoothing her hair down her back, Sevila lifted one shoulder, touching her chin to it in a roguish sort of shrug. "They tried to entomb me like one of their immortal god kings. Wrap me in gauze made of river reeds, and pickle my organs in jars after removing them with hooks from my nostrils. All that nonsense. On my journey back north, I stopped through Avaza, and that's how I stumbled across you."

Staring at her, Aurel tucked her neatly folded cowl and headwrap into one of the saddle packs in order to grasp her gently by the knee. "How on earth did you manage to escape that?"

She seemed utterly bewildered by Aurel's gesture, raising her eyebrows at Aurel's hand, but for all that she did not kick their hand away. Instead, she continued riding as though nothing had changed, a breeze trailing along the edges of her long dark hair. "I struggled until I sliced my hand open with one of their instruments, and managed to summon a human spirit. It got me out of the city in exchange for ten sleek heifers sacrificed beside the great river, Spine. A cheap price to pay, really. Especially since I just stole them from the king's herd, and called it good."

With a parting pat against her thigh, Aurel lowered their hand, and said, "Well, I for one am glad you're here."

Sevila hummed, a wordless contemplative noise. "You'd be the only one, I imagine."

"I'm sure that's not true."

"Your optimism is as touching as ever," Sevila replied, her tone dry.

They fell into a companionable silence as they continued on, broken only by the stamp of footsteps, the creak of armour against leather, and the rickety groan of passing carts as merchant caravans travelled towards Faros. The soldiers earned their fair share of staring from imperial citizens making their way along the same roads, yet still Aurel felt as though every eye fell upon them and Sevila for far longer. Even here in a crowd, the two of them could not escape notice.

"I wish you had a body," Sevila mused aloud, breaking the silence abruptly, and toying with the leather reins, her wrists resting on the high pommel of her saddle. "Then I could work out whatever this is between us."

"What do you mean?"

"Sex, darling," she drawled. "I must have finally lost my mind, and grown physically attracted to a great churl like you. It's the only explanation." Sevila drummed her fingers against the saddle's cloth-wrapt pommel, tapping out a staccato rhythm. "I could find you a nice, pretty body just for an evening. Perhaps two. It might even be fun."

Aurel recoiled, aghast. "What? No!"

She blinked down at them, as if surprised by the severity of their repulsion. She frowned, "Well, why ever not?"

"None of *that*—" Aurel waved their hands as if fending off a blow, "— interests me. Not in the slightest."

"You only say that now because you don't have a body. If you did, I reckon you'd sing a different tune," Sevila replied, her own words lilting in a sing-song manner.

"No, thank you," Aurel said flatly and firmly. "And for the sake of our friendship, I'm changing the topic."

Sevila rolled her eyes. "Ugh. Fine."

Aurel peered around, down the long column of men and women at arms. Just a few rows ahead they could see a cluster of red-cloaked Healers, their scarlet-breasted mantles oiled and draped over hardy leather armour. "Why were we placed here? Why in the middle of the line?"

Sevila jerked her head in Cosmas' direction. "She wants us on display."

With a grunt, Aurel muttered, "I can't imagine we strike notes of inspiration into the hearts of her troops."

"On the contrary. What better way to flaunt her powerful allies?" When Aurel shot her a confused look, Sevila laughed softly, a wry chuckle. "After all you've seen, and you still don't fully grasp your potential. It's almost cute." She did not have to lean down far to stroke aside a wisp of ink smoke that curled from

Aurel's cheek. "You could pluck a kingdom from the vine of the world. All it requires is that I will it."

As Aurel stared up at her, their footsteps slowed, and Sevila's horse came to a halt beside them. Behind, the line of soldiers was forced to stop as well, and Sevila paid them no heed. Further along the line, Cosmas' head jerked up and she kicked her mount to a canter, riding up alongside the column of soldiers.

Sevila straightened in the saddle, pulling her hand away to grip the reins tight. "Ah, Cosmas! Come to regale us with tales of your past conquests on the battlefield? I could use a bit of reassurance, to be frank."

"No. You're holding up the line." Cosmas reached over, and with the flat of her hand smacked Sevila's horse above its tail so that the animal jerked into action once more.

Sevila squawked gracelessly, and sawed at the reins, but her horse leapt forward, racing ahead. Aurel had to school their features to hide a grin, but Cosmas did not bother. She laughed loudly, boisterously, when Sevila yanked so fiercely on the reins her horse reared up on its hind legs, nearly throwing her off in the process. Seeing their commander's lively attitude, a few of the soldiers joined in the levity of the moment. One of them even went so far as to lend Sevila a helping hand, grabbing the horse's tasselled halter with an apologetic grin.

Cosmas urged her own mount forward, riding past Sevila and further along the line. Sevila watched her go with a sour look, reaching up to tuck a lock of hair behind her ear. When Aurel rejoined her, walking alongside her horse once more, Sevila grumbled under her breath, "She really must be feeling nervous."

"Why do you say that?"

"She is only ever cheery like this as a front." Sevila jerked her head in Cosmas' direction. "She's not the gambling sort, and she doesn't like our chances of winning."

Aurel looked over the heads of the soldiers, seeing Cosmas riding further along the column and chatting with a few of the men. In this environment, surrounded by her troops, she all but beamed — the confident tilt of her chin, the easy grace with which she handled herself atop her horse, quick to smile, quick to laugh.

Everything she hadn't been while cooped up in the bureaucracy of Faros.

"And, as the gambling sort," Aurel asked Sevila, "what do you think of our chances?"

Sevila shot Aurel an impish grin. "I like them even less than Cosmas."

X

Onwards they marched without a glimpse of Theodoros and his men apart from tracks in the ground and tales from passing merchants, whose stocks had been raided before Cosmas could get to them. Every day, they journeyed further west, and everyday Cosmas' scouts on horseback returned with reports on Theodoros' movements. Some days they reappeared on the horizon looking bored and sun-stricken from the long hours spent riding across the plains. Other days they rode up holding their flanks, nursing wounds, fletched arrow shafts bristling from their shoulders and backs. They would deliver their reports, gasping for breath, as they were pulled from their saddles and tended to by spirits summoned by the army's Healers.

On one such occasion, Sevila sat atop her saddlebags on the ground, eating half a loaf of bread, and watching impassively as Cosmas stood over the scout, waiting for his report.

"What happened?" Cosmas asked. Her arms were crossed, and her face stony, but she spoke in a gentle tone.

"We came across— " The scout grimaced past the pain, hissing through his teeth as the Healer prodded at the flesh around the arrow shaft in his shoulder to gauge the severity of the wound. Taking a deep breath, the scout continued, "We came across some of the Fourteenth's scouts. There was a skirmish. But something strange happened."

Cosmas did not prompt him to continue, simply held her silence until he did so.

"I reached for my bow, but the string had gone dry and snapped." The scout turned his face up to Cosmas, one of his hands balled into a fist. "I checked it just this morning! It was fine, then!"

Cosmas tried to soothe him. "Perhaps it snapped during your ride. These things happen."

"I'm telling you: it was fine!" he insisted, growing agitated. "Someone must have meddled with it!"

Hearing this, Sevila went very still. Aurel glanced at her to find that her eyes had narrowed, honed to a sharp edge. For a moment, she squinted at the scout, then caught sight of Aurel watching her. Flashing a grin that was meant to be disarming, she took another bite of bread. Perhaps Sevila was growing easier to read — the tightening of skin around her eyes, the stiffness of her shoulders. Or perhaps Aurel had grown used to her many feigned expressions, picking them out as if they were rotten fruit in a barrel of wares.

"Again, with your hair-brained theories!" One of the fellow scouts came over, her square-jawed face rugged and weather-worn. "Give it up, Lysandros! You let your bowstring get dry on the march!"

"I didn't!"

When Lysandros jerked forward to shoot a glare at the other scout, the Healer placed a firm hand on his chest and ordered, "Don't move."

The other scout turned to Cosmas with a lazy salute in greeting. "He's paranoid. Ever since he skirmished against a horselord years ago."

Lysandros snarled as the Healer snapped off the arrow shaft, leaving a jagged bit of wood poking from his shoulder. "They're unnatural! And we're getting closer!"

"Alright. That's enough" Cosmas' voice hardened to a brook-no-nonsense tone, and both scouts cut their bickering short, going silent the way squabbling children might when confronted with a wrathful parent.

The Healer rummaged around in his pack for materials, muttering alongside the clatter of reagents, the rustle of dried leaves and roots. When he withdrew a sun-bleached bone, Sevila leaned forward atop the bulging saddlebags, and said, "You need a clavicle, not an ulna. Were you raised in a barn?"

The Healer shot her a dirty look, but begrudgingly went back in his pack searching for the proper bone.

Cosmas scowled at Sevila, who shrugged. "What? I was right, wasn't I?"

Closing her eyes and steeling herself with a deep breath, Cosmas turned back to the others. "Lysandros, thank you for bringing this to my attention. Helena, don't you have work to do?"

Helena saluted once more, sharper this time, before striding briskly away, the quiver strapped to her hip slapping against her thigh as she walked. The Healer reached out, and cut a careful incision into the back of Lysandros' arm, and a dribble of bright red blood spooled forth. Using the tip of his thumb, the Healer sketched a few words onto the clavicle, which dripped onto the ground in a hiss of steam. When he cast the clavicle onto the ground with a murmured chant, a circle of shadow and blood rippled outward, turning the earth to liquid darkness.

The soul of a lanky, ape-like creature clawed its way to the surface, its eyes like bright lanterns into the void. It turned its gaze upon the Healer, who held out his hand. "A goat slaughtered for you, if you heal this man's wounds."

In response, the chimp chattered back at him, leaping up and down on the ground.

"Greedy little thing," Sevila muttered with a smirk. She brushed her hands clean of crumbs, and said around the last mouthful of bread, "I like it already."

The Healer ignored her, and instead scowled at the chimp. "Fine. Two. That's as much as I'll give you. Do we have a deal?"

The chimp's face split in two, like ink carved with a grin of needle-like teeth — an eerie, coal-bright smile. Both the Healer and Cosmas shuddered at the sight, and Aurel stared, taken aback. Leaping forward, the chimp clasped the Healer's hand before turning towards Lysandros. It touched his shoulder and back, tracing the wound with inquisitive fingers. Lysandros winced, but did not move. In a flare of fiery light, the arrow shaft slowly began to turn, pulling from his body with a gentle corkscrewing motion and — as they watched — leaving knitted flesh behind.

The moment the deed was done, the chimp let the offending arrow fall to the ground, and rounded upon the Healer with a burst of insistent chatter. "Yes, yes," the Healer groaned, rising to his feet, and leading the chimp away to, presumably, fulfil his end of the bargain.

Cosmas patted Lysandros' shoulder, brusque. "You've done well. Rest up. And let the others know to avoid any skirmishes until we draw nearer to Pala. We can't have our resources whittled away before we even get to the siege."

With a respectful bow of his head, the scout murmured a hasty, "Of course," before re-joining the rest of the troops.

Sevila watched him go with a careful, narrowed gaze. "He's right, you know."

Cosmas frowned at Sevila, who continued, "We're getting closer, but not to the Helani."

Rubbing at her forehead, Cosmas sighed, "Why am even surprised that this is your fault somehow? I should have known."

Sevila deflected the accusation with a shrug. "You're going to regret bringing me along."

"And why is that?" Cosmas asked, then added, "Apart from the obvious reasons."

In reply Sevila only smiled, a keen-edged self-deprecating sort of grin. "You'll see."

Cosmas' expression turned guarded and suspicious. "What is that supposed to mean?"

Rather than answer, Sevila stood, pulling her veil up and obscuring much of her face. She turned to Aurel, and announced, "I'm hungry. Let's see if these muscled louts have anything better than dried fruit and stale bread."

"Sevila!" Cosmas growled. When Sevila continued to ignore her, and started walking away in search of food, Cosmas looked to Aurel. "See if you can wring an answer out of her, won't you?"

Nodding, Aurel hastened after Sevila, who strode ahead, her pace brisk. As they walked through the camp, making their way towards where a group of soldiers were starting fires and pulling out rations from their packs, Aurel said, "You know, if you told her, she might be able to make preparations for whatever it is we're going to face in the capital."

"There is no preparing. Not for this." Sevila's stomach growled, and she grimaced, stopping abruptly to clutch at her abdomen.

"Are you alright?" Aurel asked. They placed a hand on her shoulder.

She waved their concern away, but did not brush aside their hand, muttering, "Fine. I'm—" With a sudden wince, she took a deep breath, and straightened. Her golden eyes gleamed, and she looked over her shoulder off into the distance, westward where Pala and battle awaited them. "I'm getting very close."

Ӿ

At the end of the sixth day of marching — a mere day and a half from the capital by Cosmas' exacting standards — the soldiers were joined by reinforcements from the east, which was cause enough for relief to flow throughout the ranks. The sun had begun to slip down towards the earth, but light still shone across the rolling plains between Faros and Pala. In the distance, the mountains leading the horizon south streamed with flossy late-afternoon sunlight, their peaks abloom with a burnished glow.

They stopped. They made camp. They settled themselves around their individual camp fires behind the temporary wooden reinforcements erected all around them, and when they opened their packs to reach for their rations it was to find that everything had gone rotten. A rumbling murmur wound its way through the ranks alongside the putrid stench of mould and fetid meat.

Sevila was calmly brushing out her hair, when Cosmas stalked towards their little fire, stationed a few strides away from the nearest soldiers. She walked, flanked by two high ranking officers, whose taut expressions were the only indication that this bizarre event had disturbed their confidence. When the three of them passed by their watching troops, the two officers straightened their shoulders, and their faces grew harder around the edges, as if to shield themselves from scrutiny.

Coming to a halt beside Sevila and Aurel's fire, Cosmas kept her voice low when she growled, "This is your fault."

Sevila paused in her brushing to run her hands through her hair, and feign boredom. She pretended to ignore Cosmas even as she answered, "Unintentionally."

"Make it stop," Cosmas said. A few soldiers wandered a bit closer, trying to overhear the conversation, but Cosmas' officers warded them off with glares and barked orders.

Raising one eyebrow, Sevila dragged the brush through her hair once more. "I can't."

"Can't? Or won't?"

Rather than answer, Sevila set aside her brush, and turned to Aurel. "Darling, do you have the—? Oh, thank you." She took the pins Aurel was already holding out for her, and began twisting her hair into a neat bun at the base of her neck.

"Sevila," Cosmas prompted, her voice sharpening.

With a roll of her eyes, Sevila said, "There's nothing to be done, and the closer we get to Pala, the worse it will get."

"You—!" Cutting herself off before she could shout, Cosmas glanced towards the other campfires, pursing her lips. When she continued, it was in a hushed tone. "Tell me what's happening, at least."

With her hair firmly pinned in place, Sevila patted it before leaning back against the saddlebags, stacked atop one another like a small hillock of pillows. Their contents rustled and clinked. "Just reality fraying at the edges a bit. I caused a few hiccups in the fabric of existence the last time I was in the same vicinity as my soul, as well."

"Like what?" Aurel asked.

"Oh, you know." Sevila waved her hand in a vague gesture. "The river, Spine, ran red with blood. A swarm of locusts devoured crops. Livestock were riddled with plague. And—"

She fell silent, looking off into the distance behind them. Both Aurel and Cosmas turned to watch a shadow creep towards the army, sweeping across the land. Soldiers stood at their campfires, and pointed towards the heavens, an anxious murmur rushing through the ranks. In the sky, the moon moved in front of the sun, an eclipse casting an unnatural darkness that cloaked the earth in an ink-black silence.

Gesturing towards the sun and moon over the horizon, Sevila said weakly, "Yes. And that."

"And there's no controlling it?" Cosmas asked softly, still staring at the eclipse, limned in a coronal glimmer of light. She looked away quickly, and rubbed briskly at her eyes.

Sevila shook her head. "Not that I'm aware of." When Cosmas' expression grew drawn and pinched with worry, Sevila added, "If it's any consolation, it will affect Theodoros as equally as it will affect us."

"Well, now I'll rest easy," Cosmas replied dryly.

"I thought sleep was a long-forgotten memory of yours," Sevila drawled.

With a faint grunt, the corner of Cosmas' mouth twitched in an uneasy smile. It faded quickly, and she shook her head, clasping her hands behind her back in an officious manner. "Be ready by first light. I've given the order we're to march earlier than intended. We will arrive in Pala by tomorrow."

Sevila did not answer. Her mouth thinned, and she nodded in mute understanding. Cosmas inclined her head towards Aurel in farewell before turning and striding away once more, re-joined by her officers, and issuing orders. Aurel watched her yellow-dyed cloak snapping behind her, and where she walked the soldiers straightened in her wake. When Aurel turned their attention back to Sevila, she had drawn her legs up beneath her, arms crossed, hunched and staring into the fire. In the sudden darkness, the flames cast pale shadows that coveted the hollows of her cheeks and the sharp corners of her chin. Here, travelling across the sands, and gilded in cool moonlight, she appeared normal, at ease, drawn, tired, human. The sudden nearby yelling of soldiers startled her, and she jerked. Her eyes blinked open, and another set of eyelids shuttered vertically, almost too fast to discern.

"What's it like?" Aurel asked. When Sevila scowled in puzzlement, Aurel added, "Being a god?"

Sighing, Sevila leaned back, tilting her head to the side as she studied the fire. "It's not what you think. We aren't all powerful or all knowing. We have different relationships with things like death and time and space, but the rest is just— " She waved one hand, waggling her fingers and grimacing. "It's like having a very specific compulsion. You know, I once walked the entire breadth and length of the Ular mountains without stopping, all because I couldn't help it. In the end, I looked back, and saw bloody footprints in the snow — I'd lost my toes somewhere along the way. And a few fingers, I think." She chewed at her lower lip thoughtfully. "It's difficult to remember those times. You sort of live in an eternal trance. Like finally scratching an itch, except the itch has been driving you mad for decades, and never goes away. Also, the itch is an aspect of nature, and— " Cutting herself off, she grumbled, "This metaphor is quickly deteriorating."

"No, I think I understand." Aurel watched her, curiosity driving them to ask, "What about cities? Are there whole cities constructed by gods?"

Rubbing at her brow, Sevila muttered, "Why on earth would gods need cities? And since you have a habit of taking my rhetorical questions literally — the answer is: no. That's like asking if the sun, or the rain, or the personification of time wanted to build a city."

"Did you not have a place to congregate and mingle?"

"Most us don't really get along," Sevila said dryly. "By that I mean we typically hate each other. Or, at least, I hated the rest of them."

"Were you ever worshipped?"

"Ugh. Yes." Sevila propped her arms behind her head, and closed her eyes. "I have a group of damned annoying followers spread out across Aegryph and the empire. Desert nomads that only go into cities once a year. They literally follow me around, or at least they try to. I managed to shake them a few decades ago. Last I heard, they were out looking for me to the south somewhere."

"What's it like to—?"

Before Aurel could finish, Sevila cut them off. "OK, no." She held up her hand and glared sternly at them. "No, no, no. *No.* I'm done. I know that we are— " she stilled struggled to say the word 'friend' and instead choked out, "— *what we are,* but you need to give me some time to adjust. Space out your questions by a few years or so. That should be enough for me to grow used to this whole arrangement of ours."

"A few *years?*" Aurel gaped at her. "This is assuming I'll still be around for that."

"Well, I— I mean—" Sevila cleared her throat, and glanced aside. "Won't you?"

"If everything goes according to plan, then I'll have my body back and will die in a few years. You said so yourself."

Sevila blinked, and the blank expression on her face was as close as she came to appearing stricken at the thought of something.

"Right. Of course." She looked away. The firelight illuminated the slope of her profile in rich amber hues. "I guess I'll have to find another travelling companion, then. I don't know if I can enjoy travelling alone — not like I used to."

Aurel frowned in confusion. "Why?"

Sevila gave them a pointed look.

"Oh," Aurel said, very faintly.

"Mmm," Sevila hummed. Silence stretched between them, teeming with all the unspoken things they dared not breach. Until finally Sevila murmured in as soft a tone as she could muster, "If you're expecting me to somehow change, suddenly to be a better person or —"

"I'm not."

She looked at Aurel, and her eyes trapped the low firelight like a resin. "Good. Because I am going to disappoint you."

Aurel smiled. "I know."

Chapter 15

The eclipse followed them all along the plains towards Pala, tracking their movements, and shadowing their steps like a mote in the eye of a vengeful god. A preternatural darkness hung over the land, and the air was stitched through with shadow. Everywhere the army marched, silence trailed in their wake. Birds fell quiet upon the branch, all manner of livestock and wildlife went still, and the only sound was the brush of a faint wind tangling the tall barley, and the stamp of a thousand thousand booted feet marching in unison towards the capital.

The soldiers marched alone, carrying only what equipment they needed while the train of supply carts followed miles behind them, bringing up the rear. In the distance, the mountains crept closer, while at their feet the capital straddled a river which ran from those glacial heights towards the sea. At the mountains' peaks, a veil shimmered with thunder, stretching towards the low-slung sky, a wall of light that crackled like lightning, and shielded the empire's borders from the Helani horselords to the north and west. In the valley, Aurel's eyes pierced through the darkness; they could see Theodoros' troops fleeing just ahead towards the safe retreat of the city gates.

At the front of the column, Cosmas made a sharp motion with her hand, shouting orders to her second-in-command, who in turn rode off with the cavalry. Wheeling away from the rest of the army, the cavalry thundered down the plain. They quickly caught up with Theodoros' forces, not engaging or riding boldly through, but skirmishing briefly before veering off to flank once more, harassing, stalling them. Still, Theodoros' men continued their retreat. Slowly, they crouched their way behind shields and tightly knit groups of infantry that bristled with spears.

With another gesture from Cosmas, archers positioned themselves perpendicular to the cavalry, firing into the ranks of Theodoros' retreating flank, forcing his troops to twist out of position or otherwise risk collapsing to a rain of fletched arrows. As the soldiers withdrew, they stepped over the bodies of the fallen, leaving behind a field littered with the dead. Only, some of the men rose to their feet once more, arrows falling harmlessly to the ground, leaving not even the trace of a wound. Half of the archers, when they reached for ammunition, found only empty quivers. Others found live snakes writhing and hissing in place of arrows, and, screaming, they flung down their bows and quivers to the ground.

On the field below, Aurel watched in puzzled disbelief as chaos unfolded. Reality ran at its most ragged. Men died, then got up again as though nothing had happened, their wounds healed. Others staggered to their knees before ever reaching the enemy, clutching swords and arrows that sprouted from their chests as if planted there by fortune. On and on Theodoros pulled back towards the city, his seasoned troops threatening to buckle beneath the strain of Cosmas' advance. Behind him the front gates groaned open, and the enemy forces slipped inside, sequestering themselves away before Cosmas' infantry could engage them.

Glowering beneath her helm, Cosmas swore under her breath.

Aurel looked up at her and asked, "What's happening?"

In answer, Cosmas simply glared at where Sevila sat atop her horse nearby — beneath her bone-stitched veil, Sevila's expression was inscrutable — before jerking on the reins of her own mount, kicking the sleek dark beast into action. She rode off along the ranks, shouting orders to officers. "Keep moving forward! The supply chain and siege weaponry will be here shortly! I want every entrance to the city secured before they arrive! Have it done within the hour! Bottle up the river and the sally ports! Nothing passes in or out of the city unless I know about it! Helena!"

The scout from before cocked her head in Cosmas' direction, a bored tilt of her chin in acknowledgement.

Cosmas yanked on the reins to stop her horse before the scout. "What do your sources on the inside say?"

Helena shrugged. "Nothing good, General. The Fourteenth has cut off all communications, and throttled any dissent within the city. They're a zealous bunch. They won't be easy to crack."

"Then get a bigger hammer," Cosmas growled. "If we can convince someone to switch sides and open a back door, we'll take it. I don't want any more blood spilled than is absolutely necessary. And when we do get in, there'll be no looting, under any circumstances. Understood?"

With a salute, Helena said, "Yes, ma'am."

Nudging her horse along, Cosmas pushed ahead, continuing to deliver commands with the seamless confidence of a person used to being obeyed at every turn. As the army moved into the sloping valley that stretched before the capital, securing the area and hunkering down for a siege, Sevila rode ahead, kicking her horse towards the city, and leaving Aurel behind without a word of explanation. Trapped in the fastidious military routine of preparing camp and holding ground, Aurel tried to stay as out of everyone's way as possible. Once, they offered their help with pitching tents, but the soldier in question simply shook his head, nervously proclaiming he needed no aide until Aurel gave up and went off in search of Sevila for company.

They found her at the fore of the front lines, between the army and the city walls. She had dismounted from her horse, swinging down from the saddle in favour of tracing the ground with unsettled footsteps. Today, as she had done so for the entirety of the last day, Sevila wore her veil up, obscuring her face. Her horse grazed nearby, its back laden with bags, but she ignored it, not bothering to unpack like the rest of the army. Instead, she paced. From the moment the troops stopped moving and began hunkering down into place for the oncoming siege, Sevila prowled at the boundary between army and city with the lithe restless energy of a creature locked away in its cage.

When Aurel approached, she did not stop. Hands clenched at her sides, Sevila seemed to quiver, her shoulders and the length of her spine racked with fine shivers. Around her eyes, the skin appeared dark and bruised. Her fingertips trembled, and though she wore long sleeves clapped with lengths of costly gold, the mottling could be seen extending to her wrists, flaking at the edges as though she had been caught mid-molt. Ever since the eclipse, she had kept her silence clutched close to her chest like a fan of gambling cards. When prompted, Sevila spoke only in monosyllabic grunts and pithy turns of phrase. When more was required of her, speech felt drawn out, strained and folded and tempered, as though she had to pry individual words from the bellows of her lungs with coal-bright blacksmith tongs.

Aurel stopped nearby, but remained a few paces off, hesitant to breach the space around her. Standing this near, even Aurel could feel a slight crawling sensation where their gut should have been. "How are you feeling?"

Sevila's gaze flicked in Aurel's direction briefly — the passing dart of a gold-touched glance, brighter, more lustrous than usual — before looking off into the distance once more, tracking along the walls and then to the mountains beyond. "Not good."

"When did you last eat?" Aurel asked as they walked towards Sevila's horse. They unbuckled one of the leather-sewn saddlebags, reaching inside only to recoil in disgust. The food Sevila usually stowed away — like a greedy shrike hanging its prized kills from the highest branches — had devolved into a seething mass of insect larvae that crawled and writhed. When Aurel jerked away from the saddlebag, dropping what had once been a bundle of fruit bought at the grand Farosian markets, the throng of flies and maggots squirmed along the ground, bursting at Aurel's feet.

Sevila eyed the mess with a keen quality to her gaze, something not repulsed but avid and yearning lurking there, as though she were actually tempted to eat. "I'm not that desperate," she drawled. Then, after a long pause, she added in a voice nearly too low for Aurel to hear, "Yet."

When Aurel had first seen her back in the dimly lit desert abattoir, dust had clung to her travelling silks, and she had engoldened in the glow of sunlight at her back, alive with saffron and copper and rich warm metallics. Now, rain clouds bloomed on the horizon above the mountains, dead soldiers littered the ground at her feet, and Sevila wore silks the colour of age-darkened oxblood. She looked drawn. She looked worn and skittish. She looked at the city walls with the same unease of a person chained and cuffed and dragged to the headsman's block.

Weakly, though they knew the soldiers' rations would have fared no better, Aurel offered, "I'll see if I can find anything in camp."

"Don't bother. There will be nothing." She stared up her pacing once more.

"Just—" Aurel motioned towards her with a helpless calming gesture of their gauntleted hands, "— stay there. I'll be back."

Every soldier Aurel approached however, shrugged and held open their ration packs to reveal that their stores of food were just as afflicted. The whole camp, the city, the fields, and the river turned up empty, decaying, or festering with vermin. Fish showed their shiny white-scaled bellies, and floated in the broad river, bloated with rot. Blight and fungi clutched the crops in the surrounding countryside. Even the water tasted sour, and Aurel saw soldiers screw up their faces in disgust with every swig from their iron reinforced water skins. Eventually Aurel returned, empty-handed, to where they had left Sevila, but she was nowhere to be found. Her horse pawed at the dusty ground, lipping at a tuft of grass only to spit it out with a shake of its head.

An irrational fear gripped Aurel then. Sevila was gone. She had left again, this time well and truly never to return. Looking around, Aurel craned their head, using their great height to their advantage. A few passing soldiers shot Aurel curious glances, and one — the scout, Lysandros — even dared to approach.

"You looking for someone, spirit?" he asked, his tone cautious. He kept his distance, remaining just out of reach, as though afraid Aurel would suddenly grab him.

"Yes," Aurel said. "Have you seen Sevila?"

"The scary little necromancer?" Lysandros jerked a thumb over his shoulder. "I saw her making the rounds not long ago."

Relief flooded through them, and Aurel relaxed. "Ah, good. Thank you."

With a nod, Lysandros turned to leave. Before he could take more than a few steps, Aurel called after him, "Is there anything I can do to help?"

Lysandros paused. He looked at Aurel with raised eyebrows, his expression guarded yet puzzled. "What do you mean? Haven't you already been allocated a task?"

Aurel shook their head.

If anything, Lysandros only seemed more suspicious at this. "Then, why are you here?"

Spreading their hands in what they hoped was a pacifying gesture, Aurel said, "To help in any way I can."

"No, I mean — why are you *here?*" Lysandros gestured towards the earth at Aurel's feet. "Why were you summoned? What's your contract?"

At that, Aurel did not answer.

Scrubbing a hand through his short hair, Lysandros sighed. "Never mind. Don't tell me that. It's best I don't know, anyway." He waved for Aurel to follow him and started walking along. "Come on. The artillery should be arriving soon. I'm sure the engineers could use a hand moving all the heavy equipment. And bring your Mistress' horse; it should be stabled with the others."

Despite the horse's balking, Aurel grabbed its reins, and led it along after the scout. "Thank you."

As the day crept onward, the sun never dipped towards the horizon, remaining fixed at its zenith in the sky, hidden behind the dark-blotted face of the moon. The rest of the army caught up, re-joining their forces, the soldiers began to light fires, and set up siege weaponry, begrudgingly allowing Aurel to lift and drag the heavy machinery for them. From the walls above looking down, the campfires would have appeared numerous as grains of sand along a wind-swept desert plain, burning bright as distant stars. For two days, this continued: the movement of troops, the careful planning, and always the waiting. And for all that time, Aurel kept an eye out for Sevila, checking that she had not left, offering their services wherever anyone would take them, or otherwise keeping out of the way.

All around the camp, Cosmas could be found — issuing orders, plotting strategy and tactics with her officers. She saw Aurel working alongside her men, and raised her eyebrows by way of greeting. Carefully placing down one of the onagers as directed by an engineer, Aurel offered her a little wave in return. She and Helena stood near enough that Aurel could overhear their conversation, even as an engineer asked Aurel to angle the onager a few paces to the left.

"Spit it out, Helena," Cosmas sighed. "You've never had trouble telling me your mind before. Heaven forbid you stop now."

"Some of the men are getting antsy," Helena admitted.

"I told you, I'm going to rotate out groups back east every half day, as we've been doing. You will not starve. Not on my watch."

Helena shook her head. "It's not about the food this time. It's that woman — that Aegryphan necromancer you brought with us."

Immediately, Aurel froze, and Cosmas' spine stiffened.

"Excuse me," Aurel murmured to the engineer they had been assisting, and walked towards Cosmas. The engineer muttered something under his breath, but did not openly complain.

Cosmas straightened, eyes darkening, and said slowly, "What about her? Has she done something?"

"In a manner of speaking? Yes and no." Helena glanced over her shoulder as if to check that Sevila herself was not lurking nearby. "She's done nothing but circle the camp for two days straight. After I noticed something amiss, I had a few of my men watch her. She just keeps walking round and round, muttering to herself, and biting her fingers until they bleed."

Cosmas tongued at the inside of her cheek. "Have you spoken to her?"

Helena snorted with incredulous laughter. "Fuck, no! She makes my skin crawl just looking at her. Plus, I like my limbs arranged just the way they are."

Mouth tightening, Cosmas nodded sharply. "Leave it to me."

"General," Helena said before Cosmas could stride off. "What is she?"

Both Cosmas and Aurel went very still. Aurel tried catching her eye, but Cosmas refused to look at them. Instead, she studied Helena, and asked in a slow, contemplative tone, "What exactly do you mean by that?"

Helena's dark eyes darted between the two of them, narrowing. "She's not military, that much is obvious. So, what is she? A College turncoat?"

Cosmas fixed Helena with a long look before answering. "She's an ally." Turning away, Cosmas said over her shoulder, "Aurel, with me, please."

Offering Helena an apologetic shrug, Aurel followed. Together they walked through the camp towards the outer fringes. There, they found Sevila. She walked, her steps brisk and hurried, as though she had a destination but no way to reach it. The soles of her leather-bound shoes had started to patch with wear, torn along the edges from her constant pacing these last few days. Even when Cosmas approached, she did not stop. Hands clenched at her sides, she instead circled back and forth, treading land as though treading water.

Crossing her arms, Cosmas watched Sevila for a moment, her expression unreadable. Then, she said, "You have my troops on edge. Why don't you stop? Sit. Try to relax. We're doing everything we can."

When Cosmas gestured back towards the camp, Sevila merely glanced where she indicated before looking away with disinterest, and continuing to pace.

Cosmas' brows furrowed, and she snapped, "What on earth is wrong with you?"

Sevila kicked up plumes of dust as she walked, scraping her heels against the ground. "Nothing."

"If it's going to affect the siege even more than it already has, then I have a right to know." Cosmas stepped forward to place a hand on Sevila's shoulder, in as much a soothing effort as it was to stop her ceaseless pacing. "We're working together now, whether we like it or not. If there were any time to withhold secrets, now is not it."

Sevila's eyes brightened, seared to a burnished gold. She had gone stiff under Cosmas' touch, wary as a wild animal. She pushed away Cosmas' hand with her own, and the skin of her knuckles and wrists appeared more mottled and bruised than before, as though she were in the process of shedding to reveal some new form beneath. "The effects of my soul are limited, but being this close to it, I still feel—" she began to pace once more, clenching and unclenching her hands, "— *urges.*"

"And it will become worse?" Aurel asked.

"The closer I get, yes — just as you've already seen." With an absent-minded wave, she gestured to the sky above, towards the recent battlefield and the lay of the land that stretched before her, and which shifted in constant turmoil, a stewing undulating rupture in which reality attempted to tear itself in twain and simultaneously mend itself together again.

Cosmas did not look around, instead staring fixedly at Sevila, her dark brows knit in contemplation. With a nod at Sevila's veil, Cosmas said, "Let me see you."

Sevila froze. She went too still, too rigid, unreality overcame her like a statue given warmth. Her eyes flickered between Cosmas and Aurel, a nervous weighing of their expressions, before she reached up a trembling hand, and tugged down the veil in a rustle of bone. A rush of air hissed between Cosmas' teeth at the sight. Sevila's skin clung loosely to her skull, glossy with a feverish patina. Her jaw moved with a series of dislocated jerks, and when she swallowed, the muscles of her throat constricted and clicked like the spines of a snake pushing its latest meal down its long body. All along her neck, sweeping up from her chest like an infection, the mottling had spread in a scale-like pattern, her skin an eggshell cracking along the edges. Her human veneer clung to its precarious hinges, and beneath something monstrous peering through.

"If we put your soul back into your own body," Cosmas said, watching Sevila with a sickened kind of horror, as if unable to wrench her gaze away, "then what would happen?"

Sevila smiled, and the result was grotesque; she carved human expressions upon her face the way a butcher carved meat from the bone. "Even now, you'd need more than mortal tools to kill me, Cosmas. Once reunited with my soul, your only effective weapons against me are your teeth."

Cosmas looked sick at the very thought. Clearing her throat, she asked, "And how long will this ritual of Isidore's take?"

Licking her chapped lips, Sevila held up her hand, showing three fingers, which she'd gnawed to ragged stumps, only to regrow flesh again and again. "Two days and three nights. The same as a severing ritual. On the final night, it will be too late. Assuming Isidore started the ritual the moment he entered the city, we have maybe half a day at most to get inside and stop him."

"I was hoping you wouldn't say that." Sighing, Cosmas rubbed at her eyes beneath the nose bridge of her helm. "You do realise that a siege takes months, yes? Without food on either side, the siege won't last as long as usual. Still— " She thumbed at the pommel of her sword, and squinted towards the city walls, just out of range of enemy archers. "These things take time."

Sevila blinked. "You're joking."

"No, I'm not. What did you think was going to happen?"

"You're the military mastermind here! I'm a god of hunger and travellers, not warfare! If you wanted to starve a city, then sure! I'm the one you ask! As for all of this—!" Sevila waved her hand, and grimaced towards Pala. "This was best left to one of my more belligerent cousins."

"And you always said I had the large family," Cosmas quipped. "Starving a city is one way we could go about it. Controlling their water would be a great tactical boon. Otherwise, it's up to them to surrender."

"Well, can't you speed things up?" Sevila started to sound panicked as well as ill.

"And how do you propose I do that?"

"You—" Sevila started to say, pausing to chew at her lower lip. Her teeth ripped the soft skin ragged. "— You have necromancers among your ranks."

Cosmas let out a huff of laughter. "So does Theodoros. Necromancy can only do so much, especially when the enemy can match us blow for blow. At some point, it always boils down to manpower."

"Yes, but we have—" Sevila stopped, and turned. She looked directly at Aurel, who gazed back at her in bewilderment. Then, she breathed, "I'd say a battle for an empire and a god soul is cause enough to use the full force of our contract, wouldn't you, darling?"

Aurel stared at her, then took a tentative step back. "You can't mean—?"

"Sevila, don't do anything rash," Cosmas warned.

Sevila's eyes glowed, forge-bright, hypnotic, and molten. She stared at Aurel as though they were a wellspring in a desert, and she were a wanderer dying of thirst. "Oh, we're well beyond all that now. What would it take, I wonder, to bring those walls crash down around Theodoros' ears? Or perhaps I'll just have you kill everyone inside. That would certainly solve all my problems."

Cosmas' hand clenched around the hilt of her sword, and though she tried to keep her words level and calm, an unnerved note entered her voice. "There are innocent people living in that city. At least a few hundred thousand of them. I won't let you stain the soil with that kind of bloodshed."

"At my best, I'm well beyond caring about what you think. And in case you haven't noticed," Sevila gestured sharply towards her face, "I've had better days."

"We can get through this," Aurel said. "We can find another way."

"You say that, and yet here we are."

Behind them, Helena approached, remaining a cautious distance away so as not to intrude. Immediately, Sevila yanked back up her veil to cover her face before Helena could see her. The furtive action made Helena's expression grow only that much more curious, though she masked it well.

"General?" she began, but Cosmas waved her off without glancing over.

"Not now, Helena."

Refusing to back down, Helena insisted, "You're going to want to hear this."

The three of them turned. Helena stood a few paces off, escorting a stooped old man through the camp. He wore nothing but white — white upon white — pale moonstones and lustrous pearls set into silver bands at his fingers. His scraggly ivory-coloured beard hid his mouth, and his hooded eyes roved with a sea-tarnished lack of pigment. Upon seeing him, both Cosmas and Sevila twitched in surprise.

Cosmas stepped forward, hand balanced on the pommel of the sword at her hip. "You're a long way from the safety of your emporium, Constantius. Or have you started to peddle your black-market wares to desperate soldiers as well as unsuspecting citizens?"

Constantius bowed his head, sweeping a hand over his heart in a polite gesture. "Anyone who can pay a fair price has a place in our shops."

"How did you even manage to get out of the city?" Cosmas asked.

"I escaped notice and misfortune only by a fingernail." His beard twitched with a smile. Aurel and Sevila exchanged a glance, and Sevila clenched her hands into trembling fists.

"Whatever it is you're selling," Cosmas said, her voice as flinty as her gaze, "we're not interested."

"I couldn't help but overhear snippets of your conversation, and my sisters have informed me that Theodoros has contracted with a certain soul." He gave Sevila a long, pointed look. "I may be able to help solve your little conundrum."

Eyes narrowing, Cosmas jerked her head towards Helena. "Take your leave."

Helena arched an eyebrow, but saluted and did as she was told. Waiting until she was well out of earshot, Cosmas lowered her voice. "I was never under the impression that you and your siblings cared who was in power."

"We remember dealings with gods. This god in particular." He nodded at Sevila, who maintained her silence. "She was known to us before she took this form. We would see that her soul is stopped before it could ever be reunited with a body, no matter the cost."

Cosmas grunted. "And you've come to offer me access into the capital out of the goodness of your heart? Somehow, I find that hard to believe. What's your price?"

"The god soul in question," Constantius said. "We want it."

All three of them stared at him in shock, utterly speechless. Beside Aurel, Sevila quivered with barely contained fury, her eyes wide. At her feet, the grass slowly withered, embrowning itself in the cracked clay earth, tinged grey at the tips, scorched near to ash. Cosmas flinched away from the air around Sevila, lifting a hand to her own throat and grimacing with a pained swallow. Constantius, meanwhile, appeared entirely unfazed. He folded his hands together beneath the long sleeves of his white robes, so like those Aurel had worn to the imperial funerary rites not long ago.

"Forget it," Sevila snapped. "We'll find another way in."

"And waste such a valuable contract?" Constantius tsked, clucking his tongue against the backs of his teeth. "Seems like such a shame. Let's hope you don't need it later to thwart the Lord Regent and the High Priest's lofty plans."

Over the bone-stitched cloth of her veil, Sevila glared, her eyes alight. Once they might have gleamed like fountain coins, but now they seared, bright and cold as golden starlight. "Don't test me. Not today. Not now. I've maintained our relationship over the centuries because it was useful to me. You and your siblings may hide behind guises, but never forget that I know what you are."

He spread his hands, and bowed his head somewhat, but never flinched beneath her unblinking stare. "We only want to safeguard it. In our hands, your soul will be shielded from the world properly this time. If you had approached us before, we might have been able to prevent this unfortunate series of events in the first place, but as usual, you trusted no one."

"Because I can never be sure you wouldn't sell so grand a prize to the highest bidder." Sevila snapped. "The very act of an exchange is in your nature."

With a shrug, Constantius replied, "All of us can only be what we are. And what of your nature, Hunger-Bearer? Would you risk seeing the world consumed over the shadow of a doubt?"

Rather than answer, a sound escaped Sevila, a low gravelly growl, wisped through with echoes of shadow like the thrum of water at the bottom of a well. She did not, however, say no.

"You're not seriously considering this?" Cosmas said, her tone accusing. Hand gripping her sword, she looked to be a heartbeat away from drawing it.

"It's my soul, isn't it?" Sevila said, not tearing her unwavering gaze from Constantius. "I'm the only one with the right to bargain with it."

"Damn it, Sevila, if you're just doing this now out of spite—!"

But Cosmas cut herself off when Sevila stepped forward. Lowering her veil, Sevila bared her teeth in a gruesome smile, her teeth long and yellowish and sharp, blood-slicked from chewing off half her own tongue while they had spoken. It was still regrowing when she offered her hand, clasping Constantius' in an iron-clad grip, and saying in a voice hushed yet firm, "I accept. You get our army into the city, and you can have my soul for safekeeping."

He returned the smile, but when he tried to retract his hand, Sevila tightened her hold. Constantius winced, gritting his teeth when the air filled with the snap of bone. She tugged him closer, and stared at the exposed flesh of his neck, her eyes roaring with a hunger as though a banquet had spread before her. "If I discover that you've done anything more with my soul than hide it away from the world, I will find you, and there is no power on heaven, earth, or beyond that can save you."

She released him, and he snatched his hand away, hiding it back beneath the long white sleeves of his robes, but not before Aurel saw a crackle of black and scarlet energy lace across his skin, re-aligning the broken structures of his hand. Constantius bowed his head, and there was not even the faintest hint of reproach as he said, "Bring whatever forces you require to the easternmost wall along the river. I've arranged for the postern there to be opened in two hours."

He left, returning to Helena, who watched the conversation from a discrete distance, no doubt eavesdropping. Cosmas watched him go with a pensive expression, the planes of her face as angular and unyielding as ever.

Aurel turned to Sevila, who had immediately lifted her veil, and struck up her pacing the moment Constantius had turned to leave. "How can you know he and his sisters will keep their word?" Aurel asked. "This is not a true contract, since you already hold one with me."

"You're not wrong, but the Constantine Siblings are not what they appear to be. If they have struck a bargain, they will keep it. Bah!" She flung her hands in the air as if shaking them dry. The dark cowl around her head shadowed what could be seen of her face, so that her eyes seemed to peer from the depths of a great shadow. "The sooner we do this, the better. I'm famished."

"Only a few hours, he said." Cosmas grimaced, then tugged her cowled helm more firmly into place over her head. "We'll need to move quickly to mobilise the troops in time. Helena!" She strode off after Constantius. "Send word out! I want all the onagers and catapults ready to attack the north-westerly gate as soon as possible!"

Helena frowned in confusion. "North-westerly? But he said—" She cleared her throat and changed what she was going to say before she could admit to openly eavesdropping. "I mean— "

"I know what you meant. Just see that it's done. I want the bulk of our troops at the north-westerly gate so that Theodoros and the Fourteenth legion thinks that's where we're planning on launching our attack. Meanwhile, I will lead a small force through the postern, and secure the gate from inside. Once the gate falls and we invade, the city falls."

Mulling over this plan, Helena asked, "And if the Fourteenth continues to fight, even after it's clear they've lost?"

Cosmas jaw tightened, and she said, "Then we kill them until they stop fighting. Either way, the city will be ours."

As Cosmas tramped away, delivering commands, and calling for her horse to be saddled and brought to her, Helena did as ordered. With a last wary look over at Aurel and Sevila, she jogged off to relay Cosmas' orders to the rest of the troops, chain mail glinting in the low light of the eclipse over her leather hauberk. In the distance, a great groan of wood and iron, a gnashing of gears and wheels as the siege engines were moved into position, pointing at the gate, which faced north-west towards the black mountains bearing their crown of thunder.

Sevila had begun to chew at her fingers again. Blood dripped in a slow sluggish line down her knuckles. She watched soldiers rush past with the furtiveness of a wolf in the midst of a flock of sheep, consumed only with thoughts of its own appetite.

Gently, Aurel reached over, and clasped her by the wrist, urging her arm down and her hand away from her mouth. She would not look at them as Aurel lifted her veil back over her face. Taking her trembling hand in their own, Aurel pulled her along towards the eastern gate, where Constantius awaited them. "Let's go."

Chapter 16

The unnatural stillness hung over the land like a funeral shroud, and beneath it Cosmas' army toiled. Meticulous, it arranged itself in neat rows, sprawled in front of the capital gates, and Pala rose before them. Its walls lacked the sheer size and strength of those in Faros, but with the proper fortifications and resources it could withstand a frontal assault for months if not years. Twin towers loomed over the gates, bristling with archers and infantrymen, waiting for the coming attack while Cosmas' army lingered just out of reach. The gates themselves narrowed, only just wide enough for two caravan lines to pass through at a time, funnelling any attackers into a slender point.

Cosmas made them wait until they heard the roar and crash of projectiles, flames rolling over the rooftops, stone thundering into the reinforced gates. The force of the blows shuddered through the city walls. Dust shook free of the stone, and fire rained down from above, launched over the walls and onto the buildings below. One of the siege engines exploded, groaning and twisted from an excess of tension that snapped their wooden rivets loose and flung sharp chunk of wood like shrapnel into the surrounding engineers. Others cast great rocks that fired in a triangular shape and ripped a hole through the gates, only for the entrance to seal itself shut once more. Theodoros' necromancers worked quickly with the Fourteenth, striking bargain after bargain to keep the enemy out.

At the easternmost wall, Constantius knocked a rapid staccato pattern against the iron railings that barred the postern. A collegiate robed figure, hooded and veiled, appeared behind the railings like a spirit summoned. Their eyes glinted, large and dark between strips of black cloth, taking in the sight of Constantius and who he had brought to the postern gate. Cosmas stood, flanked by Aurel and Sevila, and behind them a small group of imperial soldiers waited, numbering no more than twenty-five.

The figure said nothing, merely looked at Constantius, who nodded as if in confirmation. Then, the figure pulled out a chained chatelaine, and fiddled with an assortment of keys before unlocking the gate, bar by bar. Cosmas glanced at Sevila, but her expression was hidden behind the bone veil, and her fingers clacked as she wrung her hands together in constant motion.

When at last the postern was opened, the figure stepped back to let Constantius through the gap in the fortified walls, small enough that when Aurel followed Cosmas, they had to stoop and turn sideways in order to avoid scraping their pauldroned shoulders against the stone sides. The soldiers gave Sevila a wide berth as they funnelled into the city, shuffling as close to Cosmas as possible. One of them stood too close to Sevila, and inhaled sharply, covering his mouth with his hand as if to refrain from gagging at the very nearness of her. If Sevila noticed, she gave no indication. Instead, she turned her gaze towards the north, lifting her head like a hound scenting the air for blood, and in the unnatural dim of the eclipse her eyes cut like lanterns through the gloom.

Constantius exchanged a few murmured words with the nameless priest, their voices hushed. When Cosmas cleared her throat, and gave them both a pointed look, the priest went quiet, and glared at her.

Constantius turned his attention back to her, but not before gesturing towards the priest with a soothing motion of his hands. "You have what you bought, General. The main gates, where your army awaits, are that way."

"And who is this?" Cosmas jerked her chin towards the priest, who made no noise nor motion at being so addressed.

Constantius' beard twitched in a placating smile. "I do not disclose the information of other clients. Though you may rest assured that the College shares some of your reservations where our dear High Priest is concerned."

With a contemplative grunt, Cosmas swept her gaze over the priest before turning to Aurel and Sevila. "This is where we part ways. Do you know where you're going?"

Aurel looked to Sevila for confirmation, but when she continued to stare off into the distance, they nudged her with their elbow. In a movement too fluid, too controlled, she tore her gaze away, bringing the full weight of her attention back to the matter at hand, forgetting to feign unnecessary actions like breathing or blinking. For a moment, she did not answer, before finally she said in a voice that rasped, "Yes."

The crash of the onagers echoed through the streets. A few of the soldiers peered in the direction of the noise, but Cosmas ignored it. She frowned, reached out to touch Sevila, then thought better of it, and let her arm fall back to her side. Lowering her voice so that her soldiers couldn't hear, Cosmas said, "I never thought I'd say this but I wish you would say something vulgar and witty. It would make me feel better about this whole situation, knowing you were still your old self."

The bruises hollowed Sevila's eyes and brow, and the bone sewn into her veil rattled as she cocked her head to study Cosmas, fixed and unblinking. "You have never met my old self, though you might just do that."

Cosmas smiled grimly. "I hope not."

The nameless priest was listening to their interaction, watching Sevila with an odd expression, but when she glanced over, the priest flinched as if burned. Another crash rattled the far gate, the sound rumbling through the earth, vibrating up along their feet.

"I should go." Cosmas clasped Aurel by the arm, nodding to both of them. "Good luck."

Then, with a brisk gesture towards her soldiers, Cosmas left. She drew one of her swords as she strode away, and her men followed suit. Together they fanned out along the street and made their way towards the main gates, where the rest of her army lay in wait. Without a word, Sevila set off to the north, not waiting to see if Aurel trailed after her.

Before Aurel could follow, Constantius spoke. "Don't forget: you will need to trap the soul inside something. A box. A jar. Anything you can find."

Nodding in understanding, Aurel turned and trotted off after Sevila.

Her paces seemed to lengthen the further they walked, growing fluid and liquid-smooth, a serpent's glide over the ground. With every step, the world began to twist, folding in upon itself. Not far into the distance, tongues of flame thrashed from rooftop to rooftop, spreading across the city, fire hurled by the onagers and catapults over the walls in clay jars filled with oily pitch that clung to every surface and set it alight. The fires sprawled, racing rapidly ahead, devouring buildings, melting the painted plaster from their walls to reveal the wooden structures beneath. The air shimmered with a veil of heat and haze as people fled their houses, pushed ever westward, away from the invading force hammering at the gates.

"I have never seen fire act like this," Aurel murmured, slowing their steps as the two of them approached the end of a street, fighting against the opposing flow of people. The flames did not seem to flicker so much as they dripped upward, a river of heat given flesh. Sevila however did not slow her steps. Aurel reached out to grab her, pull her back from the conflagration, but she slipped from their grasp.

Glancing over her shoulder, Sevila said, "Stay close to me."

Hesitant, Aurel did so. As they walked forward together, step in step, Aurel stared. The fire shied from Sevila's presence, retreating before her in a wave. She did not spare the flames a second glance, continuing to stride ahead, and when they passed through to the other side of the broad avenue, the flames closed ranks behind them to form an impenetrable wall once more. Here the street was empty, the city's residents milling around side alleys to flee the fire's spread. Sevila strode onwards, while ahead the street sloped towards the low-slung, marble-clad imperial palace.

Sevila muttered something to herself, low and hushed, sounding absent, as though distracted. She kept her hands clenched into fists, nails biting into her palms and dripping red to the gold bands of rings around her fingers. She inhaled, a noise sharp as a hiss, rattling as the tail of a snake. Guarding the entrance of the palace, no less than eight members of the Fourteenth legion stood. Their oiled military cloaks had once been a handsome scarlet, but years in the field had dyed them a muddied ochre red. They talked amongst themselves — pointing to the fires, to the invasion of the easternmost gate, to the mountains crackling with their crown of lightning — but the moment they caught sight of Aurel and Sevila, they all went quiet.

One of them, a grizzled veteran with a scar running along his lip, fixed his mail-cowled helm back into place before addressing them. "You there!" he called out, resting a hand on the hilt of his sword in a threatening motion. "The palace is strictly off limits! If your homes have been affected, then you may seek refuge in the garrison quarters to the west with the others!"

Sevila did not break her stride.

Maintaining the same pace, Aurel lowered their voice, "What's the plan?"

She did not answer. She simply stared ahead, intent and hard as cold iron.

Seeing Aurel and Sevila approach, the soldiers drew their swords. One of them — the veteran closest to Sevila — stopped before he had taken more than a few steps forward. He clutched at his stomach, at his throat. He fell to his knees, and when he opened his mouth to scream, a boiling of black flies poured from him. They crawled beneath his skin, creeping from every orifice, their wings buzzing with a series of sharp metallic series of clicks, filling the air with an eerie whine. In horror, the other soldiers stumbled back, their faces slack, their eyes wide. When he slumped to the floor — a withered, desiccated husk — they turned and fled.

Dried blood seeped from beneath his corpse, thick and oozing, seething with flies. Sevila stepped over his body, tracking black and bloodied footprints in her wake. The insects perched on her shoulders, crawling along the edges of her veil, embedding themselves in her clothes and her cowl. She seemed not to notice them. She took an abortive step after the fleeing soldiers, a lunging motion as if she were reining in a sleuth-hound from giving chase. Aurel placed a hand on her shoulder, and their wrist was swarmed with flies. Resisting the urge to wave them away in disgust, Aurel squeezed gently. They were about to ask if she was alright when, with a shudder, Sevila shrugged their hand off and headed into the palace.

Inside, the vaulted ceilings barrelled high overhead. Pillars of inflexible marble clapped their arches, strung together with long lines of brightly coloured mosaics — bold blues and yellows in patterns at once floral and geometric. Hunting scenes were depicted across the far wall, men of the court with burgundy half-capes flung over their shoulders, women on horseback draped in lush riding silks, dogs on gem-studded leashes rushing through the tall grasses, leading the hunting party to their quarry: a stag with a twelve-pointed rack of antlers, its flank pierced with arrows, dripping bright splotches of blood at the base of an oak tree. As the two of them rounded the corner down another hall, Aurel turned to peer over their shoulder, and there along the wall behind them was a corresponding mosaic. The same scene except the court members were replaced with faceless gods, and instead of the hart, a man clutched his soul to his chest as if to tether it in place.

The further they delved into the palace, their footsteps echoing down the abandoned marble hallways, the more Sevila deteriorated. She began to sweat. She gripped at her stomach, and her breathing grew laboured. Reality unhinged its jaw and swallowed her whole. Her form started to flicker at the edges. Gold glinted at her wrists, burned in her eyes, pooled in her footsteps. She was limned in light with a face of ink-blackened stars, otherworldly as a coronal eclipse, or the collision of planetary bodies. She slouched through the towering tesserae-sheathed halls like a mirage, a blurred and vaporous vision spied by desert mystics across the blistering sands. Whenever she stumbled, Aurel hesitated to touch her.

Straight and true as an arrow, Sevila led them through the palace, ducking down servant's vestibules and side corridors lit with braziers and torches that curled with smoke, hanging the air with a curtain of sparks when she strode past. Down they spiralled, heading further into the bowels of the palace until the rich marble floors and mosaic walls gave way to unpainted, unpatterned stone, then to old brick foundations, cracked with the weight of centuries.

The palace had been emptied of all staff, all servants, all soldiers. Solitude haunted the place like the ghosts of its past rulers. Everywhere Aurel looked, familiarity scratched its nails down the space where their spine should have been. Memory was a faint pricking of feeling, like the drag of a needle across crushed velvet. Almost without thinking, Aurel lifted their hand to trail the leather palm of their gauntlet across a squat pillar, searching for even a hint of physical sensation to ground them.

Outside the enormous carved doors of the imperial mausoleum, two soldiers stood sentry. Immediately they drew their weapons, bared iron blades glinting in the low torchlight. Aurel moved forward as one of the soldiers leapt towards them and swung his sword down in a heavy blow. Aurel caught the sword in one hand, and with the other they effortlessly picked the soldier up by the scruff of his neck. Tearing the sword free from the soldier's grasp, Aurel tossed him aside with enough force that he slammed against the wall and slumped to the floor with a groan of pain, unconscious. When Aurel turned, they froze, stunned.

The other soldier's helm had been ripped off and cast away. A sword sprouted from Sevila's chest, buried to the hilt just below her breastbone, the gore-slicked point protruding through her ribs and back. She had tackled the soldier, grappling him to the ground, pinning him between her knees. His body bloated with rot. Her eyes had gone wild, pupils narrow and slitted to the breadth of a knife's edge. His throat was gone, a gaping maw of dark fresh cruor, and Sevila snarled, teeth sharp and bared, the lower half of her face a smear of blood. Redness dripped along her jawline. She was attempting to tear through his armour with her bare hands, panting with the sheer force of her hunger.

"Sevila!" Rushing forward, Aurel pried her off the corpse. She struggled against them, straining and gasping, but Aurel held her fast. "We're almost there. Come on. You can do this. Just a little bit further."

After a moment, she stopped struggling, though her eyes remained fixed on her latest meal; she quivered, every muscle held tense. Carefully, Aurel reached around and tugged the sword from her chest. Sevila made no noise, no grumble or hiss of complaint or pain. The blade caught on the edge of a rib before slipping free painted not with blood but with a glistening ichor, black and thick as a starless night, and Aurel tossed it aside in disgust. Before it could even clatter to the ground, Sevila's wound had healed shut. When Aurel placed her delicately back on the ground, she nearly toppled over, precarious as a child's marionette doll, a gathering of limbs and taut string. Keeping an arm around her shoulders, Aurel led her towards the door, carrying her through the threshold and into the imperial mausoleum, where Isidore and Theodoros awaited them.

In a great groan of rusted hinges, the carved doors—banded in thick iron—swung inward. Inside, a great dome capped the circular room, the ceiling above a panoply of volcanic glass around which the entire palace had been built. Niches lined the walls, rising up towards the heavens, and in each enclosure there was contained a vase of imperial remains, burnt to ash to escape possession. Wax masks, cast and moulded from the faces of the deceased, bore an uncannily lifelike resemblance to the dead. Behind each, a flame flickered, so that the walls were lined with a sheath of glowing spectral faces.

In the very centre of the room, Isidore knelt at the edge of a circle drawn in blood, careful lines scrawled with pinpoint precision, archaic words painted with fingertips dripping and red. The bodies of two men had been drained and discarded to one side, their corpses cast half in shadow, half in light. A cavalcade of candles danced with flame around the edges of the circle, interspersed with bronze lamps filled with oil. The candles sagged, half-melted. Pale wax oozed down their narrow stems, clustering together in meres of liquid heat. The air resounded with a murmur of chanting. Isidore's mouth moved, ceaseless and droning, intoning a language half-forgotten by its people, preserved in the summoning of the dead.

Aelia Glabas sat in the circle's centre, tethered there by lines of blood as though by chains. Her eyes stared blankly ahead. She would blink and breathe at precise intervals, her chest rising and falling as though even such simple actions required conscious thought. Her black robes pooled at her ankles. Her wrists perched at her knees. The gash across her chest cast shadows along her collarbone, a fish-bone shaped wound ragged from the knife, like a corpse exhumed and autopsied to determine cause of death.

Sword drawn, hilt clenched in one hand, Theodoros stood between the ritual and the door. In his other hand, he held a clay jar, simple and painted with red figures on a black geometric background. In any other circumstance, Aurel's eye might have passed it right by. It looked like something that belonged in any common household, containing cheap wine from the coast or beer from Aegryph.

Upon seeing him, Sevila jerked out of Aurel's grasp, taking a lunging step toward him with a wordless hiss. Immediately, Theodoros held the edge of his sword to the clay lid, cocking the blade back and forth, threatening to open the jar.

"Stay where you are, please," he said, his voice carrying a note of forced calm. "We wouldn't want to let this out too early now, would we? After all, with the ritual incomplete and with you here, it might just decide that reuniting with you is the path of least resistance."

Sevila froze, rooted to the spot, and staring at the jar in his hands.

Theodoros smiled, a triumphant tilt at the corner of his mouth. "Back in Faros, I'd wondered who you were, and the truth of that might have eluded me had you remained silent. Of course, it figures that only something so drastic as this would grab your attention. Gods are a naturally fickle lot — but soulless half gods?" His sword touched the jar's lid, scraping against the pottery. "It's no wonder this empire has sunk so low."

For the first time since outside the palace Sevila spoke, and her voice coiled with smoke, rasped through with mist. "You would lay blame at my feet, when there are men like you running amok?"

Theodoros sneered. "At least men like me try to do something about it, whereas you — you, who have all the power of the world at your fingertips — do nothing."

At that, Sevila laughed, a harsh and ugly sound that echoed throughout the mausoleum chamber, clashing with Isidore's arcane cant. "You cannot even conceive of it, can you? That perhaps your actions — not my inaction — is what caused all of this."

"At least I tried."

Sevila's lip curled. "And failed."

With a grim smile, Theodoros replied, "We'll just see about that."

Stepping forward to stand beside Sevila, Aurel spoke, and when they did so Theodoros' face flickered with some fleeting emotion Aurel could not pin. "Cosmas will have secured the gate by now. Her army will be pouring into the city as we speak. You have lost, Theo."

"I don't care." Theodoros tapped the flat of his blade against the jar. "With this, I have all the protection I need."

Shaking their head, Aurel insisted, "It will betray you. It will lie and cheat and worm its way out of whatever contract you two have struck the literal moment it is able to do so."

"That is a risk I — we —" he gestured to Isidore as well, "— are willing to take. Without Isidore, I never would have found this god in the first place. I never would have been able to strike this bargain, and protect this empire."

Voice gentle, Aurel said, "You are not protecting this empire. You are dooming it."

All pretences of calm abandoned him at Aurel's placating tone. His face contorted with fury, with frustration. Knuckles white around the hilt of his sword, he gestured with it, sharp slashes of the blade gleaming in the candlelight as he spoke. "I could not stand idly by and watch everything I hold dear fall into ruin! We needed a plan! We needed action! Iustina would have had us stand still and do nothing, while our enemies washed over us, wave after wave!"

"So, this was your answer?" Aurel asked, pointing towards the body of Aelia Glabas seated on the ground amidst a network of bloodied lines like the fine red silk of a spider's web. "To kill your empress? To kill me? There must have been another way."

"You're right. There is another way." He jabbed the tip of his sword in Sevila's direction. "Put her in your place. Let her be reunited with her soul, and answer for her actions. For once in her miserable half-life, let her do some good for this world."

Aurel expected Sevila to scoff, expected her to laugh, to rage, to sneer, to defend herself, and spout excuses. Aurel did not expect her to remain silent, to look contemplative, even resolute.

"No," Aurel said, voice firm. They stepped between Theodoros and Sevila. "Absolutely not."

"We could—" Sevila licked the residue of blood from around her lips, her neck still stained with traces of red smeared across her skin. "We could do it. I could order you to dispose of me afterwards, and it would work. It would solve all your problems."

"No!" Aurel repeated, and the word echoed, reverberating off the walls, making the flames flicker atop their wicks. "After all we've been through, it wouldn't feel right."

Turning to stare at Aurel in utter bewilderment, Sevila's brows furrowed. She fought for speech, struggling for understanding, "But — your body, the empire — this is all you've ever wanted!"

Aurel shook their head. "Not at the expense of someone else."

"Damn you!" Sevila snapped. "I'm trying to do right by you! Is this not how it works?"

Looking between them, Theodoros frowned, his eyes narrowing in confusion. "In a matter of months, you've—?" He let out a bark of bitter, incredulous laughter. "You've managed to gain the sympathies of this soulless wretch of a god?"

When Aurel tried to speak, Theodoros muttered, "No, of course, you did. I shouldn't even be surprised. All my life I called out for a god and nothing answered, while somehow you stumble upon one against all odds and curry its favour." His words sharpened. His teeth clenched. He clutched the jar as if holding himself back from smashing it on the ground, and when next he spoke he addressed Sevila. "I did everything right! How many cattle could I have slaughtered to simply gain your attention? And I wasn't the only one. Everyday — still! — the people line up at the temples, and seek you out for a contract! Where were you? Unshackling yourself from your duties?"

"You act as if I was somehow obligated to answer!" Sevila growled. "How arrogant! How like a human!"

Theodoros' face darkened. "Because you were! You still are! That is how it works! We make contracts, and we each uphold our ends of the bargain! You had the power to help us, and yet when we needed you most — you were gone."

"Well, congratulations. You now have my full attention. Is it everything you ever dreamed? Do I inspire you with awe and glory?" Her eyes and voice had taken on a lidless, hypnotic quality, her face a mask like those surrounding them along the walls, uncanny in its hyper-realism, as though she had carved herself a human likeness, as though at any moment she might reach up and peel it away from her skull. She sounded discordant, her voice a wine-dark fathomless echo, and when she smiled, her face seemed to split itself into a cloven thing. Something slick and black writhed where her tongue should have been, caged behind long sharp yellowish teeth. "Go ahead." Sevila nodded towards the jar. "Open it. Put me in that circle in Aelia's place. Reunite me with my soul, and witness the rebirth of a deity. Then we'll see how much you want my attention."

He did nothing. Licking his lips nervously, he shifted his grip on the jar.

"That's what I thought." Sevila stepped forward, and the very walls seemed to hold their breath, the waxen masks of the dead watching events unfold. "I may not be the god you want or even need, but I am the god you have."

From across the room, Isidore's chanting reached an inharmonious pitch, notes overlapping and coursing through the air. Theodoros glanced over at him for just a moment, but it was enough.

Aurel gripped Sevila's shoulder. "He's stalling. We need to move. Now."

"You think I don't know that?" Sevila growled, not taking her eyes off the jar in Theodoros' hands.

Taking a deep breath, Theodoros raised the jar above his head, and flung it to the ground at his feet.

Abruptly, the chanting ceased. The air went still and hushed and stale. Every flame in the room was extinguished. From the shattered clay fragments, a light emerged, pouring itself forth and taking shape. Theodoros' eyes widened and he took a step back, his face painted with horror. It was as if this were his first time seeing the god soul in its true form, as if he had only cracked the lid of the jar by a sliver to speak to it in the past, like a child peering through his fingers at a nightmare. The light unspooled, unfurled, a six-winged silhouette with a gaze cold, distant, and incandescent as a star. Looking at it hurt. The sensation lanced through Aurel's chest. The soul burned with a radiance so intense the world faded away to a white noise, a roar of blurring sound like the din of crashing waves, or the eruption at the birth of a planet. Its face defied description, a flame constantly shifting and all-consuming, branching out in a lash-bright crown of splendour, like the sun cresting over the horizon and washing the shadows of night from the land.

Wrenching their gaze away, Aurel found Sevila, Theodoros, and Isidore all staring at the god soul spreading before them. Where Theodoros and Isidore's faces were painted with terror, with horror and dread, Sevila looked windswept and yearning, her eyes bright, her face suffused with an answering blaze of grandeur. The sword hung slackly from Theodoros' fingers, its iron tip grazing the stones at his feet. Something dark stained the heavy cloth of his breeches, running down his leg and pooling at his ankles; he had soiled himself.

Striding forward, leaving Sevila near the door, Aurel clapped Theodoros by his armoured shoulder, pulling him around, forcing him to look away. He looked dazed, blinking the light from his eyes even as the god soul continued to expand itself above the ritual circle. "Please, Theo. There is still time." Aurel squeezed, imploring, "Don't let it have me."

He stared at them, and some brief emotion once again crossed his face before he could get it under control once more. He looked away, jaw clenched. The sword trembled in his grasp. "Auntie—" Theodoros choked on the term of endearment. He could not look Aurel in the face. "I'm—"

"Don't." Aurel held up one hand to halt his words. "Don't say it. Do not say it. The only thing I want to hear from you is—"

And here Aurel could not continue. Tripping over the words like a sandal snagged on the lip of a staircase, they shook their head. "Tell me I was awful," Aurel finally said, and their voice broke. "Tell me it was because of something I did. Tell me I deserved it. I could stomach it then, knowing that somehow you did this — all of this — because I failed you."

Now, Theodoros stared at them, his eyes dark and bright all at once, reflecting the glimmers of light caught in the melted pools of wax atop the marble floors. "No," he croaked, tightening his grip on the sword. "Your only failing was being there, at the wrong place, at the wrong time."

Aurel released him and took a step back, gesturing to where the god soul took its final shape, blotting out any shadow, making the ground quake. "Look at it. Is this really what you want? Help me stop it. Don't let it have my body."

The god soul was reaching down, extending a clawed limb towards the body of Aelia Glabas. It tipped her chin up and caressed her dark, lined cheek. The ritual circle pulsed with a glowing energy. Theodoros swallowed thickly. Moving forward, he hefted his sword, lifting it into the air as if to bring it down and cleave through Aelia's head before the god soul could complete the ceremony and possess the body. A cry of anger shouted out, and from the edge of the circle, Isidore staggered to his feet and rushed forward, a ceremonial bone knife glinting in his fist. Before Theodoros could bring down his blade, the point of Isidore's knife found a gap in Theodoros' armour, piercing deep into his neck with a bloom of red.

From the god soul, a wailing screech smote the air, making the walls tremble, making the very earth shudder and groan. Cracks appeared in the brick beneath their feet, great fissures criss-crossing all along the floor. Some of the death masks fell to the ground and broke. Others melted. The air teemed with a deep and tangible furore, thick as ash flecking the sky. Theodoros' body slumped, lifeless, to the ground as Isidore tugged his bone-knife free in a rush of blood.

The god soul rounded on Aelia, curling in upon the body. As it did so, Isidore stumbled a few steps back before tripping on his heels. The knife clattered to the ground, and he scrambled off on hands and knees to escape the boundaries of the ritual circle, leaving Theodoros' body twitching on the floor. The god soul ignored him, ignored anything else apart from the body, bearing down upon Aelia. When it touched her, Aelia opened her mouth to shriek, but no sound came out, no scream, no whimper, no rush of breath. The god soul pushed its hand through her chest; it opened its form like a maw and devoured her whole.

Aelia's body bloated with light, ruptured with it. Her face, her torso bursting like the rind of overripe fruit, an outward collapse spilling out radiance, flooding with brightness, with fire and transcendence. The ground seized and shook, and Aurel staggered back, reeling. Jars from niches along the walls crashed to the ground, shattering with ash. The vaulted ceiling cracked and ruptured, raining down chunks of volcanic glass. On the other side of the circle, Isidore ducked beneath a ledge, seeking refuge from the falling debris along the far wall.

A hand at Aurel's gauntlet, and Sevila tugged them around. "Get it out of her!" Sevila yelled over the din, her voice panicked.

"But we need three days to perform another ritual! How do I—?" Aurel began, but before they could finish the sentence Sevila gripped their arm and pulled, forcing Aurel to hunch over so that they were face to face.

Her eyes burned, and she hissed. "I order you to get my soul out of her as quickly as possible! Whatever it takes! Do it now!"

The full weight of their contract settled around them like a noose. Aurel could feel it squeezing tight, their chest constricting the way it had so long ago in the desert, where Sevila had first grasped their hand and plucked them from the shadows. Fire and salt and shards of black glass rained from the sky. As if controlled by a series of strings, Aurel turned, jerked into action, moving across the room without really seeing it, wholly focused on the task at hand, on the command given. In the wake of Sevila's orders, reality crumbled.

In the ritual circle Aelia thrashed, hovering above the ground, and every movement sent ripples tearing through reality.

The god soul within her twitched its new limbs like someone shrugging into a new cloak, testing the limits of the seams. Bone and muscle and sinew pressed beneath her skin, flame-bright, filling the air with the stench of cooked flesh. Aurel reached out and grabbed her. She seared in their hands, burning up from within. Her skin went translucent. She should have blighted Aurel from existence at the first touch, but Aurel tightened their grip, placed a hand over her head, and reached beyond her.

Light welled up in Aelia's throat. It overflowed from her mouth, from her nostrils, from her eyes. It peeled off her sun-burnished skin in tines like the lazy coil of steam brightening the mephitic maw of a mountain. Aurel could feel the pressure of it build in their own chest, threatening to boil over, to consume them raw. Sulphurous fumes twined from the fissures in the earth. There, surrounded by the imperial dead beneath a sky scorched with streaks of flame in the face of an eclipse-blackened sun, empowered by the full force of their contract, Aurel pushed the god soul from Aelia's lungs. It was exhaled in a wail of light, bright skeins rushing into the air like the cascade of water, silver, and gold.

Aurel released Aelia, watching only the pure and formless fire suspended above the palm of their hand; her body curling into a charred and withered carcass. In their grasp, the god soul convulsed. Folding their palms around it, forcing it to take the shape of their fingers, Aurel cupped the god soul in their hands. It streamed fire through the gaps in Aurel's gauntlets, fighting to be free but unable to combat the contract Aurel had struck with its rightful owner. Glancing around for some kind of container in which to hold it — a jar, a bowl, anything — Aurel's glowing eyes caught sight of one of the many bronze lamps fringing the circle of blood on the floor. Carefully, gently, they tipped their hands, and poured the god soul inside, sealing it shut with a twist of a brassy lid.

Cradling the lamp to their chest, Aurel turned. Sevila was staring at them, her expression inscrutable. The mottling remained, eating away at the edges of her skin, bruising her joints, and making her tremble. Still, even with the god soul trapped inside the lamp, its power bled out into the surroundings.

Aurel took a step forward and nearly tripped over the remains of their own body, smouldering beside the body of Theodoros Glabas. "Is she—?"

"Dead?" Sevila finished for them. "Oh, yes. Very much so. But it was not entirely your fault. My soul was promised a body, and a body it would have. Even we could not breach this contract. The ritual was already complete."

"This isn't how I imagined it would happen."

Sevila moved forward. She lifted her hands as if to cup Aurel's between her own, but flinched away from the lamp. "What else did you imagine? We've won."

"I know, but—"

Before they could finish, a sound from the far side of the room grabbed their attention. Both Aurel and Sevila looked over to find Isidore clambering from behind a pile of rubble. He coughed up plumes of dust into the ink-dark spirit hand that fixed itself to the stump of his arm. Somewhere along the way he had lost the simple headdress of black cloth that normally obscured his head and eyes. With his head of thinning hair, he appeared to be little more than an elderly man.

Crouched on his hands and knees, Isidore's coughs gave way to hacking laughter.

"What are you laughing at?" Sevila snapped.

He pointed upwards to where the ceiling had once been. Both of them craned their necks back to look upward. Aurel's eyes widened. There in the sky, their own silhouette continued to burn, a towering figure of fire slowly dimming, fading to sparks now that the fight was won.

"They saw," Isidore croaked, still laughing. "Everyone saw. Tonight, a battle of gods set the stars alight. People will flood into the temples. They will speak of this for generations to come."

Aghast, Aurel raised a shaking hand to cover their face. "I —I must have — I must have been awful."

"No, no," Sevila breathed. She sounded soft and awed, as if filled with gentle wonder. "You were beautiful, darling. At last everyone saw you as I do — your true potential."

Aurel lowered their hand when Sevila touched them on the wrist, her fingers trembling and a tender look setting her eyes alight to a burnished gold. She spoke in a faint whisper, "My beacon of light."

Epilogue

Cosmas personally cut out Isidore's tongue. She had Helena pry his tongue between his teeth with blacksmiths tongs better suited to clamping the red-hot iron of a horseshoe. Then she kindly asked to borrow Helena's knife, and jammed it into Isidore's mouth, slicing cleanly and quickly.

"What will happen to him now?" Aurel asked, watching grimly on as Isidore slumped to the ground, panting and choking on the blood brimming at his teeth like a wellspring.

Cosmas tossed his tongue into the coals of a nearby brazier, where it spat and hissed amidst the flames. She cleaned the knife and her hands upon the edge of her cloak before handing the knife back to Helena, who gave the blade an expert flourish before tucking it away once more. "I may not be able to legally kill him or even replace him until he dies of natural causes," Cosmas said, "but I can ensure he never poses a threat to the empire. He'll live out the remainder of his days on an island small enough to walk in less than an hour, cut off from the rest of the world. And when he finally dies, I'll ensure the College replaces him with someone more suited to the position."

With a wordless jerk of her head, Cosmas gestured for Helena to take Isidore away. The scout pulled him up to his feet, and hauled him off, shoving him into a stumbling walk. Chains clanked as he moved, arms manacled across his chest and a great slab of iron binding his lone hand so that he could not even scrawl gestures or words. His spirit appendage had been banished the moment Cosmas had found the three of them emerging from the palace. Onward he shambled, and still his head tracked the movements of soldiers as he walked. All who passed him lowered their eyes so as to not meet his sightless milk-blind gaze.

"Everyone saw what happened." Cosmas' eyes flicked to the bronze lamp in Aurel's grasp — Sevila refused to touch it, and her own gaze would shy away whenever Aurel gestured with it in their hands. "I'm not sure what it looked like to you, but to everyone in the city, it appeared as an apparition in the sky, two beings of fire and motion warring together, and only one emerging victorious."

"I'm—" Aurel shuffled their feet beneath her scrutiny. "I'm sorry."

With a snort of amusement, Cosmas waved their concern away. "Don't be. You know what they're saying?"

Aurel shook their head.

"That I won because a god was fighting on my side." Cosmas' mouth quirked up at the edges in a wry smile.

Sevila scoffed, pretending to be more interested in cleaning her nails free of old encrusted blood, than in their conversation. She still wore her veil up, shielding her mottled skin from prying eyes. "And you let them think such rubbish?"

Grinning at her, Cosmas countered, "Are you telling me they're wrong?"

At that, Sevila frowned and lowered her hand. "Well, technically—" she admitted in a low grumble, "—I suppose they're correct. In only the loosest sense."

Turning her attention to Aurel, the hard plains of Cosmas' face gentled. "I wish we could have done more to save your body."

Aurel ran their thumbs along the burnished metal of the lamp, and murmured, "There's nothing to be done. I cannot be reunited with a body without severing someone else's soul from it. I won't subject anyone else to this fate."

Nodding, her eyes grave and dark, Cosmas said, "I understand. With your permission, I would like to have your remains cremated and entombed in the imperial mausoleum, beside the ashes of my family. Once we rebuild the mausoleum, that is."

Aurel blinked. "I'd like that. Thank you."

"Which reminds me." A strangely wicked gleam flashed across Cosmas' gaze. She looked at Sevila. "I've also thought of the perfect way of showing my deepest gratitude for your help."

Sevila narrowed her eyes in suspicion at Cosmas' tone. "What is it? You sound far too cheery."

"I have decided to beseech the nobility and insist that you be named among the ranks of the highest class of aristocratic *Illustris*. Purely titular, of course, but it is a great honour all the same. I'm sure you'll be fending off more marriage proposals in the next fortnight than you would have received in a lifetime. Congratulations." with a smirk, Cosmas clasped Sevila by the shoulder, "Your name will only ever be remembered as a hero of the empire."

Sevila gaped at her in abject horror. When Cosmas let go of her and began to stride away, yellow military cloak billowing in her wake, Sevila called after her, "That was a joke, yes? Cosmas? *Cosmas!*"

"Is this a bad time?" said a soft genteel voice near Aurel's elbow. Turning, they saw Constantius standing there, calmly watching the goings-on.

"There you are!" Sevila rounded on him. She waved towards the lamp in Aurel's hands with a grimace of distaste. "Get rid of that thing already, won't you? The sooner the better."

Constantius' bushy ivory-streaked brows rose. "Oh? Not long ago, you weren't so eager for your soul to fall into the hands of me and my siblings."

"I've had a change of heart," Sevila drawled.

"Capricious as ever. That's what I like about you, Hunger-Bearer. One can always count on you to be unpredictable."

Holding out his hands towards Aurel, Constantius waited. Hesitating for but a moment, Aurel passed the bronze lamp over to him. Just as his sisters had done before him, he inspected the payment with a critical gaze. Then, breathing in deeply, his eyes bled briefly black at the edges, and with a sly turn of his wrist the lamp vanished.

The effects were instantaneous. Sevila exhaled, a low release of breath, as the bruised mottling at her skin retracted. With a sigh, she pulled down her veil and worked her jaw, wincing as she rubbed at her chin. Her eyes dimmed to their usual glittering gold, while high above and far beyond the moon shivered at its apex in the sky. Slowly, ever so slowly, it shifted, sliding away from its position in front of the sun. A sliver of light washed over the land, broadening to an arc that cleared darkness from the sky. All around them, the soldiers and citizens stopped what they were doing, craning their necks and pointing, among them a shout going up to the heavens, relief sweeping through the fallen city.

Nodding his head towards Aurel and Sevila in a shallow bow, Constantius murmured, "Always a pleasure doing business with you."

And without further comment, he left. Both Aurel and Sevila watched him go, ambling through the ruins of the capital and disappearing into the crowd.

"You know," Sevila began in a musing tone, still rubbing at the crux of her jawline, "I rarely rue the bargains I've struck, but that one —" She shook her head and waved her hand in a dismissive manner. "Ah, well! Trouble for another day!"

"What will you do now?" Aurel asked. "I seem to remember you mentioning sleep for a week after this whole affair was finished."

With a roguish grin, Sevila lifted one of her shoulders in a lilting half-shrug. "I might travel east and visit the backwater that the old capital has become. And after that — who knows? I shall go wherever I like."

She looked out across Pala, at Cosmas conferring with Helena and Lysandros and her officers, at the soldiers working together to douse the flames and rebuild what structures that had been destroyed in the tumult. Behind her the palace sprawled upon its series of arched columns, a maze of empty marble at the heart of the capital city. Sevila pretended to not notice Aurel's presence when she said, "I'll understand if you want to stay with Cosmas, and help her rebuild an empire under Zoe. Though it goes without saying that I shall need a companion of my own. Travel isn't what it used to be, you know."

Aurel smiled. "Cosmas has enough support without my help. Besides, someone has to keep you honest."

Sevila elbowed them, feigning indignance. After an amiable silence between them, she said slowly, uncertainly, the words ungainly in her mouth as though she were still puzzling through their meaning herself, "I'm sorry about your body."

Aurel placed a hand on her shoulder, and gave a gentle squeeze. "And I'm sorry about your soul."

"Bah! I'm far better off without it!" She waved Aurel's concern aside, then shot them a sidelong glance. "Would you prefer I call you Aelia from now on?"

"No. I like the name you've given me. It suits me."

"As you like." Covering her face with her veil once more, Sevila strode off down the main avenue. "Though, while we're on the topic, I must admit — I still fancy you calling me 'Mistress.' It always has such a lovely ring in your voice, darling."

With a rueful shake of their head, Aurel followed. "Not on your life."

Together, they set off through the city and the roads beyond. The moon was full in its descent. The sun rose. In their fields, the crops tinged with new green life once more, and the river flowed clean and true. On the horizon, the veil of thunder that crowned the mountains along the edge of the empire in an impenetrable aegis flickered and died.

And atop a distant peak there rode a lone horseman.

END

Made in the USA
Coppell, TX
16 September 2023

21654795R00173